A Piazza
for
Sant'Antonio

A Piazza
for
Sant'Antonio

Five Novellas of 1980s Tuscany

Cover Photo: Church of San Biagio, Montepulciano
© Cisek Ciesielski-Fotolia.com

PAUL SALSINI

iUniverse LLC
Bloomington

A Piazza for Sant'Antonio
Five Novellas of 1980s Tuscany

The author gratefully acknowledges the work of Douglas Preston and Mario Spezi in their book "The Monster of Florence: A True Story" [© 2008, Grand Central Publishing] which provided invaluable information for the novella "The Monster."

iUniverse books may be ordered through booksellers or by contacting:

iUniverse LLC
1663 Liberty Drive
Bloomington, IN 47403
www.iuniverse.com
1-800-Authors (1-800-288-4677)

ISBN: 978-1-4917-3188-8 (sc)
ISBN: 978-1-4917-3189-5 (e)

Library of Congress Control Number: 2014906817

Printed in the United States of America.

iUniverse rev. date: 04/15/2014

For Barbara
Jim, Laura and Jack

Also by Paul Salsini

Stefano and the Christmas Miracles

The Temptation of Father Lorenzo: Ten Stories of 1970s Tuscany

Dino's Story: A Novel of 1960s Tuscany

Sparrow's Revenge: A Novel of Postwar Tuscany

The Cielo: A Novel of Wartime Tuscany

Second Start

Author's Note

And so, the stories continue. What began as a single novel, *The Cielo: A Novel of Wartime Tuscany*, became a trilogy with *Sparrow's Revenge: A Novel of Postwar Tuscany* and *Dino's Story: A Novel of 1960s Tuscany*. Then the stories became a series with *The Temptation of Father Lorenzo: Ten Stories of 1970s Tuscany*, and now they continue with this collection of novellas.

Yes, these people are still in my head and wanting their stories told. I thank them all for the opportunity to bring them to life again.

And, again, I must thank my wife, Barbara, my daughter, Laura, and my sons, Jim and Jack, for their support and encouragement; also Dulcie Shoener, who made valuable suggestions, to my driver/ interpreter in Italy, Marcello Grandini, and to my cousin, Fosca, who started this all with her stories. *Molte grazie!*

Contents

Donna's Famous *Cucina*

"DONNA!" EZIO CRIED, lifting up a page from the *International Herald Tribune* that had come just that day. "Look at this!"

"What?" Donna rushed from her desk to stand behind her husband.

"It's her, isn't it?"

"It's an old picture but, yes, it's her all right," Donna said.

"I don't like the headline," Ezio said. "I mean, 'Ditzy English Writer Dies at 94.' Where'd they come up with that? She wasn't ditzy. Well, not really."

Donna looked at the photograph again. "No. I would have preferred 'Eccentric.'"

"'Eccentric' probably wouldn't have fit in the space, but 'ditzy'?"

"Poor woman. Read it aloud," Donna said, settling into the chair opposite her husband.

"It's not very long. She deserved a longer one. Let's see."

He began to read.

Lady Alexandria, who wrote dozens of historical novels under the pen name Hortense McParpson, died 24 January at her home in Kensington Square, London, after a short illness. Her age was given as 94, although some sources gave it as 98 or 99.

Born in London, Lady Alexandria did not begin writing until she was in her early sixties. She specialized in novels about members of various European royal families, some of them obscure, and they became immensely popular. Her novel about a cousin of Mary of Scotland, "Mistress to the Kings," was made into a popular film that has become a cult classic.

A strong, forthright woman, Lady Alexandria was known for attempting to inhabit her characters while she was writing, often adopting their speech and habits and wearing similar clothing. Some people found this disconcerting, but she said she could write more authentically because of it.

Although she published a best-selling novel almost biennially, she suddenly stopped writing in 1977, and never explained why she abandoned the unfinished manuscript about Eleonora di Toledo de Medici that she had begun during a summer in Italy.

Lady Alexandria's long-estranged husband, the Viscount of Purefoy, died in 1979. Her only survivor is her adopted son, Giancarlo, who had served as her chauffeur in Italy. She left her entire estate to the Resthaven Nursing Home west of London, where she had spent many hours volunteering since her return from Italy.

"Poor Alex," Donna said. "But she had an exciting life and I'm glad we got to know her a little."

"Great lady," Ezio said. "Can it really be, what, five years ago?"

"Yes, 1977. I wondered why we didn't get a note from her at Christmas. She always wrote about how she was so happy volunteering at Resthaven. She used to sing little songs and read to the patients. It gave her great comfort. I think it meant more to her than all the success she had as a writer."

"Well," Ezio said, "at least some of us know why she stopped writing while she was here."

"Yes. When she took care of dear Annabella she realized how she had neglected her own mother and that there were more important things in life than writing about Eleonora di Toledo de Medici."

Ezio laughed. "Remember? We never knew whether to call her Lady Alexandria or Hortense or Eleonora so we settled for Alex."

Donna smiled. "I'll never forget going to her room that first morning and finding her all dressed up in a Renaissance costume just like Eleonora. I didn't know where I was, here at the Cielo or in a sixteenth-century palazzo in Florence."

Ezio read the obituary again. "Did you know that she had adopted Giancarlo? That lazy guy who kept lurking in the background?"

"No! She never wrote anything about him. I've never understood why this thirty-something guy would stay with this old lady all this time. And why did she keep him?"

"Well, he must have had something to offer her, but let's not think about that."

"I'm sure," Donna said, "he was just waiting for her to die so he could inherit everything. And she must have been very wealthy, considering all her books. And the movie rights."

Ezio laughed harder. "But it all went to a nursing home! Good for Alex! I can just imagine Giancarlo's reaction when he found out. She had the last laugh."

"I hope she is at peace," Donna said. "She was her own best character."

Ezio folded the newspaper, put it aside and picked up his briefcase. He had become principal of the school at Reboli and had schedules to make out. Donna went back to her desk.

"You know," she said, "it's only the end of January and we're getting a lot of reservations for the summer already, more than last year, I think."

"And we can be eternally grateful to Lady Alexandria for telling the world what a wonderful place this is. She told everyone!"

"If it wasn't for her," Donna said, opening an envelope, "we might not have anybody."

She smiled as she scanned a letter from a man from Paris and read it to Ezio.

"*Monsieur et Madame.* We have heard about your charming villa from a friend who had the pleasure of staying there last year and my wife and I would be most grateful if you could accommodate us for three weeks this summer, beginning on 15 July 1982. We look forward to your prompt reply. *Recevez, je vous prie, mes meilleures amitiés.*"

"I wish people wouldn't call this place a villa," Ezio said. "It's an old farmhouse, that's all. Just a farmhouse."

"Well, they don't seem disappointed when they get here. Here's another one. He's in Germany and says his cousin Fredric von (something . . . can't read the writing) was here two years ago. Do you remember a Fredric von Something?"

"Sure," Ezio said. "The guy who snored so loud all the other guests complained."

"Here's what he says: '*Sehr geehrter Herr Maffini.*'"

"Not *Frau* too?" Ezio asked. "Oh, well, probably a German thing."

"'August 6. Rooms for three. For four weeks. Reply immediately!'"

"Yes, sir!" Ezio said.

They were interrupted by the telephone.

"Who could be calling this late at night?" Ezio wondered. "I'll get it."

After the initial greeting, he mouthed to Donna that it was a call from the United States. There were numerous interruptions because of faulty translations and telephone connections, and when Ezio put down the receiver he told Donna that the caller was the agent for an actress who had a minor, but unforgettable, role in the film about the cousin of Queen Mary that was based on Lady Alexandria's novel.

"He says they're filming a new movie in Italy and this actress has been very bothered by the *paparazzi*," Ezio said. "She wants them kept at least a thousand feet from here, so I guess it's OK for them to follow her to a thousand feet. I imagine they'll be camped out at that first bend down the hill. Anyway, she wants the whole month of September, apparently after a shoot near Siena, and she wants all the rooms."

"There goes September," Donna said.

Ezio began turning off the lights. "Oh, and the agent said her entourage will include three men. Separate rooms, though."

"Is one of them named Giancarlo?" Donna asked.

IT HAD TAKEN a lot of convincing for Ezio Maffini to agree to open the Cielo to summer visitors a half dozen years ago. The place, he said, was too far up in the hills and the road was too rough. That's true, his wife, Donna Fazzini, and their friends Paolo Ricci and Lucia Sporenza said, but the road could be fixed. Then he argued that there wasn't anything to do in the village of Sant'Antonio. But, they said, people could go to Lucca. Also, he maintained, the four-hundred-year-old farmhouse needed too much work. Teaching at the school in Reboli took a lot of time. Well, they insisted, others could help with the work.

Their biggest argument, the one that finally convinced Ezio, was that the Cielo was indeed so isolated that it would appeal to those who did not want to be going places and seeing things when they were on vacation. They would come just for the peace and quiet. And that's exactly what the eccentric author Lady Alexandria/Hortense McParpson/Eleonora/Alex was looking for that first summer, a place where she could write in isolation. She went away so enchanted that she told all her friends, business associates and everyone else she knew.

That first year, with Lady Alexandria staying in one room and Giancarlo in another, did not strain the capacity of the old farmhouse. And since Donna brought the lady's meals to her room and Giancarlo ate elsewhere, there was no burden on the kitchen or dining room.

After the following summer, when the place was filled most weeks, Ezio and Donna knew that they would have to make major changes. First, there wasn't room for everyone at the dining room table, which had been left when Donna and Ezio moved into the farmhouse in the late 1950s. It had shown its age even then. The guests had to eat in shifts, which meant that the food got cold and lost its flavor. Some of the guests grumbled.

So when the season ended in late October, Ezio and Paolo put on their carpenters' aprons, sawed long thick boards and carved table legs and then made chairs. The new table could seat twelve, maybe even fifteen people.

Then the real problem had to be faced. How was Donna expected to cook a meal in a kitchen geared at the most for five or six guests? The stove and refrigerator were much too small, and there wasn't much workspace.

They looked at the possibilities of expansion. An addition was out of the question, so the only feasible solution would be knocking down the wall between the kitchen and dining room and making one large room that would stretch the length of the first floor.

"It would be like farmhouses were in the past," Donna said. "A place where the family would spend all the time, cooking, eating, playing games in front of a huge fireplace."

"But mostly talking."

"Yes," Donna agreed. "A true *casa*. Won't it be fun for people from different countries to sit around the table and get to know each other? And for us to listen to all that?"

"Say, aren't we going to have the television set blaring? It wouldn't be an Italian kitchen without a television set."

"No!" Donna said. "No television. These people are coming for peace and quiet. They won't want to watch TV."

"But I love those new disco shows," Ezio teased.

"Then you can go to Paolo and Lucia's and watch them."

With the help from Paolo and four other friends in the village, the wall was knocked down and the old stones and debris cleared out in less than a day. Then, once the remaining walls were replastered that winter, a set of cupboards soon stretched along one wall. The floor was repaired with tiles Ezio discovered in the barn. A second refrigerator was added. An eight-burner stove replaced the small one. A dishwasher occupied a corner, and some days two or three loads were required. A large table provided room for rolling out pasta.

The renovations that winter sometimes did not go smoothly, and there were tensions. In more than twenty years of marriage, Ezio and Donna rarely had disagreements and never fought, but pressured by the workload, they became testy.

"Didn't you hear me?" Donna shouted from the bottom of the ladder one day that winter.

"No!" Ezio was repairing a hole in the roof.

"Well, I've been calling and calling."

"I didn't hear you! What about?"

"We have to go to the village and get more flour. I can't make pasta without flour."

"I've got to finish this before it starts to rain. Can't you go?"

"I've got chicken on the stove! I can't leave it!"

Ezio threw his hammer to the ground, barely missing Donna, climbed down the ladder and got into his truck. "*Merda!*" he muttered under his breath.

That night, they ate in silence, but when Donna was washing the dishes, Ezio came up from behind and hugged her. "I'm sorry," he said.

"No, I'm sorry," she said, tears in her eyes. "Let's not do that again."

"Never."

But three weeks later, there was another flare-up. Donna had returned from Lucca where she had picked up new curtains for one of the guest rooms.

"I don't see the nails," Ezio said as he rummaged through the packages.

"Nails? What nails?"

"The nails I need for the new door."

"You didn't tell me to get any nails."

"I told you!"

"You didn't!"

"I did!"

And it went on like that for a while until Ezio stormed out the door and got into his truck and Donna ironed the curtains on the table. This time it was her turn. *"Merda!"*

That night, they made up again.

"What's happening to us, Donna?"

She moved closer to him on the couch. "I don't know, but I sure don't like this."

"Is this all too much for us, Donna? We don't have to do this, you know."

"I know. But we wanted to. And we've already done all this work."

"Doesn't matter," Ezio said. "We've only done this for two summers. We could stop."

"But we're already booked for this summer. Almost all summer."

He put his arm around her. He was fifty-five then and Donna fifty-six. With long walks in the Tuscan hills and diets of simple but hearty food, they looked, and felt, at least ten years younger. Only a few streaks of gray brightened her blond hair, and his black curls were speckled with white. She had put on a few pounds, but still kept a figure he loved. Many things had changed over more than two decades of marriage, but two things had not—the sparkle in their eyes when they saw each other, and their love, which only deepened with the years.

They knew they could soon ease into a long retirement. In a few years he would retire from the school with almost a full pension so they could travel. But they had never settled for an easy life, and were excited about starting a new, exciting chapter in opening their home to guests.

They looked out over the now-vast living room, lit only by moonbeams breaking through the dusty windows.

"It does look good, doesn't it?" Ezio said.

"And it's going to look better when we're finished."

"OK, let's finish. Let's welcome our guests this summer. And let's not fight anymore. Deal?

"Deal."

But both of them had a hard time getting to sleep that night.

IN THE FOLLOWING YEARS the four guest rooms at what was now advertised as "The Cielo, Your Home Away from Home" were empty only when there was a last-minute cancellation. Enthusiastic guests told friends who then came and told their friends. An English travel magazine mentioned it briefly in a "Places to Stay in Tuscany" article, and that prompted a magazine published in New York to send a reporter who wrote a long feature story about the place. Although the writer mistakenly said that the farmhouse had been destroyed in World War II and had been rebuilt, she headlined her piece "Heaven on Earth."

"Wow!" Donna and Ezio said together when they opened the magazine, sent by yet another former guest.

The Cielo also had to credit tourist agencies and tour guides who recommended the place to travelers. One in particular, Marcello from Florence, not only brought tourists but also stayed in a separate room. Marcello enjoyed the quiet, which was a contrast from his hectic trips to Milan and Rome, and he encouraged tourists to go to the Cielo just so he could stay there. He brought in so much business and Donna and Ezio liked him so much that they refused his payment.

With eight or more guests in the four rooms at a time, the little patio was frequently fully occupied, and Ezio not only had to supply more lawn chairs but he also had to enlarge the entire area.

Amazingly, there was little conversation among the guests as they lay so close together. Part of that may have been because they had arrived from such varied places as Frankfurt, Copenhagen, Stockholm, Munich, Edinburgh and even New York and Los Angeles, so there was a language problem. But, more likely, each of the visitors simply wanted to bask in the sun, and few used the tiny pool.

Some discovered paths that led up into the mountain behind the Cielo. One young couple found an old stable and took along books, cheap wine, bread and cheese for picnics. A French visitor carted a folding chair and wrote in his notebook for hours in a grove of old olive trees. A delicate woman from Scotland unfolded an umbrella and her sketchpads in a clearing and drew vistas that she hoped to sell to a shop in Glasgow. A young man, the son of an American couple, took his guitar to an abandoned farmhouse.

Mostly, they lived in their own worlds, but, as Ezio and Donna had hoped, at night they gathered in the *casa*, and visitors from as many as five or six countries managed to have lively, if confusing, conversations with a lot of hand-pointing, nodding and dramatic gestures. Ezio and Donna loved to sit with this group, learning about other countries and customs. Visitors invariably wanted to know more about their hosts. They were fascinated by Donna's early career as a marble worker in Pietrasanta and Ezio's life as a member of the Resistance during World War II.

"You've been through so much," an elderly man from Venice said one night. On his previous three visits to the Cielo, his wife had accompanied him, but she had died last winter and he made the trip again in her memory. "But you are still together. Treasure that, Donna and Ezio, treasure that."

"We will, Signor Ventucci," Donna said. "We know we have each other, and that's the most important thing." She squeezed Ezio's hand.

"Your marriage is strong. I can tell. The important thing is to trust each other. My wife and I, well, we had our difficulties every now and then, but we always trusted one another."

"We think we do," Ezio said.

Eventually every night, the conversation got around to Donna's meals. *"Magnifico!"* they all declared. That was exactly the word that Lady Alexandria had used for her recommendations.

Donna explained that her meals were examples of the simple Tuscan *cucina povera*.

"Literally, that means kitchen of the poor, or peasant cooking. We use what's on hand, in the pantry or in the garden, and what isn't expensive at the market."

"Whatever it's called," a businessman from Cologne said, "it's fantastic."

Then the amateur cooks in the group wanted to know what ingredients Donna used, and some became bolder. It started with Elsa Schoendorf, the owner of a bookshop in Boston. After an exceptionally fine *gnocchi di spinaci e ricotta* one day and a *cinghiale al vino* the next, she asked Donna if she could watch her in the kitchen.

"I've always fancied myself a good cook," she said. "In fact, I'm rather famous for it, if I do say so myself. There was even a write-up in the *Globe* about one of my dinner parties. But you! You, Donna, are truly exceptional. I would be honored if I could just stand behind you while you prepare a meal or two."

Donna did not like the idea. For one thing, she didn't really have recipes, but simply used long years of experience and intuition to tell her how much of this, how much of that. For another, she was sure diners did not want to know what went into a dish or how it was prepared. And finally, she considered cooking a meal an intimate relationship, something between her and her ingredients. Having someone else in the kitchen would be an intrusion.

But she reluctantly agreed. After all, Elsa Schoendorf was a friendly person and also a paying customer.

The next morning she was surprised and dismayed to find that Elsa had brought her newfound friend Max van Oberling, a book dealer from Amsterdam, with her.

"All right," Donna reluctantly said, "today I'm going to make one of the staples of *cucina povera*. It's Tuscan bread soup."

"Oh," Elsa said, "I've had that in restaurants. They always use the same word. Rustic."

"Yes," Donna said. "We are the rustic ones, aren't we? Sorry I'm not wearing my peasant dress and a kerchief over my hair."

"I'm sorry," Elsa said. "I didn't mean . . ."

"That's all right. I understand. And Tuscan bread soup really is a peasant soup. OK, let's get to work. Max, chop up these two red onions and then that celery. And then dice these tomatoes. All of this is from our garden, by the way."

Max set to work.

"Elsa, drain those cannellini beans. They've been soaking overnight. Then chop that parsley, the garlic, and these rosemary and basil leaves. I'll cut up this bread. Now here's the secret. The bread has to be stale. I mean really stale. If it's not, it's going to lump up. I've had these chunks left over from our meals last week. We Tuscans don't let anything go to waste."

Donna poured olive oil into a heavy pot and added some of the garlic and herbs, and then the tomatoes and water. When everything came to boil, she turned the burner down.

"Now we let it simmer for a half-hour."

Donna gave a tour of the kitchen while they were waiting—the new pots and pans, cookware, cutlery, fancy knives. "These knives are the best part," she said. "We got them when we remodeled."

She fingered them like precious jewels.

"When we first bought the farmhouse, there was only a range that burned wood, which they called a *cucina economica*, because the people before us still used the fireplace. We installed a gas-burning stove, but we knew it wouldn't be big enough for all you people. So now we have this mammoth thing." She looked into the pot on the stove.

"OK, now we add the bread." She threw in the chunks and then started adding chicken stock, stirring all the time. More chicken stock. More garlic and herbs. A cup of red wine. More stock.

"You have to get the bread really soaked and let the flavors mesh with each other, that's why we're adding more stock."

"It smells wonderful," Max said.

Donna turned off the burner. "Well, we're done. Let's bring it in."

"*Stupendo!*" the guests cried after one spoonful.

"I can't believe it," Donna told Ezio that night. "The bread soup is so easy. Anyone can make it. They don't need me to tell them."

"Did you mind having visitors in the kitchen? You know how you resisted that."

"It was all right. I guess they made me feel like I know something."

"Donna, Donna." He kissed her. "You do. You really do."

THE NEXT DAY, with Elsa and Max again hovering over her shoulders and even taking notes, Donna opened a large bag of cornmeal.

"Today we're going to make another one of the most traditional dishes in Tuscany, something people here have been eating for centuries. It's always classified as peasant food, just like the bread soup, but I know that some fancy restaurants serve it and consider it a delicacy. Polenta."

"Oh, polenta," Elsa said. "I've tried that and it never comes out right. It's either lumpy or so hard I have to cut it with a butcher knife."

"I had it once," Max said. "Didn't like it. Too gritty. Maybe because it was served with liver and onions and I hate, absolutely hate, liver and onions."

"Well, let's just try it," Donna said. She poured nine cups of water into a big heavy pot and turned on the burner. "I just love my new stove!"

When the water was boiling, she turned the heat down to a simmer. Then she threw in some salt and took cornmeal by the handful and slowly added it, letting it flow through her fingers.

"Don't you measure?" Elsa was aghast.

"It's about three cups. I can guess. OK, this is crucial. You have to stir it as you're adding the cornmeal. I use this long wooden spoon. If you keep stirring, you won't get lumps. Oops. There's a lump."

She stirred more vigorously.

"Isn't your arm getting tired?" Elsa asked.

"In my previous life I was a marble cutter in Pietrasanta."

"You're making that up," said Max, who hadn't heard her story before.

"Unfortunately, no." Donna continued to stir for about twenty minutes more. "OK, it's done."

She took the pot to the pasta table and poured it out.

"You're pouring it on the table?" Max was incredulous.

"Don't worry. It's clean. I washed it. I know some women put it in a pan, but I've always just used the table. I think it tastes better for some reason."

Donna spread the mixture around into a perfect circle. "You could use a rolling pin, but I just use my hands. I'm making it about two inches thick. OK, it will be cool in about five minutes. Then we can cut it up into pieces. Rather, *you* can cut it up. Then sprinkle some Parmesan on it."

Elsa and Max obeyed.

On another burner, Donna had a mushroom sauce simmering. "We can pour this on top of the pieces. Just mushrooms, an onion, celery, garlic, red wine, parsley. I'd tell you how much of each, but I just guessed. I'm sure you can figure it out."

Elsa and Max weren't sure of that, but a half-hour later, as platters of polenta were passed around the table, there were exclamations of "*delizioso!*"

After everyone had eaten, Elsa helped Donna take the empty plates back to the kitchen and then volunteered to help wash and dry the dishes. The dishwasher wasn't big enough.

"That's very kind of you," Donna said. "Thanks."

Suds up her arms, Elsa began to talk about all the wonderful Italian cookbooks she collected and how she loved to simply read them, even if she didn't make any of the recipes.

"Sometimes the photographs of the meals are so beautiful, I think I could eat the food right off the page. There was one that I liked, a plate of *chicken cacciatore* placed on a bench outside a farmhouse—just like here. It was taken at sunset with the Tuscan hills in the background. Oh, my! I tell you, that photo took my breath away so I cut it out and had it framed. It's right above my desk in my study."

Donna laughed. "Why would anyone let the chicken get cold by having its photograph taken?

Elsa smiled. "I guess you wouldn't understand."

They were almost finished with the dishes when Elsa said, "Donna, have you ever thought of writing a cookbook? You are such a marvelous cook. I'm sure people would want to read it."

"Me?" Donna said, taking off her apron. "I couldn't write a cookbook. I wouldn't know where to start. I don't have anything written down. I just put in what I think should be put in and I guess I just have a sense of how long to mix, how long to cook. No, I could never do that."

Elsa stacked dinner plates into a cupboard. "Donna, have you ever heard of Julia Child?"

"Julia Child? Um, vaguely. She's American, right?"

"Well, you'd certainly know her if you were in America. Where to begin? Well, first Julia—everyone calls her Julia—moved to France with her husband and while she was there she wrote a really important cookbook, *Mastering the Art of French Cooking*. It was seven hundred and twenty-six pages!"

"Good God! Sounds like she made cooking a lot of work."

"No. That's the thing. She wrote it so that anyone could understand how to make these really marvelous French meals. I've used it myself several times, though I must say I never have great success."

"There. You see?"

Elsa ignored her. "And you know what? Then Julia had a television show and actually cooked on the show!"

"Before everyone? Good God!"

"You won't believe how successful it was. Everyone watched it. I mean everyone. Partly that was because she was so funny and made little mistakes sometime. But her meals were fantastic. It was great fun."

"I'm sure. I can't imagine someone going on television and cooking a meal. I mean, that's something you do in the privacy of your kitchen. Except for you and Max, of course."

"Well, Julia introduced America to real French cooking with her French cookbook. Wouldn't you like to introduce people to real Italian cooking?"

Donna closed all the cupboard drawers and made sure all the burners were off. She wiped the last crumb from the pasta table. She switched off the lights and took off her apron. "No, Elsa, no."

"Donna," Elsa said, "would you at least think about a cookbook? Really. I mean, I think I could help. I'd love to! I could watch you and take down the measurements and the mixing times and the cooking times. You know, it would be fun!"

"Elsa, you're very kind and that's very thoughtful. But no, it sounds like just too much work."

Elsa kissed Donna on the cheek. "Think about, Donna. Think about it."

That night, as Ezio read a new history of the Italian Resistance and Donna opened more requests for reservations, she said, "You know, I think I'm starting to enjoy cooking for this group. They seem so appreciative, not just of the food, but how I tell them to prepare it."

"Maybe you're the one who should have been a schoolteacher."

"Oh, no. I'd never be able to do this as a class. But you know what? Elsa, that nice woman from Boston, well, she was helping me clean up today and she suggested that I write a cookbook. She told me about a cookbook she has with beautiful photographs. And about a woman from America, Julia Child, who wrote a book about French cooking. She said it was very popular."

"Donna! Lucia and Paolo have been telling you to write a cookbook for years, but you've never listened."

"Ezio. I can't write a cookbook. Everything's in my head. I have no idea about exact amounts. If I wrote something wrong, people would make it and get sick and it would be terrible. I would be sued!"

"Donna, you won't be sued because someone made a bad soufflé. What did you tell Elsa?"

"Exactly what I just told you. But she wouldn't listen. She said she would watch me and write down how much of this, how much of that, how long to do this, how long to do that."

"That sounds like a perfect solution."

"So you're going to gang up on me, too."

"I wouldn't put it that way. But you have to admit that you've got some very original recipes and I for one think many people would want to try them. I'm sure there would be a publisher."

Donna was silent for a long time. "But who would we get to take photos?"

"Ha! You are thinking about it!"

"And who would take notes when Elsa leaves?"

"I'm sure Lucia would love to do that."

"I couldn't ask her. She's so busy."

"Doing what? Donna . . ."

"I don't know, Ezio."

"I do. I can see the book right now. And I know just the title: *Donna's Cucina.*"

ELSA HAD LESS THAN THREE WEEKS left in her stay at the Cielo, so Donna felt pressured to make as many different meals as she could. Elsa diligently took notes as Donna came up with one exquisite meal after another. *Pollo arrosto* and *melanzane* and *costolette di vitello alla capricciosa* and *bistecca con pomodori arrostiti* and *costoletta di maiala alla saltimbocca* and *risotto con gamberi e capesante.* And on and on.

"My mouth is watering just watching you," Elsa kept saying. Each day, guests greeted each new delicacy with more cries of *"Magnifico!"*

Unsure of some of the directions, Elsa started to ask questions. "Do you think that was a half teaspoon or three quarters?"

"Um, I don't know. I'll have to measure. Three quarters?"

"Should that boil for fifteen or twenty minutes?"

"Let's try fifteen and see if it's done."

The more specific the recipes became, the more Donna worried that they might not be accurate.

"What if these are totally wrong?" she asked Ezio almost every night. "I mean, I've never measured out things before."

"You know what? I bet your publisher will test the recipes before they print them."

"Really? They do that?"

"I'm pretty sure. They want the recipes to be accurate, too. They want to stand behind a cookbook with recipes that people all over the world will be making—your *costolette di vitello alla capricciosa* and *risotto con gamberi e capesante* and all the others."

"People all over the world! Oh, my God!"

When Elsa regretfully packed up to leave, Donna was almost in tears. "What am I going to do without you? You've saved my recipes so many times!"

"I'm sure Lucia will do just fine. Just relax, Donna. Pretend that nobody is watching you."

"How in the world could I do that? You've been hovering over me like a shadow. I get so nervous I don't know what I'm doing."

"Just relax, just relax. And I have some good news. Max says he knows a publisher in Rome who he thinks would love to publish your book. He's going to contact him as soon as he gets home. Isn't that great?"

"I don't know, Elsa. Sometimes I think I should never have started on this."

Elsa kissed Donna. "Just relax, Donna, just relax. It's going to be just wonderful. Remember Julia Child."

"Great. Threaten me with Julia Child!"

Of course, relaxing was impossible, and Donna spent each evening going over each recipe trying to figure out if she should change the amount of one ingredient or another, or alter the time for each direction even a fraction. She was so lost in thought that she shut out everything else.

"Donna," Ezio said one night, "I saw Paolo today and he wondered whether we wanted to go to Lucca to see a movie one night next week."

No response.

"He says he wants to see *Gandhi*. Remember we talked about it when it came out? That we'd want to see it? It's gotten great reviews."

No response.

"Donna?"

No response.

"Did you hear me?"

"Yes, yes, of course I heard you. You said we should go to a movie. Ezio, I'm so busy I can't think of going out. How could you even think of asking me to do that? Just let me work on this, OK?"

"OK. Fine. Forget it." Ezio went back to his book but he couldn't concentrate. Increasingly, he worried that he and Donna were talking less and being silent more when they were together. What he thought would be an exciting adventure for both of them had turned into heavy work for his wife and not much fun for him.

He could, he supposed, go back to his own project, one that he had started six years ago but had worked on sporadically ever since. It seemed like a good idea, a historical novel about a group of people trapped in a farmhouse much like the Cielo during World War II. Some of the characters were based on people he knew in Sant'Antonio who had actually been trapped for three months in the Cielo while the war was going on all around them. His own role as a member of the partisan resistance would be featured, if fictionalized.

Since the war was over for thirty-seven years, he had to refresh his memory. He read dozens of books about the war, about the Nazis in Italy, about Mussolini, about the partisans. He even talked to a few people who had been in the war, members of the Resistance or in the Italian Army, but found that their memories had, at best, faded. He knew some of their stories were patently false.

The writing had gone well at first, but then he felt there were too many characters in the book and he didn't know what to do with them or where the story was going to go. He certainly didn't know how he would end it. He had enjoyed writing his memoir, *A Time to Remember*, about his days as a partisan in the war, but that was many years ago and this was fiction. It was a lot more challenging.

So he put it aside on the pretense that he had "writer's block" and that if he read more novels he would find more inspiration. He was currently reading Vasco Pratolini's *Cronache di poveri amanti*, having just finished Pratolini's *Il quartiere* and *Cronaca familiare*. Ezio liked the way Pratolini handled so many characters and kept them interesting.

Maybe he should go back to his writing now, Ezio thought. Donna would probably not even notice.

Meanwhile, tensions in the kitchen increased when Lucia arrived to take Elsa's place in taking down the recipes.

"Donna, I didn't quite see that. Was that one cup or two?"

"Two, Lucia."

"And was that one sprig or two of parsley?"

"Two, Lucia, two! Could you watch a little more closely? I'm nervous enough without having to go back over everything."

"OK, OK. I'll try, but I've never done anything like this before."

"OK."

Now Ezio worried that Donna and Lucia, close friends for so long, would have a falling out over the project. "*Donna's Cucina from Hell*," he muttered.

By the end of the summer season, Donna had completed sixty recipes, which she thought would be more than enough to fill a book. She figured it would be a small book, not seven hundred pages like Julia Child's. Now, night after night, she pored over the recipes, again and again and again. She sat at her desk in a corner of the living room. Across the room, Ezio was in his chair attempting to write on a yellow legal pad. They didn't talk much.

In early December, they received good news.

"Donna!" an excited Elsa said on the phone. "Max just called me. He found a publisher! Roma Editore! They're one of the biggest publishing houses in Italy! They want to publish your book of recipes! And they'll take photographs! They want you to submit a manuscript. As soon as you can! Oh, and they want you to write an introduction to each of the recipes, something that will make people understand what the meal is all about. You can do that, can't you? I'm sure you can."

Donna hung up the phone. "Oh, my God!"

OVER CHRISTMAS and into the new year, Donna struggled with the introductions to the recipes. Soon, she panicked.

"I don't know what to write about," she finally wailed to Ezio. "Can you help me? Please!"

"Donna, you know I don't know anything about cooking. When you're busy or away or something I make myself some pasta. That's about all I can do. And sometimes I burn that."

"Come on, Ezio. You're a writer. You can imagine some things, can't you?"

Her husband was actually pleased to have an excuse not to do his own writing. "OK, come on over and we'll see what we can put together."

Donna gathered her notes and sat across from Ezio. "I was working on this one, *risotto con gamberi e capesante,* and I couldn't come up with anything. I mean anything!"

"Risotto with shrimp and scallops. That should be pretty easy."

"For you, maybe."

"How about," Ezio said, "if you described the history of rice in Italy. I talk about this in my Rome to Renaissance class. The kids love it. The Romans had rice, you know. They got it from India. But they used it only for medicinal purposes to settle upset stomachs. But there are records of rice pottages from the Middle Ages. They boiled rice until it was soft and mixed in almond milk or cow's milk. We're not sure when rice was actually first grown in Italy, but it was probably in the late fifteenth century. The Duke of Milan claimed that he sent a single sack of rice to the Duke of Ferrara and twelve sacks were harvested. Imagine. And then . . ."

"Ezio! No one wants to know about the history of rice in a cookbook!"

"Why not? I think this stuff is interesting."

"Well, I don't. Let's try another. *Melanzane.*"

"Eggplant! Did you know that in the nineteenth century people in Florence shunned eggplant? They thought it was 'Jewish food.' How they arrived at that conclusion, I don't know. But anyway . . ."

"Ezio, people don't want to read about what Italians thought of Jews in the nineteenth century. Please!"

Ezio sighed. "All right. One more and then maybe we should wait until tomorrow."

Donna went through her notes again. She was very discouraged. "OK. *Bistecca con pomodori arrostiti.*"

"Steak with tomatoes and peppercorns. Well, that should be easy. I mean, when you think of Italy, you think of tomatoes, right? At least other countries think of us that way. But in America they slather it all over their pasta, when they should be using just olive oil. Remember that guy from Chicago last year who couldn't believe that? He said they used tomato paste on everything. He said . . ."

Donna put a paper clip on her notes. "Why don't you go to bed, Ezio? I want to work on these things a little more."

Donna went to bed late and got up early. She had decided to write short personal essays before each recipe. For *risotto con gamberi e capesante,* she wrote about having shrimp in a restaurant for the first time and thinking that she should eat the whole thing, tail and all. She was so embarrassed when her dinner companion said that just wasn't done. For *melanzane,* she wrote about the first time she had eggplant and didn't like it much. She thought it was too stringy. But now it was one of her favorite foods and she used it as much as she could. And for *bistecca con pomodori arrostiti,* she remembered how steak was such a rarity during the war and that one Christmas her father brought home a small piece from the butcher shop and it was the best treat she had all year.

When Ezio came down for breakfast, he asked how she was doing.

"Fine. I'm doing fine, thanks," she said, not looking up. "I think I'll skip breakfast. I want to work on these some more."

"OK." He scrambled a couple of eggs and toasted some bread, trying to be as quiet as possible, but he dropped the frying pan too hard into the sink. "Sorry!" he called out.

He sat for a while with his legal pad and tried to pick up his writing from the day before. Nothing came.

"I think I'll go down to the village," he said, putting on his coat. "Need to get some things. Want me to get anything?"

No response.

"OK, see you later, OK?"

"OK."

Driving his truck down the winding road to Sant'Antonio, Ezio suddenly felt some remorse. "She's under a lot of strain. I should be helping her more. I should be more understanding. This is a really bad time. It shouldn't be that way."

At Manconi's, he picked up some veal cutlets. Maybe, he thought, Donna could show him how to make *costoletta di vitella.*

"Thanks, Anita," he said as she tied a string around the package. "How's little Marianna?"

"Just great! She's two years old now. She's walking all over and talking and talking. We're so proud of her!"

Ezio liked talking to Anita and her husband Mario Leoni. They were both two of the smartest students he'd ever had.

"Kids sure grow up fast," he said. "I remember when Marianna was born. Everyone in the village was so excited. There hadn't been a baby born in Sant'Antonio in so many years . . . ."

Ezio was interrupted by Signora Cardineli, who asked Anita for a small amount of hamburger meat for her cat.

He picked up his package. "Well, I think I'll stop to see Mario."

"Stop in again!"

At the *bottega* across the way, Mario Leoni was furiously ringing up the cash register with three people waiting in line and an elderly man shouting questions from the rear of the store.

"I guess I'll come back another time," Ezio thought.

As long as he was in the village, he decided to see Paolo and Lucia. They should be home and he needed someone to talk to. Paolo had sold his *pasticceria* in Reboli and spent his days now driving up and down the Tuscan hills on his motorcycle. But Paolo was just leaving his house.

"Oh, Ezio. Good to see you. Gotta run over to Lucca. Lucia's got a whole list of things for me to get."

"OK. Just thought we could talk for a while."

Paolo strapped his helmet on. "Not right now. But later! You could go inside and talk to Lucia, but you know how she feels about Donna right now. Taking down those recipes wasn't much fun for Lucia. Maybe you'd better wait."

"Right. I'll come back down in a day or two."

"Do that."

Paolo got on his motorcycle and Ezio got into his truck and the two men drove off in different directions. Suddenly, Ezio felt very alone.

AT THE END OF JANUARY, Donna finally typed up her manuscript on Ezio's big black typewriter. This had involved retyping a page numerous times because she thought of something to be added or deleted. Sometimes that meant retyping the following page and the page after that.

"I'll never finish this," she complained to Ezio.

"You can still quit, you know."

"Not after I've come this far."

"Suit yourself."

After she sent it off to Roma Editore she thought she could forget about it, but found herself awake at night worrying over one ingredient or another. She didn't have to wait long. Less than two weeks later, she received a call. Could a representative from Roma Editore come to see her?

She had expected a wispy little bookish agent but instead she greeted a tall, well-tanned man of about forty-five. He had curly black hair and soft blue eyes.

"Signora," he said. His teeth gleamed as brightly as his Italian shoes. "I am Antonio Palmeri, here to talk about your wonderful cookbook. I am so pleased to meet such a lovely lady. You are going to be a very big author."

Donna, wondering if he held her hand longer than necessary, introduced her husband. Ezio murmured a *buongiorno*, shook the man's hand and went to sit in his chair, where he picked up his legal pad.

"Don't you want to join us, Ezio?" Donna asked.

"I think you can take care of it."

Donna shrugged and sat down with Antonio Palmeri at the dining room table.

"Signora," Signor Palmeri said, opening his briefcase and spreading papers across the table, "we want you to know that we at Roma Editore are very excited about your book. I must say, more excited than any other book we have published in a long time. So! We are going to pull out all the stops, as we say. All the stops! Every year we publish a big beautiful book before Christmas. This year we were planning on a book about Siena, wonderful photographs and essays. Well, the author for whatever reason has not come through on time. But then your book fell into our laps, so to speak."

Signor Palmeri paused for breath and then continued. "Signora, we want your book! Not just because we need it, but because we think it is a wonderful book. And we want it to come out as quickly as possible. In fact, before next Christmas!"

"Before next Christmas?"

"Signora, that's how excited we are. But you leave the details to us. We will figure it out. Now we know that this is your first book, so we want to work with you very closely so that it is exactly the way you want it to be. Roma Editore will go out of our way to make you happy with the product. And I'm sure you will be."

He smiled again.

First, finances were discussed. Donna was to receive fifteen percent of the sale of each book.

"So if we price your book at, say, 26,000 *lire,* you will receive 3,900 *lire* each time. For every one hundred books sold, you will receive 390,000 *lire.* For every one thousand books sold, you will receive 3,900,000."

Donna's head was spinning. She looked across the room at Ezio, who had closed his eyes but looked very pale.

"I . . . uh . . . I don't know what to say," she told Signor Palmeri. "That's more money than, than, well, I don't know. My husband has been a schoolteacher so we're used to living on that."

"Italy does not pay our teachers very well," Signor Palmeri said. He smiled again. "But, you know, we can't really tell how many copies of your books will be sold."

"Maybe only ten," Donna said. "We don't have many relatives. Maybe a few people in the village."

"Or maybe a million," Signor Palmeri said. "That would mean . . ."

"No!" Donna interrupted. "I can't think about it. This is much too much to think about."

"Well, then, let's talk about other things," Signor Palmeri said.

He went on to describe how Roma Editore would test every recipe and that Donna would be frequently consulted if there were questions. He assured her that each of her recipes would turn out well. He said that the company had many photographers and that one in particular was especially good at photographing meals in various exotic settings.

"He is just amazing. You will love his pictures."

"This is going to take a long time, isn't it?" Donna said. "I mean, taking all those pictures."

"Not so long. As I said, we are very interested in your book and will have a team of editors working on it. I don't see why your book could not be released before Christmas."

"That sounds like a long time from now. Well, I'm not going to even think about it during that time."

"That is a good idea, because after the book comes out we will plan some extensive publicity, no? We will arrange for you to be interviewed by some good writers from all sorts of newspapers and magazines, from the very sophisticated to the very popular."

"But I'm so shy. I won't know what I could say."

He smiled again. "Just talk about your wonderful meals and the way you cook. People will love to read that. And they will want to know about you and how you live, up here in this beautiful farmhouse. Oh, and I believe we can do a little television. This would be a perfect setting."

"Television! Here? Oh my God!"

Why did he smile so much, Donna wondered.

"I'm sure you will do just fine," he said. "Well, I must be going. But first I need you to sign a few papers here."

He dug out a thick stack of papers. There were three sets, each with twenty-five pages.

"This is your contract, Signora. This says we will publish your book and it outlines the royalties you will get. There are a few other details, but you don't have to worry about them. Now if you will just sign here and here and here, all three copies."

Donna's hand was so shaky she wouldn't have recognized her own signature.

He put two sets of the papers back in his briefcase and left the other on the table. "Signora, it was such a pleasure to meet you. And your husband, too, of course. I hope we will meet again. Very soon." His smile was even brighter.

Signor Palmeri had put on his coat and was about to leave when he turned back.

"And we will arrange for you to visit some of Roma Editore's many stores so that you can talk about your book and autograph copies. We have stores all over Italy."

"Stores? Autograph copies?"

"Of course. This has become very popular in America now. When authors publish a book, they go to bookstores and there's a little program in which they talk about their books and read sections from them. Then people buy the books and the authors autograph them. This increases the sales of the books and it lets readers get to know the authors a little."

"But I don't want to be known, Signor Palmeri!"

"Please, call me Antonio. We will be talking soon, I'm sure. Goodbye, signora. Oh, and goodbye, signor."

He kissed her gently on both cheeks. Ezio didn't look up.

Closing the door behind their visitor, Donna confronted her husband.

"Ezio, don't you think you were a little rude? You could have been more pleasant to the man."

"I was pleasant."

"You sat in your chair all the while. You could have joined us. You would have had questions."

"Seems like you were taking care of everything pretty well."

"I didn't know what to say. Now I'm sure I'll have a million questions. And all this stuff, interviews, television, bookstores. Ezio, I don't know if I can do this.

"I'm sure the handsome Signor Palmeri, Antonio, will be happy to help you."

Donna turned abruptly and went into the kitchen.

Over a mostly silent supper that night, Ezio asked Donna if she'd like to go to a movie in Lucca.

"*La Notte di San Lorenzo*. About the partisans in the war. Directed by the Taviani brothers. I really want to see this, Donna."

"I'm too tired, Ezio. You go. You can tell me about it."

"OK, I think I will."

Ezio had never gone to a movie by himself before. That night he did.

WITH GUESTS SCHEDULED to arrive in less than two months, and a busy summer ahead of them, Donna and Ezio tried to put thoughts of *Donna's Cucina* aside.

"We'll put it on the back burner," Ezio said.

"Very funny."

There was work to do. Painting doors. Repairing the roof. Replacing panes in two windows. Fixing holes in the road. Not to mention straightening cupboards and shelves, washing all the floors, cleaning the bathrooms, filling the little pool, washing and ironing the curtains. And that was just what needed to be done the first week.

"Well, I'm exhausted," Ezio said as he collapsed into the couch one night.

"Me, too," Donna said. "Think we'll be ready in time?"

"We always are."

"Somehow."

Donna snuggled up to her husband and he put his arm around her. "This is good, isn't it, like it was before?"

He kissed her forehead. "Yes."

Donna's Cucina seemed like a cloud far in the distance. They never talked about it.

Their first guests were a couple from Belgium who had come twice before; an elderly single man from Spain; a middle-aged couple from Japan, the Cielo's first Japanese visitors; and a young man and woman from Liverpool.

Since she was freed from the pressure of writing down recipes, Donna happily made one of her specialties after another, more assured than she had ever been. "I think I'm actually enjoying cooking now," she thought as she stirred a mushroom sauce over chicken breasts.

"Magnifico!" all the guests shouted.

Perhaps because the weather was so nice all summer, not hot and with little rain, almost all the guests seemed to be in a great mood while they were there. A few exceptions: a cranky old British lady who didn't understand why the place didn't serve tea in the afternoon, and a teenage boy, brought unwillingly by his parents, who played his transistor radio much too loud.

But those were exceptions. "This is our best summer yet, all around," Ezio said.

Donna agreed.

She had received only three phone calls from the publisher with questions about recipes. "I can't believe that's all they found," she worried.

"You obviously tested them well yourself," her husband said.

In the second week of July, Antonio Palmeri called. Proofs of her cookbook were ready. Could he bring them to her the next day?

Ezio was not excited about the visit. "Couldn't he just mail them?"

"Sounded like they had a deadline and they needed the proofs read as soon as possible. Anyway, it shouldn't take long. Maybe he'll just leave them and I'll mail them back to him."

"Or maybe he'll have to make a second visit and pick them up."

"Ezio. You don't like Antonio, do you?"

"I didn't say that."

"No, but I sure get that impression. You barely talked to him when he was here the first time."

"Look, he's representing the company that's going to make you millions and millions of *lire*. Why should I resent that?"

"See, there you go. That sarcastic tone again."

"Donna, I'm very proud of you, I really am. It's just that this is all leading us down a new and different path and I'm not sure I like it."

"Ezio, I'm scared, too. A couple of years ago, we were so happy just managing this place and enjoying all our visitors. Well, most of them. Now, it's changed. But it's kind of exciting, isn't it?"

"I guess."

Ezio wouldn't admit it to Donna, or even to himself, but one reason he resented Donna's cookbook was that his own writing was at a complete standstill. After many drafts, he had completed five chapters and had gotten the characters from the village to the farmhouse where they would be trapped for three months. He had described the tensions between some of the characters and had introduced a farmer who would be their friend and benefactor.

But he didn't know where to go from there. Should he have the war come nearby? It seemed too early for that. Should he have the village priest get involved with the partisan resistance? That would take the focus off the farmhouse. Should he have a partisan visit the farmhouse? He knew that the partisan would be based on his own involvement during the war and he had a difficult time thinking about that.

So he put it aside when the tourists started arriving and, although he had plenty of time at night, he always said he was too busy to start writing again. He'd wait until fall, knowing that he'd be occupied with school then.

When Antonio Palmeri arrived the next day, Ezio shook his hand and said he really had to do some work in the back.

The visitor again held Donna's hand for an inordinate amount of time. "Signora, it is such a pleasure to see you again."

Donna freed her hand and led Antonio to the kitchen table. There, he opened a large box and spread out page proofs.

"Of course," he said, "we have a team of professional proofreaders who will go over every line, every word, with a fine-tooth comb. But we wanted you to see this, too. The type size is exactly right, no? The margins are not too wide and not too narrow, yes? And the recipes themselves are highly readable for the busy cook. Don't you agree?"

Donna had read hundreds and hundreds of books, mostly novels, but she had never seen proofs of their pages. Now she was looking at her own writing and it was overwhelming.

"Yes . . . yes . . . it all looks very good."

"But now, here is the best part. Look at these photographs. Aren't they magnificent?"

"Oh, my."

After each meal was made in a test kitchen, the photographer had placed the dishes in an unusual setting—a picnic table, the top of a marble column, on a silk bedspread, at the entry to a church.

"I can't believe these colors. They are truly magnificent, Signor Palmeri . . . Antonio. My meals have never looked so good."

"Good enough to eat? That's what we want to show. That people will look at these photographs and immediately go out and buy the ingredients and make the meal. They won't be as good as yours, of course, but they can try. Signora, this is going to be a wonderful book and we can't wait until it's published."

"Before Christmas?"

"Now we think as early as October. We hope so. Then it will be ready for Christmas giving."

"Oh, my."

"There's one more thing. You notice that the cover is not yet ready. We do that separately. I have seen the initial proof and I must say, I've never seen such a cover so astonishing. People will look at it and immediately want to buy the book."

"I . . . I . . . can't wait to see it myself."

"If all goes well, I should be able to bring you a copy in about a month, perhaps the middle of August."

That would mean, Donna feared, yet another visit from Antonio Palmeri. Won't Ezio be excited about that?

They pored over the pages for several hours. Donna could find nothing that had to be changed, but Antonio pointed out a small indent here, the wrong font there. He sat so close to her that she had to keep moving. Finally, he packed up the page proofs.

"I will see you in August," he said. "I will count the days." That smile again.

"Thank you for everything, Antonio. Goodbye."

"My friends call me Tony," he said.

"Goodbye, Antonio."

After he left, Donna looked in the mirror and found that her face was flushed.

When Antonio returned in August, Ezio again found an excuse to leave Donna with the publishing agent, though he did look long and hard at Antonio before going out the door.

"Now then, let me show you the cover," Antonio said.

If breaths could be taken away, Donna lost hers at that moment. The cover's photograph showed Donna's *bistecca con pomodori arrostiti* arranged on an ancient plate that looked as if it had come from Roman times. The plate rested on a gleaming white marble balustrade. The steak glistened under juicy ripe tomatoes and on top of leafy green lettuce leaves. A half-filled glass of red wine stood at the side. In the background, golden hills of Tuscany, dotted with cypress trees, glowed in a setting sun.

In Roman type at the top were the words *Donna's Cucina,* and at the bottom, Donna Fazzini.

Donna's eyes filled with tears. "Oh, Antonio, it's so beautiful."

She suddenly hugged him, something she would ordinarily never do to someone who was almost a stranger.

"I'm glad you like it." He held her close and was about to kiss her hair when she broke away.

"Thank you, Antonio. I'm so glad you brought the cover for me to see. It's beautiful. The book will be out in . . ."

"October for sure."

"Good. Now I have many things to do. Thank you for coming."

She opened the door. Surprised by the abrupt farewell, Antonio took his leave. Donna held on to the table. Her legs felt wobbly.

"Oh, my God! I should have showed the cover to Ezio. What was I thinking?"

DONNA TRIED TO AVOID counting the days until October. That wasn't a problem when there were still guests at the Cielo, but after the last of them, two nuns from Canada, left the third week of September, she kept looking at the calendar nailed to a kitchen cupboard.

No word the first week of October. No word the second. "I thought he'd call by now," she thought. "Maybe they're having trouble. Maybe they decided not to print it."

By Thursday of the third week, she considered calling Antonio, but then he suddenly appeared at the door.

"*Buongiorno,* Signora!" She could not get over his gleaming smile. "I thought I would bring you a copy of your wonderful cookbook myself!"

He held her hand and then put his arm tenderly around her shoulder, withdrawing it quickly when Ezio came up behind his wife.

"Ah, Signor," Antonio said. "It's good to see you again." He offered his hand, which Ezio shook quickly.

"And here it is!" Antonio took his package to the kitchen table and carefully unwrapped the brown paper. "*Magnifico!*"

Speechless, Donna put her hand to her mouth. Ezio looked at the book, but didn't say anything.

"Well, this is just one copy. I have one hundred more in my automobile, and I will bring them in now. Perhaps you would like to give them to your friends?"

"We don't have one hundred friends," Ezio said.

"Thank you, Antonio," Donna said, but she looked at her husband. "That's very kind. I'm sure we will be happy to give them to our friends."

With twenty-five books in each box, Antonio lugged four boxes from his car. "Well, then, I will leave you to look at your cookbook yourself. To devour it, if I may say so."

"Thanks so very much, Antonio," Donna said with a quick handshake.

"I'm sure you have other things to do, places to go," Ezio said.

"Yes, yes, of course. Well, I will also leave this with you." He pulled an envelope from his jacket pocket. "This is a list of interviews and appearances we have scheduled. We discussed this before, remember? I have booked very nice hotel accommodations for you all the way. Please call me if you have any questions, otherwise I will be in touch with you in about a week."

"Thank you again, Antonio," Donna said.

After he had left, Donna finally picked up her book, carefully opening the cover and turning page after page. Ezio looked over her shoulder.

She went back to page seven. "Ezio, I want you to read this."

"Acknowledgments. OK. Let's see."

I want to thank so many people for helping write this, my first cookbook, well, actually, the first book I've ever written. I want to thank my father, who was my own wonderful first cook and whom I miss very much. I am also grateful to the generous visitors at our farmhouse who gave elaborate, if undeserving, praise for my meals, and particularly to Elsa Schoendorf and Lucia Sporenza, who carefully took down all the notes needed for my recipes.

But mostly I want to thank my dear husband, Ezio. He has silently suffered through my pangs and passions as I wrote this book and I owe him so much. He has been a rock to me. I love you, dear Ezio.

Ezio suddenly hugged his wife, pulled her face to his and kissed her.

"Donna. I don't know what to say."

"You don't have to say anything. Just believe me."

He kissed her again. "I believe you. And, Donna, I'm very proud of you and I'm sorry I've been such an ass about this."

"Let's just move on, OK?"

"OK."

She looked at the boxes of books. "Oh, my, what are we going to do with all these?"

"I guess we suddenly realize we don't know many people."

"Well, we could keep them here," Donna said, "and give them to our guests next summer."

"They may have already bought one."

"I guess we'll just store them all someplace. We can put one under that table leg that's too short."

Ezio started unpacking the books.

"Oh, I'll mail one to Elsa," Donna said, "but here's what I need to do right now. Lucia and I have hardly spoken since she worked so hard taking down the recipes. I want to take one of these to her."

"I'll go with you. It'll be good for the four of us to sit down together again."

Paolo had just returned from a trip to Massa and was taking off his motorcycle helmet.

"Ezio! And Donna! Well, Lucia will be hap . . . surprised to see you."

Lucia was in the living room trying to mend a rip in Paolo's jeans.

"Lucia," Paolo said. "Look what I found on our doorstep."

Lucia saw Donna but didn't get up. "Hi, Ezio," she said.

So it was up to Donna to make the first move. She sat in a chair opposite a friend she had not spoken to in months.

"Lucia, first I want to apologize. I know I was not nice to you when you were helping me with the recipes. In fact, sometimes I was very rude. I know that. I suppose I could say that I was tense and nervous because I wanted everything to go just right, but that was no excuse for behaving the way I did. I'm sorry, Lucia. Can you forgive me?"

Lucia put down her mending. "Well, I've been thinking about this, too. I've never held a grudge before and I didn't know what to do with it. But now I know I should have been more patient and understanding. I know you were nervous and under a lot of stress. I should have taken that into account. Of course, Donna, I forgive you."

"Do you think we can be friends again?"

"Of course."

The two women reached over and held hands. Both were crying.

"OK, now that we got that settled," Paolo said, "what's that in that package, Ezio? Cookies, maybe?"

"No, sorry. Actually, Donna wants you both to have this."

When Donna unwrapped her book, both Lucia and Paolo were afraid to touch it.

"Oh, my," Lucia said. "It's so beautiful. I had no idea it would look like this. It's . . . it's a real book, Donna!"

"Yes, it is," Paolo said. "Look, Lucia, it has a cover and pages and . . ."

"OK," his wife said, "you can stop teasing now. Donna, thank you." She kissed her friend.

Over coffee and biscotti, the four friends had a lot of catching up to do, but eventually the talk turned back to Donna's book. Donna explained that the man from Roma Editore had left an envelope that contained a list of interviews and appearances. She hadn't looked at it yet.

"Donna!" Lucia said. "You're going to be interviewed? You're going to bookstores to talk? Well, I know the first thing you have to do. Donna, you have to do this."

"What? More cooking?"

"No! You have to buy some new clothes. Something, well, a little more stylish, Donna. I'll go with you! We'll go to Florence, not Lucca, there's nothing there. I've heard of this great shop on Via Tornabuoni. And it's not too expensive either. Now it's late fall, so you shouldn't wear bright colors. I think you'd look very nice in a dark green or gray, a suit perhaps. Maybe a little hat, too. And you could brighten things up with a scarf. Yes, a colorful scarf. We could go this Saturday, I don't have anything else to do. It'll be so much fun. I haven't gone shopping like this in years, I never buy anything new . . ."

IT WAS LATE when Donna and Ezio returned to the farmhouse, and they were very tired, but Donna remembered the schedule Antonio had left. She pulled it out of the thick envelope and promptly dropped it.

"Oh, my God!" Donna said.

"Pretty hectic?"

"Oh, Ezio, look at this!"

It was more than a schedule. It was a detailed ten-page list of the events Antonio had scheduled for Donna in the next four weeks. In a separate letter he wrote that Roma Editore wanted to do as much as possible for the Christmas buying season and that *Donna's Cucina* would be the centerpiece of its campaign.

"We know you will agree," he wrote.

"I'm not at all sure about that," Donna said. "Read it to me, Ezio, I can't bear to look at it."

Ezio held the first page to the light. "He says he's scheduled interviews with magazines first because they will have Christmas deadlines soon. Let's see. Good grief, he's scheduled the first one for next Tuesday. Someone from *Panorama* will come here."

"My God, that's the most widely read paper in the country. But it's mostly photos, right?"

"Guess you'd better go to Florence this weekend to get those new clothes."

"Oh, Ezio."

"Now on Wednesday, there will be a writer from *L'Espresso.*"

"Another big one."

"He's given you Thursday off, but on Friday it's *Oggi*'s turn. I think that's kind of a gossip magazine. I wonder who they'll send."

"I've never even heard of it."

"Well, a week from Monday, this is interesting. *Famiglia Cristiana.* The Christian Family? What's that got to do with a cookbook? I guess Antonio thinks good cooking is good for the soul. OK, now we get into newspapers. On Wednesday, someone from *La Repubblica,* on Thursday, *Corriere della Sera.* Well, he's got the big ones. On Friday, *La Nazione.* That's in Florence. And on the following Monday, there will be a writer from *La Stampa.* I guess that's it for magazines and newspapers."

"So all these magazines and papers are going to send reporters here and interview me? What in the world am I going to tell all these people, Ezio? I don't know what to say."

"Just answer their questions. Just talk about how you love to cook and how people have loved your meals. That's right, isn't it?"

"Yes, but it seems like boasting."

"Donna, you want people to buy your book. The articles in these newspapers and magazines will let people know about it and then they'll buy it. It's called marketing."

He turned to the next page. "Oh, look, here's your schedule for your readings at Roma Editore bookstores. Good grief, I didn't know they had this many. It's actually a tour, Donna. You'll be gone, let's see, ten, eleven days. You start in Venice, then Padua, then Bologna, up to Milan, down to Pisa, then Florence, Perugia, Siena and you end up in Rome on November 20."

"No! We've only been in Pisa and Florence and Siena and Rome. And never for very long."

"You'll be staying in hotels."

"Good God! I hate hotels. Remember that awful one we stayed at in Rome?"

"Just think of the Cielo as a sort of hotel."

"Well, hardly, Ezio. How will I get to these places? Will you take me? I don't want to take trains and buses, and I certainly don't want to drive myself. Will you come with me, please? I'm going to be a nervous wreck. Oh, this is terrible."

Ezio kept reading the schedule, and finally put it down.

"Donna, I can't get away from school now. There's so much going on with the Christmas pageant coming up and everything else. Anyway, there's no need for me to drive you. The very handsome Antonio Palmeri is going to be your driver."

"Oh, no!"

"Oh, yes. He says he has booked two rooms in each of the hotels. He says they're adjoining, in case you have questions. He says there will be time in each city to do a little sightseeing. And he assures you he will find excellent restaurants for you, though he says they will never match your cooking. This guy is something else."

Donna didn't, couldn't say anything. Ezio walked to the window and looked out over the valley. A full moon shone on the miniature houses in the village below and it should have been a peaceful scene, but Ezio's heart was racing.

"I don't have to go, you know," Donna said. She hardly heard her own voice.

"Of course you have to go. It's all arranged. Signor Antonio Palmeri has taken care of everything. Every minute. You can even go sightseeing with him during the day and sleep in adjoining bedrooms at night. It will be a wonderful trip for you. Just wonderful."

"Ezio . . ."

"No, go. You deserve this. You did all that work on the book. And it's a great book. You'll have fun. Really."

"Ezio . . ."

"Are you worried about me? Come on. I'll be fine. I can take care of myself. I can make my meals. I love pasta. And I'll be busy at school."

"Ezio, really, I don't have to go. If the book sells ten copies I'll be happy."

"Donna, did you look at the contract you signed?"

"Contract?"

"Yes, that thick stack of papers you signed when the handsome Signor Antonio Palmeri came here the first time. You were so excited about having the book published, I don't think you ever read it. Well, I did. Let me get it."

Ezio went to the desk and opened a drawer. "Here . . . here on page twenty-four. You the undersigned agree to take part in any publicity campaigns that the party of the first part, that's Roma Editore, requests. And here you are, undersigned."

"I didn't know that!"

"Well, you agreed. You can't back out now."

Donna burst into tears. "I didn't know . . . I should have read that . . . interviews . . . readings . . . hotels . . . away for ten days . . ."

"And all with handsome Antonio Palmeri. Oh, he signed his name Tony."

CALLING THE TRIP FRIVOLOUS, Donna allowed Lucia to take her to Florence on Saturday, driving to Lucca and then taking a train the rest of the way. They went immediately to Via Tornabuoni. Donna didn't like trying on clothes to begin with, and resisted Lucia's effort to spend hours with one outfit after another. She finally decided on a dark gray suit, a green dress with a gold trim, a navy suit with white piping and a fitted dress in deep violet. Lucia wanted her to buy at least four more outfits, but Donna declined.

"Lucia, I'm going to have a different audience every night. Every outfit will be new to them. Why should I have so many?"

"The people may be different, but don't you want to look nice for you?"

"Lucia, I don't care how I look. Especially now."

"Especially now?"

"Yes."

"You mean because of Ezio, right? I thought there was something going on between you two. I could just tell, I'm funny that way. Want to tell me about it?"

"No."

"Donna, you've always told me everything."

"We'll work it out, Lucia. Don't worry about it."

They traveled home in silence.

The following Tuesday, the first interviewer arrived. To a man, and woman, every writer who came to interview Donna in the next weeks spent the first fifteen minutes complaining about the road to the Cielo. "How can you drive on those sharp turns?" "Shouldn't there be a fence so that cars don't fall into the valley?" "What if another car comes at you? There's no room!" "How many people have been killed going up and down that road?"

Two of the writers, both men, were so worried about making the treacherous return trip that they hardly asked any questions about Donna's cookbook.

A couple of the others, young women apparently on their first assignments, were more interested in Donna's career as a marble worker in Pietrasanta than in her cooking ability.

"I have no idea what these people could write about," Donna told Ezio.

Ezio wasn't around when the writers came. If he wasn't at school, he seemed to vanish into thin air.

"Ezio," Donna said after the third day, "I wish you would stay around to help me. I don't know how to handle these people, I don't know what to say."

"It's your book, Donna."

"I know, but . . ."

"It's your book."

"OK," she said, "are we going to go through that again? I thought we'd settled that. I don't know what's going on in your mind, Ezio, but you certainly aren't supporting me now."

"I thought I'd been like a rock. Seems like I read that somewhere."

"Well, I meant that. Then."

"Donna, just do the interviews and go on your wonderful trip with Signor Antonio Palmeri. We'll talk when you get back, OK? I'm going to bed now."

Later, when Donna crawled into bed next to her husband, she thought he must be sleeping because he didn't move. She lay on her side, staring at the wall. She wondered if she and Ezio would ever work it out.

On November 10, Antonio Palmeri arrived to take Donna on her bookstore tour. He remained in the car while Ezio waited at the door.

"Well, I'm off," Donna said. "Wish me luck. I'll call every night."

He kissed her lightly on the forehead. "No need to call. You'll be busy. I'll be fine."

Donna could feel tears welling in her eyes as Antonio opened the door of the red Maserati for her. Ezio saw that he whispered something to her but couldn't tell her reaction. Soon the car disappeared down the road.

He went into the kitchen and warmed a cup of coffee. He looked out the window over the valley for a long time. He turned on the television and turned it off. He picked up a Vasco Pratolini book, read five pages and put it down. He dug out his legal pad and stared at the blank pages.

"I think I'll go for a drive," he thought. When he returned he could barely remember where he went.

That night as promised, Donna called after her first appearance at a Roma Editore bookstore.

"Ezio, you should see Venice! It's everything we ever imagined. It's like a picture book come to life. I watched the gondolas go by. I sat in St. Mark's Square tonight. It's really fantastic!"

"How did the reading go?"

"OK, I guess. There were about thirty people. I think Antonio expected more. They asked a few questions and I think maybe ten or twelve books were sold."

"Seems like a lot of work to sell ten or twelve books. How's Antonio?"

"I haven't seen him much. I wanted to be alone and just walk and discover things on my own. I thought I'd get lost, but I didn't. I'm very proud of myself."

"How was dinner with Antonio?"

"I got back late from my walk so I didn't have dinner with him. He must have gone to bed."

"So you haven't spent much time with him?"

"Not at all. Just at the reading. Why?"

"Oh, nothing. Sounds like you're having a good time, Donna."

"I am. But I miss you, Ezio."

"I miss you, too, Donna."

It was late, but Ezio suddenly had an idea on how to solve a problem with his story. He picked up his legal pad and wrote furiously. He was still writing at 2 a.m.

Donna's excited phone calls continued in the next days, through readings in Padua, Bologna, Milan and Pisa. She'd seen the basilica in Padua! The colonnades in Bologna! The cathedral in Milan! The leaning tower in Pisa! She went on and on.

At home, even though he was tired after a day at school, Ezio had never written so intensely, and so well. By the time Donna had gone to Florence he had written four more chapters. And he liked them.

But she didn't call from Florence.

"Maybe she got back to the hotel too late," he thought. "Well, I won't worry about it. She's fine."

The next night she didn't call from Perugia. Ezio thought of calling her hotel, but changed his mind. "She can take care of herself. And she'll be home in a couple of days."

He couldn't wait for her call from Siena. He and Donna had visited it three times, becoming more enchanted each time. They planned to spend a week there next year.

But she didn't call. "Well, I'm sure she'll call from Rome. And anyway, she'll be home in a few days."

His writing was now at a standstill. He couldn't think about writing another sentence. He was now convinced that something had happened in Florence.

WHEN DONNA DIDN'T CALL from Rome, Ezio called her hotel. She sounded very tired and strained, almost as if she'd been crying.

"Glad I got you, Donna," he said. "What's wrong?"

"Nothing's wrong, Ezio."

"You must be so tired from seeing everything. How much did you see? The Colosseum? The Forum, the Pantheon, Trevi Fountain? You couldn't have had time to go to the Vatican."

"I didn't see any of that, Ezio."

"Really? You were at the reading all day?"

"No, just tonight."

"What did you do during the day?"

"I stayed in the hotel."

"All day? You went to Rome and you didn't see anything like we did the last time?"

"No."

"Were you with Antonio?"

"Ezio, I'll be home tomorrow night. Bye."

Ezio thought it odd that when Antonio drove Donna back the next night he simply brought her suitcase in and left without saying a word. "Just as well," Ezio thought. "Hope I never see that asshole again."

When he turned around, he saw that Donna had already gone into their bedroom and was undressing.

"Tired?"

"Exhausted."

"Do you want to talk?"

"No."

"OK. Get some sleep."

"I will. Thanks."

Donna slept so late the next morning that Ezio had already made a trip to the village to get bread, eggs and milk and then worked on the fence in the back. She came into the kitchen at noon, eyes puffy and her hair uncombed.

"Don't look at me," she said.

"I'm just glad you're back."

"So am I."

"Want to talk about your trip?"

Donna poured a cup of coffee and sat at the kitchen table, barely noticing what was in the newspaper Ezio had left for her.

"Something happened, right?" Ezio said. "When you were in Florence? You didn't call after that."

"Ezio, I can't talk about it yet."

"Have you been hurt? Should you see a doctor?"

Donna laughed. "A doctor? What's a doctor going to do?"

"I don't know, but then I don't know what the problem is. Did Antonio do something? That bastard."

"I don't blame Antonio, Ezio."

"Blame? What blame? What happened? Tell me, Donna."

"Ezio, I can't talk about it yet. I only got up because I have to tell you something that's going to happen, something I don't like very much at all."

"Couldn't be any worse, could it?"

Donna described what would happen shortly after Christmas. A television crew from one of the new networks in Rome would come to the Cielo and film a program in which Donna would make one of her meals. She would have to go slowly and describe the ingredients and the cooking times. All this would take place in a half-hour. The film would be used by the producer to find a sponsor and if one were found it would become a regular feature on television.

"Wow," Ezio said.

"Ezio, I really don't want to do this. I don't want to be on television! But Antonio says it's in my contract."

"I guess it is."

"Ezio, do you know what he said?"

"That you'll be just great?"

"No! He thinks that if this works out and they can get a sponsor I can be the Julia Child of Italy!"

"Really?"

"Don't laugh. That's what he said. Oh, Ezio! I don't want to do this. I don't want to be the Julia Child of Italy. I don't want to be the Julia Child of Sant'Antonio!"

"OK, Donna. Settle down. You said 'if this works out.' Well, maybe it won't work out. Maybe they'll find out it's too complicated to bring all their equipment up here or that our kitchen isn't the place for a television show. Or maybe they won't be able to find a sponsor. So it may not work out."

"Or maybe they'll think I don't have the personality to be on television."

"Donna . . . ."

"Elsa says Julia's funny and she has a personality. I don't have any personality."

"Donna . . ."

She was weeping now and he put his arm around her. "Let's just forget about it. This isn't going to happen for weeks."

Of course, they couldn't forget about it, and their Christmas was the worst they ever had. Antonio sent a box of newspapers and magazines with articles about Donna, but she didn't even open the package. They didn't go to Midnight Mass with Lucia and Paolo, and didn't exchange little gifts with them as they always did when their friends came to the Cielo on Christmas. The dinner Donna prepared was perfunctory, just slices of ham she had in the freezer, lumpy mashed potatoes and peas from a can. Ezio bought a package of cookies from Leoni's for dessert.

Not even the traditional toast with *Brunello di Montalcino* could cheer things up.

"There's snow on the side of the mountain," Paolo observed during a long silence.

No one commented.

"I think it will go away by the end of the week," he said.

Lucia went on and on about a little boy named Pasquale who was running down the road with his dog Bruno that morning. "He's such a cute little boy."

Silence.

"Want to watch television?" Ezio asked.

No one replied.

"All right," he said. "Elephant in the room. Anyone want to talk about Donna's television program? It's going to be January 10. They called today."

"Oh, Ezio," Donna said. "Don't call it that. I'm just going to make a meal and it will be filmed."

"On a television program," Paolo said. "Say, what are you going to make? Can we come by and have some? You're not letting it go to waste, are you?"

"I don't know," Donna said, "Maybe the *costolette di vitello alla capricciosa* or the *bistecca con pomodori arrostiti*. I'll have to think about it. Someday."

"I have something to say," Lucia said. "Donna, I think you should get a new dress. The ones you bought in Florence are OK for night, but this will be during the day. You need something lighter, more cheerful. I can't think of anything you have like that. Yours are all too . . . well, plain. You need something that will stand out more.

Now I remember another shop on Via Tornabuoni, just a few doors down from that other one . . ."

"I'll have a look in Lucca, Lucia," Donna said. "Maybe I'll get sick or something."

January 10 finally came and Donna and Ezio waited at the window all morning, and then most of the afternoon. Finally, a small Fiat and two huge vans lumbered into the Cielo's tiny parking lot. A scruffy man who hadn't shaved in days got out of the car and introduced himself as the producer. After haranguing Ezio about the drive up the hill from the village, he helped his crew unload what seemed like tons of equipment and took it all into the farmhouse.

"By the way," the man said, "we got a late start so we'll be staying here tonight and shooting tomorrow morning."

The rest of the crew trailed him into the farmhouse. A young man who looked like he just graduated from college was the director. Two older men were the cameramen. A middle-aged woman would handle the lights. Last was a young woman, about twenty-five, with long blond hair and lots of lipstick. She wore a short yellow dress with red striped leggings. Getting out of the car, she tripped on a cobblestone and reached out for Ezio's hand.

"Oops!" she said. "Lucky you were there."

He held her hand and guided her to the door, wondering why she had the tattoo of a star on her neck

"Are you the husband?" she asked.

"Yes." He thought his voice sounded strange.

"I'm Marta. I'll be doing your wife's makeup."

"Actually, Donna hardly uses any makeup."

"Well," she said, "for television she'll need special makeup. Don't worry. I know how to do it."

She tossed her hair and squeezed Ezio's hand. "After I put your wife's makeup on I really won't have anything to do. I'd love to see the grounds. Maybe you could show me?"

Another smile, another squeeze of Ezio's hand. He felt like a schoolboy.

THE PRODUCER HAD SAID that filming would start at 10 o'clock. Having spent the night tossing and turning, Donna slipped out of bed at 6 so she wouldn't wake Ezio. She went into the kitchen and started the cappuccino maker, then pulled out most of the ingredients for the meal she would make on television. She had decided to make *petto di pollo toscano con pasta,* but she kept the chicken breasts, purchased the day before from Anita at Manconi's, in the refrigerator.

Then she waited, and waited.

At 10:30, the sleepy-eyed producer arrived downstairs, followed by his crew. By the time lights and cameras were set up, it was almost noon and they were finally ready to shoot.

Despite Donna's protests, Marta applied makeup not only to Donna's face but also to her hands and arms. She also applied liner to her eyelids. "We don't want you fading into the background," Marta said.

"I look like a whore," Donna said, staring into a mirror.

Her work finished, Marta found Ezio standing in the back of the room. "Hi!" she said. "My, you're looking good today!" She patted his arm.

Ezio wore a blue work shirt and jeans, something he wore every day. "Um, thanks," he stuttered.

"I'd really love to go for a walk. It's so sunny. It looks so beautiful outside."

"It's pretty cold for a walk."

"Don't worry, I've got something warm." She rushed to her room and returned wearing a thin pullover, bright red with big yellow sunflowers. "There. I'm ready to go!"

"You're going to be cold," Ezio said. "This is January in Tuscany, not in Rome, you know."

Ezio pulled his heavy winter coat off the hook near the door and put on his woolen hat and gloves.

She thrust her arm in his. "If I get cold you can put your arm around me."

Ezio's face was as red as her pullover as Marta pulled him out the door.

In the kitchen, Donna watched the entire scene. "What in the world is that all about?" she wondered. "Where are they going?"

She didn't have time to think. The young director wanted her to lay out the ingredients on her table. She obeyed. He presented her with a script for the introduction, but added, "We've never done a cooking show like this so this is basically up to you. Try to be as informal as possible. Just imagine that you are describing what you're doing to a friend. Pretend we're not here."

"Right," Donna said.

Looking at the four bright lights and the two cameras, one for long shots and one for close-ups, Donna found the whole scene surreal, but all she could think of was Ezio and Marta going off into the cold.

"OK!" the director said. "Ready, set, roll 'em."

Donna looked nervously into the camera, reminded of the frightened deer in the headlights of her car last week. But she glanced down at the script, trying to sound natural.

"*Buongiorno!* My name is Donna Fazzini and, um, I want to welcome you to my kitchen. *Donna's Cucina.* Yes, that's the title of my new cookbook, which I wrote."

"Well, that was dumb," she thought. But she continued.

"And today I'd like to show you how to make a recipe in the book. I've chosen a very simple one because Tuscan cooking is simple cooking, and if you'll just follow along, I think you'd enjoy making this, too."

She stared blankly into the camera. The director gave her a thumbs-up.

"Today," she said, "we are making *petto di pollo toscano con pasta.* As you know, this simply means Tuscan chicken breasts with pasta, so doesn't that sound like fun?"

Why in the world did she choose this, she wondered. It was Ezio's favorite recipe. She had made it just before going on the tour. She managed to pull a skillet out of a cupboard and placed it noisily on a burner.

"First we will take this big skillet—it's my favorite one that I use all the time—and we will pour in some virgin olive oil and get it hot. There. Then we will sauté a cup of chopped onions, a cup of chopped yellow peppers and a cup of red peppers. This will take four of five minutes until everything is tender."

Perhaps if she talked a lot she wouldn't think about other things. She went to the refrigerator and pulled out two chicken breasts.

"Aren't these lovely? I bought these chicken breasts yesterday from my friend Anita Manconi, who has this wonderful little butcher shop in the village. My husband and I like to go there . . ." She stopped suddenly and noticed the director shaking his head.

"Now . . . now," she stuttered, "we have to flatten these chicken breasts. Some people like to slice them, but I prefer the old-fashioned way. I put each chicken breast between sheets of waxed paper, like this, and I simply pound them with a meat mallet. If you have any hostility, this will be a way to get it out."

She thought she might be using more force than she usually did.

"All right. Now we place the chicken breasts in the skillet and we add all these things, which I've already measured out. First we have five diced tomatoes—you can use a fourteen-ounce can—and then two-thirds cup of chicken broth. There."

She was talking very fast now. "Then add a tablespoon of balsamic vinegar, three-fourth teaspoon salt, one-fourth teaspoon sugar—yes, sugar—and an eighth of a teaspoon of pepper. We will let this all simmer for twenty or twenty-five minutes.

"Now while that is going on in that pot, I have water boiling in this big pot. Yes, we will make pasta. You may prefer spaghetti or some other pasta. Really, you could use any kind. My husband and I prefer linguine . . . ."

She suddenly stopped and stared into the camera. The director began waving his arms. She continued. "So, so, yes, linguine is what we will use today."

Donna sprinkled some salt into the water and poured in two handfuls of the pasta. She was clearly unnerved, and turned to face the camera, tears in her eyes.

"Well, I think you know what to do next. When the pasta is done, pour it into a bowl and serve the chicken breasts on top of it. OK? *Bon appetit!*"

She walked out of the kitchen and into the dining room, out of sight of the camera.

"Cut!" the director shouted. He ordered the lights turned off.

"What the hell?" he shouted. "Why didn't you finish? We only shot about twenty minutes and this is supposed to be a half-hour show."

"I couldn't . . . I couldn't go on."

Donna steered herself to a chair and sat down. Her hands were trembling, her legs weak.

"OK, OK. You were doing fine until then. Maybe we can find a sponsor with just this. We'll let you know. *Merda!*"

She could hardly hear the crew members wrapping their long cables and dismantling their equipment. She didn't see them cart all their boxes and crates out the door. When they had finished, they grabbed their coats and ran to their vans.

"Where's Marta?" one of the light men asked.

"I thought she was with you," the director said. *"Merda!"*

It had been more than three hours since Ezio and Marta had left for their walk. They now showed up at the door, Marta wearing Ezio's coat and looking flushed and happy. She hugged Ezio, whispered something in his ear, gave him back his coat and dashed into the waiting car.

Ezio took the coat and hung it on the hook near the door.

"Ezio!" Donna said. "What on earth?"

"I don't want to talk about it."

YEARS LATER, if they talked about it at all, Ezio and Donna always referred to it as "the night of a thousand confessions."

It came two months after Donna's television taping, a time when tensions between the two ebbed and flowed until there were breaking points. Most of the time, they maintained an almost complete stony silence, acknowledging each other in the mornings and at night, but keeping their lives separate. They prepared their own meals. They went to bed and got up at different times and were careful not to move into the other's space during the night. If one or the other had to run an errand, a note would be left.

Donna became absorbed in keeping the records of book sales up to date and filing press clippings without looking at them, but she often just stared into space. Ezio found reasons to stay late at school and, when home, established a working area in a corner of the basement. He set up a small table and brought books and clippings and his big black typewriter. Whenever he tried to write he found an excuse to put his notes in order first. In two months, he had completed only the draft of one chapter.

They both looked very sad.

In early February, Donna received a one-sentence letter from Antonio. "I regret to inform you that sponsors have not been found and therefore a television cooking show will not be produced."

She laughed. "Well, thank God for that. Strange letter, though. I guess he's upset, too. Hope I never hear from him again."

She left the letter on the kitchen table for Ezio to see. Neither mentioned it.

Lucia and Paolo knew something was obviously wrong and, together, they tried to help. Since they hadn't been invited to the Cielo, they asked Ezio and Donna to visit them in Sant'Antonio. The meeting was less than revealing.

"I was thinking about the good times we used to have on New Year's Eves," Paolo said. "We all made resolutions. Remember that? Donna? Ezio?"

Donna and Ezio nodded, but didn't say anything.

"Do you ever hear from that young German couple who stayed at your place last summer?" Lucia asked. "They were so entertaining. I never knew two people who were so much in love. Any word from them?"

"No," Donna said.

"Nothing," Ezio said.

After about an hour, Ezio said he needed to get home. Wanted to do some writing. Donna said she had to work on her recipes.

They drove back to the Cielo in silence.

With the tourist season about to begin in mid-March, there was a need for more communication. Donna saved her questions so she could ask them all at one time.

"There's a couple who want to bring their two kids, two and four. What should I tell them?"

"Tell them they're welcome, but there won't be much for the kids to do. Tell them to try Alfredo's over near Camaiore. They've got a little playground."

"This man says he's a vegetarian."

"Up to you on whether you want to make special meals."

"This woman from France says she wants utter quiet."

"If there are kids scheduled during her time she'd better make other plans."

Their first guest was scheduled to arrive on March 12. Her name was Fredricka VandenBloom, who had been a friend of Lady Alexandria/Hortense/Eleonora/Alex in London and had come the first time years ago on her insistence. Since then, she had stayed for at least two weeks four times over the years, and Donna and Ezio greatly enjoyed her company. They would laugh about their mutual friend's eccentricities and always ended with tearful remembrances.

Donna and Ezio knew they did not want Fredricka VandenBloom to experience the tensions between them. On the night before their guest arrived, they sat across from each other at the kitchen table. Donna had made only pasta.

"Ezio," Donna said.

"Donna," Ezio said simultaneously.

"I want to . . ."

"I want to . . ."

They stopped and couldn't help but laugh.

"I guess we both want to say something," Ezio said.

"Yes. And it's about time."

"Well . . ."

"Well . . ."

"Let me go first," Ezio said.

"No, let me."

"OK, if you want to."

Donna pushed her plate away and pulled it back. She arranged her fork and knife on top, removed them and put them back. She looked at her nails and plucked at a cuticle.

"OK, here goes. Yes, something happened in Florence between Antonio and me. But it's not what you're thinking. Well, back to the beginning. As you may have noticed, from the very first day, Antonio seemed to be flirting with me."

"I noticed."

"I let it pass. I thought, here was this sophisticated guy from Rome. I always heard men from Rome acted that way, so I didn't think anything of it. And besides, I was so worried about the book and the book tour and the interviews, well, I didn't notice some things. Sure, I wanted him to like me. I wanted the book to be a success. Yes, I know I hated all the work I had to do to write it and get it in shape, but I liked the way it turned out. And I was proud of it, I really was."

Ezio rearranged his own plate. "You had a right to be. It's a great book."

"I was worried about going on that book tour with him. I mean, what were we going to do all day together? We don't have anything in common. And at night. Separate rooms, but he made a point of having them adjoining. But I thought, nothing is going to happen. My God, I'm more than ten years older than he is. And here I am, this dowdy woman who can't keep her weight down. And I'm from a tiny village in Tuscany. Surely he's not going to make any moves on me.

"Well, the first few days went well. We were cordial. We met in the breakfast rooms in the hotels and talked a little about what happened at the bookstores the night before. Then I said I wanted to explore the city on my own—Venice, Padua, Bologna, Milan, Pisa. He always said he wanted to go along, to point things out to me because he'd been to every one of these places many times. But I always said no, I wanted to be alone.

"Oh, my God, Ezio, each of these places was so beautiful. Venice! Oh, my. I'd see things and I'd think, 'Oh, if only Ezio could see this,' and then I'd think about how we hadn't been getting along so great, and I'd feel bad. And I began to notice that Antonio was becoming even more friendly. But I always ignored him, I really did."

She paused and went to the sink to refill her water glass. Sitting down again, she ran her finger around the rim of the glass.

"And then we got to Florence. I had noticed that he had become more insistent about showing me all the sites. And I knew there would be so many things to see and I'd never find them on my own and we had only a few hours. So I said OK. We went to the Pitti Palace, and the Duomo and the David in the Accademia. We saw Dante's house and the spot where Savonarola was executed. Antonio had stories about everything.

"The book talk that night went well, but it was only about 9 o'clock when we finished, and Antonio said he wanted to show me the Arno. The river looked so pretty in the moonlight and we walked on this long street next to the river. Remember when we walked on it, Ezio? We were only married a year then.

"I stumbled a little on the cobblestones and Antonio put his arm around me. I thought, well, OK. Then he thought we should have a drink, so we went to this little place near the Ponte Vecchio and I had something. I don't know what it was, Antonio ordered it."

Donna smoothed out the tablecloth and fiddled with a loose thread.

"So we got to our hotel, got our keys from the desk clerk, and took the elevator upstairs. When we got to our rooms, I said I had a very nice time and I'd see him in the morning. But then he opened the door to his room and said I should see the view. He said we could see the Duomo all lit up. My God, how could I have fallen for that? I mean, really. It was like one of those trashy novels I used to read.

"Well, I went in. OK, I'm going to go fast here, Ezio. We looked out the window. I saw the Duomo. He put his arm around me and turned me around. He kissed me, gently at first but then harder. I was trying to resist, but I don't know, somehow I kissed him back. I don't know what I was thinking. I know that I liked being in his arms, so warm, so gentle. And he was whispering things to me, I don't know what. I don't know what I was thinking, Ezio."

"Bastard," Ezio said.

Donna could feel tears welling in her eyes.

"He was starting to unzip the back of my dress and I suddenly realized what was happening. I don't remember what I said. Maybe I didn't say anything. But I grabbed my coat and ran out of there. I could hardly find the key to my room in my purse and then I could hardly unlock the door. Finally I did. I threw myself on the bed. And I cried. I didn't sleep all night."

Ezio tried to reach across the table to hold his wife's hand, but she was searching for the handkerchief in her apron pocket. "Bastard," he muttered again.

"Let me finish," she said. "We hardly spoke to each other for the rest of the trip. I don't think we spoke a word all the way home from Rome. You saw his note. He's apparently given up on me, and I don't care.

"Ezio, for months I've been trying to understand what that whole thing was all about. The thing is, I know I might well have let him . . . let us . . . well, you know. Yes, for a minute I liked what was happening. I liked being held in his arms. I had been very lonely for a long time . . ."

"Because of the way I was acting," Ezio said.

"No. Well, yes. No. That was part of it, yes, but part of it was that I was so wrapped up in this damn cookbook that I wasn't paying attention to what you were doing. And I know that was making you lonely, too. We were two people living separate lives in this big house. So when Antonio kissed me, I sort of felt like I was a real person again. And, yes, I suppose I was a little flattered that a younger guy would want me. My God, I'm not a schoolgirl. I don't know, Ezio, I'm so confused . . . ."

She made no attempt to hide the tears that ran down her cheeks and onto her dress. This time, Ezio grabbed her hand and gripped it hard. He had tears in his eyes, too.

"It's OK, Donna, it's OK," he said. "I need to tell you about me."

"It can't be any worse."

EZIO BEGAN TO PACE the kitchen floor. He checked the stove to see if the burners were off. He opened and closed cupboard doors. He poured himself a glass of grappa, and then sat down again.

"Donna, remember that girl who came with the television crew, the one who did your makeup?"

"The one who made me look like a whore? How could I forget?"

"Marta, that was her name."

"It was pretty obvious that she was flirting with you."

"I knew she was."

"But you let her?"

"Donna, I don't know what I was thinking. I know I was all mixed up at the time. You were so involved in your book . . ."

"So it was my fault?"

"No! You had a right to be. It's a wonderful book and you worked so hard on it. You needed to do those interviews and go on that book tour. Even the television taping. No, it wasn't you. It was me. For a while I thought maybe this was seven-year itch, but good God, I'm a little late to be having that, right? It would probably have happened even if you weren't involved in the book."

"What happened, Ezio, what happened?"

"OK, from the beginning. I was lonely, too. You don't know how many times I went to school and sat in my office and looked out the window. Or how many times I went to the village and made an ass of myself by trying to talk to people. I'd go over to Paolo and Lucia's. Paolo was always on his bike going off somewhere. Lucia didn't want to talk to me."

"Because I treated her so badly. What a mess, Ezio, what a mess."

"And another thing. I thought if I could write my novel, that would make me feel better, but every time I tried to write, nothing would come, or else I wrote such stupid stuff I threw it out. And then I would feel even worse, so after a while I didn't even try to write anymore. I've only written six chapters, Donna, and I'm not sure where to go from here. I may never go back to it."

"Ezio, you must!"

"OK, here's another thing. I haven't wanted to admit it, but it's true. You were getting all this attention, you were a star . . ."

"Ezio, really."

"Well, you were. Big book, interviews, book tour, television. Me? Principal of a tiny school sitting around watching his wife become famous. Yes, I admit it, I was jealous."

"Oh, Ezio."

"Yes, jealous. Like a schoolboy. Well, anyway, here comes this girl, literally falling down on my doorstep, who seems interested in me. God only knows why. I mean she's, what, twenty-five years old and I'm fifty-nine, my hair is turning gray, my knees are getting bad, I can't work like I did before . . ."

"But you've kept your shape, Ezio. Thin as a rail like your father. Blue eyes. Great smile. You don't look anywhere near your age."

"Oh, stop it. I have no idea why she flirted with me. Maybe she goes from town to town making conquests she can boast about to her friends. 'I met this old guy in this village in Tuscany and you should have seen how I wrapped him around my little finger.' All her friends would have a good laugh. Well, you saw what happened. She wanted to go for a walk after she'd done your makeup."

"Like a whore."

"It was a stupid idea, cold as hell out there, but we went. We walked up the hill and she was shivering so I gave her my coat. I wouldn't call what she was wearing a coat. We got to the hay barn and she was still shivering. She wanted to see what was inside. Never been inside a hay barn before, she said. So I opened the sliding door and we went in. It was actually kind of warm in there, the horses' heat and all.

"She wanted to sit down, so we sat on a pile of hay. Oh, Donna, this is so awful. Like one of those bad movies they make in America. She sat next to me. Real close. No, I didn't move away. She . . . she . . . held my face and kissed me. I didn't respond at first, but then I kissed her back, real hard. I didn't know what I was doing but I ran my hands up her back and hugged her close. For a minute, Donna, I wanted her. I really wanted her."

Ezio got up and began to pace the kitchen again.

"And then, I don't know, I thought, 'What the hell am I doing? This is insane.' So I got up and pulled her up and threw my coat back on her and pulled her all the way down to the car. And that's why I had hay all over me when I came in."

"You did? I didn't even notice."

"Well, I did."

He sat at the table again. "There you have it. The whole story."

"Just like mine," Donna said.

"I suppose so, but somehow I feel mine is worse. I mean for a minute, I really wanted her, Donna. I've never—ever—wanted another woman since I married you. I've never even thought to look at another woman."

"And I never thought I'd look at another man, Ezio," Donna said softly. "And for a minute I wanted him, too."

They held hands across the table.

"I feel so guilty," Ezio said.

"So do I."

"Guess it's because we're Catholic."

"I doubt that," Donna said. "Anyway, I feel guilt, shame, remorse, humiliation. You name it."

"I've got the same list."

"So," Donna said, "I suppose some people would think what happened was pretty petty. I mean for both of us, it was just a matter of a minute or two, right?"

"Yes, right."

"But for me, this was something major. I'd never done anything like that before."

"I hadn't either."

They sat in the dark for almost a half-hour, the only sounds the crackling of dying embers in the fireplace.

Then Donna got up. "But you know something, Ezio? I think I love you more now than I ever did."

He got up and took her in his arms. "I feel the same way about you, Donna."

"Do you think we can go back to the way we were?" she said.

"It's not going to be the same because we'll always have these memories," Ezio said. "But we'll get past it, won't we?"

"Yes," Donna said, "I think we will."

Hand in hand, they walked to the window and gazed at the moonlit valley. In the distance, an owl screeched and Ezio gripped his wife's hand harder.

"Donna, remember what that man from Venice told us that summer? The one who had lost his wife?"

"Yes. He said we had to trust each other. I'm going to do that."

"I am, too."

Ezio started turning off the lights. "We'd better get to bed. Fredricka VandenBloom is supposed to be here about ten tomorrow morning. And I want to get up early."

"Why?" Donna asked.

"I think I've figured out what should be next in my novel. I want to write it before I forget."

"It's going to be a great novel, Ezio."

"Well, I'll tell you one thing. If I do finish it—big if—and if there is a publisher—another big if—I'm not going to do a book tour or, God forbid, go on television."

"Ezio! You'd look great on television."

"Yeah, right."

"And you know what, Ezio? If my book sells at all, and we get some royalties, I want us to go to Venice. Just the two of us. OK?"

"Yes!"

Little Fly

"PASQUALE!" HIS MOTHER SAID, "how many times do I have to tell you not to go past her house? You know what happens. She yells at you and you run away and then you fall down."

"But I was just walking past . . ."

"Yes, I'm sure you were just walking past, just like you were just walking past last week when this happened. It happens every time."

"But . . ."

"Last week you tripped and fell and it was the right knee, now it's the left. Hold still. I need to put this Mercurochrome on it."

"Mama, it wouldn't have happened if her cat didn't hiss at Bruno. Ouch! That stings."

"Only a little. So what happened this time?"

"Me and Bruno were walking past Signora Cardineli's house and . . ."

Serafina Marincola placed a patch on the scratch. "There. You're sure you weren't running? You know that's when you fall."

"OK, walking fast. Anyway, Bruno saw Signora Cardineli's cat on the porch . . ."

"And?"

"And Bruno barked and Alessia hissed and Bruno barked and . . . Mama it was so funny!"

"I'm sure. Don't touch the scratch, Pasquale."

"And then Signora Cardineli came out of the house and she picked up Alessia and yelled at Bruno to stop barking but he didn't and then she yelled at me to go home and never come by her house again."

Serafina put the Mercurochrome bottle back in the little first-aid kit and into the kitchen cupboard. "Which is exactly what I've been telling you and telling you. You can go another way to the woods. Go around the church."

"But this way is faster!"

"By what? Ten minutes? As if a seven-year-old needs to be in a hurry to get anywhere."

Pasquale jumped down from the stool. "Oh, and she called me that name again."

Serafina sighed. "Well, Pasquale, don't listen to her. You're not a *terrone*. You're a fine young boy. Now go in the backyard and play with Bruno. And don't go out on the street! It's almost dinnertime. My God, I'll be glad when school starts again next week."

Serafina turned her attention to the task of unpacking groceries that had been interrupted by her son's sudden appearance. She'd just returned from shopping at Manconi's and Leoni's, where Signora Della Franca had again ignored Serafina's greeting. Serafina had muttered and continued shopping.

Pork sausages. Lengths of salami. A pound of goat cheese.

"Damn that Signora Cardineli," she seethed.

Two packages of fusilli. Two loaves of bread. Three big melons. Cookies for the kids.

"Damn that Signora Della Franca."

She had just hidden the cookies on the top shelf when her husband returned from work, receiving the customary kiss and hug.

"You look tired, Salvo. Hard day?"

"Not bad. It got hot out there the last few hours. Where's everybody?"

"Francesco's with Farid and Clara's with Samia. Pasquale is in the back with Bruno. At least he's supposed to be. He had another run-in with Signora Cardineli again today."

"Again?"

"Bruno and her cat went at it. Pasquale tripped and fell when he ran away. Scraped his knee a little."

"Maybe someday he'll learn not to go past her house."

"She called him *terrone* again, but he didn't seem to mind."

"Maybe he doesn't know what the word means."

"Well, I know what it means. And I hate it! Salvo, I just hate it!"

"Serafina, just ignore Signora Cardineli. Let's make dinner."

Serafina and Salvo prepared the meal in silence, although Salvo tried to ease the tension by humming, and then singing, old Calabrian songs. Serafina didn't even smile. When the children were gathered, she filled their plates and poked at her own. Aware that their mother was upset, Francesco, who was thirteen, and Clara, who was twelve, tried to make up for it by talking louder and faster than usual. Pasquale listened and laughed but hardly said a word.

Serafina took a long time doing the dishes while her husband worked a jigsaw puzzle with the children and got them to bed. Later, Salvo could tell she wasn't paying much attention as she sewed a rip in Francesco's jeans, and he finally put his newspaper down.

"Still thinking about what Signora Cardineli said?"

"Yes."

Salvo reached over and held her hand. "Serafina, don't let what she said get to you like this."

"Salvo, I still get angry when this happens. We've been in Tuscany for almost five years now. You'd think people would accept us. But no. I feel like we're still outsiders, the way people look at us, or the way they ignore us, like Signora Della Franca today. We're still *terroni*, those dirty people from the South. My God, it's 1983. When is Italy going to solve its North and South problems?"

"I know it's hard here for you, *cara*," Salvo said. "You're stuck in this house all day and when you go out you expect people to be nice to you. And they aren't."

"They don't even say hello. They're so rude. Signora Della Franca. You would think she'd know my name by now. I'm sure I see her three or four times a week. If not in Leoni's then Manconi's or . . ."

"Serafina . . ."

"And in church! We see her every Sunday in church. She sits just across, one pew up, and we have to get in line together when we go to Communion."

"Serafina . . ."

"Whenever I try to talk to her she looks right through me, like I wasn't even there. Other people do that, too. It makes me so angry."

Salvo sighed. "Well, Serafina, I think we just have to make the best of it. We have each other. We've got the kids. We've got a nice house now."

"After all the work you put into it."

"The kids seem happy, Francesco and Clara anyway. Who knows what Pasquale is thinking? He's so quiet."

Serafina tied the last knot and put Francesco's pants down. "Salvo, have you ever thought about moving back to Calabria?"

"Serafina! What are you talking about? We can't go back to Calabria. We're living in Tuscany now."

"Sometimes I miss it, Salvo. I miss my mama. She's eighty-eight now. She doesn't have long. I miss my sister and all those kids."

"Serafina, think of why we came up here in the first place. There was no work in Corigliano. We were living with your mother in her tiny little house. You were arguing all the time. The kids were fighting with their cousins. We had to get out of there."

"But now I miss her. I don't think I'd argue anymore."

"And what would I do for work? I just did odd jobs there, nothing steady. I know my job here doesn't pay that much, road crews never get paid much, but it's steady work except in the worst weather."

"I know . . ."

"And what about the kids? The school at Neboli certainly is better than the one in Corigliano. Just yesterday, Ezio told me he heard that Francesco was one of the best students in his mathematics class. We don't want the kids to go back to that little one-room school where they didn't even have enough books to go around, do we?"

"I know . . ."

"Serafina, you know there was another reason why we moved here."

His wife looked away. "Yes. Pasquale."

USUALLY, SALVO'S SNORING didn't bother Serafina, but after tossing and turning for a long time, she got up, went down to the kitchen and made a cup of tea. Early frost on this chilly September night had whitened the window overlooking Via Giacomo Matteotti outside. Serafina found it amusing that a village of two hundred people would have streets with names. She couldn't remember the name of the street where she had lived in Corigliano.

"I should remember that," she thought. "But it seems like a long time ago."

She did remember coming to Sant'Antonio. Salvo's cousin Amadeo had been urging him to move north for years. Amadeo had first moved to Naples, then to a village outside of Florence and then to Camaiore, not far from Lucca.

"You've got to get out of Calabria," Amadeo kept saying. "You know there aren't any jobs there. Think of your kids. Think of your wife. She looks very tired, Salvo. You owe it to her. Come up to Tuscany. I'll look for a job for you. There are lots of little villages around here. You don't want to live in a city."

When Amadeo found out about a job on the road construction crew where he worked, he immediately called Salvo. "I found a job for you! Come right away!"

Salvo took the train as far as Florence, then a bus to Camaiore. Amadeo gave him a tour of villages in the area, Massorosa, Fabbriche, Pescaglia. When they drove through Sant'Antonio, almost missing it because it was so small, Amadeo suddenly screeched the car to a halt.

"Look! There's a 'For Sale' sign."

Even if Salvo had not lived for fifteen years in a tiny, cramped house in Calabria, this place looked like a mansion. Three stories high, with fine masonry and ornate doors and window frames, it was the most imposing house in Sant'Antonio.

Serafina remembered when Salvo called her. "Serafina, you should see it! It's huge! A big kitchen. A separate living room. A sunroom. The kids will have their own rooms, Serafina! There's an attic where they can play. And a big backyard. With a huge oak tree. And there's furniture! Kind of old, but we can use it. And the price! Serafina, it's been on the market for years. The woman who owned it died, and the bank wants to get rid of it. OK, it needs a little work, but Amadeo says he'll loan us the money. Serafina, we can afford it!"

What Salvo didn't tell Serafina was that the refrigerator, the sink and the stove badly needed replacing, that there was a major leak from one of the bathrooms down the living room wall, and, worst, that pipes had frozen in a recent winter and flooded the basement. Salvo would spend all of his free time during the next three years making repairs.

Serafina remembered how excited Francesco, Clara and Pasquale were when they arrived, running up and down the stairs, looking in every closet and every cupboard and drawer. Serafina and Salvo had just held hands and watched them.

Over the years, they discovered reminders of the previous owner. At least a dozen old pink nightgowns were hidden in the back of drawers and even under a loose floorboard. Tiny statuettes and medals turned up under chair cushions. Empty lipstick holders were stashed in kitchen cupboards. Francesco discovered expensive women's shoes stuffed under his mattress.

"Oh, you'll probably find a lot more," her neighbor, Lucia Sporenza, told Serafina. "Annabella, well, Annabella was not quite right in her last years. Poor thing. But she was a lovely woman, and we all miss her very much."

Ah, Lucia. At first, Serafina was pleased to have her and her husband, Paolo, as her neighbors. Lucia knew everything! She told Serafina so many little details about everyone in the village that Serafina couldn't keep anyone straight.

But Serafina wondered about some of the things Lucia said.

"We're so pleased that you came here from Calabria," she announced at their first meeting. "My son, he lives in Florence, married a girl from Calabria. Dark skin, but a lovely girl. At first we wondered, because Dino was dating this other girl from Lucca, and we thought he'd marry her. So when he married Sofia, we were surprised. Francesca's so light. But we like Sofia anyway."

She smiled slightly.

"And she makes such interesting meals. I had never tasted Calabrian food before. I mean, it's not like we make here in Tuscany. Will you still be making your Calabrian dishes now that you live here? I don't imagine we have what you need. I hope you'll come to know how we eat here in the north. I can give you some recipes if you like.

"And, you know, there's a nice family from Algeria down the street. They have a boy and girl about the same age as yours, Farid and Samia. I'm sure you'd like to meet them. They're foreigners, too."

That was only the start of it. Every time Lucia introduced Serafina to one of the villagers, whether it was at Leoni's or Manconi's or at church or even on the street, she always made the same point.

"This is my new neighbor, Serafina. She's from Calabria, but I know we're all going to love her."

"But? But?" Serafina told Salvo every time it happened. "It's like I'm an exhibit, that I'm not even human. And the way people stare! You'd think they'd never seen a person with dark skin before."

"I bet a lot of them haven't," Salvo said. "They'll get used to us."

Rinsing her teacup as she looked out at the moonlit street, Serafina realized that things hadn't changed much. Just last week, Lucia said she thought it was so nice that little Sant'Antonio had a family from Calabria, a family from Algeria, a divorced woman with children and two homosexual men.

"Paolo always says we're a melting pot," she said, laughing.

Serafina didn't know what to say. And since then she had avoided her neighbor.

Drying her hands, Serafina heard a noise upstairs. She found Pasquale roughhousing with Bruno.

"Pasquale! It's 2 o'clock in the morning. What are you doing?"

"Me and Bruno were just playing."

"Go to sleep, Pasquale."

SERAFINA TRIED NOT to wake Salvo when she returned to their bedroom, but she tripped and a lamp fell over.

"What?" Salvo mumbled. "What? Why are you up?"

"Pasquale," his wife said, crawling alongside him. "Playing with Bruno."

"In the middle of the night? What's that kid going to do next? Let's get some sleep."

Serafina kissed her husband and turned over. But now she couldn't stop thinking about her little son.

Pasquale had been born five weeks prematurely, on Easter Sunday, so of course he was named for that great feast day, *Pasqua*. At only four pounds, two ounces, he had struggled for the first months of his life and remained in Saint Anna Hospital in Catanzaro for six weeks after his birth. Serafina and Salvo took turns staying with him day and night.

Because he had trouble sucking, a feeding tube was placed through his nose and into his stomach. He had trouble breathing, and the doctors said he had respiratory problems. They called it RDS or HMD, but Serafina and Salvo didn't care what it was called. They only wanted this tiny baby to breathe on his own, not with the help of a ventilator. It broke their hearts to see his little brown body, naked except for a big white diaper, connected to tubes and dwarfed by the breathing machine.

"I can't stand it," Serafina cried, falling into her husband's arms.

"He's going to get better, I know it." But Salvo couldn't and didn't know it.

Once, when Pasquale was off the ventilator but still in Saint Anna Hospital, Serafina bent down and suddenly screamed. "Salvo, he's not breathing! He's not breathing!"

Nurses came running, but by the time they came, Pasquale was taking breaths again.

"This happens," a nurse said. "It's called apnea."

While she restored the ventilator, Salvo hugged his wife. "He's going to get better, *cara,* I know it."

Finally, they were allowed to take Pasquale home, where they tried to make a safe, quiet corner for him in their bedroom. When he cried during the night, which was often, they rushed to his side. As he grew older, they became frantic every time he coughed or sneezed.

"Do you think we'll ever stop worrying about Pasquale?" Serafina asked one night as she slumped, exhausted, into her chair in front of the television. The boy was three years old then.

When Pasquale had trouble reading simple signs, his parents took him to a doctor in Catanzaro who fitted him with glasses, round ones with wire frames that made the boy's black eyes seem even bigger.

Then Salvo heard about the job opening in Tuscany.

"We have to get out of Calabria," he told his wife. "We have to make a change. Amadeo checked on baby doctors. There are good ones in Lucca, and Florence is not that far away. There's a good hospital in Lucca and of course in Florence. The first thing we'll do is find a good baby doctor, someone who can help if Pasquale gets sick again."

When they arrived in Sant'Antonio, they quickly found a doctor in Lucca who examined the little boy, prescribed some medicine and asked that he be brought back for checkups every month. Francesco and Clara were enrolled in the school in nearby Reboli, and Pasquale, then four years old, stayed at home. He didn't have much to do, but played with toy trucks, drew pictures with his crayons and watched children's shows on television.

Perhaps because of the medicines and his greatly improved appetite, Pasquale grew stronger and stronger. With Bruno, a terrier of unknown ancestry that Salvo found wandering on the highway, he raced up and down the hills near Sant'Antonio. His feet hardly touched the ground.

Salvo and Serafina called him *moscerino*, the little fly.

And climb trees? The boy loved to climb almost anything, but his favorite was the big oak tree in the backyard. One branch stretched right to Pasquale's window and Salvo made a platform in the crook of branches twenty feet off the ground. The boy called it his tree house. He thought it was neat that he could climb to it either from the ground or through his window, and he would take his toys, a blanket, a sandwich and even Bruno and spend the day there.

"What do you do up there in the tree?" his mother asked him one day.

"Nothin'."

"Nothing? You just sit there?"

"Yes."

"What do you see?"

"Um. Lotsa stuff. Mama, I see the birds and the bird nests and the mama birds feeding the baby birds and sometimes squirrels come to visit and there are these big leaves that have things like veins in them and, Mama, I can see above our house and all the other houses and way up to the church and to the hills where Francesco goes and, Mama, I can pick acorns off the branches and you can take them apart and there are seeds inside and . . ."

Serafina hugged him then. "Pasquale, Pasquale, I don't think there's ever been a boy like you."

But it was not only his size that made Pasquale different from other children. For reasons his parents didn't understand, his skin was considerably darker than that of his brother and sister. Predictably, he became a curiosity in Sant'Antonio. The villagers could get used to the darker skins of the rest of the family, but they couldn't stop staring at the chocolate-brown boy who darted past their houses. Everyone was too polite to say anything. Except Lucia.

"Serafina," she said one summer day on the street in front of their houses, "I was just thinking. It must be nice for Pasquale not to worry about getting sunburned."

Serafina rushed her son back into her house.

Last year, the boy was enrolled in *Prima Classe* in the school in Reboli. He was smaller than any other child in his grade, and so shy that he stood in a corner of the playground while the other children kicked a soccer ball around. Some of the children were afraid to go near him. The bolder ones went up and touched his face or arm. Pasquale closed his eyes and let them.

He did, however, do well in his classes, especially reading, and he seemed happy.

"He's a very smart child," his teacher said. "You can be very proud of him."

Salvo and Serafina, who could never figure out what was going on in Pasquale's head, celebrated the end of the school year by buying the boy a strawberry gelato.

Next week, Serafina knew, Pasquale would be starting *Seconda Classe*. She wondered what changes it would bring.

ON SUNDAY, the family filled its usual pew near the back of church for Mass. Salvo and Serafina stayed mostly awake during another of Father Sangretto's sermons, which had grown increasingly longer and more repetitive as his memory failed. Francesco manufactured a paper airplane out of the church bulletin, Clara chipped at her fingernail polish, and Pasquale seemed engrossed in the statue of Saint Anthony.

"Look at Pasquale," Salvo whispered to his wife. "Do you think he's praying?"

"I don't think so. But who knows what he's thinking?"

And when Serafina went up for Communion, Signora Della Franca again looked past her.

On Monday, Salvo and Serafina shooed their children out of the house and to the bus stop on the next street.

"Bye!" the children shouted.

"Have a good first day at school!" Salvo called. "Make lots of new friends!"

"Be careful, Pasquale!" Serafina said.

"Thank God," she sighed when they were out of sight. "I've been waiting for this day since June."

"Why don't you not do anything today," Salvo said. "Just relax."

"You know I never relax."

"OK, see you tonight."

He kissed his wife and, lunch bucket in hand, went out the door.

The day went by too quickly. The children's rooms needed straightening and she had to run to Manconi's for hamburger meat. Salvo had bought a grill this summer and the family would have a barbecue to celebrate the first day of school. Salvo enjoyed roasting or, as his wife said, burning sausages and hamburgers on the grill in the backyard.

Straightening Pasquale's room, she discovered a wooden cigar box under his bed. Inside, she found three brittle oak leaves that had turned a brilliant red, a robin's egg, a bit of moss, three shiny acorns, two smooth stones, Bruno's old collar, a Saint Christopher medal, fourteen coins and a soiled holy card of Saint Joseph.

"What a cute little boy. Sometimes I just want to hug him and hug him."

Late in the afternoon, Francesco and Clara swept in the door first, chattering about seeing their friends from the other villages for the first time since vacation began.

"And Maria has new earrings and she wears lipstick," Clara said. "Mama, can I wear lipstick?"

"Twelve-year-old girls do not wear lipstick," her mother said.

"And Mama," Francesco said, "Bernardo said he got a BB gun for his birthday. I'm going to ask Papa if I can get one."

"You can ask, but I don't think he's going to say yes. Where's Pasquale?"

The boy shuffled in just then and tried to get past his mother. "Mama, I'm going up to my tree house for a while."

"Why? Did something happen in *Seconda Classe*?"

"No."

"Then why are you going up to your tree house?"

"Just want to."

Serafina looked at her son climbing the stairs. "Something must have happened."

She kept looking at the boy as they prepared for the outdoor barbecue. He didn't help load the charcoals as he usually did, he didn't want to turn the burgers over and, worst, he left most of his meal on his plate. Even the potato chips, which Francesco quickly devoured.

While the others cleaned up, Pasquale gathered Bruno in his arms and climbed to his tree house again. His parents waited until

Francesco and Clara were watching television inside before they stood at the base of the tree.

"Pasquale," Salvo shouted, "did something happen at school today?"

"No, nothin'."

"You sure?"

"Yes."

"Do you like your new teacher?" his mother called.

"He's OK."

"Do you think *Seconda Classe* will be too hard?"

"No."

"Do you feel OK? You hardly ate any dinner. Aren't you hungry?"

"I'm OK."

"You sure?"

"Yes."

Serafina tried another tactic. "Do you want to come down and watch TV with your brother and sister? There's probably a good show on."

"No."

"Are you going to stay up there all night?" Salvo asked.

"No."

"When are you going to come down?"

"Dunno."

"OK then," Salvo said. "Don't stay up there too long. It's going to get cold when the sun goes down."

"OK."

Salvo and Serafina held hands as they returned to the house. "Good God," she said. "Something happened at school. I know it."

"Let's see if the kids know something."

They found their older children in front of the television.

"We need to talk to you," Salvo said. "This is important."

They didn't look up.

"Turn off the television. *Laverne & Shirley* again? Don't you ever get tired of that stupid show? Now listen. Did something happen at school today with Pasquale?"

"I dunno, I didn't see him much," said Francesco, fiddling with the remote.

"He's in the little kids' classes," Clara said, brushing her hair for the seventh time that day. "We're on the other side of the building."

"What about on the playground?" Serafina said. "Did you see him on the playground?"

"The little kids play on the other side," Francesco said. "I'm with my friends."

"And I'm with my girlfriends. We don't watch the little kids."

"And he was fine on the bus?"

"He sat in the back."

"OK, OK. Don't you have homework to do?"

"Not today!" they both said.

As Salvo put the grill away, Serafina looked out the kitchen window. She could see Pasquale still up in the tree. He was lying on his back, apparently with his eyes closed.

"Poor Pasquale. Something's going on."

The following nights were the same. Pasquale came home, went to his room before dinner, hardly touched his food, then went to his tree house until it was time to go to bed. Salvo and Serafina became more and more concerned. They decided that he really needed to make friends in the village, even though there were only a couple of children his age.

"Look," Salvo told Francesco, "on the weekends, can't you take Pasquale along when you play with your Algerian friend? Would that be too much to ask? He wouldn't be a bother."

"Papa," Francesco said, "me and Farid like to go into the woods and find stuff. We're not going to take a little kid along. He wouldn't keep up. He'd get lost, and then what would you say?"

"Clara," Serafina said, "couldn't he go along when you play with Samia?"

"Mama! Samia and me have lots of stuff to do. We stay in her room and do stuff. We don't want a boy around. A little boy!"

"All right, all right," Serafina said. "Have it your way."

Deflated, Salvo and Serafina decided to try Pasquale again. Since it was raining, they found him in the attic playing catch with Bruno.

"I swear, if something ever happens to that dog, Pasquale will be in real trouble," his father said.

There was only one window in the attic, and they could see dark clouds rolling in from the hills. They coaxed the boy to a corner and sat on old trunks that were still filled with the dresses and hats of an elderly woman.

"'Squale," Serafina said, "Bruno is a lot of fun for you, isn't he?"

"Yes, Mama."

"I'm glad we got him for you. He likes you better than the rest of us."

"He's my best friend."

"It's nice that you have a good friend, Pasquale," Salvo said, "but don't you think you'd rather play with another little boy?"

"No."

"Wouldn't it be fun to have a friend? You could play ball, you could play games."

"No."

"What about Manfredo?" Serafina said. "I think he's seven years old like you. You know, the son of Bernadetta Miniotti. They live at the edge of the village."

"No."

"Or," Salvo said, "Mustafa. The brother of Farid and Samia. I think he's eight years old or so. You could go along when Francesco and Clara go over to their house but you'd have to stay out of their way."

"No."

Serafina saw tears in her son's eyes and tried to pull him onto her lap.

"Pasquale, is something wrong? You don't seem happy lately."

The boy squirmed away. "Mama, Papa, can I go to another school?"

"Another school?"

"Yes." His voice was so soft his parents barely heard it. The clouds were thick outside now, plunging the room into darkness

"'Squale," his father said gently, "what school? There aren't any other schools around here. Just the one in Reboli. There just aren't any others."

Tears now flowed down Pasquale's cheeks and his mother lifted him onto her lap. "It's all right, *caro*, it's all right."

Salvo took off the boy's eyeglasses and put them in his pocket. "Can you tell us, my *moscerino*, why you want to go to another school?"

"It's OK. Never mind. Forget I asked."

"But Pasquale, if there's a problem at this school, we want to know."

"No. There's no problem."

"Are you sure?"

"Yes."

The rain, which had been soft at first, now beat the window in pellets as mother, father and son sat huddled in a corner of the attic.

"I guess we're not going to get an answer, Serafina."

AFTER DINNER the following Monday, the children hunched over paper and schoolbooks as they did their homework on the kitchen table. Francesco was using a small calculator for his math problems, Clara had an atlas open in front of her as she tried to answer geography questions, and Pasquale had a workbook about Italy's history.

"Need some help, Pasquale?" Salvo asked.

"No. I'm all right. Can I go to my room to finish?"

"Why would you want to do that? You kids need to stay here so your mother and I can answer questions, help you when we can."

"Not that we can do much anymore," Serafina said from the stove where she was picking off burnt lasagna from the oven. "Those problems are getting too hard for me."

Finishing the dishes, Salvo happened to look at Pasquale's workbook and stopped short.

"Pasquale. Why is that page covered with black marks? Did you do that?"

The boy quickly closed the book but didn't say anything.

"Pasquale? That page has black marks all over. It looks like a crayon. You can't even see the questions. Why did you do that? Were you upset?"

"I didn't do it," Pasquale said softly.

"You didn't? Then who did?"

Pasquale turned the book over and over.

"Pasquale," Salvo said, "who made the marks in your book?"

"I don't know."

"You don't know? How could you not know? Did you leave it somewhere?

"I don't know." The boy struggled to hold back tears.

"You don't know if you left it somewhere? Pasquale, I think you know what happened. If somebody is marking up your book, then you can't see the questions and then you can't write the answers. That's pretty mean for someone to do that. I think you should tell us who did it."

Pasquale stuffed his fists into his eyes, trying to hold back tears.

"OK, OK," his father said. "If you don't want to tell me, OK. But please don't protect someone who did it. That person is likely to do it again. Now here, let's see if I can read the questions and you can answer them."

Francesco and Clara had long finished their homework and were back in front of the television when Salvo settled down next to Pasquale and put his arm around the boy. It took a half-hour longer, but eventually he made out all the questions and Pasquale had no trouble answering them.

On Wednesday, the problem wasn't a schoolbook. It was Pasquale's shirt, the first new one he had had in years since he always inherited Francesco's clothes even though they were too big. Serafina had just bought the shirt in Lucca, and this was the first day the boy wore it to school. It was a splendid shirt, blue plaid with a white collar, and Pasquale looked very proud in it.

But when he came home that day, he darted past his mother and up to his room. When he returned, he wore an old brown shirt that had been in a drawer.

"Pasquale!" Serafina said. "Why aren't you wearing your new shirt? You looked so nice in it."

"I, um, I just thought I'd change."

"But where's your new shirt?"

"It's . . . it's in the laundry."

Sure enough, Serafina found the shirt on top of the laundry basket next to the washing machine. It was no longer a blue plaid; instead, dark chocolate stains covered the front and the white collar.

"Pasquale! What happened to your shirt?"

"I, um, I spilled chocolate milk on it."

"Chocolate milk? You don't drink chocolate milk. You hate chocolate milk."

"Well, I, um, had some today in the lunchroom and it spilled. It will come out, won't it?"

"I don't know. That's a pretty bad stain. I'll try. Now why don't you go walk Bruno before dinner."

When Salvo came home from work, Serafina told him the plaid shirt story.

"That's very odd," he said, holding the shirt up to the light. "I don't think he spilled milk on this shirt. I think someone threw chocolate milk at him."

"Who in the world would do a thing like that?"

"I guess we'd better ask."

They found Pasquale lying face down on his bed, his head in the pillow. Crouched on the floor, Bruno looked worried. Salvo sat on one side of the bed, Serafina on the other.

"Pasquale, please," Serafina said. "We know something is happening at school. Can you tell us about it?

A long pause, and then a muffled voice from the pillow. "Don't like it."

"What don't you like about it, Pasquale?" Salvo said. "Don't you like your teachers?"

"They're OK."

"Is there too much homework? You seem to do it pretty fast most nights."

"No."

"Are the classes too hard?"

"No."

"Do you have fun on the playground?"

Pasquale waited. "No," he whispered.

"Are the games on the playground too hard?"

"No."

"Are the other kids fun to play with?" Salvo asked.

Pasquale didn't answer.

Serafina stroked her son's back. "Pasquale, your father asked if the other kids are fun to play with. Are they?"

The boy shook his head.

"Oh. I see. 'Squale, is somebody giving you trouble at school?"

The boy's shoulders shook and he buried his face further into the pillow.

"Is it a boy?" she said.

Pasquale sniffled.

"It's OK, *caro*. It's OK."

Salvo patted his son's back. "It's OK, *moscerino*. Can you tell us the boy's name?"

His parents waited patiently. They could hardly hear Pasquale's muffled response.

"Rocco."

"Rocco?" Serafina asked her husband over Pasquale's sobs. "Do we know who that is?"

"I don't think so," Salvo said.

"Is he the one who made marks in your history book? Is he the one who threw chocolate milk on your new shirt?"

Serafina and Salvo thought they saw their son nod.

WITH PASQUALE STILL LYING on his bed and still crying, his parents interrupted Francesco and Clara watching *Dallas*.

"Who is this Rocco boy at school?" Salvo asked. "What do you know about him?"

"Rocco?" Francesco said. "Rocco Mazzei? Everybody knows Rocco Mazzei."

"Everyone knows him?" Serafina said. "Why?"

"He's in *Seconda Classe*, like Pasquale. He should be in *Terza Classe* but he was held back. He's a troublemaker."

"And," Clara said, "He's very rich. His father drives a big new car. It must have cost a zillion *lire*."

"What does the boy look like?" Serafina asked.

Francesco and Clara exchanged glances and laughed.

"He's this big kid, bigger than any of the others. He's got these little teeny eyes and these big ears. He looks like a kid in a cartoon."

Francesco laughed some more.

"And he smells!" Clara said. "One day I had to walk past him in the hall and I could smell him a mile away."

"Like garlic or something," Francesco said.

"Worse than that," his sister said. "Yuck!"

"Why would Pasquale be afraid of him?"

"I dunno," Francesco said. "We don't hang out with those little kids."

While Francesco and Clara went back to watching television, their parents sat at the kitchen table.

"Who else can we ask?" Salvo said.

"No one who will talk to me," Serafina said. "You know the people here."

They thought for a while.

"We don't even know the teacher's name," Salvo said. "Wait! Ezio's the principal of the school now. He should know something."

Ezio Maffini and his wife, Donna, were among the few people in Sant'Antonio who'd welcomed Salvo and Serafina and their family when they first arrived in the village. They helped them move furniture, invited them to dinner and called frequently to make sure everything was all right. Salvo and Serafina wished they could know them better, but they lived in a farmhouse at the top of a hill.

"Is it too late to call?"

Salvo picked up the phone and began dialing. "Only 8:30. They're probably just sitting around reading or something . . . . Ezio . . . Ezio Maffini? *Ciao*. It's Salvo Marincola down in Sant'Antonio. How are you tonight? . . . Fine, just fine . . . . She's fine, too. And Donna? . . . Good, good . . . . Listen, I want to talk to you about a kid in your school . . ."

Smoothing out the flowered tablecloth, Serafina could hear only half of the conversation. Then her husband hung up the phone and sat down.

"Ezio said he doesn't want to spread gossip," Salvo said, "but that because of what has happened to Pasquale, he thinks we ought to know what he's heard. Rocco's parents moved to Reboli just before school started last year. His father is some sort of executive at Fiat and spends most of the time in Turin. He comes to Reboli on weekends. Rocco's mother mostly stays inside their home and no one knows very much about her. Rocco is an only child. He is obviously very spoiled and wants his way. He's not a very good student and doesn't turn in his homework. When he does, it's sloppy. He was held back this year because he failed the final examinations. Rocco's teachers have told him the boy's sort of a troublemaker in class, talks out loud and makes rude gestures. Oh, and Ezio says he picks on other kids, especially little kids."

"Well," Serafina said, "are they going to do something about him? How can the other kids learn with a kid like that around?"

"Ezio said the teachers have tried. He said they've tried to talk to his mother, but she doesn't seem interested. And his father isn't around much, of course."

"Great. Well, something has to be done, Salvo. They can't let a kid like that run their school, can they? Did you tell him how Pasquale is so afraid of him?"

"I told him everything. Ezio said he would call Pasquale's teacher right now and try to find out what's going on between Rocco and Pasquale. He said the teacher is new and this is his first job. He said at least they could separate the boys. They've been in alphabetical order."

A half-hour later, Ezio called back. The teacher, Salvo told Serafina, agreed to separate the boys in the classroom tomorrow morning but he couldn't promise to keep them apart on the playground.

"Salvo, do you think we should go to the school and talk to the teacher?"

"Let's see how this works out, Serafina."

"I just feel so helpless. Poor little Pasquale."

"Serafina, I've been thinking. He's seven years old now. We've protected him all his life . . . ."

"We had to, Salvo. He was so sick."

"But he's not now. The doctor says he's healthy. He's small, but he's healthy. Look at the way he runs and how he climbs. We'll never know what's going on in that head of his, but I don't think we can protect him all the time. We have to let him grow up. And if he runs into trouble, well, he'll have to learn how to handle it."

"And if someone is mean to him, picks on him? What's he supposed to do then?"

"He has to learn to be more aggressive."

"Aggressive? You mean if this big Rocco kid hits him, little Pasquale is supposed to hit him back? Salvo, please . . ."

"I don't know about hitting, but we can't be at his side forever protecting him. He has to grow up and help himself."

"But he's so little . . ."

"He's always going to be smaller than a lot of guys, Serafina. We have to accept that. And he has to accept that. And live with it. He's going to face obstacles, sure, but we can't be around to protect him all the time. Serafina, we're not going to be around forever. You know that."

"Poor *moscerino*."

THE NEXT AFTERNOON, Serafina was amazed to see Pasquale coming home smiling, and even laughing a little.

"Hi Mama!" he shouted. He put Bruno on a leash and led him out for a walk along the little river that ran through Sant'Antonio.

When she told her husband when he came home, Salvo grinned. "Do you think?" he said.

"Let's hope," his wife said.

At dinner, Pasquale had just gotten his plate of pasta when he piped up. "Listen. I have a good joke!"

"Tell us the joke, son," Salvo said.

The boy jiggled in his chair. "Why did the teacher wear sunglasses?"

Salvo scratched his head and looked at the ceiling. "I don't know, Pasquale. Why did the teacher wear sunglasses?"

"Because the students were so bright!" The boy almost fell off his chair laughing. "So bright! Get it?"

Serafina and Salvo also laughed uproariously. "We get it, Pasquale," Salvo said. "I've never heard that joke before!"

"Oh, Papa, you have, too," Francesco said, getting a kick under the table from his father.

When she tucked him in for the night, Serafina kissed her son. "You had a good day, didn't you, *caro*?"

"Yes, Mama."

"You'll have another one tomorrow."

Pasquale was equally happy on Friday night, and had two jokes to tell.

"Which side of the chicken has the most feathers?"

The boy could hardly sit still.

"The top?" Serafina asked.

"Nooooo! The outside! The outside! The outside!"

Salvo slapped the boy's back. "That's so funny, Pasquale!"

"Wait," the boy shrieked, "I've got another one. What do you call a fish with two legs?"

Salvo thought a long time. "I don't know, I don't know . . ."

"A two-knee fish! Get it? A two-knee fish. A tuna fish! A tuna fish!"

Even Francesco and Clara giggled, and Salvo and Serafina were laughing so hard tears streamed down their faces.

"Who told you all those good jokes, Pasquale? Or did you make them up?"

"No, Giuliana told me."

"Giuliana?"

"She's just a girl in my class. She sits next to me now."

When the children were in bed, Serafina and Salvo celebrated their relief with a glass of wine.

"Oh, my God," she said. "I think he's OK now. He's happy, he even tells jokes. Separating him from Rocco was all that was needed."

"And he even has a little friend."

"Think we can stop worrying, Salvo?"

"I don't know, maybe. We'd better wait a few days and see what happens. They might still run into each other on the playground."

"Pray to God he's OK."

The weekend was uneventful. Pasquale and Bruno ran through the hills and avoided Signora Cardineli's house. He spent hours in his tree house. Francesco and Clara were gone most of the time, Francesco hiking with Farid and Clara secretly experimenting with makeup at Samia's house. Serafina, however, was upset again when her greetings were ignored by Signora Della Franca and Signora Rizzo when she went to Manconi's for meat for the hamburgers. Salvo failed to burn any sausages in his Sunday night cookout.

But on Monday, Pasquale came home with tears running down his face. His mother tried to stop him, but he ran to his room and flung himself on the bed. Bruno crouched nearby, whimpering.

"'Squale, what's wrong, what's wrong?" Serafina sat on the edge of the bed.

He refused to answer. Stroking his back, she noticed his book bag on the floor.

"Oh, my God! It's all right, *caro*, it's all right. You just stay here. I'll bring you something to eat later."

She took the book bag downstairs to show her husband.

"*Merda!*" he cried.

In large black letters on the back of the bag: *TERRONE.*

"It's getting bad again," Salvo said. Serafina had burst into tears and was huddled on the sofa. "Feed Francesco and Clara, Salvo. I'm not hungry."

On Tuesday morning, it took an hour of his parents' urging and the promise of treats when he came home to get the boy on the school bus. Salvo was about to leave for work when Serafina asked him if she could have the car that day.

"Can you call Amadeo?" she said. "He can give you a ride."

"Why do you need the car all of a sudden?"

"I, uh, I need to go to Camaiore to . . . to pick out some cloth for curtains for Clara's room."

"Today? It can't wait till next week?"

"I think . . . I'm sure they have good sales on Tuesdays."

When Salvo had left, Serafina ran to Leoni's. She didn't know how long she'd be away and would need a snack or something in the car. She arrived at the shop just as Signora Cardineli and two other women, Signora Della Franca and Signora Rizzo, were about to leave.

"*Buongiorno, signore,*" Serafina said brightly.

All three women gathered up their shopping bags and swept past her. Serafina muttered a choice expletive under her breath.

With a *panini* at her side, she drove off, not west to Camaiore, but southeast to Reboli. She had no idea what she would do when she got there, but she knew she had to be near Pasquale.

She left the car in one of the last remaining spaces in the parking lot overlooking the playground and maneuvered her way to the fence. No one else was around on this sunny but chilly October day. Should she go into the school and look for her son's classroom? She wasn't sure where it was. And what would she do then?

After a half-hour, her dilemma seemed resolved. A door opened and a teacher led a string of children onto the playground. Serafina scanned the group for signs of a small dark-skinned boy. This must be *Prima Classse,* she thought, not his.

Then the door opened again and another teacher, a young man who didn't seem old enough to control a classroom, led a balky group onto the playground. At the rear, Serafina saw a boy with dark skin who was smaller than the rest. Her heart skipped a beat.

When the kids started playing soccer, she watched as her son stood near a wall at first, but then kicked the ball when it was sent to him. Tentatively, he joined in the game. He was actually playing with the other children. Serafina could feel tears welling in her eyes.

Then another boy, a heavy kid bigger than the others, bumped into Pasquale. Serafina was sure it was intentional. Pasquale fell down and the big boy leaned over him, saying something she couldn't hear.

The game continued, with the big boy continuing to jostle Pasquale. Where was the teacher? Oh, over there against the wall, smoking a cigarette.

When the recess finally ended, Serafina saw the big kid shove her son against a wall, put his face up to his and force something into Pasquale's hand. She saw her son look at it and cram it into his pocket. She saw him wipe his eyes on his sleeve.

"Oh, Pasquale!" she whispered. "What did he say? What did he do?"

She was tempted to leap over the fence and run to the playground, but the teacher had led all the children back into the school. She looked at her watch and knew that she had to get back to Sant'Antonio before Salvo found out.

It was probably only her imagination, she thought, but the school bus that afternoon seemed unusually late. Pasquale shot through the door and up to his room before Serafina could grab him. She found him again face down on the bed.

"Go away!"

"Pasquale, please!"

"Go away!"

Again, Pasquale hardly touched his dinner and when he was finally persuaded to get into his pajamas and into bed, his mother dug into his pants pocket.

"Oh, no! No!" She ran downstairs to where Salvo was cleaning the kitchen.

"Look at this! Look at this!"

"What is it?"

"Just look."

"Oh, my God!"

SALVO TURNED THE PIECE OF PAPER over and over in his hand. "Are you sure this was in his pants pocket?"

"Yes, I'm sure."

"Did he tell you it was there?"

"No, but I knew it was."

"How did you know that?"

Serafina hesitated. "I saw Rocco give it to Pasquale and he put it there."

"What? You saw Rocco? Where? When did you see him do that?"

"Today, on the school playground."

Salvo tried to make sense of this. "Serafina, I thought you went to Camaiore to buy cloth for curtains today."

"Well, I didn't. I'm sorry, I lied. But I don't care. And I don't care if you get mad at me. I needed to be at the school today, Salvo. So I went there. Somehow I needed to be near Pasquale. I don't know why, I just did. And I knew you wouldn't want me to go. If you want to yell at me, go ahead."

Salvo looked at the paper again. "I'm not going to yell at you. I'm not mad at you. How could I be mad at you? I just can't believe what it says here. Are you sure it was Rocco? Are there other big kids in that class?"

"Not like him. I'm sure it was Rocco."

"Didn't the teacher do anything? What kind of a teacher is it that lets one kid bully another?"

"The teacher looked like he was twenty years old. Probably just got out of school and this is his first job. He wasn't even looking at the kids. He was leaning against a wall smoking. I bet the kids run wild in his class."

"Running wild is one thing. This is another." Salvo looked at the paper again. "The kid can't even spell."

He stared at the scrawled writing. "N-I-g-R-r b-a-B-y"

"Well, maybe he can't spell but we know what he means," Serafina said. "We've got to talk to Pasquale about this."

The boy lay on the bed, staring at the ceiling. Bruno was at his side.

"'Squale," Salvo said, "you have to understand that what Rocco did was a very bad thing. We don't know why he did it, but it was mean and cruel and we are so sorry."

"We don't want to make excuses for him," Serafina said, "but some people might say that maybe he is embarrassed because he doesn't look good, that he's ashamed of being so big, bigger than anyone else in your class. But what he did was very, very wrong."

"Or maybe," Salvo said, "his parents don't treat him right. He doesn't get any love, like we love you. Maybe all he feels is hate. Think that could be true?"

They could barely hear the boy's whispered response. "Yes."

"Or," Serafina said, "maybe he just wants to be noticed. He wants some attention."

Salvo took the boy's hand. "So he takes it out on someone smaller, like you. He thinks he can get away with it because you wouldn't get back at him. So he marked up your book and he threw chocolate milk at you and who knows what else he's done. He's got to have done other things because you've been so unhappy, you've been unhappy since the beginning of school."

"The note," Pasquale whispered.

"Yes, the note," Salvo said. "Calling you a baby was the worst thing he could think of calling you."

Pasquale looked away. "He called me something else. Something even worse."

Salvo and Serafina didn't know how to respond to that.

"Yes," his mother said, "and that was really very, very ignorant."

"Mama, how come you and Papa and Francesco and Clara don't have dark skin like me? Why am I so dark? Why am I the only one?" Pasquale began to sob.

"Honey," his mother said, "I don't know why that is. Remember your cousins in Corigliano? Some of them were lighter and some were darker. Remember Diego? He's as dark as you are. And Maria, too. But nobody paid any attention because a lot of people are dark in the South. Here in the North, it's more noticeable."

She put her hand on the boy's head. "People come in all different colors, *caro*. I think when God looks down he sees people all over the world who are in all different colors and shades. Some are light, some are dark and everything in between. I think God is so pleased with what He sees, and He loves them all, every one of them. It doesn't matter."

"I don't think so," Pasquale said.

"Well, we do. And you know what? We think that God especially loves people who are treated badly by other people. I bet, when He saw Rocco write those words, that He felt very bad and He thought, 'Pasquale is someone who is very, very special to me. I love him very much.'"

"And, 'Squale," Salvo said, "you know that we do, too. We love you so much, sometimes it hurts."

Serafina took her son in her arms and Salvo gathered them both in his. Salvo and Serafina were still sobbing when they left the little boy huddled in his bed.

Downstairs, while Salvo paced the worn rug on the living room floor, Serafina stared out the window. On the Via Giacomo Matteotti, Lucia and Paolo were strolling arm and arm down the street. So were Signora Rizzo and her husband, followed closely by Signora Della Franca and her husband. On any other night, Serafina and Salvo would also be making the ritual Italian evening walk, *la passeggiata*.

"How can everyone act so normal, like nothing has happened?" she wondered. "The world isn't the same anymore."

"Not for us," Salvo said. "And not for Pasquale."

Serafina looked out the window again. "I hate these people, Salvo! I hate these people!"

"Now Serafina . . ."

"I know, I know, Rocco did this, not Signora Cardineli or Signora Della Franca or not Lucia. But they're mean in their own ways, Salvo. Don't you see that? Stupid little Rocco might have written those horrible words, but these people think the same way . . ."

"Not everyone, Serafina. And not everyone is as bad as that kid."

"Oh, I know, you're going to tell me about Donna and Ezio again. Sure, there are exceptions, but there are so many people in the North who can't stand the people in the South. It's been going on forever, and I don't want to be part of this great melting pot, as Paolo calls it. I just want to raise my family and live a peaceful life and not have to worry about my children being called . . . being called . . ."

Serafina was sobbing now, and Salvo took her in his arms. He stroked her dark hair but he didn't have any words.

"I should have known what to expect," Serafina said. "Josefina and all the others, they told us not to move to the North. They told us we wouldn't be welcome. They told us we would run into this. They told us we'd be called *terroni*."

"Yes, and we were," Salvo said.

"But 'nig . . . nig . . .' I can't even say the word. I don't think they even say it in America anymore."

They sat on the sofa, hand in hand, not knowing what to do, what to say. Serafina put her head on her husband's shoulder. It was dark outside now, but they didn't turn on any lights, as if it were somehow safer to remain in the dark.

"Salvo," Serafina said, "would you think again about moving back to Calabria, back home?"

Her husband knew this was coming, and he didn't know what to say. Maybe his wife was right. Maybe they shouldn't endure the prejudice around here any longer. But what was the alternative? To go back to their threadbare existence in Corigliano? To live in poverty, hand to mouth?

"I don't know, Serafina, I just don't know."

"Would you at least think about it, Salvo. For me? And especially for little Pasquale?"

Salvo hugged his wife. "I don't know, Serafina. Sure, it's hard for Southerners in the North. You think I haven't heard people talk about my skin color behind my back? You think I don't have to work harder because otherwise they'll say I'm lazy? You think I don't have to watch what I wear because if I wear something that looks good they'll say I'm trying to look like a Northerner and if I wear something bad they'll say I'm just a dirty Southerner?

"But think of what we'd be giving up. I've got a good job. We've got this great house. We even have a good car, well, better than that heap we had there. We never had any of that in Corigliano. I know it's been hard sometimes, but isn't it getting better?"

"No," Serafina said. "No, it's not."

Salvo hesitated. "I don't know. This is one incident, one kid, one bully. Do we really want to change everything because of this?"

"I think we should, Salvo."

"Well, let's talk to the teacher before we decide anything."

ON WEDNESDAY AFTERNOON, Salvo and Serafina sat in their car in the school parking lot in Reboli and waited for the bus to leave for Sant'Antonio. They had told Francesco and Clara in the morning that they wouldn't be home when they returned from school and that they should keep a close eye on Pasquale.

When the bus had left and they entered the school, they found that the halls were decorated with artwork the pupils had made, delicate landscapes and bold portraits near the upper grades, gaudy sketches near the lower grades. The room for *Seconda Classe* was near the end of the hall, and they found Nico Orsini leaning back in his chair, his feet on the desk, with a cigarette in one hand.

"Yes?" He made no attempt to stand when they entered.

"*Ciao*," Salvo said. "You're the teacher for this grade?"

"Yeah. That's my job."

"We are the parents of Pasquale Marincola."

"Pasquale? Oh yeah, the black kid."

Salvo made a move forward but Serafina held him back.

"We want to talk to you about our son," she said.

Nico finally put his feet down and riffled through a folder. "Your son. Your son. Pasquale. Pasquale. Yes. Well, you should know he's not doing so good."

"What do you mean? He does his homework every night."

"He does? Well, he doesn't seem to be turning it in."

"Of course he turns it in!" Salvo said. "What do you think he's doing with it?"

"I don't know. But I have no record of homework for the last two weeks. None."

Serafina grabbed her husband's arm and leaned up to whisper in his ear. "Salvo. I bet Rocco steals his homework before he can turn it in. Oh my God!"

Red-faced, Salvo turned back to the teacher, who had lit another cigarette. The tattoo of a snake wound around his wrist.

"We want to talk about another kid. Rocco. Rocco Mazzei."

"Oh, Rocco. Funny kid. Likes to make jokes. You know his father? Really nice guy. Says he's going to get me a job at Fiat. Then I can get out of this fuckin' school and . . ."

"Here," Salvo said, throwing a piece of paper on the teacher's desk. "Rocco wrote this and gave it to our son. Do you think that's funny? Tell me, do you think that's funny?"

Serafina was afraid her husband was going to hit the teacher.

"What? Well, Rocco isn't so good at spelling."

"It's not the spelling, you goddamn stupid idiot!" Salvo yelled. "Don't you think that's a cruel, mean thing to call our son? Don't you think it's cruel when this kid marks up our son's books and throws milk at him? Don't you think it's cruel when this kid steals his homework? Well, what do you think?"

Nico Orsini stood up. "Hey, I don't have to take this crap from you! I don't get paid enough fuckin' *lire* to have to listen to you yell at me. I'm not responsible for what one kid does to another. Parents need to control their kids. Now get out of here now!"

Serafina grabbed her husband's fist, which was aimed straight at the teacher's face. "Salvo! No! Don't make this worse. Let's get out of here."

Serafina drove on the way back to Sant'Antonio. She had never seen her husband so angry and was afraid he'd go off the road.

"All right," Salvo said when they got back in the kitchen. "I guess I give up. We'd better tell the kids."

Francesco and Clara were again in front of the television set.

"Where's Pasquale?" Salvo asked. "We told you to keep an eye on him."

"He's in his tree house," Clara said. "He's there all the time."

"Well," Serafina said, "we have something to talk to you about."

They did not take the news well.

"No! No! No!" they shouted in unison.

"But . . ." Salvo said.

"No!"

Salvo tried to calm them down. "Will you just listen for once? We all know that the move to Tuscany has been hard, especially for your mother. She doesn't have any friends here. In fact, some people are downright cruel. We just feel we're not welcome and we're uncomfortable about that. We feel we'd be happier back in Calabria, with our own kind of people."

"But we've made friends!" Francesco said, his eyes filling with tears. "Farid and me are best friends. And I have other friends at school. Antonio and Luigi and Guido . . ."

"And me and Samia are good friends," Clara said. "And I hang out with other girls at school. Elizabetta and Patricia . . ."

"I know, I know," Serafina said. "But you had friends in Corigliano, too."

"Mama," Clara said, "that was almost five years ago. We don't know those kids anymore."

"You'd get to know them again."

"No."

"Well, can't you just think about it?"

"I don't want to think about it," Francesco said.

"Me neither," Clara said.

The silence in the kitchen was deafening.

"Pasquale," Francesco said. "It's about Pasquale, isn't it? That's the reason. He doesn't like it here so all of us have to suffer."

"It's not that he doesn't like it here," Salvo said. He couldn't bring himself to talk about the note.

Tears flowed down Francesco's cheeks. "No, it's because another kid teases him. Isn't that right? Well, he'd better learn to live with that. He's little and he's dark and he always will be and he's going to be picked on and I don't see why the rest of us have to sacrifice for him. I'm not going to do it. I'm not going! I'm staying here!"

Francesco stormed to his room.

"Clara," her mother said, "can't you at least think about it?"

"Mama, Mama. I don't want to go back there. I really don't. I like it here! Please!" Tears streaming, the girl followed her brother up the stairs.

Salvo held Serafina close. "Maybe with time . . ."

"I don't know."

Salvo put his arm around Serafina and held her close. Then they suddenly realized that someone else was in the room.

"Pasquale! What are you doing there? What did you hear?"

HE DIDN'T CRY when his parents asked him what he'd heard, but he didn't say anything, either. He didn't cry when they helped him get into his pajamas after he refused to have a snack before bedtime. He didn't cry when they tucked him in and said, "Good night and try to get some sleep."

But now, with moonlight creating a square on the wall opposite his bed, he let the tears flow.

*I can't stay here anymore. My brother and sister hate me. Rocco bullies
me and I can't stand to go to school any more. Old Signora Cardineli calls
me a* terrone. *So does Rocco. I am a* terrone. *I know what that means.
I'm black. And I'm a nigger. I don't know what that means but it must
be really bad. I don't belong here. Everyone else is white. Real white. I'll
miss Mama and Papa. I'll miss my tree house. But I'll take Bruno. He's
my best friend. We'll find someplace to go. We can take care of ourselves.
I have a ton of* lire *in the box under the bed. We'll be OK. But I'll wait
until it's light. I don't want to go out at night. There are scary things out
there at night.*

THROUGHOUT THE NIGHT, Serafina and Salvo took turns
checking on Pasquale. Even well after midnight they found him wide
awake, staring at the ceiling. It looked as though he'd been crying,
but he denied it.

"Go to sleep, *moscerino*, go to sleep," they kept saying.

For the rest of the night, when they checked, he did seem to be
sleeping.

"Thank God," Serafina said. "Maybe we can get some rest now."

Not for long. The telephone rang much too early.

"What? What?" Salvo took the pillow off his head. "What's
going on?"

"It's the phone," Serafina said, groping for the clock on the stand
at the side of the bed. "Good Lord, it's not even 5 o'clock. Who could
be calling at this hour?"

"I'll get it." Salvo rolled out of bed, grabbed a robe and stumbled
downstairs.

"*Pronto!* What? . . . Wait . . . Wait . . . Talk slower, I don't
understand . . . Where . . . OK, we'll be right there."

"What? What?" Serafina cried as she rushed down the stairs.

"It's Pasquale. Signora Cardineli says he's in her backyard. He
fell off her roof."

"What? He's in bed. I know he's in bed. He's sleeping."

They ran up the stairs. Pasquale's bed was empty, the window
open.

"He must have climbed out to the tree house and then jumped
down. And Bruno's gone! Oh my God!"

They threw on the clothes they wore the day before and rushed out to the car. The sound of car doors slamming must have awakened Lucia Sporenza next door.

"What's going on?" she shouted from her upstairs window. "Where are you going?"

"Signora Cardineli's! Pasquale's hurt!" Salvo shouted as he drove off.

"Well, all of Sant'Antonio will know that in five minutes," Serafina said, still easing into the passenger seat.

It took less than five minutes to drive to Signora Cardineli's house on the other side of the village. They found the old woman seemingly frozen still, clutching her cat. She wore an old woolen jacket over a pink nightgown, and shiny pink slippers covered her feet. Her thin white hair was wound in big curlers.

Pasquale lay at her feet. The boy's head was at an awkward angle and his left leg was twisted under his right. His eyes were closed, his brown skin turned ashen. Bruno hovered nearby, whimpering.

Salvo bent down and held his son's shoulders. "'Squale, 'Squale, what happened?"

There was no movement. Salvo put his ear against the boy's mouth.

"He's breathing. We've got to get him to the hospital."

Frantic, Signora Cardineli tried to explain. "I always get up early and this morning I went out to get the milk bottle for Alessia and she got out and then she climbed up the tree and you see that branch, it goes over to the roof and she got on the roof and she's never done that, never, and I called and called for her to come down and she wouldn't and I didn't know what to do and I was crying and crying and then this little black boy came along with his dog and for once the dog didn't bark and I told the boy that I couldn't get Alessia down and he said he'd climb up and get her and he did and Alessia jumped down but the boy, the boy, he was trying to climb down and he fell, he fell off the roof. Oh, he's going to be all right, isn't he? I'm so sorry, I'm so sorry."

Salvo and Serafina didn't hear half of what she was saying because they had bundled Pasquale into their car and were already on the road to Lucca. Bruno had bounded in behind them.

While her husband kept the gas pedal to the floor, Serafina sat in the backseat, holding her son. She wiped the boy's forehead with a handkerchief. He was cold.

"Oh, Pasquale, Pasquale. What were you doing up on the roof? What were you doing at Signora Cardineli's house? Are you upset because of what Francesco and Clara said? They didn't mean it, *moscerino*. They didn't mean it. Oh, *caro*, we love you so much, we love you so much. Please, can you open your eyes, please!"

Serafina's tears fell on the boy's curly black hair.

Nurses were just arriving at the Hospital Campo di Marte when Salvo screeched to a halt in front of the emergency entrance.

"Help me, please!"

Three nurses summoned a gurney and rushed Pasquale through the doors, with Serafina and Salvo close behind.

"Bruno, you stay in the car and be quiet," Serafina shouted over her shoulder.

"The nurses will help you, 'Squale, the nurses will help you." Salvo leaned down as his son was wheeled into the emergency room. He had not opened his eyes or shown any sign of life since they found him under the tree in Signora Cardineli's backyard.

A doctor pushed his way through. "Please stand back, Signor, Signora, we have to take care of the boy."

Holding hands, Salvo and Serafina stood against the wall, trying to see what was going on and feeling very helpless.

"Please God, please God," Serafina whispered.

They saw the nurses take Pasquale's clothes off, his good shirt, the one that now showed only a few signs of chocolate milk, his short pants, his shoes and socks. Salvo and Serafina couldn't help but remember the little body in a diaper, attached to tubes and machines, only seven years ago.

Seeing their son like this, they collapsed in tears into the hard wooden chairs against the wall.

When nurses rolled in a screaming girl of about ten, Serafina suddenly remembered. "Francesco and Clara! They're home alone."

"We can call Lucia later," Salvo said. "She can get them off to school. We need to stay here."

Serafina began to pray. "Holy Mother, Holy Mother . . ."

It seemed like hours, but in reality it was only twenty minutes before a doctor stood before them.

"Signor, Signora," he said, "we need to take X-rays and make other examinations. We will take him into another room. Please go into the waiting room. A nurse will show you. We will let you know what we find out."

"Doctor, Doctor," Salvo said, "how serious is it?"

"We can't be certain until we have completed the examinations."

Serafina grabbed his arm. "It's serious, isn't it?"

"Keep praying, Signora."

OBVIOUSLY, the clock in the waiting room was broken. Every time Serafina looked at it, it was only a minute later. Now it was 6:15. She was sure that it was 6:14 the last time she looked and that was a half-hour ago.

"Salvo," she said, "tell someone the clock is broken."

Salvo didn't hear her. He was pacing back and forth, back and forth, so often that the worn carpeting threatened to tear. Every fifteen minutes he sat down, wiped his forehead, and began pacing again.

The family of the screaming girl—her parents, two sisters, a brother and a grandmother—occupied all of the chairs on the opposite wall, waiting for her results. The mother, the sisters and the grandmother sobbed loudly.

In a corner, an elderly man crouched in a chair, murmuring "No, No, No, No . . ."

A young couple held on to each other on another side. Both were crying. The woman held a blue baby blanket.

"That was us," Serafina told her husband.

She couldn't help but notice that although there were plenty of chairs next to her, no one came near.

"*Terrone*," she muttered.

She looked at the clock again. 6:45. "Oh! Francesco and Clara! We should call now!"

Salvo turned toward the door. "I'll call Lucia. There's a phone down the hall."

"Oh," she called after him, "and better let Bruno out so he can do his duty."

Salvo did that first, and Bruno obliged, hopping back into the car when he was finished.

No one answered the phone at Lucia's, so Salvo called his own number and she answered there.

"Salvo!" she cried. "Where are you? What happened? How's Pasquale? I've been worried sick."

Salvo gave the little information that he had, and Lucia said she had come over a half-hour ago and was making breakfast for Francesco and Clara. Francesco wanted to talk.

"Papa, what happened? Where are you? How's Pasquale?"

Salvo went through the same limited answers.

"Papa, I'm sorry! I'm sorry! I didn't mean what I said!"

His father could hear him crying and his sister sobbing in the background.

"It's OK, Francesco. We'll talk about it later. Now we have to worry about Pasquale. Go to school. I'll call you later, OK? Put Lucia back on the line."

Assured that the children would get off to school safely, on time and with lunch bags prepared, Salvo went back to the waiting room. All the members of the family of the screaming girl were now on their knees, praying loudly. The old man continued to mutter "No." A young mother, looking very haggard, had joined the group on a bench near the window. She tried to feed a squirming baby from her breast, a toddler crawled on the floor and a boy of about two jumped up and down. All the children were screaming.

"Salvo," Serafina said, "come sit with me. I don't want to be alone."

Her husband joined her on the green plastic couch, coffee stains stretching down the sides. "He's going to be all right, *cara*," he said.

"That's what you kept saying when he was in the hospital the last time."

"And he did get better, right?"

"But this seems so much worse."

"I know, I know."

Serafina's handkerchief was soaked, and Salvo gave her his.

"The poor kid," she said. "He's been through so much. Rocco. And the kids last night. If only we had closed the door he wouldn't have heard what they said."

"We couldn't have known he was there."

"If only we had stayed with him through the night. He wouldn't have gotten out. And Signora Cardineli? I told him over and over not to go by her house. Where was he going? At that hour?"

"We've never known what goes on in his little mind," Salvo said.

"Oh, Salvo, what are we going to do?"

"We have to wait to see how he is. We have to wait . . ."

All of the women in the family of the screaming girl had now taken out rosaries and were praying loudly. "Our Father . . . Hail Mary . . ."

"Merda!" Salvo said. "Who believes in God at a time like this? How could He do this to our little boy, our *moscerino?*" For the first time, Salvo broke down and sobbed. Serafina put her arms around him. They didn't speak.

A grim-faced young doctor came through the swinging doors and approached the young couple on the other side. It was clearly bad news. The husband helped his wife, who could barely stand, follow the doctor back inside.

"Oh, Salvo," Serafina cried.

"Cara, cara."

"I can't stand it."

Now another doctor came out and talked to the old man. The man smiled through his tears as the doctor led him through the doors.

It was 9:38 when another doctor appeared in front of Salvo and Serafina. She was a stocky woman, about fifty years old, with short dark hair. Her surgical mask hung around her neck. She pulled up a chair so she could face them.

"Signor, Signora," she said, "I am Doctor Ramonoli. With several other doctors, we have made a preliminary examination of your son. Let me tell you about the situation. Your son has had a very bad fall. Very bad, and he has many injuries."

"What? What are they?" Salvo asked.

"Well, he has many bruises around his chest and there is a slight fracture of a rib, but that will heal on its own."

"Thank God," Serafina said.

"Then he has a fracture of the femur in his left leg. That's the thigh bone. A fracture like this is usually caused by an automobile accident or a fall, and I understand that he fell from a great height."

"A roof," Salvo said.

"The way we treat such fractures," the doctor continued, "is to insert a flexible rod into the hollow of the center of the bone."

Serafina gasped.

"I know that sounds painful, but the thigh bone heals and we remove the rod after time. Your son is young and I don't see any problems in his getting the full use of his leg again."

"Thank God," Serafina said.

"Now another problem. When your son fell, he probably reached out with his left hand and so there is a break in the forearm. This may require surgery to realign the broken bone, but perhaps he can just wear a sling for a while and it will heal by itself. Again, your son is strong. So we'll wait on that.

"Good," Salvo said.

"Now for the most serious injury suffered by your son."

Serafina grabbed Salvo's hand. "Most serious?"

"Your son fell very hard on his head. We may think that the head is so strong that it can't be injured, but that's not true. Your son has suffered what we call a traumatic brain injury or TBI. We are concerned about blood flow and pressure within the skull. Fortunately, we now have the technology to see what is going on inside the brain, and our hospital is fortunate enough to have one of these new machines. It's called a CT scanner. These have been in use only in the last decade. We will use the results of that test to determine how to proceed.

"So for now, what we need to do is keep a very close eye on your son and keep him stable. We have moved him to a private room. He will probably remain unconscious for some time, how long we don't know, but it may be long, very long. But we will be monitoring him constantly. Do you have any questions?"

"No," Salvo said. "Please let us see our son."

IT LOOKED LIKE any other hospital room. The walls were painted a neutral beige. A painting of a Tuscan landscape decorated one wall.

A small crucifix hung above the bed. Four nurses hustled from one side to another, sometimes bumping into each other.

Salvo and Serafina could hardly find their son on the bed, surrounded as he was by equipment they could never understand. But there he was, covered from the waist down by a white sheet that made his skin appear even darker. His left leg, encased in a white cast, was raised by a pulley attached to the ceiling. A thick cast covered his left arm, which was folded on his chest. Wires were attached to his head and an oxygen mask covered much of his little face. His eyes were still closed and he seemed to be sleeping. Or worse.

"Please," Serafina cried to a nurse, "he's OK, isn't he?"

"We're monitoring him closely," the nurse said, writing notes on a lined pad.

"He doesn't look like he's in pain," Salvo said.

"He's heavily sedated," Doctor Ramonoli said. "We must keep him still at this point."

Serafina leaned down. "Can you hear us, Pasquale? It's your Mama. Papa is here, too. We're going to stay with you now."

Salvo bent down on the other side of the bed. "'Squale, can you give us a sign that you can hear us, maybe move a finger?"

No response.

"Signor, Signora," Doctor Ramonoli said, "you can see that we have a team of nurses taking care of your son, and I will be here regularly. I'm afraid we can't allow you to stay in here long. You're welcome to stay in the waiting room, and we will call you if there are any signs of changes."

"We can't stay with him?" Salvo was almost shouting.

"Please!" Serafina cried. "Please!"

The doctor's tone softened and there was a glimmer of a smile. "Well, if one of you wants to stay at a time, you could sit over in that chair in the corner. But please don't attempt to get near your son. We need to keep constantly monitoring him."

"You stay first," Salvo said. "I'll be in the waiting room."

He kissed his wife, took a long look at his son and closed the door behind him.

In the waiting room, the family of the screaming girl had now left, but the mother with the baby and two young children remained in a corner. The baby was asleep and the toddler had curled up on his mother's feet. The older boy was still jumping up and down and crying. In stark contrast, an elderly woman wearing a dark blue dress under a swath of fur and a pearl necklace read from a magazine. She might have been waiting to enter a theater, and Salvo couldn't figure her out.

He remembered that he hadn't called his boss, and then had to wait for the phone while a teenage girl, her hair in spikes, finished a call, apparently with her boyfriend. It took a long time for his boss to answer.

"Luigi? Salvo here. Listen . . ." He explained why he hadn't shown up for work. "Thanks, Luigi. I'll be back to work as soon as I can. I'll let you know."

When he returned to the waiting room, the woman with the three children was gone. In her place, a man about thirty years old tried to read a magazine to a young girl on his lap. A teenage boy slept on a chair next to the elegant woman.

Salvo resumed his old place. He picked up a magazine, flipped through its pages and put it down. He pulled out his cigarette pack but decided against it. He leaned back and closed his eyes but couldn't sleep. He tried to imagine what had brought each of these people into the waiting room. He noticed that no one sat near him.

"*Terrone.* Serafina was right."

In Pasquale's room, Serafina tried to figure out what each of the nurses was doing. At first, when a nurse took notes from a monitor, she asked what the numbers meant. The nurse smiled but did not reply. When another nurse wiped Pasquale's forehead with a towel, Serafina said, "Can I do that?" but the nurse shook her head.

The hours dragged on. About 3 o'clock in the afternoon, she went out into the waiting room and Salvo replaced her. They agreed that they would each spend about an hour with their son. They didn't go to the cafeteria for dinner. Neither was hungry and, anyway, they didn't want to risk being away if something changed.

At 5 o'clock, Salvo called home and Lucia answered.

"Salvo! What's going on? How's Pasquale? We've been worried sick. Where's Serafina? Where are you calling from?"

"Lucia, Lucia, let me answer."

Salvo gave a very limited answer, afraid he couldn't remember all the things that were wrong with his son. Then Francesco got on the phone again.

"Papa, how's Pasquale? I'm sorry, Papa, I'm sorry. What's going to happen?"

"We don't know, son. Just eat what Lucia has made for you, OK? What are you having tonight?"

"She brought over some ravioli she had in the freezer."

"Well, eat whatever she gives you. Then do your homework and go to bed. You and Clara can watch television a little. I don't know when we'll be home. Maybe not until tomorrow. We have to get Bruno home. He can't stay in the car for another day. You can make your own breakfast, right? OK then. Put Lucia back on . . . . Lucia, how can we thank you?"

"It's nothing, Salvo. Glad to do it. Paolo is here now. We'll help the kids with their homework and get them to bed. And we'll see that they get off to school OK in the morning. Don't worry!"

"We won't, Lucia. I'll call you tomorrow. *Molte grazie*, Lucia, *molte grazie*."

Salvo went back to change places with his wife and told her that the kids would be all right.

"I wonder why Lucia is being so nice to some *terroni*," Serafina said.

THEY TOOK TURNS staying with Pasquale throughout the night. Nurses came and did what they had to do and left. Serafina tried to pray but her mind went off to a million other places. Salvo, his eyes watering, simply looked lovingly at his son.

They tried to sleep in the waiting room but could not. A stream of other people, relatives of patients brought to the emergency room, came and went. They always sat on the opposite side of the room.

At 7 o'clock in the morning, Salvo drove back to Sant'Antonio to deliver Bruno. The dog seemed happy to be home at last, bounded up to Pasquale's room, curled up on the bed and went to sleep.

Lucia was in the kitchen making breakfast for Francesco and Clara.

"Papa!" the children cried. They both hugged him.

"OK, OK," Salvo said. "I'm here just for a little while. I need to get back. I don't want to be away too long. Pasquale's the same. No sign of change. He's just lying there, hooked up to a bunch of stuff. The nurses are good. Someone's there all the time. The doctor comes a lot and talks to the nurses."

"But what is Pasquale saying, Papa?" Clara asked.

"*Cara,* he's not saying anything. He's unconscious."

At this, both children began to sob.

"Papa, it was because of what we said, wasn't it?" Francesco said through his tears.

"It was, wasn't it?" Clara said.

"We don't know," Salvo said. "We don't know. But what you said was very cruel and I don't have to scold you about that. You obviously know it."

"Papa, I'll never say anything like that again!" Francesco said.

"Me neither," Clara said.

"Good. Well, finish your breakfast and go off to school. Try to concentrate. Your mother and I have enough to worry about without having to worry about how you're doing in school."

Salvo conferred with Lucia, who assured him that she and Paolo would be back in the evening to prepare dinner, help the children with their homework and get them to bed.

"*Molte grazie,* Lucia," Salvo said. "We'll always remember this."

"It's nothing. Now go back to the hospital."

"Papa!" Francesco shouted as Salvo got into the car. "When can we go to see Pasquale?"

"Only me and your mother are allowed now. Maybe later. Be good!"

Nothing had changed when Salvo returned to the hospital. Another family had taken over the waiting room, this time an ancient *nonna,* a man of about sixty with a long beard, a younger woman, perhaps his daughter, and two squalling children. They were in the midst of a bitter argument, apparently blaming one another for an accident. Four generations, Salvo deduced, waiting for someone.

"Any change?" he asked his wife when he entered Pasquale's room. Her eyes were red from crying, her hands red from rubbing.

"Nothing. Oh, Salvo, if only he'd make a movement, move a finger, a toe, anything. This is like watching a . . . a . . . I can't say it."

"Don't think it. Look, the respirator shows that he's breathing. Remember when we sat by his side in the hospital in Catanzaro? How we watched the respirator?"

"They said he had RDS then. Now they say TBI. Why can't these people talk in words we understand instead of letters?" She began to sob again.

Salvo stood in back of her chair and massaged her shoulders, but there was nothing he could say.

After a long day, about 7 o'clock in the evening, when both Salvo and Serafina were in the room, a nurse suddenly called another nurse. They huddled over the little boy, and his parents struggled to see what was going on. Then Doctor Ramonoli arrived and there was much whispering.

"Excuse me," Salvo said. "What's going on?"

Doctor Ramonoli pulled down her surgical mask. "We thought there was a movement, but we may have been mistaken. He's still the same."

The doctor left, and the nurses resumed adjusting machinery, checking tubes and wires and taking notes.

"'He's still the same, he's still the same.' That's all they can say?" Serafina moaned.

"It's better than he's getting worse, isn't it? We have to keep up our hopes."

Salvo did not say this with much enthusiasm.

Two hours later, nurses again gathered around the boy's bed, only to shake their heads and leave again.

"It's this waiting and waiting," Serafina said. "If only . . . if only . . ."

"Maybe tomorrow," Salvo said. "I'll call home again and make sure the kids are in bed by now."

Lucia assured him that Francesco and Clara had eaten all their dinner, had done their homework and had gone to bed quietly. Also, Paolo had walked Bruno and the dog was sleeping again on Pasquale's bed.

"OK," Salvo said. "We're going to stay here tonight. Maybe Serafina will come back in the morning. Thanks so much again."

AT 2 IN THE MORNING, Serafina had curled up on the wooden chair in Pasquale's room and drifted off into a restless slumber. A little boy was running, running, running through the woods, a shaggy dog behind him. The boy was singing! She couldn't make out the words, but it must have been a happy song because the boy was laughing and the dog was barking. They came to a tall tree and the boy started climbing. He was so fast! He got to the first branch, then the second, then the third. He moved out on the branch and it suddenly splintered. The boy fell. The sound was so loud Serafina wakened, hearing herself crying out, "Oh, no!"

Five nurses surrounded Pasquale's bed, furiously adjusting tubes and monitors. Serafina could barely see through them but knew that something terrible was happening. Then she saw the little body convulsing. A nurse adjusted the respirator. Another refastened the wires on his head. A third checked the plasma drip behind him.

"What's happening?" Serafina cried. "What's happening?"

"Please, Signora, please stand back."

"But I want to see! I'm his mother!"

A nurse ushered her to the door. "Please, Signora, wait in the waiting room. You can't stay here now."

"But I have to!"

"Please, Signora."

Salvo was dozing on the green couch. No one else was in the waiting room.

"Salvo! Salvo! Something is happening. They won't tell me. They won't let me stay . . ."

Her husband folded her in his arms. "No, no, no,"

They clung to each other for more than an hour. Finally, Doctor Ramonoli stood before them, her face haggard.

"Your son has had a very bad episode. He is more stable now. We are monitoring. That's all I can say." She turned to leave.

"Doctor," Salvo said, "will this happen again?"

"We don't know. We are monitoring."

When she left, Serafina saw that the doctor's shoulders were shaking.

"What are we going to do, Salvo?"

"We're going to wait."

And that's what they did. Hour after hour. At midmorning, Salvo was allowed back into Pasquale's room. The boy looked the same.

Hour after another hour. The clock barely moved. The waiting room filled with more families, many of them sobbing, and then they left, only to be replaced by others. No one sat near Salvo and Serafina.

At 6 o'clock, Salvo called home. "Lucia, it looks like Pasquale is going to be in the hospital for a long time." His voice began to crack.

"Oh, poor little boy."

"I don't know when we'll be home, Lucia. Can you manage things OK?"

"Of course! Of course! Don't worry. The kids are fine. We'll be fine. I did a little cleaning and some laundry. Just stay with Pasquale. You need to be there."

But Lucia wasn't sure things would be fine. She was tired. As soon as she hung up, and settled Francesco and Clara in front of the television set in the living room, she got on the phone again.

"Ezio? Lucia here. Can you and Donna come down to Salvo and Serafina's now? Good. *Grazie.*"

A half-hour later, the two couples sat around the kitchen table, out of earshot of Francesco and Clara, who were deeply involved in a television show.

"Salvo says Pasquale's going to be in the hospital for a long time," Lucia said. "Now Paolo and I don't mind coming over here morning and night to take care of the kids and we do a little cleanup and today I did laundry. But I was just wondering . . ."

"Lucia always is just wondering," Paolo said.

"Well, I was just thinking about when Annabella was sick."

"Yes!" Donna said, "and we all came over to help her. We took turns, seven of us, one each day. In this very house."

"It worked out very well, I thought," Lucia said. "And our husbands didn't seem to mind."

"Of course not," Ezio said.

"Well," Lucia said, "I wonder if we can get a group together and help out Serafina and Salvo. I know they'd appreciate it."

"Great idea, Lucia," Donna said. "I'm willing. I've got time. Let's get seven women together."

Besides Lucia and Donna, that meant five women would be needed. Donna pointed out that although it had been only seven years since Annabella died, not all the women in that group were around anymore.

"Rosa and Fausta and Flora have died, and Sabina is living with her daughter in Lucca and Viola with her sister in Pisa. Poor things, they're suffering like Annabella now."

They thought of other women who might help.

"I suppose Anita Manconi," Lucia said, "she's young, but she's got the meat market to run and she has that little girl."

"No," Donna said. "I think she's busy enough."

They thought some more.

"Well," Donna said, "there's Bernadetta Miniotti."

"The divorced woman," Lucia said.

"Well," Donna said pointedly, "some people might bring that up. She's awfully nice, and her kids are in school. I think she'd like to meet some new people."

"I'll call her," Lucia said.

"And," Donna said, "there's Fatima Issiakhem. Her kids are in school, too."

"Farid and Samia are best friends of Francesco and Clara."

"Yes, it's about time we got to know her, don't you think, Lucia?"

Lucia was about to say something, but Paolo answered for her. "I'm sure Lucia would love to get to know her," he said.

They counted: Lucia, Donna, Bernadetta Miniotti and Fatima Issiakhem. Three more were needed. They finally decided to ask Signora Bruni, whose husband had recently died and was reportedly looking for something to do, and Signorina Cesi, a retired schoolteacher who had moved into Flora Lenci's house.

"That's six," Donna said. "One more."

"Well, I hate to suggest . . ." Lucia said.

"I think you're thinking what I'm thinking."

"Yes. Well, I'm sure she feels guilty about all this, the way she treated that poor little boy, so maybe this will help make up for it."

"OK," Donna said, "I'll call Signora Cardineli."

NOW IT WAS NOT JUST HOUR AFTER HOUR but day after dreadful day. Pasquale showed no sign of improvement, but Salvo kept saying, "He's not getting any worse," and Serafina would start to cry.

And then it became week after week. They drove back and forth from Sant'Antonio to Lucca so often they could do it in their sleep, which, unfortunately, they sometimes almost did, careening away from oncoming cars. Serafina stayed with their son through the day, and Salvo went to the hospital after work, remaining until morning. They got to know the nurses, and Doctor Ramonoli became even more solicitous, sitting with them for long periods to explain what was happening.

But not much was happening. Pasquale's parents wondered whether this might go on forever, and they would have to eventually take him home and care for him themselves. Serafina shuddered when she thought of that.

"Poor *moscerino*," Salvo kept saying.

At least they didn't have to worry about Francesco and Clara or what was happening at their home in Sant'Antonio. Lucia and Donna and their crew of women not only kept the children well fed and cared for, but they also seemed to actually enjoy the housework.

"I like coming over here," Lucia told Donna one day. "It's easier cleaning this house than mine and it gets me out of my own house."

Serafina and Salvo continued to thank the women profusely. "*Molte grazie, molte grazie, molte grazie.*"

"I don't know what we'd do without them," Serafina told Salvo. "Now I know there are some nice people in Sant'Antonio."

"Well, that's one good thing that's come out of this."

"The only good thing," Serafina said.

One morning, Serafina came downstairs to discover Signora Cardineli in the kitchen, about to make breakfast for Francesco and Clara. It was the first time the women had seen each other since that terrible day when Pasquale fell off the roof, and Serafina couldn't help but remember all the times the woman had called her son *terrone*. She knew that if her son had not been such a good boy he would not have climbed up to rescue the cat and that's why he had remained in a hospital bed for weeks. But she also remembered the frail old woman holding that cat and sobbing over Pasquale's tiny body.

"Oh, Signora Cardineli," Serafina said, her voice without emotion. "Thank you so much for everything you're doing. You've been quite wonderful. Francesco and Clara will be down any minute."

"I'm so sorry about your son. How is he?"

"He's the same, Signora Cardineli."

"No change?"

"No, Signora Cardineli. Thank you for asking. Again, thank you for coming over to help." She picked up her purse and started for the door.

"But, Signora Marincola, may I say something?"

"What is it, Signora Cardineli?" She had not turned around.

"I mean . . . I wanted to say . . . Please, could we sit down for a moment?"

Serafina put her purse down. "All right, but just for a moment. I need to get to the hospital."

"I understand, and I thank you."

Reluctantly, Serafina sat opposite the visitor at the kitchen table. "And you wanted to say?" she said.

"Signora Marincola, I just want to say . . . well, I just want to say how sorry I am for calling your son that awful name. I don't know. I've always lived in Tuscany. I suppose I could say that I didn't know any better. But I know that's not an excuse. There is no difference between people who are from Tuscany and people who are from Calabria. The color of our skin makes no difference. I know that now. Your son taught me that. What a wonderful little boy. I'm so grateful to him, not just for rescuing Alessia but for teaching me about accepting people. And I'm so sorry, so very sorry."

The woman had been wringing her hands throughout this, and now she brought them to her face to wipe away her tears. "Please forgive me, Signora Marincola."

Serafina had hardly slept and was exhausted. Now, she couldn't hold back her own tears any longer. She reached across the table and held Signora Cardineli's hands.

"I forgive you, Signora Cardineli," she whispered.

"Oh, please, call me by my name. It's Pasqualina."

"Like Pasquale?"

"Yes. I was born on Easter, too."

"Oh, my." The women couldn't help laughing.

"And please call me Serafina."

"Now," Pasqualina said, "I want to give you something. I've been waiting until I saw you."

She went to her shopping bag in the corner and took out a plastic bag.

"I found this on the ground after you took your son away that morning. I think he'd like it when . . . when . . ."

Serafina looked inside the bag and pulled out the wooden cigar box containing Pasquale's treasures, the oak leaves, the stones, the robin's egg. Serafina counted the *lire*. "He wouldn't have gotten very far on this," she said. There was also a ragged small ball. "Bruno's favorite toy. He wanted Bruno to have something, too."

Both women were now sobbing. Serafina stood and hugged her guest. "Thank you, Pasqualina, thank you so much."

Serafina was still wiping away tears when she entered Pasquale's room just as the nurses had gathered round his bed. Salvo was trying to see what was going on.

Five weeks, four days, three hours and twenty-four minutes after he fell from Signora Cardineli's roof, little Pasquale had slowly opened his eyes. Just a little, but unmistakably a movement.

"Look!" a nurse said. "Are you sure?"

"I'm sure," another nurse said.

"What? What?" Serafina cried. She ran to the bed and grabbed her husband's hand. The nurses let them get near, and together, they leaned down. Serafina kissed her son's forehead. Salvo touched his shoulder. There was no recognition.

"Perhaps we were mistaken," a nurse said.

"Maybe tomorrow," another said.

But then there seemed to be movement again. Serafina held one of the little hands, Salvo the other.

"It's Mama, Pasquale."

"It's Papa, *moscerino.*"

"Can you say Mama?"

"Can you say Papa?"

The boy's lips moved ever so slightly, and he started to say something, then stopped. Then his lips quivered again. They leaned even closer.

"Say something, 'Squale."

They could hardly hear him.

"Bruno."

TWO WEEKS LATER, Francesco and Clara were allowed to visit their brother. They entered the room slowly and quietly, not sure what they would find. Pasquale was no longer on a respirator and the wires had been removed from his head, which rested on two pillows. His left arm was in a cast and his left leg was still raised on a pulley.

"Hi," Francesco said.

"Hi," Clara said.

"Hi," Pasquale said.

Serafina pushed them forward. "Show your brother your presents."

Francesco stood on one side of the bed. "I brought you a coloring book and crayons. I know you only have one hand but you can still color, can't you?"

Pasquale smiled, a crooked smile since the left side of his face was still a little paralyzed. "Sure. Thanks."

Clara stood on the other side. She brought a framed photo of Bruno, which Salvo had taken. The dog was looking into the camera. "Look, he's saying, 'Come home,'" Clara said.

"No, no, don't cry," Serafina said, seeing tears welling in her son's eyes. "You'll be coming home real soon."

"Now," she added, "don't you have something to say to your brother?"

Francesco looked down on the bed, his hands fidgeting behind his back. "Pasquale, I . . . I'm sorry for what I said that night. I didn't mean it. You are the best little brother I ever had. And . . . and I love you."

He touched the cast on his brother's arm. "Hey, can I write my name on your cast?"

"Sure!" Pasquale said. Francesco took a red crayon and did just that.

Clara had a prepared speech. "Pasquale, I want you to know that I have always liked you a lot even though sometimes you are a pill but I forgive you for that and I hope you will forgive me for what I said. I'm really sorry. There."

Pasquale smiled at his sister. "You can put your name on my cast, too." Which she did, with a blue crayon.

Serafina added her name, in orange, and Salvo found room for his, in black.

Two weeks after that, with Doctor Ramonoli and the nurses waving goodbye, Pasquale left the hospital and came home. Francesco and Clara had rolled out a long piece of brown wrapping paper that they got from Anita Manconi and hung it between two trees in front of the house. "Welcome Home Hero!" it said.

Inside, everyone cheered as he hobbled through the door. He still wore the cast on his arm and was using a pint-sized crutch. Lucia and Paolo were there, along with Donna and Ezio. Signora Miniotti brought her three children, Mandina, Manuela and Manfredo. Fatima and Mohammed Issiakhem were with their kids, Farid, Samia, Hakeem and Mustafa. Signora Bruni and Signorina Cesi were in the doorway to the dining room. In the back, Pasqualina Cardineli tried to be invisible.

Bruno, kept in the kitchen until now, bounded out, almost knocking his master down. Pasquale picked him up and the dog licked his face, one side to the other.

"Bruno, Bruno, Bruno."

There was strawberry cake with strawberry frosting and strawberry gelato. "I know you don't like chocolate," Serafina said.

"But I love strawberry!" Pasquale said. "Hey, I have a strawberry joke."

"Pasquale, how do you know a strawberry joke?" Francesco asked.

"Remember when Giuliana came to see me in the hospital last week? She told me a joke."

"Tell us the joke, Pasquale," Salvo said.

"What did one strawberry say to the other strawberry?"

No one could possibly know the answer.

"If you weren't so sweet, we wouldn't be in this jam!"

Everyone in the room dutifully convulsed.

"Get it," Pasquale said, "in this jam, in this jam?"

"That's very, very funny," Salvo said, tickling the boy under his good arm.

With everyone laughing so hard, no one heard the sleek, white Lancia Delta pull up in front of the house. A grim-faced man, about forty years old with thinning hair and a tiny mustache, and wearing an expensive black suit, was soon at the door. A boy about eight years old trudged behind him. The boy was bursting out of his clothes.

"Signor Marincola?" the man said when Salvo opened the door. "I am Pietro Mazzei, and this is my son, Rocco. We are sorry to interrupt your festivities here, but Rocco wants to say something to your son."

No one said a word when Signor Mazzei and Rocco entered. Pasquale sat in an overstuffed chair, Bruno at one side and his crutch on the other. His father pushed Rocco forward.

"Tell Pasquale what you want to say, Rocco."

Rocco edged slowly to Pasquale's chair.

"Pasquale, I . . ."

"Go ahead," his father said. It was a command, not a request.

"Pasquale, I'm sorry for all the bad stuff I did to you and for calling you names."

"More, Rocco."

"It was mean of me to do that. I don't know why I did. It was just that you were so little and it was easy to pick on you."

"More."

"I want to ask you if there is anything I can do to make up for what I did."

Pasquale looked at this boy who had terrorized him. He should have been angry, but instead he saw a kid who deserved pity, not hatred.

"It's OK," Pasquale said. "I forgive you."

"*Grazie,*" Rocco said, using his fist to wipe his eyes.

"Hey, want to sign my cast?" Pasquale found a green crayon in his box and Rocco scrawled his name in the only available space.

Signor Mazzei took his son's hand and turned to Salvo. "Signor, I want to apologize myself for my son's behavior. Words cannot express how I feel, how I'll always feel. Again, forgive us for interrupting your party. I'm pleased to see that your son is doing well. Rocco won't be in school when he returns because we are moving back to Turin. My wife needs, um, some treatment and Rocco should be in a school where there will be, shall we say, more discipline. Thankfully, I've found such a school there."

He glanced at Rocco, who looked petrified.

"Thank you for coming, Signor," Salvo said. "Thank you for coming. My wife and I and especially Pasquale appreciate it."

With second helpings of cake and gelato making the rounds, Lucia got into a lively discussion about Muslim clothing with Fatima Issiakhem. Signora Bruni talked about life in Camaiore with Signora Miniotti. Paolo, Salvo and Mohammed Issiakhem discussed Paolo's new motorcycle, and Ezio told Salvo and Serafina that Nico Orsini, Pasquale's teacher, would not be returning to the school next year.

"We had to honor his contract for the rest of this year, but after June, he's gone. And I can guarantee that Pasquale won't have to worry about him."

It was quite noisy, and Serafina tapped a coffee cup with a spoon to get some quiet.

"I don't want to interrupt, but since we're all here, I would just like to say something. Salvo and I, and also Francesco and Clara and of course Pasquale, are so very grateful for all that you have done in the last couple of months. We just couldn't have pulled through without all of you."

There were murmurs of "It was nothing" and "We were glad to do it."

"But I also want to say something else. Before all this, before little Pasquale here decided to fall down and break practically every bone in his body . . ." She leaned down and kissed her son on the top of his head ". . . before all that, I was having some real problems living in Sant'Antonio. Salvo and I moved here from Calabria so that we could have a better life for our kids, and it has been good for them.

"But lately, it hadn't been so good for me. There were some people who called us bad names and some who didn't seem to want to have anything to do with us. I was very hurt and depressed. In fact, I asked Salvo several times if we should move back to Calabria."

There were cries of "No, No." Salvo put his arm around his wife.

"Of course, what happened to Pasquale was not a good thing, but I see now that sometimes good things come out of bad things. Every time I came home during the last weeks and I found what Fatima or Bernadetta or Lucia or Signora Bruni or Donna or Signorina Cesi or Signora Cardineli had done here, making dinners for the kids, cleaning the house, doing the laundry, ironing, shopping, oh, so many, many things, well, I was so grateful."

Serafina's voice was breaking but she continued. "And I know now what wonderful and kind people you all are. And I thank you from the bottom of my heart. We love being in Sant'Antonio."

Now there were cries of "We love you, too" and "We will always be friends." Salvo went around shaking hands and everyone hugged Serafina.

Then everyone noticed that Pasquale, tired from his hospital stay and perhaps because of one too many pieces of strawberry cake, was yawning in his chair.

"We really have to get going," Donna said.

That was the cue for everyone to leave, though there was much talk of offering to help more and meeting one another soon. Pasqualina was the last to go out the door.

"Signora Marincola . . . Serafina . . . I wonder if I could say something to Pasquale."

"Of course."

She bent down. "Pasquale, I want you to know that I am very sorry for calling you that awful name. It was very mean and cruel. Can you forgive me?"

"Sure," the boy said.

"And I want to thank you so much for rescuing Alessia that day. But, oh, I'm so very, very sorry that you fell. I would never have let you on the roof if I had known that. Can you forgive me for that, too?"

"Sure."

"And I've been thinking. Sometime, when you're better, would you like to come over and have a treat, cookies or something . . ."

"Strawberry ice cream?"

"Well, of course. And you could play with Alessia. I know she'd like that. I'm just getting too old to play with her."

"Could I bring Bruno?"

Serafina put her hand on her son's shoulder. "Pasquale, do you think that's a good idea?"

"Sure. I think Bruno and Alessia should be friends."

The Monster

IF FATHER LORENZO didn't exactly hate hearing confessions, he certainly didn't look forward to them. He remembered telling his late superior, Father Alphonsus, that it was one of a priest's most painful duties.

"All those people with their little sins," he remembered saying.

He never knew how to respond to some of those "little sins." Should he make light of what these people said? After all, they must think their sins were important or they wouldn't be there. Should he consider these transgressions as more serious than they were? He couldn't help but think that in the whole range of what was sinful, they were on the very low end.

It was another Saturday afternoon and time for him to go out and listen to more of these minor matters. Now that he was only part time at the Basilica of Santa Croce's soup kitchen, the new superior at the church, Father Frederico, wanted him to be more active in the parish.

"We're losing too many priests," Father Lorenzo was told. "We need you."

And so it was not only daily Mass and confessions, but also weddings and funerals and marriages and baptismal preparations and visits to the sick, not to mention trying to induce the poor people of the parish to please put a little more into the collection basket because God knows we need it.

Father Lorenzo draped the purple stole around his neck and strode out into one of the massive church's side chapels. Temperatures outside had already soared near one hundred on this sultry late August afternoon, and even the basilica's thick walls couldn't completely suppress the heat. Fanning themselves with their handkerchiefs, three elderly women were already lined up beside the confessional, with another half dozen kneeling in prayer nearby.

He knew confessions should be anonymous, but of course he recognized most of the women since they attended daily Mass and, although they had little to confess, showed up for the sacrament every Saturday afternoon. He kept up the pretense of anonymity by averting his eyes as he walked past.

Entering the confessional, he sat down on the worn purple cushion and slid open the latticed door on the window on the right. A black curtain concealed the woman behind it, but there was no doubt it was Signora Amalia Fazzari, fifty-eight years old but so heavy that she looked ten years older. Because of a heart condition, she breathed heavily, and Father Lorenzo knew that she again had linguini with lots of garlic for lunch.

"Bless me, Father, for I have sinned," she wheezed.

"Bless you, Signora. Tell me what you want to confess."

It was the same every week. She had yelled at her husband too much, "but he never listens to me." She had insulted her neighbor Signora Tomasselli, "but she said she thought my towels were getting too thin." She had actually slapped the little girl in the piazza who was snickering "for no good reason when I walked by."

Father Lorenzo felt his mind wandering. He wondered if he had remembered to order more bread for the soup kitchen. He thought he should find out more about the couple in his matrimony class because the young man did not seem at all eager to get married. And there was that mysterious leak under a gutter outside his office. Need to call someone . . .

Suddenly, something Signora Fazzari was saying brought him back to reality. It was new.

"So you know, Father, I have this daughter, Maria. We never thought we'd have a child, but then she came along and now she's seventeen years old. So pretty. You wouldn't believe she was my daughter, certainly not Guido's daughter.

"Well, you know, she's so pretty that all the boys are after her. I try to keep her at home, I tell her to dress more modestly, but she wears these little things, short skirts, blouses that you can see everything. She has all the boys going nuts.

"Lately, I know she's being going out with one boy, Pietro. He seems like a nice boy, I guess, but he's only nineteen years old. I know his mother, his father died years ago. Pietro is always hanging around and they go to Maria's room and I hear them talking and laughing and I'm not sure of what they're doing but I can guess. But at least I know where they are."

Father Lorenzo interrupted. "What are you trying to tell me, Signora?"

"Well, Father, it's just that on Saturday nights I know that Maria and Pietro drive out to the country. He has this old beat-up Fiat that he bought from a friend. Black, with a broken window. They drive way out in the country north of Florence. I know, I asked Maria. She says they go to a disco bar and then they drive to this place where other young people go.

"Father, I know what's going on when they get there. I was young once, you know. I know they park and they do things they shouldn't be doing, not when she's only seventeen and he's only nineteen."

Father Lorenzo interrupted again. He could hear coughing and mumbling and knew the other women were getting impatient in the waiting line. "What are you getting at, Signora?"

"Well, last Saturday I told Maria I didn't want her to go parking with Pietro anymore, especially on Saturday nights. So last Saturday night, after I went to confession, she and Pietro stayed in her room all night. I could hear them. Guido could hear them. He got so mad he was ready to go in there and stop them but I told him no, it was better that they do it at home than out in some lovers' lane. They didn't come out until Sunday noon! Father, they didn't even go to Mass!"

"What are you confessing, Signora?"

Signora Fazzari's voice was breaking. "Father, is it a sin for me to tell them they can do it at home? I know they are committing a sin. But am I guilty, too? I mean, I did it for their own good. I mean, there have been twelve! Twelve, Father! All in lovers' lanes. And all on Saturday nights!"

She was sobbing now.

Father Lorenzo suddenly wished he could talk to Father Alphonsus about this. Certainly he would have sage advice. But a fall down the stairs had taken the life of the wise old priest three years ago.

Everyone in Florence knew what Signora Fazzari was talking about. For ten years now, a serial killer had preyed on young couples making out in cars in remote regions outside of Florence. There had been at least six incidents and twelve victims. In most cases, the killer had shot both the boy and girl and then brutally hacked off the private parts of the girls. All Florence was terrorized, with rumors and accusations rampant. Now there were posters and postcards everywhere—a staring eye surrounded by leaves and the words *Occhio ragazzi!* "Watch out, kids!"

What should he tell Signora Fazzari? Her daughter and the boy were no doubt committing sins, but how serious were they, really? The signora was only acting like a mother, trying to protect them from a terrible threat. Now, in the summer of 1985, there hadn't been any killings for more than a year, but who knew when the killer would strike again? Mothers all over Florence were telling their daughters, and their boyfriends, to stay home on Saturday nights. Then the mothers looked away and said a prayer, and as soon as they could, they went to confession.

Father Lorenzo could not decide how to respond, so he avoided answering her questions. "Signora Fazzari, through the ministry of the Church may God give you pardon and peace, and I absolve you from your sins in the name of the Father, and of the Son, and of the Holy Spirit. For your penance, say the sorrowful mysteries of the rosary. Go now."

He made an abbreviated version of the sign of the cross, slid the window door shut and shuddered.

"*Il Mostro di Firenze* . . . the Monster of Florence is taking all our lives."

MORE THAN A WEEK LATER, after a busy schedule of Masses and meetings, hours at the soup kitchen and marriage preparation sessions, Father Lorenzo was still struggling with Signora Fazzari's questions. He pondered them again over his morning brioche and cappuccino.

He knew what some of his priest friends would tell her. The boy and the girl are committing sins and so if you let them do those things under your roof you're committing sins, too. You're just as guilty. Yes, you can make them stay at home because surely there is a danger from the killer. But they mustn't go into the bedroom. Never! Have them watch the television with you. Have them play *briscola* or some other card game with you. Or just sit and eat and talk, like good Italians. Understand?

Father Lorenzo should tell the signora that? About a boy of nineteen and a girl of seventeen? Some priests, he feared, lived in another world.

He was well-aware that most young people in Italy lived at home until they married, and many married late. Until then, they had no private place to get to know each other really well. As a result, secluded wooded areas, dirt roads, even cemeteries around Florence were well-known as trysting spots. Couples would spend the evening at the movies or at discos, then drive to places where they could accomplish what they wanted to do.

Like everyone else in Florence, Father Lorenzo also knew that this practice was so widespread that it resulted in a subculture of Peeping Toms, lecherous men who found some sort of gratification by watching what they themselves could not do. Some of these voyeurs carried night vision cameras, and they were so experienced that they knew the areas where the "best action" could be observed.

"Sick, sick, sick," Father Lorenzo said, often to himself, but sometimes aloud, when he thought about this.

And for ten years these young lovers were not only preyed upon by dirty old men, but by a killer.

He wished Father Alphonsus were here. His cappuccino was cold now, and he'd lost any appetite for the brioche. He felt the need to pray.

Only one person was in the Medici Chapel of Santa Croce when he entered, a large woman seated in the back. He slipped past her and knelt in front of the della Robbia altarpiece of the Madonna. Whenever he was disturbed or questioning, the Virgin's kindly face seemed to give him peace.

"Our Father, who art in heaven . . ."

He had only begun the second sorrowful mystery of the rosary when he became aware of sniffling, wheezes and gasps from the back of the chapel. He turned around.

"Signora Fazzari? Here on a Monday morning?"

The woman wiped her eyes. "I couldn't sleep, Father. I couldn't sleep all last night."

The priest put his hand on her shoulder. "Your daughter?"

"My husband. Father, Guido did a terrible thing. He . . . he . . ."

"Go slow, Signora."

"Sunday morning, when Maria and Pietro were still sleeping in her room, he went in there. Oh, Father, it was terrible. He grabbed Pietro and he threw him downstairs and out in the street and he told him never to see Maria again. The poor boy. He was out in the street in his undershorts and all the neighbors could see him.

"And poor Maria. She was hysterical. She kept fighting Guido, screaming and scratching at him. Guido pushed her back into her room and got a key and locked the door. And then, oh, Father, it was terrible. Maria tried to climb out the window even through she only had her nightgown on. Guido ran downstairs and stood beneath the window so she couldn't jump out. All the neighbors were out watching. Oh, Father, I was so ashamed."

Signora Fazzari had to pause for breath. Father Lorenzo sat down next to her and put his arm around her shoulder.

"Well, Pietro finally drove away because Guido kept yelling at him, and Maria . . . Maria hasn't come out of her room since then. Guido's gone to work now so I came here. I thought I could pray, but I can't, Father, I can't."

"Try to become calm, Signora. Here, use my handkerchief."

For more than an hour, the priest sat with the stricken woman, hardly saying a word. All he could think about was how Florence had changed. What was once a serene, if somewhat arrogant, city was now gripped by fear and hysteria. Florence had survived the devastating flood of 1966. Would it survive the Monster?

Father Lorenzo remembered exactly when he first heard about the serial killer. It was Monday morning June 8, 1981, and he had been unpacking bread in the soup kitchen, ready to make soup for the daily noon meal. He remembered that his back began to hurt so he sat down on one of the long benches to take a break.

That is where his friend Dino Sporenza found him.

"Father, Father!" Dino was out of breath. "It's terrible. Oh my God. Oh my God."

"Sit down, Dino, catch your breath. What in the world?"

Dino's words came in spurts. "Father, remember that nice young woman . . . who brought . . . who brought dresses and other things to the soup kitchen . . . so, so we could give them to the poor? She worked at Gucci in Florence. I remember she came . . . she came at least three times. Carmela Di Nuccio was her name. She was 21 years old."

"Sure. I remember. Carmela. Very pleasant. And quite pretty. I remember one time she told me she was going out with a guy and it was getting serious. What about her?"

"Yesterday morning, a man was taking a walk in the country, they said he was an off-duty cop, just taking a walk. This was near Via dell'Arrigo. You know where that is?"

"Sure, south of Florence, I've been there. Pretty rugged. Lots of vineyards and olive trees. There's a medieval castle nearby. At the top of the hill you can see the Duomo in Florence. Why?"

Dino paused to catch his breath again.

"The cop saw a car parked alongside the road. He knew that this was an area where young lovers went on Saturday nights, but normally they were all gone by Sunday morning. So he went up to the car and saw a man sleeping in the backseat of the car. Only . . . only . . . he wasn't sleeping, Father. He had a bullet hole in his forehead."

"My God."

"So the cop left and called headquarters. When the other cops arrived, they looked all around and found the body of a woman down a steep bank about twenty yards from the Fiat. It was . . . it was . . ."

"Carmela?"

"Yes."

Father Lorenzo closed his eyes and mouthed a silent prayer.

"They found her purse nearby. It was empty."

"God in heaven!"

"It gets worse, Father. When the cops looked at the body, they found that her jeans had been pulled down and . . . no, Father, I don't want to go on . . ."

"Take it slow, Dino, take it slow."

Dino swallowed hard. He whispered the rest. "They found that her private parts had been cut out and taken away."

"Oh, my God! Poor Carmela."

Neither spoke for a while, unable to imagine the horrific scene. Dino sat with his head in his hands; Father Lorenzo dug out his rosary but couldn't get past the first Our Father.

"Dino," he finally said, "who was the boy?"

"His name was Giovanni Foggi. He was 30 years old and worked for the electric utility. They were supposed to get married."

"Oh, my God. How do you know all this, Dino?"

"It's in all the papers today. Big headlines. Didn't you see them?"

"You know I don't read the newspapers, Dino, and that's the reason why. Do the cops have any clues?"

"They're not saying if they do. But one of the papers says that this is similar to those killings six years ago near Borgo San Lorenzo. Remember that?"

"North of Florence, yes. A boy and a girl. Terrible thing."

"The girl was shot and then stabbed ninety-seven times. Ninety-seven! How could somebody do that? How could anybody do that?"

"And some people doubt that there's a devil in the land, Dino."

"And you know what else? That killer shoved a grapevine up . . . up that girl's private parts. It was still there when the cops found her. So that's why they think it's the same killer. They've got a name for him now."

"I'm afraid to ask."

"The Monster of Florence."

NOW, SITTING ON THE COLD BENCH of the Medici Chapel with his arm around Signora Fazzari, Father Lorenzo shivered when he thought of that conversation. He felt tears gathering in his own eyes. So many victims, he thought, so many victims, one of them right here next to him.

The first two killings were followed by another and another and another.

On October 23, 1981, a couple about to be married, a workman named Santino Baldi, 26, and a telephone operator, Susanna Cambi, 24, were shot to death and stabbed in a park near Calenzano northwest of Florence. Susanna's pubic area was cut out, just like Carmela's, but this time the killer carved out a bigger area. Authorities said the same type of knife was used, a scuba knife.

On July 19, 1982, a mechanic, Paolo Mainardi, 22, and a dressmaker, Antonella Migliorini, 20, were shot while parked on a country road in Montespertoli southwest of Florence. Antonella died almost right away but authorities said Paolo was able to start the car but then got stuck in a ditch. The killer shot him again but didn't kill him. After Paolo was found the next morning he was taken to a hospital but he died there. He never regained consciousness so he was never able to give any information about the killer. Antonella was not mutilated. Authorities believed it was because they were parked near a busy highway, Via Nuova Virgilio. The same gun was believed used in all of these killings because of a special mark on the bullet casings.

On September 9, 1983, two German tourists, Horst William Mayer and Uwe Rüsch, both 24, were shot to death in their Volkswagen bus near Via di Giogoli southwest of Florence, Authorities theorized that the killer was deceived by Rüsch's long blond hair and build, thinking he was a girl. Authorities said it was the same gun, a .22 automatic Beretta.

On July 29, 1984, a student, Claudio Stefanacci, 21, and a barmaid, Pia Gilda Rontini, were shot to death and stabbed in Stefanacci's Fiat Panda parked in a wooded area near Vicchio di Mugello. The boy was still in the car and the body of the girl was nearby. She had been stabbed a hundred times and besides cutting off her private parts, the killer ripped off her left breast.

When the authorities were able to connect the killing of Carmela and Giovanni at Via dell'Arrigo to those six years earlier near Borgo San Lorenzo and then to the next murders, Florence knew that it did not just have a murderer on its hands, it had a serial killer. Because the shell casings were the same, authorities knew that the same gun was used, that the same method was used and that similar, if not identical, attacks were made on the female victim.

But it had taken a long time for Florence to believe it was home to a serial killer. Italy just didn't have such things. England had Jack the Ripper; France, the French Ripper; Germany, the Vampire of Dusseldorf; the United States, the Boston Strangler and Chicago's Richard Speck.

This didn't happen in Italy. And certainly not in Florence. Father Lorenzo and Dino were talking about that one day after he had consoled Signora Fazzari once again. They had escaped the heat in an alcove of Santa Croce.

"Father," Dino said, "I can't believe this is happening in Florence. Florence! Of all places! The city of Michelangelo and da Vinci and Botticelli and Machiavelli . . ."

"And the city that expelled Dante . . ."

"And Brunelleschi and Donatello and Galileo and Lorenzo the Magnificent . . ."

"And the Pazzi family that tried to kill Lorenzo the Magnificent in the Duomo . . ."

"And Petrarch and Giotto and Ghiberti and Fra Angelico . . ."

"Dino, Dino, Dino. Stop. Don't you realize that Florence has always been a city of severe contrasts? It has some of the wealthiest people in Italy and some of the poorest. It has benevolent laws and hardened criminals. Yes, it produced all those grand and brilliant people, but there has always been a dark side, too. Just look at what Savonarola did. Frightened the city so badly by stirring up such a religious fervor that his enemies finally hung him and burned his body right there in Piazza della Signoria. Every time I see the plaque that marks the spot where he was hung I think of how extreme Florence has been. This is a beautiful city, Dino, the cradle of the Renaissance, of art, of culture, of architecture, of literature. But it's also a harsh and demanding city. Maybe only Florence could produce such a Monster."

Father Lorenzo's voice cracked and he rubbed his hands together. Dino had never seen him so distraught, not even during the devastating flood of 1966.

Both of them were aware of the wild rumors and lurid speculation that continued to spread throughout the city. The police were inundated with anonymous letters that accused fellow Florentines of these heinous acts. When *La Nazione* published an article with a headline "The Surgeon of Death Is Back," everyone thought that a well-known doctor was the Monster. Specifically, the rumor mill zeroed in on a prominent gynecologist whose wife, it was falsely claimed, found the missing portions of the female victims in her refrigerator. After a crowd gathered in front of the doctor's house, the chief prosecutor had to go on television to discount the rumor.

"I think the paranoia is getting worse," Dino said. "There hasn't been a killing since last July, and people are just waiting for another. They look at every face in the street thinking, 'Maybe he's the

Monster.' My God, just the other day there was this woman in the piazza who was looking and looking at me. Then she came up close and stared into my face. Then she turned around and walked away. Father, I don't look at all like that guy in the sketch. OK, I'm about the same age, forty years old, and my ears stick out, but whose don't? I've got a full head of hair and it's blond, not black, and my eyes don't look anything like his. Good God!"

"I hate to admit this," Father Lorenzo said, "but I've been wearing my robes more now. People don't stare at me as much. I guess they think a priest couldn't be the Monster."

A cleaning woman walking by the alcove stopped to look at the two men talking to each other. She looked closely at one and then the other, and then walked away.

"See?" Dino said.

"It's like we're all holding our breath, just waiting."

"When are the cops going to find the guy, Father? When? They make an arrest and they put the guy in prison and then there's another killing so it's obviously not the right guy. He's still on the loose, Father. He could be anywhere. My God, he could be out there in the middle of Santa Croce."

"Dino, Dino. Now you're getting paranoid, too."

Now in the summer of 1985, as Florence waited for the killer to strike again. Father Lorenzo could only be grateful that Maria and Pietro would not be on a lovers' lane.

SINCE HE FEARFULLY READ the newspaper every day now, Father Lorenzo's worries about Signora Fazzari were compounded the next morning when he opened the day's edition.

"No, no, no, no!"

In need of new glasses, he held the paper closer. It was just a little item, buried on page 15, and he could easily have overlooked it.

Butcher Thought by Some to Be Monster
Found Dead Hanging in His Shop

Angelo Mancuso, a longtime butcher in Oltrarno, was found dead yesterday morning hanging by a rope near the meat locker in the back of his shop.

Ever since the police posted a sketch of the alleged Monster of Florence in 1981, Mancuso had been threatened and hounded because some believed that he looked like the man in the drawing.

Mancuso always denied that he had anything to do with the killings. Police said it was clear that Mancuso had committed suicide and were not investigating further.

Mancuso leaves a wife and two children.

"No, no, no, no!" The priest was shouting now and a young Franciscan on his way to Mass stuck his head in the open door.

"Something wrong, Father?"

"Yes, godammit!"

"Father?"

"He didn't do it! He couldn't have done it! He wasn't the Monster!"

"Father?"

"This has all been a fucking lie!"

"Father, should I call Father Frederico, I'm sure he . . ."

"No, don't call Father Frederico. I don't need Father Frederico. Just leave me alone, OK?"

"Yes, Father." The young Franciscan slipped away, wondering again whether he should have joined an order that included such crazy people.

Father Lorenzo threw down the paper and grabbed his hat. "I've got to go see Angelica."

Pushing through crowds in front of Santa Croce on another humid August morning, then running along the Lungarno and shoving through the tourists on Ponte Vecchio, he got to the piazza in front of Santo Spirito in less than twenty minutes. Breathless, but he got there. At fifty-four, he could no longer run like he used to.

The Mancuso apartment was on the second floor of a three-story building on Via Maffia. He could hear screaming and wailing behind the door.

"Oh, Father! Thank you, thank you for coming." Angelica's eyes were swollen and her face flushed. She wore a faded housecoat and scruffy bedroom slippers because she didn't have the energy to get dressed. Her dark hair, usually held in a neat bun on top of her head, cascaded in knotty ringlets down her back. Filling the tiny room were relatives and friends, some holding each other and wailing loudly, some sitting or standing quietly, seemingly unable to comprehend what had happened. Father Lorenzo recognized a few of them.

Angelica fell into his arms. "Father, he didn't do it, he didn't kill anybody."

"I know that, Angelica, I know that. Your husband was a good man. I don't know how he could suffer through all this for so long."

Angelica blew her nose. "It got worse last week. I don't know why. I guess someone posted that damn sketch again. I don't know . . ."

Father Lorenzo held her close, but there was nothing he could say. What he was thinking was: "Damn, damn, damn!"

He could never understand how the police could release what they called a sketch of the Monster after the June 1981 killings. Only one man had told police he thought he saw the killer, but the man gave conflicting descriptions. The police, eager to show that they had leads, allowed the sketch to be made public.

There he was, a grim-faced man of about forty, with receding hair and very thick eyebrows. He had a strong nose, big ears and a firm mouth. His eyes were big and black.

In other words, a generic sketch that could have been of any one of hundreds of men in Florence.

Immediately, Florentines found suspects who resembled the man, and rumors spread throughout the city. Innocent men were suddenly afraid to go outside, and their wives became hysterical. A cab driver found all four of his tires slashed. A ticket taker in a movie theater received a note with letters cut from a magazine: "*Il Mostro.*" A man who worked for the utility company felt so threatened by rumors that he was the killer that he gathered his family and moved to Assisi.

And one of the rumors, likely started by a disgruntled customer, began to spread that Angelo Mancuso was the murderer. Looked at a certain way—or in the dark—he could have resembled the sketch. Also, he had vineyards near Via dell'Arrigo so he knew the area well, the gossips said. He liked to go out at night, they argued. He was often gruff with customers, they reported. And besides that, he hardly ever went to church.

After the October 1981 killings, and the publication of the police sketch, Angelo and Angelica saw a noticeable drop in customers, even though his butcher shop had always been known for its excellent meat and poultry. Little kids started to pretend that they were scared of him and then laughed and ran away.

A week after the July 1982 double murder, Angelo found the words "*Il Mostro*" painted in red letters on the front door of his shop. After the September 1983 murders of the two German boys, someone threw a large rock through the shop's window. And after the last killings, in July 1984, a crowd gathered in front of the shop. Some carried signs, "*Il Mostro di Firenze*," and when police arrived to disperse them, the crowd demanded that Angelo be arrested.

But there was no reason to arrest him. He was at home with Angelica every time the killings occurred. He had nothing to do with the terrible events.

Father Lorenzo often visited Angelo and Angelica during these years, trying to comfort them but unable to explain how people could be so stupid, cruel and vicious. He could only hope that the real killer would be arrested and convicted. Then people would know the truth.

There were arrests, yes, but no one was convicted.

Angelica dabbed her sodden handkerchief on her cheeks. "Father, I didn't know that he was going to . . . going to . . . . I had no idea. But in the last weeks he yelled a lot at me and the kids, for no reason. But at night he got real quiet. I'd ask him what was wrong and he would just stare straight ahead. I know he didn't sleep and he got up a lot. He wasn't eating either, no matter what I made. Oh, Father!"

Father Lorenzo led her to the worn and patched sofa and put his arm around her.

"I should have called you then, but I wasn't thinking. I should have called you yesterday after we found him, but . . . who knows? I wasn't thinking."

"It's all right, Angelica. I'm here now."

"Father, what am I going to do?" Angelica cried. "We have no savings. How am I going to feed Luciano and Donatella? How are we going to survive?"

Father Lorenzo held her close again and said that Santa Croce had a fund that could be used and he would personally see that she wouldn't have to worry about any of that.

Angelica blew her nose. "I'm going to miss him, Father. I know, we had our problems, but who doesn't? He was a good man, I know it. I know he loved the children. And we got along, most of the time."

She began sobbing again.

For the next hour, Father Lorenzo sat next to her, just as he had sat with Signora Fazzari, until finally realizing that he had to return to the soup kitchen. The funeral, they agreed, would be the day after tomorrow and he would be honored to say the Mass.

On the way back, barely noticing the crowds and bumping into people, he knew that something had to be done to calm this hysteria. But what? It was out of control. People weren't thinking rationally. They weren't thinking at all.

Passing a newsstand, he couldn't help but see the huge headline: *"Fratelli Vigna interrogated in omicidi del mostro."* "The Vigna brothers questioned in the Monster murders."

UNTIL THE NEWSPAPERS began publishing articles about the Vigna brothers in the early 1980s, most Florentines rarely thought about Sardinia. It was just that big rocky island off Italy's western coast where, in recent years, the northern beach areas had been developed as extravagant playgrounds for the superrich. The Costa Smeralda, as it was called, had become a destination for international celebrities and business leaders who built huge villas and spent their days on the white sand beaches and their nights in glittering nightclubs. The towns of Porto Cervo, Liscia di Vacca, Capriccioli and Romazzino prospered with this new attention.

Not so the mountainous interior. It was a region still called the *Barbagia*, a name derived from the Romans, one of the numerous invaders of this vulnerable island. But even their mighty armies were unable to conquer it.

Florentines, and Italians in general, thought of Sardinia in stereotypes: A forbidding place where the peasants spoke a strange dialect, where women wore black, and where bandits swooped down on unsuspecting travelers and robbed them. Some towns, it was believed, had resident witches. Vendettas were common.

Only a little of that was true.

Scholars called the interior region *la vera Sardegna*, the "true" Sardinia, because it preserved a pastoral lifestyle that had existed for centuries. Shepherds still guarded their flocks in the barren lands, always moving from one place to another to seek some sort of grass or stubble.

According to tradition, shepherds banded together, not just for their common good but also as a defense against marauding thieves. Even in the mid-twentieth century, it was considered a normal practice for shepherds to steal livestock from each other. The thief was considered brave and capable (*balente*) and was respected because he could get away with something.

Surrounded by craggy peaks on a high plain in the southern part of Sardinia, the village of Bellanove was in the heart of *la vera Sardegna*. It was here that the Vigna family lived and where three brothers developed their reputations.

The oldest was named Giuseppe. As a young man he was accused of raping one of his sisters and, in accordance with the Sardinian tradition, was shunned by the villagers.

The youngest brother was Frederico. He was the *balente* of the family, with a history of violence, of beating up his girlfriends, of hanging around with gangsters and of stealing sheep.

The middle one was Sergio, and he became famous for an incident in 1961. His wife was called Brunella, only seventeen years old, and there was a son, Angelo. Sergio refused to believe that Angelo was his son. Everyone knew that Brunella had a lover.

On the night of January 14, 1961, Sergio, who was twenty-four years old, was out drinking in a local bar, leaving Brunella home with eleven-month-old Angelo. Brunella went to a neighbor's house to warm milk for the baby because, she said, the propane tank at her house was empty. When Sergio returned home, he told the *carabinieri* later, he found the bedroom door closed but he could see a light underneath. He also said that Angelo's cradle had been moved to the kitchen. His statement to authorities said:

"I knocked once and called out to Brunella but no one answered. I immediately thought that she was with her lover and so I ran out of the house, fearing an attack."

Sergio ran to get Brunella's father and brother and they all returned to the house. There, they found that the propane tank had been moved next to the bed, the valve was open and the tube was under Brunella's pillow. Obviously, authorities said, Brunella had taken her own life.

No matter that only Sergio claimed that he could smell propane. No matter that Brunella had reported the propane tank empty to a neighbor a few hours earlier. No matter that Sergio was hardly the kind of guy who would allow his wife to let a lover into their home. And no matter that she had bruises around her neck and scratches on her face.

Despite the official ruling that Brunella had committed suicide, most people in Bellanove believed Sergio had killed his wife.

After Brunella died, the outcry against the Vigna brothers grew and they were compelled to leave. Sometime later in 1961, they boarded a ferry for Livorno and then traveled to Florence, where there was already a Sardinian colony.

In Florence, little was heard from Giuseppe. Frederico mostly spent time in a bar with other Sardinians and otherwise was involved in petty holdups and thefts. Sergio, the quietest of the three brothers, began work as a bricklayer.

Sergio rented a room in a house owned by a family named Mosca who had arrived from Sardinia earlier. There was a father and a son, Santino Mosca, whose wife was named Benedetta Lauri. Santino's family had arranged the marriage even though he was much older than his wife and was considered *uno stupido,* stupid.

Benedetta Lauri was not. She stole money from her in-laws and, with a voluptuous body and ravenous desires, she soon found men who could satisfy her in ways her husband could not. One of them was the friendly new tenant Sergio Vigna. When Benedetta bore a son, Nicolo, the good Sardinian women in the neighborhood counted the months and realized that Santino Mosca had been in the hospital after a motorcycle accident nine months earlier, but Sergio Vigna was very much around.

Disgusted, Santino's father threw Santino, Benedetta, little Nicolo—and Sergio—out of the house.

Later, Benedetta also took up with Sergio's brother, Frederico, the *balente,* joining him on his frequent visits to bars and getting acquainted with his gangster friends. But then Benedetta found yet another lover, Arturo Lo Russo, a married bricklayer from Sicily.

Sicily! It was bad enough if it had been someone from southern Italy, but Sicily? Obviously, this was too much for the Sardinians.

On the night of August 21, 1968, Benedetta and Arturo went to a Japanese horror movie and, with little Nicolo, six years old, in the backseat, then drove in Arturo's white Alfa Romeo to the countryside outside of Florence. A shooter and his accomplices were already there, the police said later. While Nicolo slept, Benedetta and Arturo proceeded to have sex. The boy awakened when the first shot was fired.

Four bullets were fired into Arturo's body and three into Benedetta's. Authorities later said that the shooter then handed the pistol to Santino Mosca, who fired the last bullet into his wife's body.

Little Nicolo gave conflicting accounts of what he had seen. Mosca admitted firing the gun once, but told authorities that he threw the gun into a ditch. It was not found.

Ballistic tests showed that the bullets came from a .22 Beretta.

Even Mosca realized that he had been framed. He first blamed Sergio for the killings but then claimed full responsibility. This dimwitted man was convicted of the murders of Benedetta Lauri and Arturo Lo Russo and sentenced to fourteen years in prison.

Starting in 1974 and then into the 1980s, when the other double murders began to occur with chilling frequency in the Florentine countryside, authorities sought a link to the Lauri-Lo Russo murders and they discovered what they called the Sardinian Trail.

Frederico and Sergio Vigna were obvious links, and the investigators first zeroed in on Frederico. He was near the scenes of the killings and didn't have an alibi. In August 1982, a month after the killings at Montespertoli, he was arrested for being the Monster.

But there was a problem. Frederico Vigna was in prison in September of 1983 when Horst Meyer and Uwe Rüsch were killed and still in prison in July of 1984 when Pia Rontini and Claudio Stefanacci were murdered. In November 1984, he was finally freed.

In the summer of 1985 no one was in prison for being the Monster, but authorities were still keeping an eye on Sergio Vigna. Some people thought it strange that another family member was also questioned about the killings: Angelo, the son of Sergio (or Brunella's lover) who was only a baby when his mother died (or was murdered) but was now in his mid-twenties. People said Sergio hated Angelo.

While building their files about the murders in Tuscany, although not solving any of them, authorities also turned their attention to Sardinia, in particular Bellanove, to investigate the 1961 death of Sergio's wife, Brunella.

The Sardinians in Florence watched these developments warily. For years, these simple people had come to Florence to escape their barren countryside, to find jobs and build better lives. They wanted to flee a land of thievery, vendettas and murders. Overwhelmingly, they were quiet, law-abiding citizens and they were alarmed and ashamed when the term "Sardinian Trail" was thrown around so loosely in reports about the Monster.

But they were well aware of the Vigna family, and now in Florence they were gripped by fear. No one dared to talk or reveal what they knew.

Especially Rosaria, the wife of Tomasso Nozzoli.

AFTER SEEING THE HEADLINE, Father Lorenzo realized that he hadn't visited Rosaria for some time and wondered if Dino had. A phone call brought his friend over to Santa Croce within an hour and again they escaped the oppressive heat outside in the alcove off the chapel. They mopped their sweaty brows and loosened their shirts.

"Glad you called," Dino said. "It was too hot to work today anyway."

The priest fanned himself with his prayer book. "I don't suppose there's anything new with Rosaria and Tomasso and Massimo, Dino? Have you gone over there lately?"

"I stopped there last week. Tomasso seems to be getting a little worse every time I see him. I'm not sure if he even recognized me."

Father Lorenzo shook his head. "He might have known me the last time I saw him, but I had my robes on so that may have helped."

"Terrible to get old."

"He's eighty now, I think," the priest said. "I'm only fifty-four and I find myself forgetting things. Last week I forgot to read the book for my book club. Of course, it was this new book by Umberto Eco. *The Name of the Rose.* I tried to get through it when it first came out but I couldn't, so maybe I forgot on purpose."

"Listen. I'm only forty and Sofia says I'd forget my head if it wasn't screwed on."

"Just wait, Dino, it will get worse. And Massimo? How was he?"

"Still the same. Sings his little song, plays with his little toys. It's kind of cute to see this big lug of a father and this big lug of a son sitting across the table and trying to put pieces of a puzzle together. Cute, but very sad, too. Well, at least they have each other now."

Father Lorenzo wiped the perspiration off the back of his neck. "Dino, I've said this many times. Rosaria is a saint. A living saint. I don't know what Saint Francis or Saint Catherine or any of those other saints did, but no one deserves a higher place in heaven than Rosaria. How she manages to keep that big apartment clean, and do all the shopping and prepare meals for those two big men . . . well, I don't know."

"She never seems to complain," Dino said.

"And then—and then!—she has to take care of a husband who's losing his mind and a son who lost his years ago . . . she's a saint. That's all. A saint."

Almost afraid to go where the conversation was leading, Father Lorenzo and Dino remained silent for a long time. Finally, Father Lorenzo asked: "I saw the headline today. I don't suppose Rosaria has said anything lately about . . . ?"

"No, she never does."

"She's scared to death," the priest said. "Like all the Sardinians here. They're afraid they might say something that would bring the wrath of the Vigna gang down on them. It's quite ironic, isn't it, Dino? Florentines are afraid of the Monster and Sardinians are afraid of the Vignas. And who knows, they might be the very same."

Dino got up and paced the cold marble floor. "Stupidly, two weeks ago I was over there with Rosaria and Tomasso and Massimo and I had *La Repubblica* under my arm. There was a headline with 'Vigna' in it, I don't know what the article was about. Just another one, I guess, there have been so many. Rosaria must have seen 'Vigna' and right away she got real pale and her hands started shaking. I said I was sorry to upset her and she went into the bedroom and didn't come out. I tried to play a game with Tomasso and Massimo but after a couple of hours I left."

"Something must have happened between her and the Vigna brothers, or at least one of the Vigna brothers, during those years when she went back to Sardinia, Dino."

"I know. It was when she went back home because Tomasso was having that affair. But what? She won't talk about it. In fact, she doesn't talk about Sardinia at all."

Rosaria and Tomasso had had a stormy marriage. She had left her family and come to Florence alone when she was just seventeen years old, the oldest of thirteen children. She said she had found life unbearable in the impoverished Sardinia.

Although he was considerably older, she married Tomasso, and for a while they seemed happy. They even had a little son, Massimo.

But then Tomasso began having an affair with a very wealthy principessa, and the fiery Rosaria returned to her family in Sardinia, even leaving ten-year-old Massimo behind.

"How could she leave her son with that bastard?" her neighbors wondered. "Oh well, she's from Sardinia. Who knows what they will do."

After Massimo suffered severe brain damage in a bloody soccer game, Rosaria returned to Florence in 1965 and took her son back to Sardinia. It was not until 1976, when the principessa had long been dead, that Tomasso went to Sardinia and pleaded with his wife to come back to Florence with him. Finally, she agreed.

Father Lorenzo and Dino knew that Rosaria had some terrifying experiences during those eleven years when she had returned to Sardinia, but they didn't know what they were. When news about the Vigna brothers began appearing in the newspapers, they saw a sudden change.

She never went out of the house except to do her grocery shopping, and even then she ran all the way to and from the shops, never talking to anyone. She had Dino put three locks on her door, and he and Father Lorenzo were about the only people she let in. She began to talk very softly, as if she were afraid someone might hear her, even though there were no other apartments next to theirs on Via Ghibellina.

"Sometimes I catch her doing some strange things," Dino said. "Like one time I was there watching Tomasso and Massimo and she started washing the windows. Well, only one window. She washed it and washed it like it had never been washed before. It seemed like hours. I don't think she knew what she was doing."

"She's obviously very afraid. But of what?"

"The only thing that gives her pleasure is cooking traditional Sardinian food. She says she takes after her mother and grandmother. But she hardly eats anything herself. Years ago, she was such a good-looking woman. Now she doesn't take care of herself and she can't weigh more than ninety pounds. Her dresses just hang on her. Just hang."

"Always black, too."

"I think she's about fifty-six years old now," Dino said.

"Her eyes are always red, like she's been crying. She looks about seventy."

SINCE ROSARIA DIDN'T GO TO CHURCH, the only way Father Lorenzo could try to find out what was happening was to visit her. Which he did the next day.

"Maybe this time Rosaria will talk to me," he thought.

Even though it was still early in the morning, the sun was unrelenting and Father Lorenzo arrived on Via Ghibellina with sweat stains under the arms of his brown robe.

"Rosaria, it's me, Father Lorenzo," he shouted outside the locked door of the second-story apartment. He could faintly hear Massimo singing his little song.

"How do I know it's you?" Rosaria's voice could hardly be heard.

"Because I'm the priest at Santa Croce where you used to go to Mass. I've visited you many times. Years ago, we had some wonderful conversations. Rosaria, I'd just like to talk to you."

He could hear the door latches unlock, one by one. The door opened a crack and Rosaria's gaunt face appeared.

"I'm sorry, Father. I have to be careful these days, you know. I never know who could be at the door. So many . . ."

Her voice trailed off as she led him into the dark dining room where Tomasso and Massimo were seated at the table, trying to put a jigsaw puzzle together. The shutters were closed and all the curtains were pulled tightly shut. The only light was from a single wall sconce.

"They're in here," Rosaria whispered. "I'll leave you alone." She turned and fled down the hall and into a bedroom, closing the door tightly behind her.

"But . . . but . . ."

Well, Father Lorenzo thought, maybe I can talk to her later.

"Hello, Tomasso! How are you?" The priest didn't know if he should really be talking so loud or if that was condescending.

The old man turned his head. His blank eyes brightened a little when he saw the Franciscan robes.

"Oh, Father . . . Father . . ."

"It's Lorenzo, Tomasso, Father Lorenzo. I see you are putting this puzzle together with your son. Massimo is a good boy, isn't he? It's going to be a very pretty puzzle. I like the color. And you're doing very well. You'll be finished in no time."

The puzzle, a picture of a large red flower, contained only twenty-five pieces, each about two inches. Massimo was trying to force one into the wrong place and having trouble.

"It's OK, Massimo," the priest said. "Here, do you think it might go over here?"

He guided the big hand a little to the right, where the piece fit perfectly. Massimo grinned and began singing his little song. *Nella cantina di un palazzone/tutti i gattini senza padrone . . .*

"You like singing that song about the forty-four cats, don't you, Massimo? I like it, too. And I like it when you sing it."

Massimo's grin grew wider. He picked up another piece of the puzzle and resumed his song.

Father Lorenzo sat in a chair next to the windows. Even in the dark he could tell that it was once, long ago, the home of a loving family. Against the red-striped wallpaper was a large photograph in an oval frame of Tomasso and Rosaria on their wedding day. Both were standing, he more than a foot taller than his bride. Tomasso's smile spread wide on his chunky face, Rosaria's was thin and hesitant. His suit was obviously too tight and he seemed strangled by his collar. Rosaria had a little hat atop her curls. Perhaps because she couldn't afford a wedding dress, she wore what was probably the best thing she owned, a flowered print that was popular in the 1940s.

On another wall, photos of Massimo were arranged in black frames. First as a baby with a white dress and bonnet. Then as a boy of maybe five with long curls, a tiny jacket and short pants. Then at his First Communion, clutching a prayerbook and rosary and looking very proud in his first suit. Then as a teenager in a soccer uniform, holding a ball in the air.

The photos ended there. Father Lorenzo noted that Tomasso and Rosaria were shown only in their wedding portrait.

The other walls contained the typical religious paintings found in Italian homes everywhere: A doe-eyed Mary cradling the Infant Jesus, a bloody Jesus crowned with thorns, a mystical Saint Francis holding a couple of birds. Behind each frame was a dusty palm branch from a long-ago Palm Sunday.

Father Lorenzo regretted that no one here attended Mass anymore. He thought the ritual, not to mention the sacraments, would be comforting. But Tomasso and Massimo wouldn't understand what was going on and, anyway, they didn't venture out anymore, certainly not on their own. Rosaria was too frightened to be seen in such a public place.

He looked down the hall. Tomasso and Rosaria had separate bedrooms, a condition Rosaria demanded when she returned from Sardinia. She never forgave her husband for the affair he had with the principessa and returned to Florence only because of Massimo's condition.

"If these walls could talk," the priest murmured. The family must have been happy at one time, he thought, but now it seemed possessed by some dark demons. From all the confessions he had heard over the years, he knew that almost every home held secrets.

It was approaching noon. Tomasso and Massimo had made little progress on their puzzle, which was only half finished. Neither seemed disturbed, often putting a piece in the wrong place over and over.

"The patience of Job," Father Lorenzo thought. Perhaps serenity and acceptance come with loss of memory. He wondered if he could expand on that idea for a sermon.

Outside, delivery trucks rumbled noisily on the cobblestone street. He knew he had to get back to Santa Croce but decided to try again with Rosaria. Knocking on her door, he said, "Rosaria, I don't want to disturb you, are you resting?"

Her answer could barely be heard. "No."

"I just thought we could have a little visit. It's been so long since we talked. Think we can?"

There was no sound behind the door.

"Rosaria? I wonder if you heard me. I can come another time if you want."

The door opened slightly. "No, Father, I don't want to wait for another time. Let's have a little talk now."

ROSARIA OPENED THE DOOR and led Father Lorenzo to a small chair next to the bed. She smoothed the bedcovers and sat on its edge, her tiny feet not reaching the floor.

"I'm so glad to see you again, Rosaria," he said. "It's been a long time. How have you been?"

"Well, you know . . . with what's been going on . . ." Her bony hands wound around a handkerchief.

"Tomasso looks good," the priest said, trying to keep a conversation going.

"He's getting old."

"And Massimo? He's still the same?"

"Yes, the same."

"You're a saint, Rosaria, a saint."

"No! No!"

Father Lorenzo leaned forward. "Rosaria, I know you've been upset about something. Do you want to tell me about it? I promise . . . I promise . . . you can trust me."

"I'm afraid, Father."

"I know that, Rosaria. Do you want to tell me why you're afraid? Maybe we can get some help or something."

"I don't see how anyone can help me."

"Rosaria, maybe if you told me a little more, you'd feel better. You've been holding something in for so long. It must be such a burden."

Rosaria edged herself down to the floor and walked to the window. The curtains were pulled but she fingered the heavy brocade. Turning around, she squared her shoulders. It was as if some giant boulder were about to be lifted from her back.

"I guess I should tell someone."

"Good. Do you want to start at the beginning?"

Rosaria hugged herself, afraid of what was going to be released.

"At the beginning, yes."

"Yes," the priest said.

"All right. I'm not proud of this. In 1957, I left Tomasso with Massimo and went back to Sardinia. You know that."

"Yes, I know."

"I couldn't stand it anymore. I knew what had been going on with Tomasso and that . . . that woman."

Almost thirty years later, her dark eyes flared with anger at the thought of her husband having an affair with the principessa.

"I know people wondered why I didn't take Massimo with me. He was only ten years old then. But I was so angry, I wasn't thinking straight. One day I just got up in the morning and packed my bags and went out the door. I took a bus to Livorno and then the ferry to Sardinia. I still can't believe I left my son with that man. Well, I did it, and I was miserable every day I was in Sardinia.

"I went to live with my parents. That was terrible. They didn't want me back. They kept yelling at me for leaving my husband and my child. There was so much yelling and screaming in that house I almost came back to Florence a couple of times. But I didn't."

Rosaria sat on the bed again. She was shaking now and she stared at the worn carpet on the floor for a long time. Her words came slowly.

"But that isn't what I want to talk about."

"Go slow, Rosaria, go slow."

"My parents' house was in village of Bellanove . . ."

"Bellanove? Isn't that where . . . ?

"Yes. Everyone knows that the Vigna brothers lived there. Everyone."

"Did you know them, Rosaria?"

Rosaria's eyes flashed. "Know them? Know them? We lived just down the street from those bastards. And goddamn Sergio lived right next door to us with his wife."

Even though Father Lorenzo showed no sign of shock, Rosaria added, "Sorry, Father, I get so upset when I think about them. Bastards."

He reached over and held her arm. "Take a breath, Rosaria."

She took more than one, and her eyes narrowed before she continued.

"Bastards, every one of them. Oh, the stories I could tell about those brothers. I didn't know such evil people existed."

"They do, Rosaria, they do."

"Well, this is the story." She clasped her arms even tighter around her body.

"I became friendly with Brunella, the wife of Sergio. She was a sweet girl, only seventeen years old. I knew she had a lover and I don't know why she ever married Sergio, but he had such a way with women. She would come over and sometimes we'd bake things or we'd just sit and talk. I wasn't that much older than her and we both had hard lives, with our husbands and all."

Rosaria took a long breath.

"Then Brunella had this cute little baby, Angelo. Fat, cuddly. The poor thing didn't look like Sergio, though, and he always reminded her of that. I think he hated that baby, but Brunella loved little Angelo. I think it was because Sergio was so mean and cruel to her that she found some comfort in little Angelo."

Rosaria stopped, walked to the window again and then returned to the bed.

"Brunella often came over to borrow things. That bastard Sergio wouldn't let her keep a lot of food in the house, not even for the baby. I couldn't believe it. That's how cruel he was, Father."

"Poor Brunella."

"Well, on January 14, 1961, I'll never forget the date, Brunella came over to warm a bottle of milk for the baby. She said the propane tank they had was out of fuel. Sergio let that happen a lot. He'd go out drinking and he wouldn't think about his wife and baby. He did that every night and came home plastered.

"That night, she had little Angelo in her arms and we sat at the kitchen table and we warmed the milk and she fed the baby. He fell right asleep. So then she went home and I went to bed. My father and mother had gone to bed a long time earlier.

She looked at the priest, her eyes pleading. "Here's the hard part, Father."

"Take it slow, Rosaria, take it slow."

"I wasn't sleeping very well. I could hear my father snoring in the next room. But then in the middle of the night I heard this yelling next door. That wasn't unusual. Sergio always came home drunk and he'd yell at Brunella and she'd start crying. I could hear everything even though the window was closed. This was in January and it was cold outside.

"Then, Father . . . then I didn't hear Brunella anymore. But Sergio was still yelling and screaming. I didn't know what was going on. I felt like going over there but God knows what Sergio would have done to me. So I just stayed quiet but I watched out the window. Then Sergio came out. I saw him wipe his hands on some rag. And then he looked up at my window and he saw me. I know he saw me. I jumped away and got into bed. I never slept at all that night.

"Well, the next morning I found out what happened. There were all these *carabinieri* outside, in front of their house. Sergio was yelling some more and was pacing around, putting on a big act. And then . . . and then . . . I saw four guys carrying a stretcher out of the house. And it was . . . it was Brunella, Father . . . it was Brunella."

Her tears flowed down her cheeks and onto her black dress. Father Lorenzo sat next to her on the bed and put his arm around her thin shoulders. He couldn't help but think of Signora Fazzari and Signora Mancuso and what had happened to them.

"Terrible, Rosaria, terrible."

"Two days later, the *carabinieri* came around and asked my father and mother and me if we heard anything that night. Of course my father and mother were sleeping, but I told them what I had heard. I told them about Sergio's yelling and Brunella's crying. Then they wanted to know when I had last seen Brunella, and I told them about how she came to get the baby's milk warm because she'd run out of propane fuel. They seemed very interested in that.

"And I told them about Sergio coming out of the house and wiping his hands on a rag. They seemed interested in that, too, but I was surprised they didn't ask more questions.

"Nothing came of it, though. Sergio told the *carabinieri* that Brunella had taken the tube from the propane tank and committed suicide. Suicide! Father, Brunella would never have committed suicide. She went away from our house with little Angelo so happy. She would never take her own life."

"But that's what Sergio told the *carabinieri?*"

"Yes. He said the propane tank was next to her bed and there was a tube under her pillow. But Brunella told me the tank was empty so how could she commit suicide with an empty tube? It makes no sense!"

"No, of course not."

"Well, the *carabinieri* believed him, and he was let off the hook. I don't think they even asked him about wiping his hands when he left the house. But there were scratches on Brunella's face! I saw them! I saw them when she was laid out. Everyone believed that he killed her. They started yelling at him when he went down the street. 'Murderer!' and 'Wife Killer!' Sergio got so mad. So did his brothers. They got into a bunch of fights.

"Well, it was time for them to get out of Bellanove. They moved to Florence a few months after Brunella's murder, all three of them."

"I imagine you were glad to see them go," Father Lorenzo said.

"Yes. But the night before he left, Sergio came to my house and pounded on the door. I didn't open it, but I will always remember what he said. 'I'll get you for this, you bitch.' That's what he said, 'you bitch.' He knew what I had told the *carabinieri*. It was all written down."

"You just told the truth, Rosaria. You were very brave."

"I came back to Florence once, that was to get Massimo after he hurt his head in that bloody soccer match. That's why he is the way he is today, Father, but I guess you know that."

"Yes, I know. In fact, I was at that match. It was terrible."

"Well, I went back to Sardinia but then my father died and then my mother, and my goddamn brothers and sisters wouldn't let me into the house because they didn't like Massimo. They were ashamed of him. Imagine! So I moved up to the northern part of Sardinia and we lived in a hut. We didn't have any money, but there were shepherds all around and they had a lot of needs that had to be taken care of. I guess you know what I mean, Father."

"I know what you mean, Rosaria."

"And I'm not ashamed of it, Father! I had to earn money so that Massimo and me could live and that's all I knew how to do."

"Sometimes we do what we have to do, Rosaria."

"Well, when Tomasso came to get us, this was in 1976, I didn't want to go back to Florence. I knew Sergio was here. But I had to think of Massimo, he was getting older and he needed more care. So when I came back I knew that bastard and his brothers were here, but we didn't live near them and I thought it would be all right. I mean, this is a big city, I shouldn't be afraid, right?"

"I would think so."

"Well, two weeks after I got here I was in the market and suddenly I saw this evil man staring at me."

"Sergio?"

"None other. I ran right home without even paying for the cabbage I had in my hand. And it's happened again and again, month after month, year after year. I've seen him on the street and he looks at me and stares that evil stare. I've seen him in Piazza Santa Croce . . ."

"I've seen him there, too. I know who he is."

"He's everywhere. Sometimes he's with his brother. Frederico is just as bad. And so in the last few years I've been so afraid, so afraid . . ."

Father Lorenzo pulled her closer to him. "You're a saint, Rosaria, a saint."

"Don't say that. Not after the life I've lived."

She stood up. "You're probably wondering why I'm telling you all this now, Father."

"I'm glad you did."

"Well, it's because of this."

Rosaria went to the dresser and pulled out the second drawer. She retrieved an envelope from beneath a pile of underwear. "This was slipped under our door last night."

On the envelope were letters clipped from a magazine. "rOsaRia." Father Lorenzo opened the envelope and pulled out a sheet of paper. Letters clipped from a magazine were pasted to form words. "yOur TiME iS ruNNing oUt"

"That's why I'm afraid, Father."

FATHER LORENZO fingered the letters pasted to the piece of paper as if trying to uncover a clue in the glue.

"Have you shown this to the police, Rosaria?"

She laughed. "The police? What would the police do? They haven't been able to find the Monster, how would they be able to find someone who put this under my door? Anyway, if I went to the police, Sergio Vigna would find out about it in two seconds and God knows what kind of revenge he'd take on me."

"You're convinced this is from Sergio Vigna?"

"Who else? I don't have any other enemies. He knows that I know he killed his wife. Poor Brunella. If he were brought to trial for that, I would be called to testify and I could finally tell everybody what really happened that night."

Over the course of telling her story, Rosaria's voice had become stronger. Her shoulders, under Father Lorenzo's arm, had stiffened and she no longer played with the handkerchief in her frail hands. She had indeed lightened her burden.

"Father, I have to say this. I feel better now that I've told you what happened. At least somebody else knows the truth if something were to happen to me."

"Nothing is going to happen to you, Rosaria."

"Right. Just like no one is going to put a threatening letter under my door. I know that bastard Vigna is watching me. But can I ask you to make a promise, Father?"

"Anything, Rosaria."

"If something happens to me, would you see that Tomasso and Massimo are taken care of? They can't take care of themselves. Maybe there's a convent or some place where they could stay. I know Tomasso won't be here for very long, and Massimo, well . . . Massimo would be happy anywhere, as long as he has his puzzles and somebody makes his meals. He can still take care of himself."

Father Lorenzo hugged her closer. "You don't have to worry about Tomasso and Massimo, Rosaria. I promise I'll take care of them."

Having said that, the priest wondered how in the world he could make such a promise. There weren't any convents that would take two men, and though he'd heard of places called group homes in other cities, he didn't know of any in Florence. And then he remembered someone.

"Anna," he thought. *"Dino's aunt. She's been marvelous taking care of babies at Santa Croce. And now she's started this place for old people who don't have any family. She got three other former nuns to help her. That would be the place."*

He smiled. "Don't worry, Rosaria. I know the perfect person."

"Thank you, Father. OK, now I should start making something for them to eat."

"Them? Not you?"

"I'm not hungry."

"Rosaria, you have to keep up your strength."

"I'm strong enough, Father. I'm strong enough."

"Are you going to be all right?"

"I'll be OK. I'm not going out, but I have a friend who keeps me informed about that bastard Vigna's comings and goings. She's from Sardinia, too, and she lived in Calangianus. That's near the hut where Massimo and me stayed. She knows all about me, how I made my living there, and she knows all of the Vigna brothers. So she keeps an eye on Sergio and calls me up when she hears something about him. Antonella Maruca is her name."

Father Lorenzo quickly memorized the name. For some reason, he wondered whether he might have to find her someday.

All the way back to Santa Croce, Father Lorenzo could not help thinking about what Rosaria had told him. What an amazing woman, he thought. She'd been through so much pain and heartbreak in her marriage, had endured terrible indignities in her homeland, and now she feared for her life. All because she helped a friend in need. A saint, nothing less, he thought. He felt humbled to know her.

Passing storefronts, he saw the familiar poster in shop windows, "*Occhio ragazzi!* Watch out kids! Attention!" Now, however, in the height of the tourist season, translations had been added: "*Jeunes gens, danger! Atencion chicos y chicas! Pericolo di aggressione!*"

That was necessary, he thought. Although the killings had been widely publicized throughout Europe, he knew that young people didn't read newspapers and may not have seen the grisly accounts on television.

Near a poster in the window of a shop specializing in teenage clothing, he saw two young couples, apparently college students from France. They were uniformly dressed in t-shirts and shorts and had "University of Reims" pins on their backpacks. The priest hadn't spoken French for years, but he was able to decipher the gist of what they were saying.

"It says there's a danger," a girl said.

"Of what?" the other girl asked.

"I don't know. It just says people are supposed to be careful."

"Stupid Italians," a boy said. "How should we know what we're supposed to be afraid of?"

"Maybe we're supposed to look both ways before we cross the street," the first girl said, laughing.

"Or maybe we're not supposed to give money to beggars," the second boy said. "They're everywhere."

All four laughed and the first boy started furiously rummaging through his backpack. "Hey," he said, "I can't find my *préservatifs*. I know I brought them."

"I have lots," the second boy said. "I'll give you some when we get to that place Pierre told us about, on the road to San Casciano. We're going in separate cars, right?"

"Yes, of course."

Father Lorenzo's French may have been rusty, but he certainly knew what *préservatifs* meant. Well, at least they're using condoms, he thought, but they'd better not go up to San Casciano or to any other lovers' lanes near Florence.

"Excuse me," he said, "but I couldn't help but overhear what you were saying."

The girls hid behind their boyfriends.

"So, *Père*," one boy said, "you were, how you say, eavesdropping on our conversations?"

"I'm sorry, but you were talking rather loudly. Look, that warning is there for a reason, and I think you'd better heed it."

"What? We shouldn't have sex? Look, *Père*, we're from France. That's what we do over there. Maybe your pope wouldn't like it, but . . ."

The girls giggled and the boys could barely hold back their laughter.

"That's not what I'm talking about," Father Lorenzo said. Nearby pedestrians wondered why he was talking so loudly.

"So it's OK as long as we use *préservatifs*?"the boy said.

The priest knew he was getting nowhere.

"The reason for those posters," he said slowly and patiently, "is because there is a serial killer loose in Florence. In fact, he's called the Monster of Florence."

"Monster of Florence?" the other boy said. "Really? Sounds like one of those bad movies from America."

"Listen!" Father Lorenzo said. "I'm telling this for your own good. Listen up."

The boys and girls suddenly became serious.

"There have been six incidents in the last ten years," the priest said. "Twelve people have been killed. All of them have been couples and all have been young people."

The boys put their arms around the girls' waists.

"They were all shot to death. Many, many times. In most cases, the girls were mutilated."

The boys hugged the girls closer.

"And you know where all of these killings happened?"

The French visitors shook their heads.

"On lovers' lanes outside of Florence. Every one of them."

"Every one?" a girl whispered.

"Every one. That's why Florence has put up those posters. It's to warn visitors, like you young people from France, to be on guard and not go to places where there may be danger. Terrible danger."

"And this killer hasn't been found?"

"They've made some arrests, but they've never found the real murderer."

"When was the last one?" the second boy asked.

"Last July. Almost all of them have occurred in the summer, or at least on hot nights. So we're all holding our breaths wondering when the next one will happen. Could be anytime."

The priest noticed that all four of the young people were wiping sweat off their faces.

"Thank you, *Père*," the first boy said.

"Yes, thank you," the others said.

The boys and girls crept silently away. Father Lorenzo thought he heard the girls sobbing.

"Well, maybe I've saved four lives. With or without the *préservatifs*."

FOR THE NEXT WEEK, into September, Father Lorenzo found himself consoling one stricken woman after another.

On Monday morning, even though he got there early, Signora Fazzari was waiting for him in the Medici Chapel of Santa Croce. She was in tears and breathing heavily.

Her daughter was still at home, although she came out of her room only for meals or to go to her job cleaning floors at Santa Maria

Novella. She barely acknowledged her mother and refused to even look at her father.

"Father," Signora Fazzari said, "I don't know what to do. Guido is getting madder and madder. Every time he sees Maria his face gets so red I think he's going to burst a blood vessel. He won't try to talk to her. Not that she'd listen. She'd just go to her room and slam the door. I feel like I'm always in between. I can't please Maria, I can't please Guido."

She began to cry, and once again Father Lorenzo put his arm around her.

"You've been very strong," he said. "And very patient. I know God will reward you."

Of course, he thought, it was presumptuous of him to imagine what God would do.

"And then," Signora Fazzari continued, "last night Pietro showed up. On our doorstep! Can you imagine! Now he has a motorcycle, and he came roaring down the street and parked in front of the house. It was so loud! All the neighbors came out. And Guido, well, Guido stormed out of the house and started yelling at Pietro. He even started kicking the motorcycle.

"Maria hung out her bedroom window and started calling to Pietro, and then Guido started hitting Pietro on the back and yelling at him to leave. This went on for maybe twenty minutes. Father, it seemed like two hours. Finally Pietro went away. And Maria won't come out of her room. She didn't even go to work today and you know how we need the money. I don't know what to do, Father."

Father Lorenzo could only tell the poor woman that she was doing all she could and that she had to take care of herself, eat good meals, get plenty of rest, try to pray.

"And I'm praying for you, too, Signora."

That's what he said, but he was thinking about all of the grief the Monster had caused in simple homes all across Florence. The Florentines would never be the same.

On Wednesday afternoon, Father Lorenzo visited Signora Mancuso. All the relatives had gone home after the funeral, so now it was only Angelica and Luciano and Donatella. The children, teenagers, were acting out over the death of their father.

"Luciano won't listen to me anymore," Angelica had cried the last time the priest visited. "He goes off with his friends and he doesn't come home until two or three in the morning. I know, because I wait up for him. And I know what kind of condition he's in. Father, he doesn't just drink beer, it's stronger stuff, too."

She paused and lowered her voice. "And lately, I'm ashamed to say this, I know he's smoking that stuff. All the boys have it. I don't know where they get it. They say it's all over Florence now and all the kids use it. I don't know what to do."

They were sitting at the kitchen table and Father Lorenzo got up to pour both of them more coffee.

"I suppose his schoolwork is affected," he said.

"Affected? I don't think he goes to school more than three days a week. So he's way behind in everything. The teacher came over one day. She's a nice lady but she doesn't know what to do with him. She said she has four or five kids like him but she said he's the worst. That's what she said, 'the worst.' Oh, if only Angelo were here now. He wouldn't let him get away with this stuff."

She wiped her eyes and took a sip of coffee.

"And Donatella? What about her?" the priest was afraid to ask, but did anyway.

"Don't let me get started about Donatella. The way she dresses. Little tiny skirts. And the makeup! All over her face. She doesn't know how to put it on. She says she goes over to her girlfriend's after school, but I think they hang out at Piazza Santa Spirito with the other kids. She's just turned thirteen. She shouldn't be with those older girls. But will she listen? No, she just glares at me and goes to her room and gets on the telephone. She'll call her girlfriend even though she just saw her fifteen minutes ago. Oh Angelo, what have you left me?"

Not knowing what to say, Father Lorenzo asked if Angelica had received her semimonthly check he had arranged from the church's benevolent society.

"Yes, it came yesterday. Now I can pay the rent. And buy some groceries. I don't know what we'd do without that, Father. I don't know how to thank you. Someday, I'll find a job and repay you."

"I'll make sure it never stops, Angelica."

"You're a saint, Father. Oh, if only Angelo was here. Why did he have to do that? Why did he have to kill himself like that? Why didn't he think of us? Damn you, Angelo!"

Angelica threw the coffee cup against the wall, smashing it into a million pieces. She fell sobbing into the priest's arms.

Another victim of the Monster, Father Lorenzo thought as he led her to the couch in the living room.

On Friday, Father Lorenzo spent the entire afternoon with Rosaria. While Tomasso and Massimo once again tried to put a jigsaw puzzle together, this time a picture of a cat sleeping in a basket, the priest tried to learn if she had heard anything more about Sergio Vigna.

"I called my friend Antonella Maruca yesterday," Rosaria said. "She said she's seen him across the street a couple of times lately and he seemed awfully nervous, like something was about to happen."

"What do you think?"

"Who knows? But it's been almost a year since the Monster killed, you know."

"Rosaria! Do you think Sergio Vigna is the Monster? Really?"

"Father, if he killed his wife he could kill anyone, right? Doesn't it seem strange to you that he killed his wife in 1961, that there was this killing of Benedetta Lauri and that Sicilian in 1968 that has never been solved . . ."

"That guy Mosca went to prison for a while."

". . . and that there was another killing in 1974 and then all those killings since 1981. And who was around for all of them?"

"Sergio Vigna."

"Of course."

"Well, that's not really evidence, Rosaria."

"I don't need evidence. I know what I believe. I know what I saw in Bellanove twenty-five years ago. I can still see that bastard coming out of the house and wiping his hands on that rag. And I know what note I got under my door."

"I hope we don't have another killing. Ever," the priest said.

Rosaria closed her eyes. "I hope so, too, Father. I hope so, too."

Jostling the crowds and trying to avoid looking at the posters in shop windows, the priest fingered his rosary all the way back to Santa Croce. Dino was waiting for him at the door to his office when he returned. From the look on his face, Father Lorenzo knew that something was terribly wrong.

"Father, there's been another one. A really gruesome one."

"Oh, no."

"They say it was a couple of French tourists."

"No, no, no!"

THE KILLINGS HAD OCCURRED the previous Saturday night in woods frequently used by lovers on the road to San Casciano, south of Florence. It was a lovely area, deep in Chianti country and surrounded by vineyards that produced wines known throughout the world.

"Some guy who was looking for mushrooms found a tent in the woods . . . ," Dino said.

Father Lorenzo wondered if the French students he had met earlier were campers. He supposed that they could have had a tent in one of their cars. But surely those college kids had listened to him. They couldn't have gone off into the woods after all he said, could they?

". . . it was near San Casciano . . ."

"Oh, no."

". . . and the woman's name was Nadine and she was thirty-six years old and . . ."

"What did you say, Dino?"

"I said the woman's name was Nadine."

"What else did you say?"

"I said she was thirty-six years old. Why?"

"Nothing." Father Lorenzo couldn't believe he felt relieved after learning that someone had been killed.

Dino went on to say that the woman was separated from her husband and had a little daughter who was staying with friends in France but was supposed to start school just on Monday. He said Nadine had been living with a twenty-five-year-old man, Jean-Michel, and they had been camping throughout Italy before this.

"They were each shot four times. They found his body outside the tent and hers inside."

"And the killer mutilated her?"

"Removed her vagina and left breast."

"Good God!"

"That's not all, Father. Nobody knows this, but I know a reporter who's been covering the case. He told me. The prosecutor's office got an envelope in the mail. Inside was a portion of the woman's breast."

The priest had heard a lot of gruesome things in his life, but this disclosure made him sick to his stomach.

"One more thing, Father. The envelope was addressed to the only woman in the prosecutor's office. And her name was cut out of letters from a magazine."

"Oh, my God. I've got to call Rosaria."

But before he got to the phone, it rang.

"Yes, Rosaria. Yes, I'll be right over."

Father Lorenzo found the woman sobbing and clutching an envelope. Although she had seemed stronger when he left just hours earlier, she had lost her composure and couldn't control her shaking arms.

"Here, Father, look at this."

The envelope with Rosaria's name was like the previous one, with the letters cut out from a magazine. Inside was a simple message. "WaTch oUt"

"Father, something is going to happen, soon. I know it. He knows I know he killed Brunella. He wants to silence me."

He dared not tell her about the letter the prosecutor's office had received. Yet he thought that this time she really should show the letter to the police.

"Please, Rosaria?"

"No! He'll find out, I know he will. He'll find me. Look, he's already killed two more people."

"We're not sure of that, Rosaria."

"I'm sure of that, Father. My friend Antonella called me this morning. She said Sergio Vigna hasn't been seen since Saturday morning. He didn't come home all weekend."

The priest led her into the bedroom. Tomasso and Massimo were usually oblivious to what was going on in the apartment, but he knew they'd be upset if they heard Rosaria's hysterical sobs.

"What am I going to do, Father? I have to go out. I have to do my shopping. There's hardly anything in the refrigerator."

"Rosaria, you are not to leave the apartment, at least for now."

The priest quickly thought of a plan. Dino and Sofia would be enlisted to help. They would do all the shopping and run any other errands. Rosaria would stay in the apartment for at least a week, and then they'd decide what to do next.

"Is that all right, Rosaria?"

"I guess so. It'll have to be."

Predictably, another killing after a year of anxious waiting caused fear and frenzy to spread through Florence once again. Noting that the victims were from France, the city put up more posters with vague warnings that visitors should be careful but not indicating what exact danger existed out there. Florence, after all, depended on tourists and couldn't afford to keep them all away.

Florentines never walked alone. They huddled on street corners and *caffès* discussing the latest murders, often offering opinions on who the killer might be. Sometimes, neighbors were considered likely culprits.

At the Fazzari home, Maria was told to stay in her room. Signora Fazzari even thanked her husband for banishing Pietro. "Now they can't go out," she said.

Until now, a reward for information about the killer had never been offered. That was something Americans would do, not Italians. But the government itself finally offered a reward of a half billion *lire.* There were no takers.

Meanwhile, Judge Mario Rotella, the examining magistrate, was relentlessly pursuing the Sardinian Trail connection. He tried to get Santino Mosca to reveal more about the killings of Benedetta Lauri and the Sicilian in 1968, but the confused aging man wouldn't cooperate.

Sardinians, both in their native country and in Florence, accused the magistrate of racism.

"You know those Florentines," Antonella Maruca told Rosaria. "They've always looked down on us. Now we're being used as scapegoats."

"But what about Sergio Vigna?" Rosaria asked. "He's a Sardinian."

"Yes, but we're not all like him."

In fact, Rotella zeroed in on Sergio Vigna, finally concluding that he was indeed the Monster of Florence. One powerful argument was that on the weekend that Nadine and Jean-Michel were killed, the *carabinieri* who were supposed to be following him had somehow ignored him.

"See?" Antonella told Rosaria. "I told you that bastard was nowhere to be seen that weekend. Now we know what he was doing."

The investigation of Sergio Vigna took months, but on June 11, 1986, he was arrested for murder. But it was not for any of the serial killings in Florence. He was charged with murdering his wife, the teenage Brunella, in Sardinia in 1961.

"Thank God," Rosaria cried when Antonella told her. "Now I can tell the truth about what happened that night. He'll be sent to prison and I will never have to be afraid again."

"WHY," FATHER LORENZO asked Dino, "do you think Judge Rotella charged Vigna with that old murder in Sardinia in 1961? What does that have to do with the killings in Florence?"

"The word I hear, from my reporter friend and others," Dino said, "is that Rotella has been conducting his own investigation and he thinks that if Sergio can be convicted of killing his wife, then that can be used as leverage for convictions for the murders here."

"Seem like a stretch, Dino."

"I think so, too. That killing was twenty-five years ago. How are they going to find witnesses now?"

"I might know of one," Father Lorenzo said.

Significantly, Rosaria had not received any threatening letters since Sergio had been arrested.

Now, she was so excited about being called as a witness that she was already thinking about what to wear.

"I only have black dresses," she told Antonella.

"That's good! That will make you look sincere, honest. You could wear a bright scarf with it, though, red maybe. You need a little color. And you should have your hair done."

Rosaria could think of nothing else. She even wrote down a long description of what she remembered about that night. That didn't take long since she had gone over every detail so often.

Then she discovered that the trial would not be in Florence but in Cagliari, an ancient port city that is the capital of Sardinia.

"Cagliari?" Rosaria wailed. "How can I afford to go to Cagliari? I can't even afford to buy eggs, they're so expensive now."

Father Lorenzo assured her that if she were called to testify, he would see that she would have the money for the bus to Livorno, for the ferry to Sardinia, for the bus to Cagliari and for a room there.

"I don't think you'd be there long," he said.

"I just want to be there, Father. I just want to tell the true story. I've been wanting to do this for twenty-five years."

The Italian justice system being what it is, Vigna's trial didn't begin for almost two more years, on April 12, 1988. By that time Rosaria could recite her testimony in her sleep. And there were no more killings during that time.

Although Rosaria had to wait to be called to the trial, Antonella decided to go and left for Sardinia a week before the trial was to begin.

"I'm going to get a good seat on the first day and they're not going to move me," she declared. She promised to call Rosaria with daily updates.

When the trial finally began, Antonella suffered through the first day and called Rosaria that night.

"It was mostly routine today," she said. "The judges said something, the prosecutor said something and the bastard's attorney said something. I didn't understand what was going on. But Vigna! You should have seen him, Rosaria. He was in a cage, of course."

"A cage?"

"Don't you watch television, Rosaria? Prisoners are always in cages in Italian courtrooms."

"I never watch television, Antonella."

"Well, anyway, he stood all the while. He had his fists around the bars of the cage and he just stared ahead. The judges asked him questions and he answered in this silly voice. Real high, almost as if he was a girl."

"The guy's crazy."

"But he kept calm all the while. Oh, Rosaria, the most interesting thing was this. His son Angelo was there."

"Angelo? Brunella's baby? The one we warmed up milk for?"

"Not a baby anymore, Rosaria. He's a big handsome guy. I mean handsome, if you know what I mean. He must be about twenty-six or twenty-seven now."

"So he was there to testify for his father? How could he testify for his father? He was only a baby when his mother was murdered."

"No! He was brought to testify *against* his father."

"Good Lord. I don't understand this."

"I don't either. Anyway, he's apparently been serving time for some other offense. A reporter told me that. So his hands were tied behind his back. He sat on the other side of the judges so he faced his father. But he never took his sunglasses off. Never."

"How odd."

"But you could tell he was looking at his father and his father was looking at him. This went on for hours. Hours! And there was such hate between them."

"Between father and son?"

"Who knows what goes on in that family, Rosaria. They're all filled with hate. Even brother against brother, son against father."

"I bet Angelo could kill as easily as his dad," Rosaria said.

"Well, the judges asked questions of both of them and it went on and on. But Angelo refused to answer anything. He just sat and stared. I didn't understand what was happening. They finally adjourned until tomorrow. So I'll call you tomorrow night."

"Thanks, Antonella. Oh, did anyone say when I would be called? It will take me a day to get there."

"No, nobody said anything about any witnesses. Maybe tomorrow."

Rosaria sat at the dining room table with Tomasso and Massimo. They had only a couple of puzzles and this time they were trying to put the red flower together again. It was as if they'd never seen it before.

The following night, Antonella had little to report.

"They spent the entire day going over papers. I had no idea what was going on. Then they adjourned until tomorrow."

"Nothing about calling witnesses?"

"Nothing. I'll call you tomorrow night."

Rosaria stared blankly at the red flower for another night.

The third night Antonella did not have good news.

"The judges asked if there were any witnesses and the prosecutor said there weren't any. He said that Sergio had returned home to find his wife dead that night and that he went and got her father and her brother to go back to the house with him. But both the father and that brother are now dead so there aren't any witnesses."

"What do you mean, no witnesses? I'm a witness! Why don't they call me?"

"Well, that's what I thought. I tried to stop the prosecutor on the way out but he didn't pay any attention to me."

"Antonella, please! Tomorrow morning before it starts could you please tell somebody that I know what really happened and I could be there in a day. Please!"

"OK, I'll try."

The next night Antonella had worse news.

"Rosaria, I tried to talk to the prosecutor, I really did. I told him how Brunella had come to your house and told you the propane tank was empty and how during the night you heard Sergio screaming at her and how she was crying. And that you saw Sergio come out of the house and wipe his hands on a rag. I told him all that."

"What did he say? Didn't he believe you?"

"He kept saying, but did she see Sergio kill his wife, did she see that? And I had to say that you didn't but that it was obvious that he did. But he said you weren't really a witness and that you weren't, what was the word, 'credible.'"

"I'm credible! I'm credible!"

"I'm sorry, Rosaria. It looks like they're going to end this thing tomorrow."

"No! They can't! They need to hear what really happened. I'm going to go there!"

"I'm sorry, Rosaria."

The following night, Antonella reported that the trial had ended. The judges said it happened too long ago, that there wasn't any evidence available anymore and that nothing could be proved. Besides that, there weren't any witnesses.

"I was a witness!" Rosaria screamed into the telephone. "I was a witness! Why didn't they call me?"

"I don't know, Rosaria. But Sergio was acquitted. He's free."

"No!"

"I walked out of the courthouse after him and that cocky guy actually met some reporters on the steps. Know what he said? He said, 'It was a very satisfying conclusion.' And then he walked away."

"Bastard! Bastard!"

SERGIO VIGNA not only walked away from the courthouse, he also walked away from any life he had known. Over the next months, it was reported that he returned to his hometown of Bellanove and then he simply disappeared. If anyone looked for him, and it was doubtful that many cared, he was nowhere to be found.

"He's in the mountains with all the other bandits" was the general feeling of the Sardinians in Florence.

The Sardinians in Sardinia didn't say anything.

Vigna was never seen again.

Although Florence could not have known it at the time, the Monster did not kill again after the murders of Nadine and Jean-Michel near San Casciano in September 1985. Over more than the next decade, there were various investigations and some arrests, but no one was ever convicted of being the Monster.

Gradually, life in Florence returned to normal. The posters were taken down. People stopped whispering about their neighbors. Young lovers went out on Saturday nights, but few visited the lovers' lanes outside of the city as they had before.

Signora Fazzari no longer visited Father Lorenzo every Monday morning. She still went to confession every Saturday afternoon, but her sins were again what could at best be called "venial" and not "mortal." After years of pleading, Maria was allowed to see Pietro again. Guido did not like the idea very much, but allowed it to happen.

"What can he do?" Signora Fazzari told Father Lorenzo one day. "They're old enough now to know what they're doing. Pietro seems to have a good job at that shoe manufacturing plant, so who knows? I don't mind. I'm getting old. I want to see some grandchildren, Father."

He still visited Angelica Mancuso, but not as often and only on weekends now that she was working as a seamstress in a fashion designer shop. She seemed happier now that she was earning money, that Luciano was hanging out less with his friends and going to school more often and that Donatella was learning how to dress properly.

Angelica confessed that she had met a man, "an older gentleman," whose wife had died some years ago.

"We go for walks or he comes over and I make him a good Italian meal," she said. "He likes the kids and they seem to like him. He's teaching Luciano to play chess. I don't know if anything will come of this, but it's nice to talk to a man. Angelo never liked to talk."

As for Rosaria, she coped with Tomasso during his last days, a horrifying time when he did not know her at all and had lost control of all his bodily functions. She buried him in a simple grave at San Miniato, but nowhere near the principessa's grand tomb.

"They're both dead now," she told Father Lorenzo, "I don't care what they do."

The priest and Dino knew that Massimo was becoming too difficult for Rosaria to handle alone after his father died, and so they sought help from Anna. The former nun enlisted four other former nuns and together they established a sort of visiting nurse organization. One or another of the women came to Rosaria's house Monday through Friday and took care of Massimo's needs. They also worked jigsaw puzzles with him.

This allowed Rosaria to get a job and she found one in the china shop that Tomasso once owned. The new owner had transformed it into a souvenir shop for all kinds of trinkets advertising Florence.

"A lot of the stuff is junk made in China," Rosaria confided to Dino, "but the tourists love it. Especially the Americans. They buy these little statues of David and think they're getting real marble. Or these ashtrays with the Duomo. They think they're made of brass. Oh well."

At Antonella's urging, Rosaria joined a group of women that called itself the Sardinian Ladies Society. They met at each other's homes, made wonderful Sardinian dishes, played cards and talked about life in Sardinia. It was good to hear stories about such a beautiful land that they loved so much but that had been so maligned.

No one talked about the Vigna brothers, and no one talked about the Monster.

People didn't forget, however. On the Saturday before Christmas in December of 1989, Dino helped Father Lorenzo unpack figures from the crèche that was always the annual attraction at Santa Croce.

"I hope it's over at last," the priest said, removing straw that surrounded one of the kings. "It may be only five years now since we've had a killing, but, still, it's been five years so we can hope."

"I don't know how we lived through all that," Dino said. He placed the figure of Joseph next to the empty crib.

"We lived through the flood of 1966."

Dino placed the figure of Mary across from Joseph. "That was different. We knew what we were fighting."

"And it happened only once."

The shepherds and angels were now in their proper places. Baby Jesus would wait until Christmas Eve and the three kings until Epiphany.

Father Lorenzo straightened up and stretched his aching back. "I think about Signora Fazzari and Signora Mancuso and Rosaria so often. What a terrible time they had."

"Let's hope we never have to go through that again."

Father Lorenzo and Dino stood back and admired the peaceful scene.

"There's so much evil in the world, but we have to remember that there's so much goodness, too," Father Lorenzo said.

"Let's have a good Christmas, Father."

A Piazza for Sant'Antonio

AS SOON AS HE UNTIED the string on the package and saw the cover of the new *Scandalo italiano,* Mario Leoni knew that the magazine had done it again. Every month, the tabloid used big bold type on its cover to proclaim some terrible new scandal. "The Worst Beaches in Italy!" "*Restorante* Ripoffs!" "Sex Fiends Are Looking for You!"

"I don't know how they can print this rag," Mario said as he arranged the magazines on the shelves of his *bottega.* "And I don't know how people can read this stuff. Still, there's always a line here when a new one comes out so I guess I have to carry it."

In its short life, *Scandalo italiano* had quadrupled its circulation with its sensational stories of politicians' escapades and photo spreads of naked starlets. Not to mention its front-cover "exposés" and its popular Page Three photo of a seminude "Bimbo of the Month."

Mario paused to take care of a customer. Old Signora Cardineli, accompanied as always by little Pasquale, was buying another cat toy for Alessia.

"*Grazie,* Signor Leoni," Pasquale, polite as always, said as he dangled the toy on his finger.

"You're welcome, Pasquale. Have fun with Alessia!"

Smiling to himself, Mario placed a half dozen copies of *Scandalo italiano* between *Panorama* and *Gente Viaggi,* but kept one to look at.

"Well, let's see what the big exposé is this month. 'Ten Places to Avoid in Italy!' That should be interesting. It's on page fourteen." He flipped through the pages, pausing only a second to see who this month's "bimbo" was.

He scanned through the article, discovering that the places were in alphabetical order. "Hmmm. Never heard of some of these. Maybe they made them up. They make everything up. Wait! What the hell?" He held the magazine closer.

"Good God!" he whispered, hoping that none of his customers could hear or see him. "This is terrible. How could they do this?"

Mario plucked the other copies of *Scandalo italiano* from the shelf, kicked them under the counter and ran across the street to Manconi's meat market with the single copy under his jacket.

"Anita!" he yelled to his wife. "Look at this!"

"I can't now, Mario. Wait a minute. I'm almost done with this chicken."

Anita Manconi sliced off the final wing, set the pieces on the draining board behind the display case and washed her hands. "What's up?"

"Look!"

"What?"

"The cover of this magazine."

"Oh, that awful magazine again. Why do you even carry it?"

"Look at the headline."

"'Ten Places to Avoid in Italy.' So? We're not going anywhere, are we?"

"Anita, turn to page fourteen and look at the list."

Anita adjusted her glasses and flipped the pages. "OK, 'Crude oil town in Catania . . . Fertilizer company in Mantova . . . Traffic jams in Pieve Fissiraga. Mario, why am I reading this stupid list? What do we care what this magazine says?"

"Read some more. They're in alphabetical order."

"Another and another. Oh! Sant'Antonio! Mario, little Sant'Antonio's on this list! Imagine!"

"Anita, it's a bad thing. We're listed as one of the ten places to avoid in this whole country."

"Oh."

"Look at the picture."

"My goodness, it's the rubber manufacturing plant outside of town."

"Read the caption."

"*The Amex Rubber Company is only one reason why you should avoid Sant'Antonio. Can you imagine the smells that envelop the village?*"

"Mario, that's not true. It's not that bad. Anyway, we're used to it."

"*Scandalo italiano* does this all the time. They never tell the truth. They just make stuff up to sell their damn magazine. Read the article, Anita."

Anita found the article next to the picture.

"*If you have the misfortune to travel from Lucca to Camaiore you will travel through the pitiful village of Sant'Antonio. It won't take long, because the village is so small, but do not stop! In fact, we recommend that you close your eyes as you drive through. Don't worry, you won't be arrested. As far as we could tell, there are no traffic cops in Sant'Antonio.*"

Anita put down the magazine. "Mario, that's not true either. Fernando has been our policeman for years. OK, he's a little old now but . . ."

"Read more, Anita."

"*If you do make the mistake to stop, you won't find much, if anything. There are a couple of shops, one of them a* bottega *that sells the usual variety of merchandise, from flour to flowers, but not the most basic brand of cigarette. The owner seemed particularly rude when I was there . . .*"

"Rude! Rude!" Mario shouted. "Now I know who that guy was. He came in three weeks ago. He wanted this brand of cigarettes that I never heard of and he got all huffy when I told him that."

"I'm sure you were very polite." Anita continued reading.

"*Across the street there is a meat market and for all I know it might carry quality products, but I kept wondering why such a comely young person was in charge of such an important element in any Italian's dinner menu. Shouldn't she be at home taking care of her children, if indeed she has any?*"

"Mario," Anita said. "I didn't tell you this, but that slimy guy made a pass at me when he was in the shop. His hands were all over the place and I slapped him. Now we find out he's not only stupid but sexist, too. My God, it's 1985. Women should stay at home?"

Anita's hands were shaking now, but she forged on.

"*Now all cities, towns and villages in Italy should have a piazza, right? Can you think of one that doesn't? Italy is famous all over the world for its piazzas. We invented them! Well, Sant'Antonio doesn't have one. Those two shops in the middle seem to be the last remnants of what might have been here centuries ago. But no more. There isn't even a* restorante *or a* trattoria *or even a* bar *for coffee in the morning. Can you imagine?*

There's an old well in the middle of the space but people say it has been dry for years."

"I never knew there was a piazza here, Mario."

"He may be making that up, too. Read some more."

"And every village in Tuscany is supposed to have a beautiful church, right? Well, I couldn't even find one in Sant'Antonio until I asked an old crone and she pointed me to an edifice in the fields north of the village. Now some people might find this attractive, but if ever there was a mismatch of architectural styles, this is it. Its façade is vaguely Romanesque, its interior somewhat Gothic. Whatever it is, it's a mishmash. And the interior badly needs a coat of paint.

"Also, if you're looking for a distinctive painting by an old master, as in other churches all over Tuscany, well, you'll have to look a long time here. There's only one, a ghastly portrait of the beloved Saint Francis shaving the head of Saint Clare. We cannot imagine how such a depiction helps the faithful to pray to their God. Nearby there's a cemetery, where let's hope the inhabitants of this godforsaken village can finally find the refuge they must have yearned for in life."

"How can he say such a thing?" Mario asked. "Read some more."

Anita did.

"The village itself is composed of a couple of dozen nondescript houses. Oh, the people say there is a little river running through town, but all I could find was a tiny stream with some dead fish. No, Sant'Antonio is not a place where you want to stop. In fact, it's a place to avoid. It's not a lovely hilltop town like San Gimignano orMontepulciano or Montecatini, also in Tuscany. People come from all over the world to see those places. But Sant'Antonio is, instead, as flat as your grandmother's polenta. Note that it is the only place in Tuscany on our list of places to avoid. The only one! There are only two words to describe Sant'Antonio: Dull and boring. Avoid it at all cost."

Anita put down the magazine. "Oh, my. I don't know what to say."

Mario wiped the tears from his wife's eyes. "Don't say anything. Here, give me that copy. I'm going back to the *bottega* and destroy all the other copies. I'll burn them all. People will never know what *Scandalo italiano* had to say about our wonderful village."

It was too late. When Mario returned to his shop he found that a half dozen customers had found the copies of the magazine he had kicked under the counter.

"Mario," said Signora Giovanna Alberti, "we found these copies of *Scandalo italiano* on the floor. You must have dropped them. I'll take my usual copy. Here's my *lire*."

"And here's mine," said Signora Grazia Paluzzi.

"And mine," said Signor Enrico Agosta.

Within a half-hour, the news was all over Sant'Antonio.

THE INITIAL RESPONSE, later that same day, to the *Scandalo italiano* was: "Let's find the bastard who wrote this fuckin' article and kill him."

That was the sentiment expressed by Angelo Catalino, who famously led a *banda* of partisans in the hills around Bologna during the war. He had grabbed Enrico Agosta's copy of *Scandalo italiano*, torn it into tiny pieces and thrown them down the well in front of Leoni's. Later, when no women were around, he articulated in explicit detail what he would do to the author's nether regions.

The problem was that no one knew who wrote the article. The author had attached only his initials, L.M.S., to the piece rather than his name.

"L.M.S.?" people gathered in front of Leoni's wondered. "Who the hell is that?"

"Luciando Melificio Sensibiliata?" someone volunteered, making up a name on the spot.

"Lothario Montecellino Scalionitini?" someone else suggested.

A third person in the group wanted to sue. "It's slander! He told lies about us! We should collect millions and millions of *lire*."

It was up to Ezio Maffini to make a correction. Ezio, who had a law degree from the University of Pisa but spent his life as a schoolteacher, said, "Slander is oral defamation. Something someone says aloud. This was written."

"Well, then let's sue for that, whatever it's called."

"I think you're talking about libel," Ezio said. "That's when someone writes an untruth about someone else."

"So he wrote untruths about us. We can sue. It's libel."

"I think we'd have a hard time proving that in court," Ezio said. "He gave his opinion and when you read the article, what he says is mostly just his opinions. The stuff about Leoni's and Manconi's, the houses, the church, the painting, the well, the river."

"Well, that's not right. We've got to do something. We can't let that filthy magazine get away with this."

Stella Bevetta, who hardly ever said anything anywhere, raised her hand and said softly, "I know. Why don't we write a nice letter to *Scandalo italiano* and tell them how truly upset we are by this article? And we should all sign it, every one of us. They should know how we feel. I'm sure they will listen and do something about it. They must be very nice people."

"Signora," someone said, "this is not a time to be nice. Anyway, if they publish the letter it will only call attention to the falsehoods in the original article."

"Oh."

In the days that followed, a gloom as thick as rain clouds in the middle of winter settled over the village. People didn't want to look at each other, much less talk. They made their purchases at Leoni's and Manconi's and left without any conversations. At Mass on Sunday, Father Marcello, who had replaced the ailing Father Sangretto, devoted his sermon to the need for forgiveness. He quoted Matthew: "If someone strikes you on the right cheek, turn to him the other also," but his listeners weren't ready to do that, even if they understood what it meant in the first place.

Mostly, the villagers stayed in their homes with drapes closed. A few didn't even turn on the television. "Dull and boring, dull and boring." They couldn't get the words out of their heads.

Walking arm in arm along what they still called a river, Priscilla Brancatti confided to Amalia Campolo, "You know, I hate to say this, but my cousin in Massarosa doesn't want to come here anymore. She says she always knew Sant'Antonio was a terrible place and now it's in writing so it must be true. She doesn't want people to know she has a cousin here. Can you imagine? I don't really mind. I never liked her anyway."

"I got a telephone call from my sister-in-law in Pisa yesterday," Signora Campolo said. "She said we should collect money and build a new church. She said she never liked the church and she's always hated that painting. As if we have the kind of money to build a new church. Of course, they have lots of money in Pisa."

It didn't help when the twice-daily "Visit Italy" bus traveled through the village. In the past, the tourists paid no attention to what they were seeing. Now, they hung out of windows, laughing and pointing. "Dull and boring! Dull and boring!" they shouted.

"Go to hell!" Giovanni Bertollino yelled back at them.

In front of Leoni's, as they had every weekday for years, Giovanni, Nico Magnotti and Primo Scafidi still sat on white plastic chairs from eight o'clock in the morning until noon and from two o'clock until six. Now they had something else to talk about instead of the war, Italian politics and television programs.

"Well, they can say what they want, but Sant'Antonio isn't like it was," Giovanni said. "When I was a boy we used to have fun. We played around that old well there, we fished in the river, we went into the hills. We shot rabbits and birds. Now what do kids do? They just want to drive fancy cars."

"*Boh!*" said Nico.

"And drugs!" Primo said. "All they do is take all this stuff. Then they act crazy. We never did anything like that. Maybe a beer once in a while."

"And the way the girls dress! You can see everything! It's not like it was," Giovanni said.

"*Boh!*" said Nico.

They muttered to themselves for a long time.

A saner discussion took place at the Cielo, the hilltop home of Ezio and his wife, Donna. They were joined by their friends Lucia and Paolo.

"I don't know," Donna said. "Do you think something good will come out of something bad? That's what they always say, and I'd like to believe it, but I don't think it will happen this time."

"What good could ever come out of this?" Paolo asked. "That damn article just made everyone depressed because they know it's all true. Sant'Antonio has never been a place anyone would want to visit. Never has, never will be. It really is dull and boring, you know?"

"Any place can be dull and boring, Paolo," Ezio said. "It's what you make of it."

"And this is a place we call home, Paolo," Donna said. "Remember, I moved here, you moved here. We both came here when we got married, me to Ezio, you to Lucia, and now we wouldn't think of living anywhere else, right? We've come to love it, haven't we?"

"Guess so," Paolo admitted. "I've never even thought about it until now. Damn that *Scandalo italiano!*"

"I've lived in Sant'Antonio all my life," Lucia said, "so I can't compare. But I love this village, always will. And I don't care if we don't have a piazza. What's the big deal about a piazza? As long as we've got those two shops, that's enough for us. We can go to Lucca for whatever else. And I like our church! I always find new things to look at. And that painting! The look on Saint Francis' face. It's beautiful."

"I suppose," Ezio said, "a few things could be done to make the place better. That's true everywhere. Well, maybe some big rich man will read the article and decide to put all his money into making Sant'Antonio the Cinque Terre of Tuscany."

"Oh," Paolo said, "rich man? You must be talking about your neighbor."

Ezio laughed. "Well, Paolo, he's hardly my neighbor. Lives at least ten miles from our house. I've never even seen the man. Nobody has. He never comes out. Just stays in that huge place with the high fence and the growling dogs. He's in another world, and I doubt very much if he's seen *Scandalo italiano.*"

It was a good joke to end the depressing evening.

AFTER TWO MORE WEEKS of bickering, most people in the village agreed that something should be done. Most people, that is, except Giovanni Bertollino, Nico Magnotti and Primo Scafidi, who didn't like change at all and voiced their opinions loudly from their white plastic chairs in front of Leoni's.

"Leave it alone!" one or the other would shout whenever anyone talked about an improvement.

The other villagers, while wanting to do something, were at a loss about what to do, but everyone said Sant'Antonio shouldn't wait any longer with this scourge on its reputation!

The obvious solution: Call a meeting of the comune.

The Comune of Sant'Antonio had elected a new mayor only last year after Armado Cellini, the mayor for many years, died of a heart attack. Cellini, a farmer on the northern outskirts, was never challenged and was pretty much ignored. But then, there wasn't that much to do.

Many villagers, especially Paolo, urged Ezio to run, but he refused. Although he had just retired as principal of the school in Reboli, he was accompanying Donna on many book tours, and wasn't in town all the time. Besides that, he said, he was finishing his novel and needed time to complete it. (He wondered how long he could say that he was finishing his novel, since it was actually completed but he was afraid to send it to a publisher.)

So Ezio encouraged the man who had become a teacher in the school in Reboli. Stefano Frazzetta had moved to Sant'Antonio only a half dozen years ago, so he was still considered a newcomer, but he was well-liked, playing organ at the church and goalie for the amateur soccer team. His partner, Gino Rubino, a travel agent in Lucca, was also welcomed, especially when he provided huge sheets of lasagna for the parish festivals.

Stefano declined at first on the ground that there were men and women in the village who were more experienced and knew more about the village's history and politics. Ezio agreed, but pointed out that none of them was willing to run.

So Stefano was elected unopposed in a special election, and, since Sant'Antonio didn't have a town hall, comune records were transferred from Armado Cellini's attic to Stefano's attic.

Stefano soon found that it was a position that required little attention and paid even less. Most of the work was routine, done by the legislative body, the *Consiglio Comunale,* and an executive body, the *Giunta Comunale,* and even that consisted mainly of paying bills and registering births and deaths.

But after *Scandalo italiano* nothing was routine anymore.

On August 12, a poster appeared in the comune's long-vacant bulletin board in front of Leoni's.

Attention!
Important Meeting
Comune of Sant'Antonio
12 September 1985
Church Hall
All Should Attend!

A month later, the night of September 12 finally arrived and the streets of Sant'Antonio were filled with people silently lining up to go to the church hall, the only place in the village large enough for such an event. Although most everyone knew everyone else, they barely acknowledged each other. The gloom had settled even deeper.

Father Marcello introduced himself at the door and urged everyone to return for Mass next Sunday.

"What he's really saying is we should go to church and put something in the collection box," an old man said.

The place was packed. There had never been so many people in the hall, not even for the annual *festa* on the Feast of Saint Anthony. Father Marcello had to round up three teenage boys to bring down more folding chairs from the choir loft. Ezio, Donna, Lucia and Paolo were joined in the front row by Lucia's son, Dino, and his wife, Sofia. They had come from Florence to hear about what was happening in Sant'Antonio.

Unfortunately, it had been a hot September and the place was soon filled with the odor of sweaty bodies. Some women brought fans along, others used their handkerchiefs.

Stefano sat in the middle of the long table at the end of the room, flanked by members of the *Consiglio Comunale* and the *Giunta Comunale*. He did not seem nearly as nervous as one might expect a young mayor to be on such a momentous occasion, and instead talked softly with members of the audience who came up to give their opinions.

At 8 o'clock sharp, since Stefano was used to running a prompt classroom, he called the meeting to order. He kept his own introduction brief, but members of the *Consiglio Comunale* and the *Giunta Comunale* felt obliged to describe all the wonderful things they had accomplished during their tenure.

Father Marcello got up and tried to inject the meeting with a prayer. "It's important that we ask God's blessing on what we do here tonight," he said.

"Father," Stefano said, immediately exerting his authority, "we thank you for the use of your hall, but the comune has no religious affiliation and it would be contrary to our bylaws to have any such acknowledgment at this meeting. Now, I would like to thank everyone for coming here tonight. I think you will find this a very important meeting . . . ."

He was interrupted by a man in the back of the room. "Stefano, what are we going to do about the article in *Scandalo italiano*? We're going to sue, right?"

"It's good to see you here tonight, Pietro," Stefano said. "The *Consiglio Comunale* and the *Giunta Comunale* have called this meeting to discuss the future of Sant'Antonio, not the past. Yes, we acknowledge that the reputation of our lovely village has been badly damaged, but we feel this is a time for us to come together and formulate plans for our future. Now . . . ."

"But that magazine was terrible," a woman at the side yelled out. "I agree with Pietro. Let's sue!"

Stefano talked louder. "As I said, Claudia, we are here to discuss the future, not the past. We do not want revenge. We do not want to be vindictive."

Paolo nudged Lucia. "How does Stefano know everyone's names? I can hardly remember yours."

"He's a schoolteacher," Lucia whispered. "They have all those pupils. So when they meet someone once, right away they remember the name. They have to do that."

Stefano was speaking again. "And so what I and the *Consiglio Comunale* and the *Giunta Comunale* would like to do tonight is get your ideas on how we can all be proud of Sant'Antonio again. Because I know we all love our village. Gino and I came here as strangers and you've made us feel so welcome. I know other new people feel the same way, although it may have taken a little time for some."

Here he looked at Serafina and Salvo Marincola who were sitting in the front row with their children, Francesco, Clara and little Pasquale. The family had come from Calabria and had endured intolerance and prejudice until they were accepted. Serafina and Salvo smiled.

"So," Stefano continued, "we would like to make a list of what we can do to truly make this the community it has always been. Augusto here will take down your thoughts. Just shout them out."

One of the members of the *Comunale* got up and went to a whiteboard behind the table.

For a few minutes there was much stirring and murmuring, and then the suggestions came.

"How about having a market once a month?"

"Why don't we have a real piazza?"

"Could we have a big festival every year, bigger than the *festa*?"

"Yes! A real piazza!"

"Maybe paint the church?"

"I think we need a *restorante* or a *trattoria* or at least a *bar*. There's no place to eat here."

"I would love to see a piazza!"

"A new coach for the soccer team!"

"Let's get the well working again!"

"It would be great to have a piazza like other villages!"

This went on for some time and Augusto got so tired of writing "piazza" so often that he just wrote down "p."

Stefano asked for a few more suggestions and then called a halt.

"Wonderful! These are all great suggestions. And we should probably set some priorities so that we can focus on one at a time. But it looks like one choice is the most popular. We need a piazza!"

STEFANO LOOKED OUT at the crowd, which was now happily buzzing. "So if we're going to build a piazza, what should be our next step?"

"I'm willing to help," a man on the left side cried out. "What can we do?"

"Me, too!" another man said.

"And, me!" a woman cried.

"Well, this is just great," Stefano said. "OK, what we need first is to decide if this is even possible. So I want to appoint a feasibility committee. Raise your hand if you're willing to serve. I think we should have five people."

Hands went up all over the room.

"Thanks for volunteering! OK, I'll be arbitrary. How about you, Barnardo, and you, Sebastiano, and then Mario and Anita since you were practically mentioned by name in the article. And Ezio, please be the chair."

He went on to say that the group would have two weeks to look at the comune's finances and see if at least a start could be made on the piazza.

"OK, meeting adjourned! Thank you all for coming."

In stark contrast to the way they arrived, the villagers left the hall laughing and talking. Women were arm in arm, men draped their arms over other shoulders. There was hope for Sant'Antonio.

Ezio stayed behind to congratulate Stefano on the way he handled the meeting. "Were you nervous?"

"Hell, my knees were shaking the whole time."

"Well, you did it, and that's a start."

Stefano pulled Ezio aside and lowered his voice. "Ezio, I have to tell you this because you're going to find out soon enough. The comune is broke. I mean broke. We don't have money for a piazza. We don't have enough money for a pizza. How are we going to tell these people?"

"Let our feasibility committee worry about that, Stefano. We'll let you know."

"All I can say, Ezio, is good luck!"

Ezio and Donna walked back to Lucia and Paolo's along with Dino and Sofia. Lucia made coffee and passed around a plate of cookies, "fresh from Leoni's because I don't bake anymore."

"Thank goodness," Paolo said under his breath while taking two cookies. Lucia kicked him.

"Well," Donna said. "That was interesting. You know, I've never missed a piazza here because there never was one. But now that maybe we'll have one, it's kind of exciting, isn't it?"

"I've never lived in a place with a piazza, so I wouldn't know," Lucia said. "But it would be fun. We'd have a place for a real *passeggiata*, instead of walking down one street and then another. We never see other people that way. I mean it's nice to visit in homes, but where do we get to meet new people? Or even talk to them? Everybody's always in a hurry at Leoni's and Manconi's."

"What," Dino wondered, "will become of Giovanni Bertollino and Nico Magnotti and that other guy, Primo Scafidi, if they make a piazza? Wouldn't they have to move? They've been sitting in those chairs in front of Leoni's for centuries. They'd better not be evicted."

"I think," Ezio said, "there'd be a grandfather clause that would allow them to stay."

Ezio said that when he was researching his "almost-completed" novel he came across a couple of books about the history of Sant'Antonio. One, a reprint of a volume originally published in 1847, had lithographs of a small piazza in the center of town. There were several shops and what looked like a restaurant. A well was in the middle, though it could have been a fountain.

"So it looks like we have the remnants of the piazza still with us. I never realized Leoni's and Manconi's were in such old buildings. I imagine they've been converted many times. There were other buildings around the square, what may have been a town hall and maybe a little museum. Those buildings are gone, but of course that old Travello house wasn't there then."

"An eyesore and a hazard," Lucia said. "It should have been torn down years ago."

"So," Paolo said, "we have the outline of a piazza right there and we didn't even know it."

"And besides that," Ezio said, "the drawing clearly showed that the piazza was paved in red bricks. At some point, somebody covered it all over with concrete."

"Ugly concrete," Lucia said. "Well, I hope we can dig it up."

Another book, Ezio said, was devoted to a festival, apparently the predecessor of the *festa* of Sant'Antonio.

"The book said the village was even split up into *contrada*, just as in Siena, but there were only four of them: the *Aquila*, or Eagle; the *Chiocciola*, the Snail; the *Leocorno*, the Unicorn; and the *Oca*, the Goose. And each district had an emblem and a different medieval costume. They'd dress up and come to the piazza and stage various fights. There'd be music and lots of food. Looked like fun."

"You know what, Lucia," Paolo said. "I bet you could make me a medieval outfit. Hat, shirt, tights, the whole works."

"I don't think anybody would want to see you in tights, Paolo," his wife said.

"Of course," Ezio said, "Sant'Antonio was a lot bigger then, maybe two or three thousand people. Now, what do we have, two or three hundred?"

"If that," Paolo said. "And for that we can blame the Germans."

"Or the Americans," Dino said.

"Well, bombs are bombs," Paolo said. "Doesn't matter what kind of plane they fall from."

No one wanted to talk about the war again, so they went on to talk about piazzas in general, how they were unique to Italy, with virtually every city and town, except Sant'Antonio, having one. They were the focal point of every community, a place where people gathered to talk, to shop, to dine, to play and even to pray because many had a church on the side.

And then they began to reminisce about piazzas they had known and loved.

"Ezio," Paolo said, "remember how we used to talk in the piazza in front of Chiesa di Sant'Ignazzio in Reboli after the war? Outside my *pasticceria*? Remember how I'd buy Little Dino here a chocolate cone from the *gelateria*? He'd get it all over his shirt, but that's all he ever wanted."

"You did? I did?" Dino said. "I don't remember that."

"Ezio," Paolo said, "remember how you were going through such a bad time? Terrible headaches. Very depressed, though you wouldn't admit it. Old women would look at you and say *povero sfortunato*. Poor boy. And then you made up your mind to find the collaborator of the massacre at Sant'Anna di Stazzema."

"And," Ezio said, "that got me to Pietrasanta and it was there that I met Donna." He smiled at his wife.

"And that's another piazza story," Donna said. "I used to spend my lunch hours from the marble factory in the Piazza del Duomo in Pietrasanta reading Vasco Pratolini. Then Ezio rescued me." She squeezed his hand.

"Well," Dino said, "there are a lot of piazzas in Florence, and we've been at them all. Piazza della Signoria is magnificent. There's so much history there."

"Our favorite, though, is Piazza Santo Spirito in Oltrarno," Sofia said.

"But our memories aren't always so pleasant," Dino said. "Remember in 1966, during the flood, Sofia? And how the piazza in front of Santa Croce was flooded to the second story? And how Father Lorenzo kept the soup kitchen going?"

"And how you rescued that old lady from her apartment? Everyone was so proud of you."

"I really just carried her upstairs," Dino said.

Donna said that now that her cookbook was a modest success, she and Ezio had seen many cities in Italy, and so had spent a lot of time in piazzas. "I like Piazza San Marco in Venice—except for the pigeons, of course."

She said that they liked to watch tourists in Piazza Santa Maria Novella in Florence or to have chocolate gelato in the piazza to end all piazzas, the Campo in Siena.

"Our favorite, though, is the Piazza Pio II in Pienza," Ezio said. "It's just a small space but it's surrounded by the cathedral with its bell tower on one side, the Piccolomini palazzo on another, the Episcopal palazzo on the third and the town hall on the fourth. Pienza is such a jewel. We'll have to go back soon, right Donna?"

"How about tomorrow?"

"I always hear other people here talk about piazzas," Lucia said. "Salvo and Sarafina Marincola came from Calabria and they talk about taking their kids to the Piazza Grimaldi in Catanzaro."

"And," Paolo said, "I know that Stefano and Gino go to Rome some weekends just to have a twilight dinner at Piazza Navona."

Memories flooded the room for a long time.

"So, Ezio," Lucia said, "when do you think they'll be starting on the Sant'Antonio piazza?"

"I don't know, Lucia. As I said, we may need a rich man."

THREE DAYS LATER, Stefano brought Ezio the financial books, and the new feasibility committee met for the first time at Ezio and Donna's. It didn't take long to go through the books.

"It looks," Ezio said, "as if we spent more on paving that road to Camaiore than we budgeted for, and we didn't collect as much in taxes as we expected."

"But the bottom line," Anita said, "is that Stefano was right. The comune is broke."

"What are we going to do?" Barnardo asked. "Everybody is so excited about having a piazza. They think it will happen overnight. And they expect us to do it all."

"It's all I hear about every day at work," Sebastiano said. "We'd better do something. But what?"

They all thought for a while.

"Could we level with them?" Mario suggested. "Just tell them the comune is broke so we can't do it."

"Oh, and then what?" Anita asked. "Everybody will fall back into the same depression where they were before. Dull and boring. Dull and boring. And they'll blame us."

They thought some more.

"And the thing is," Barnardo said, "they want some action now. I think we'd all be run out of town if we told them the truth."

And then they thought some more.

"Well," Ezio said, "we might do this. We could get a start on the project with some volunteer help. For one thing, we could get a group together and dig up the concrete and find out if there really are those red bricks underneath."

"And we could get that old Travello house torn down," Sebastiano said. "I can get guys from the road crew and we could do that. Take a couple of days."

"And after that?" Anita asked.

"After that?" Ezio said. "I guess we pray for a rich man to send money down from the heavens."

But before any work could be done, Ezio said, the entire space needed to be surveyed.

"How are we going to afford that?" Barnardo asked.

More quiet while they thought.

"Got it!" Ezio said. "I know an engineering professor at the University of Pisa. He always has students who need practice. I'm sure he could send a team over and they could do the work. They'd get college credit, and we wouldn't have to pay them."

"Excellent!" everyone agreed.

On Monday two weeks later, teams of young people from the University of Pisa arrived wearing helmets and orange safety vests. They brought elevating levels and telescopes; surveying tripods and surveying bipods; poles, prisms, field books and buckets of red marking paint.

With their professor guiding them, they set up stations at various spots in the space in front of Leoni's and Manconi's. It was not a large space, perhaps a thousand feet in one direction, twelve hundred in another, but it was irregular, meaning that the young surveyors had to record their findings from many angles.

Naturally, their work attracted the attention of villagers young and old. Women stopped to watch after shopping. Children tried to look into the telescopes. Giovanni, Nico and Primo amused themselves by giving instructions.

"A little to the left," Primo commanded.

"No, the right," Nico ordered.

"I think you should start over," Giovanni yelled.

The old men hadn't had so much fun since the Easter fireworks display went off a day early four years ago.

The apprentice surveyors painted red lines, letters and numbers all over the concrete space.

"Looks like a Chinese puzzle," Primo said.

Once the surveying was complete, the students left, but in their wake was the general good feeling that the piazza was on its way. After all, look at all the red paint.

"I don't know where the money is coming from," a woman told Ezio one day at Leoni's. "But the comune must have had enough to pay those students. You're doing a good job, Ezio."

Ezio smiled.

An even more visible sign of progress occurred a week later when Barnardo and his crew arrived on a Saturday to tear down the old Travello house that encroached on the space for the piazza. Thrown up after the war, it had always been a hazard, and the last family who lived there had abandoned it more than twenty years earlier. The comune had put up a "condemned" sign on it, but it still stood there, roof caving in, walls falling down, concrete steps broken. Vandals had denuded the place of everything, including the kitchen sink and the toilet.

With a half dozen garbage trucks lined up, Barnardo's team started on the roof, tossing down tile after tile. Then the walls, which collapsed after a few hammer attacks. Then the upstairs floor and then the first floor. The house had no basement. Most of the work was completed on the first day, with cleanup work on Sunday.

When the last truck had hauled away the remnants of the house, only a bare plot remained. Children quickly claimed it for a game of war.

The next project: Digging up the concrete. A sign went up on the comune bulletin board:

Wanted!
Anyone with
Strong arms!
In front of Leoni's
28 October 1985
9 o'clock

Everyone knew what the project was, and twenty men and five women reported on time, pickaxes, drills, spades and shovels in hand. Barnardo was again in charge and positioned each of the volunteers around the perimeter of the proposed piazza.

"Ready! Set! Go!" he shouted, and twenty-five backs bent in unison. When a shovel didn't do the trick, a pickax did. Or a drill.

"Whoever gets to the middle first, gets a prize!" Barnardo shouted.

"What is it?" someone yelled.

"A surprise!" Barnardo answered, and hastily ran off to Leoni's, where Mario gave him a case of Brunello di Montalcino.

"My treat," Mario said. "I'll have to figure out a way to account for this on the books."

Outside, everyone was furiously digging and chipping away at the concrete. Cheers went up when a spade hit the red bricks. Antonio and Francesca, young people who were engaged to be married, made it to the center first and happily took the wine away.

"This will be for the wedding reception," Antonio cried.

After all the chunks of concrete had been carted away, it was clear that the original piazza did have a smooth surface of red bricks, still remarkably preserved. A few bricks were missing, a few more needed repairs, but most were in good shape.

Everyone looked very pleased, and children wasted no time in hopping from one brick to another.

"It won't be long now, will it, Ezio?" someone called.

"We'll see," he replied.

On the sidelines, the feasibility committee admired the work, too.

"Looks great," Barnardo said. "Who would have thought all this could be done in just three weeks. The people of Sant'Antonio really came together."

"But," Anita said, "we should tell people that this is it. We can't let them think there will be other things happening. Stefano, why don't you tell them?"

"I guess they should be told." Stefano stood apart from the committee and looked over the crowd. He cleared his throat.

"People of Sant'Antonio," he began, "as you can see we have made a very good start on a piazza for the village. Now I have to tell you something."

He paused and looked back at the other members of the committee.

"I have to tell you . . . I have to tell you . . . that winter is approaching and so we will not be able to continue until at least March."

DAY AFTER DAY, the committee members tried to think of a source of revenue. Day after day, they couldn't come up with an idea. Meanwhile, almost every day, each of them ran into villagers who were so excited about resuming work on the piazza that they were counting the days until March.

Stefano called Ezio on a Saturday morning in late November. "Ezio, we have to do something. How about trying to get a loan from a bank? If we told them how important this is, I bet they'll be willing to come up with something."

"Not sure how we'd ever repay it, but it's worth trying," Ezio said.

On the following Monday, Stefano, Ezio and Barnardo drove to Lucca, parked outside the walls and walked to the Bank of Lucca. Although they were unannounced, a vice president agreed to meet with them. His office was filled with cigar smoke and he sat behind his mahogany desk with a *Toscano Classico* in his hand.

"Signori," he said, "you say you are from the village of Sant'Antonio?"

"You've heard of it?" Stefano asked.

"Oh yes." The man's smile was very thin. "I have read about it."

"Then you know," Stefano said hurriedly, "how important it is for us to create a new atmosphere for the village. There are many things we would like to accomplish. We would like to have a *restorante* or *trattoria*, for example. And market days once a month. Maybe even a medieval festival. The people of the village are very excited about this. We have already made a start, in fact. We've torn down an old house that was in the way and we've removed the concrete from the bricks of the old piazza. We hope the Bank of Lucca will be able to help us out with a loan so we can continue our work."

The man peered over his glasses. "We are always pleased to help local development. We have made loans for many cities and villages for projects. But of course we have to be realistic. I assume you already have some money put aside for the project already. How much do you have now in reserve?"

Stefano coughed a little, but blamed it on the smoke. "Er . . . none, sir."

"None? None?"

"No, sir."

"Then how much can you put down as collateral? I'm sure you have something."

"We are willing to work very hard and we promise to repay a loan very quickly."

"But what is your collateral?"

"I'm afraid none, sir."

"Signori, I wish you the very best in creating this piazza. Now if you'll excuse me?"

The man stood up and walked out of the room.

Stefano, Ezio and Barnardo were uncharacteristically quiet on the way back to Sant'Antonio. Nearing the village, Stefano suddenly said, "What the hell. Why don't we go to Rome?"

"You think the Italian government would give us money?" Barnardo asked. "They're so messed up they don't even know who the prime minister is one day to the next."

"Worth a try," Ezio said.

Two days later, Stefano, Ezio and Barnardo found themselves in Rome but hopelessly lost in the bureaucracy. Running from office to office, they tried the Ministry of Economic Development and were sent to the Ministry of Cultural Affairs and Activities and from there to the Ministry of Economy and Finance. When they were then sent to the Ministry of Agricultural, Food and Forestry, they decided to go home.

"Wasn't worth a try," Ezio conceded.

The feasibility committee met some more and each time ended more depressed.

In early December, Stefano received a telephone call that was both baffling and intriguing. He went to the next meeting of the committee.

"Out of the blue," Stefano said, "I got this telephone call. It was late at night, which was rather strange, but I answered, and the guy said he was Count Pietro Bartolomeo Francesco Terrasini. That's what he said. Seriously."

If they didn't laugh out loud, all of the committee members smiled.

"A count! Of course!" Sebastiano said. "That's what we need, a count. But counts are a dime a dozen. You can buy the papers anywhere."

"If he's a count," Anita said, "then I'm Princess Diana."

"Well, anyway," Stefano said, "the guy said he was executive director of the *Commissione turismo della Toscana* in Florence."

"He's from a tourist agency in Florence?" Barnardo said. "There must be dozens of them. What did he want?"

Stefano continued. "He said the *commissione* had heard about our plans for a piazza and of course they very much supported what we were doing."

"He didn't say anything about *Scandalo italiano,* I don't suppose," Anita said. "Maybe he doesn't know about it."

"Doubt that," Stefano said. "I think all Italy knows about it. But he didn't mention it."

"That was kind of him," Sebastiano said.

"Anyway, he said he called because he wondered if we planned to have a pizzeria in the piazza. I said we were considering something like that, and he said he would very much like to talk to us about a proposal."

"Proposal for what?" Ezio asked.

"He didn't say. But I said we were open to all ideas, which I think we are, so I said he could come and talk to us next week Wednesday, if that's OK with all of you."

The committee members nodded.

"I guess so," Barnardo said. "At this point we're willing to hear anybody with any proposal. I'd even listen to my dog."

The committee members agreed to meet the alleged count at Stefano's house at 7:30. At 8:15, when he hadn't shown up, they were about to leave when a black Lancia pulled up. The man was soon at the doorstep. He was about forty years old and little more than five feet, but he tried to compensate for that by wearing inch-high platform shoes, black and white and made of genuine leather.

His black hair was slicked back from his highly tanned face. He had a thin mustache and small goatee. Even though it was evening, his silk shirt was unbuttoned almost down to his navel, exposing gray chest hair and at least two gold chains with medals. Both hands were heavy with jeweled rings. His nails were manicured.

"*Buonasera*," he said by way of greeting the committee members. "I am very happy to meet you all."

Skipping the formalities, Stefano invited the man to sit and explain his proposal. Terrasini took out a folder from his briefcase.

"I should explain," he began, "that the *Commissione turismo della Toscana* has pizzerias all over Tuscany. I could read you a long list of their names but I'm sure you have been in many of them. They are all known for their fine food and service."

"Well," Stefano said, "could you mention a few, just for our references."

"Of course. For example, San Casciano, Massa Marittima, Vicchio, Colle di Val d'Elsa . . ."

"OK, that's enough."

"Well," Terrasini continued, "when I heard about the opportunity of establishing one of our pizzerias in your fine village, I jumped at the chance, and that's why I called you, Mayor Frazzetta. We would like to build and operate a pizzeria as the cornerstone of your new piazza. We have the finances, all we need is your approval."

"If you're a tourist agency," Stefano said, "why do you operate a chain of pizzerias in Italy?"

"A tourist agency can do many things."

"You can't do this just to promote tourism," Anita said. "What do you get out of it?"

"We all benefit."

"You must make a lot of money with all those pizzerias," Stefano said.

"We do all right."

"Can you tell us exactly how you make the money?" Ezio said.

Terrasini suddenly felt the room getting warm and took off his jacket. His shirt clung to his chest.

"I don't know if we want to get into mundane details," he said.

"Oh, we don't mind mundane details," Anita said. "In fact, we rather like them."

Aware of his evasiveness, the committee members began to prod more. And more. They asked about financing for construction, for maintenance, for staffing, for supplies. Terrasini tried to avoid any discussion of how the pizzeria chain worked and instead wanted to focus on the variety of pizzas offered, the décor of the interiors and the experience of the staff.

"You will love having one of our pizzerias on your piazza," he said, mopping his forehead.

"Signor Terrasini," Stefano finally said, "we appreciate your coming. We'll think about all this and let you know our decision."

After his hurried exit, Anita said, "Well, that was interesting, but I think there's something very suspicious about him and his *commissione*."

"I don't understand how a tourist agency can operate a chain of pizzerias," Mario said.

"We need to check him out," Sebastiano said. "How can we do that?"

Ezio had an immediate answer. "Dino's in Florence. He knows people. He can check."

It took only three days for Dino to call Ezio back.

"Well, to begin with," Dino said, "Pietro Bartolomeo Francesco Terrasini really is a count. Not a major one, though. He's some sort of descendant of a guy named Costanzo Ciano, who was a naval commander in World War I. Costanzo received a gold medal for his action during the war, and King Victor Emmanuel III named him Conte di Cortellazzo e Buccari. This was when kings bestowed noble titles for war heroes. When Mussolini was rising to power Costanzo became a Fascist and the leader of the organization in Livorno. He died in 1939."

"Not a very impressive background," Ezio said.

"As for the *Commissione turismo della Toscana*," Dino said, "I did find the name of his outfit on a door in a big building near Piazza Santa Maria Novella, but nobody answered the bell. I went at least four times. The last time, I asked a guy coming out if he knew anything. He said his office was next door to the *commissione*, but he's never seen anyone going in or out. So I guess Count Pietro Bartolomeo Francesco Terrasini *is* the *Commissione turismo della Toscana*."

"Obviously a front," Ezio said.

"I have a friend, Giacomo," Dino said. "He's a reporter for *La Repubblica* and he's been watching Terrasini for years. He's written dozens of stories. He says the whole pizzeria business is controlled by the mob. They control the cheese industry that supplies the pizzerias. They get kickbacks from the owners. And now, Giacomo says, they're using the pizzerias for a heroin network."

The committee members shuddered when Ezio told them of Dino's report.

"Good thing we found out," Stefano said. "Thank Dino for us."

Another possible source of revenue eliminated.

"I guess there's only one more possibility," Stefano said. "Our last chance."

Everyone nodded.

"Who wants to come with me?" Stefano said.

"Since I live the closest to him, I will," Ezio said.

"I'll come, too," Anita said.

TEN YEARS AGO, there was only one question on the minds, and lips, of everyone in Sant'Antonio: "What's going on up there?"

The "there" was the old monastery of San Gregorio Magno al Celio, founded by the Camaldolese branch of the Benedictine order in the middle of the sixteenth century. Crowning the crest of the highest hill in the region, it was a long building, with a chapel at one end, the residence of the rector at the other, and a dormitory for about twenty monks in between. The monks had hoped to produce wine from the vineyards and olive oil from nearby trees, but both ventures proved unprofitable, and the place was used for only a decade or two before the monks abandoned it and moved to Rome in 1573.

Over the centuries, the inevitable happened. The tile roof collapsed. Daring thieves carted off the stained glass windows in the night. Pigeons and small furry animals adopted the place as their home.

"We should tear the place down," the people of Sant'Antonio said. But there was no money for such a project, and it crumbled more and more every year.

But in the last decade, every morning for months and months, trucks streamed up the narrow treacherous roads to the top of the hill. Some carried equipment, others building supplies. Every evening, they returned, empty. If a villager stopped a truck driver to ask what was going on, the answer would always be: "We're fixing up the place. That's all we know."

That led to questions of why anyone would want to fix up the place and who would that be?

The answer to the first question was elusive. But Ezio, who lived about ten miles from the place and therefore was the most immediate neighbor, found an envelope at the side of the road one day. It was addressed to "Signor Bernadetto Magnimassimo."

Anyone who followed the businesses pages knew who Bernadetto Magnimassimo was. A multimillionaire, he had made his fortune in the shipping industry, turning out luxury yachts for Arab princes. Little was known about his personal life. He was born in 1909, which would make him seventy-six now. His wife had died in 1968 and in the same year he sold his empire to a Greek tycoon. He had no children and no apparent heirs. There was a vague reference in one article about his interest in obscure Italian poetry and paintings, but nothing explicit.

When Ezio revealed this information, there were more questions: Why would Bernadetto Magnimassimo move from his villa in Capri to an abandoned monastery on a hilltop in Tuscany? Why would he bother to fix up this old building when he could buy anything he wanted new? What possible use could he have for such a huge building when he was an elderly man living alone?

Villagers knew that Magnimassimo did move into the place about five years ago when his red Lamborghini was sometimes seen driving up and down the hill. Every sighting was dutifully reported. They also knew that his place was surrounded by a high iron fence and guarded by vicious dogs.

And then it was discovered that the man had two servants, Signora Amabilia Bianco and her husband, Emilio. Amabilia, always dressed in dark gray or black, apparently was the cook and housekeeper because she occasionally stopped at Leoni's and Manconi's to pick up meat or items like eggs or butter. She was always pleasant and smiling, but declined to answer questions from Mario or Anita. Emilio was the driver, wearing a gray uniform and stiff cap, but even more reluctant to answer questions.

Bernadetto Magnimassimo himself was never seen. It was reported that he never left his palatial estate at the top of the hill because he was in such deep mourning for his wife. "Poor man," the women of Sant'Antonio said. "He can have all the money in the world but he can't buy happiness. He must be very lonely."

When the feasibility committee met after the disastrous discussion with the "count," it was clear that the only alternative to find funds for the piazza was to approach Signor Magnimassimo. He obviously had money, and he was a resident of the comune. Perhaps he would at least listen to their plea.

Stefano wrote the letter:

Dear Signor Magnimassimo:
I am the mayor of Sant'Antonio. I would like to meet with you about a proposal for our wonderful village. I hope you will agree to meet with me and two of my colleagues.

Thank you very much.
Stefano Frazzetta

Surprisingly, a short response arrived three days later:

Dear Mayor Frazzeta:
2 p.m. Thursday, 23 January 1986
Bernadetto Magnimassimo

"Incredible!" Stefano said when he showed the letter to the committee. "He's had no contact with anyone in the village, he's been a recluse up on that hill and never goes out, and now he agrees to meet with us just like that? Why?"

"Let's not ask questions," Ezio said. "Let's just go."

"Agreed," Anita said.

Naturally, although Tuscany had not seen a snowflake all winter, January 23 dawned with a storm raging out of the northeast. Heavy snow covered icy roads and schools were closed. Stefano, Ezio and Anita knew they had to start out early, and they were on the road by 9 a.m.

They were off the road at 10:15, skidding into a gully before they got a fourth of the way. With Anita behind the wheel, Stefano and Ezio managed to shovel the car back onto the road and they were off again. Only to spin completely around and veer into a tree on the turnoff to the Magnimassimo place. It was now 1:10 p.m. Again, they got the Fiat headed in the right direction and nervously proceeded at the rate of five miles an hour. Breathless, they arrived at the old monastery at 1:48 p.m.

In knee-deep snow, they stomped around the iron fence, seeking a gate or at least a bell, but only hearing vicious barking dogs. Suddenly, Emilio appeared, seemingly out of nowhere, and, holding two growling dogs on leashes, let the visitors enter through the heavy iron gate. They trudged up the narrow path to the door.

"Buongiorno!" Smiling warmly but obviously not used to visitors, Amabilia ushered them into a vast, but dimly lit, parlor. "Signor Magnimassimo will be here shortly. Please sit down."

The visitors preferred to stand. The room contained only a long sofa, two upright chairs, a large desk and a long table. A thick carpet with an Oriental design spread over most of the marble floor. Three walls, covered with red damask, held large paintings of elaborate scenes from mythology.

"My God, I think these are by Giovanni Signoretti, from the fourteenth century," Ezio whispered. "I've seen only a few of his paintings. These must be very rare."

"Who's he?" Anita whispered.

"A member of what's called the Sienese School."

"Why are we whispering?" Stefano whispered.

"I don't know. Seems like the thing to do in a room like this."

On the fourth wall was a larger-than-life portrait of a woman dressed in a long white gown that ended in a short train. She was about forty years old, with short blond hair. Loops of pearls fell below her waist and she held a small book.

"*Buongiorno!*" The visitors were startled to find a tall man, well over six feet, standing in the doorway. He had flowing white hair and a short white beard. Impeccably dressed, he could have stepped out of a men's fashion magazine: dark blue pin-striped suit and vest, blue and black striped tie, gold watch chain over his chest, shiny black leather shoes. Although he leaned on a mahogany cane topped by a gold lion's head, he looked not a day over sixty.

"Welcome to my home!"

He greeted Anita first and she caught herself before she curtsied. Ezio was next, and he noted his host's firm handshake.

"And you must be," Magnimassimo said, turning to Stefano, "the mayor."

"Yes, sir. I'm pleased to meet you, sir. Thank you for inviting us, sir."

Magnimassimo held on to the mayor's hand. "And your name is Stefano Frazzetta?"

"Yes, sir."

"That is not a common name."

"There are some Frazzettas in Umbria, I'm told, but I haven't met them. They may be distant relatives."

Magnimassimo gripped Stefano's hand even tighter. "But you are the only Stefano?"

"There may be one in Umbria, I don't know. My father was named Stefano, too. He died when I was a boy."

"So you are the only living Stefano?"

"As far as I know, sir."

Magnimassimo released Stefano's hand and engulfed the mayor in his arms. "Stefano Frazzetta, you don't know how pleased I am to meet you."

SMILING AND STILL NERVOUS, Amabilia brought in a silver tray of coffee and biscotti, and Bernadetto Magnimassimo invited everyone to be seated.

"Here, Signor Frazzetta, sit by me on the sofa. May I call you Stefano?"

"Of course. Thank you."

"And you must call me Bernadetto."

"Thank you, sir."

Ezio and Anita took their places on the straight-backed chairs and, obviously excluded from the conversation, spent the time examining the paintings on the walls, especially that of the woman in white.

"Stefano, I was so pleased to receive your letter and to see your signature. I thought to myself, Could it be? Could he be the one? And you are!"

"I am?"

"Of course," Bernadetto said, "you wonder why I am so pleased to meet you today."

"Yes, I am curious, sir."

Bernadetto got up and went to the desk. He opened a drawer and pulled out a small, worn leather-bound book. "It is for this reason."

He handed the book to Stefano.

"My God, it's my thesis. You had this bound in leather?"

"Nothing is too good for the words you have written."

Stefano looked at the cover, while Ezio and Anita tried hard to see, too.

"Un esame di amore in Donna me prega"

"An Examination of Love in 'A Woman Asks Me'"

Stefano turned to Ezio and Anita. "I was fascinated with the poetry of Guido Cavalcanti at the university and so I wrote my thesis on what's called his masterpiece. *Donna me prega* is his treatise on his personal thoughts and beliefs of love."

"I'm sorry," Anita said, "but I'm afraid that I've never heard of Guido Cavalcanti."

"He lived in Florence in the thirteenth century," Stefano said.

"From about 1250 to 1300, to be exact," Bernadetto added. "Now you wonder why I am so excited about meeting the author of *Un esame di amore in Donna me prega*. Well, I have to say, and I've thought about this many times, that this is the most thorough examination of *Donna me prega* that I have ever read, and I assure you I have read countless books and theses and articles about this work."

Stefano felt his face getting flushed and he tried to hide his shaking knees, but Bernadetto went on.

"I hope you don't mind my saying that, Stefano. I was so impressed with your interpretations. They were new ideas to me. I read your work over and over and I shared them with my wife. She was also very much impressed."

He looked up at the painting and seemed to whisper something.

"Thank you very much, sir. I'm sure I don't deserve such compliments."

"I'm just telling the truth, Stefano. Now I'm sure you are curious about why I love Guido Cavalcanti's work so much. I am afraid I did not become interested in his works until I was forty-four years old. What a waste of all those years before! I remember the date exactly. It was February 2, 1953. I was inspecting several of our cruise ships in Genoa. I was with my wife . . ."

He paused, and the others looked away.

"We went out to dinner that night and afterwards we went for a walk. Well, we happened upon a bookstore that sold antique books, some of them quite rare, I believe. I was looking around and my eyes fell upon this little book of poetry on a table with other books. Somehow the book attracted me more than the others. I picked it up and began to read. And that's how I fell in love with Guido Cavalcanti."

"That's a wonderful story, sir," Stefano said.

"You see the painting? She's holding the book in her hands." His eyes teared and the others looked away again.

"Well, that was just the beginning. My wife always said I was obsessive. I began to collect as many of Guido Cavalcanti's books as I could. Then I collected books analyzing his work and it was then that I discovered your excellent book, Stefano. I found it in a little bookstore in Florence."

Stefano smiled and let his host continue.

"My love for Guido's work continued to grow. I made it a point to read at least one of his poems each night. Often, I would read them to my wife, or she would read them to me, and we would talk about them. She had such wonderful insights. I tell you, Stefano, and you, too, Signor and Signora, those were the happiest times of my life . . . ."

The others examined the patterns in the rug. They also looked at each other. Were they ever going to talk about the piazza?

Bernadetto got up and pulled another book from the desk drawer. He sat down again.

"This is one of his early poems, but I like it very much."

Bilta di donna, e di saccente corre
e cavalieri armati che sien genti,
cantar d'augelli e ragionar d'amore,
adorni legni 'n mar forte correnti,
aria serena quand' appar l'albore,
e bianca neve scender senza venti,
rivera d'acqua e prato d'ogni fiore,
oro e argento, azzurro 'n ornamenti.

Beauty of women and wise hearts
and noble armed cavaliers
bird's song and love's reason
bedecked ships in strong seas
serene air at dawn
and white snow falling windlessly
watery brooks and fields of all flowers
gold, silver, lapis lazuli in adornment.

"My God, what imagery, what phrasing! Of course, this was, as I said, in his early period when he was concerned about beautiful ladies and strong knights, when he believed that love has a philosophical component related to human intelligence and moral purity by equating it with a wise heart. But then, of course, came his involvement with other Tuscan poets in the movement called *Dolce Still Novo,* and the most famous member was . . ."

"Dante!" Stefano said.

"Of course, and Dante was not only a member of this group, but also Guido's best friend! There is no doubt that Guido had an influence on Dante's work. There are many examples, as you know since I'm sure you read Dante as well as Guido."

Stefano nodded slightly. He hadn't read any Dante since the university.

"The *Dolce Still Novo* was an important period in Guido's life, and my wife and I loved this poem in which he interprets love as a source of torment and despair in the surrendering of self to the beloved. For example, the sonnet *Voi che per gli occhi mi passaste il core* (*You, Whose Look Pierced through My Heart*)."

Out of the corner of his eye, Stefano could see that Ezio was mouthing "piazza, piazza," but how could he stop Bernadetto from going on? He had already opened another book and began to read:

Voi che per gli occhi mi passaste 'l core
e destaste la mente che dormìa,
guardate a l'angosciosa vita mia
che sospirando la distrugge amore
E' ven tagliando di sì gran valore
che' deboletti spiriti van via
riman figura sol en segnoria
e voce alquanta, che parla dolore.

You whose look pierced through my heart,
Waking up my sleeping mind,
behold an anguished life
which love is killing with sighs.
So deeply love cuts my soul
that weak spirits are vanquished,
and what remains the only master
is this voice that speaks of woe.

"Ah," Bernardetto said, "I could consider these thoughts for days. And indeed I have. Stella and I often read this poem over and over before we retired for the night."

Once again, he looked lovingly at the portrait.

"But let me read you another since I know you are also a scholar of Guido Cavalcanti's works."

Anita suddenly had a coughing fit and Bernadetto called on Amabilia to bring her a glass of water. And then he began to read another poem.

And another.

Ezio excused himself to go to the bathroom. It was as big as his own living room, with a marble floor, frescoes on the walls and elegant fixtures throughout. He couldn't wait to describe it all to Donna. But when he returned, Bernardetto was reading yet another poem. He noticed that Stefano was trying to keep his knees from shaking.

After that, there was a long discussion of *Donna me prega*. Bernadetto wanted to know how Stefano came to write his thesis, what books he had used for research, and what his professors thought of it.

"I assume your professors were most impressed," he said.

"Yes, yes, I think they were." Stefano didn't disclose that he hadn't read a single line of Guido Cavalcanti since writing the thesis.

Bernardetto offered to show everyone his library of Guido books, but it was now 7 o'clock and Ezio and Anita were getting very nervous. Bernardetto tried to insist that they stay for "a little light supper which I'm sure Amabilia can prepare," but snow was still falling and the drive down the hills might be more treacherous than this morning. Stefano tried to steer the conversation to the piazza.

"Signor Magnimassimo . . . er . . . Bernardetto, I wonder if we could talk a little about our reason for coming here today."

"Ah, yes, of course. I have monopolized our conversation because of my great love for Guido Cavalcanti and because I am so excited to meet someone who shares that love. Please forgive me. I just had no idea that the excellent author of *Un esame di amore in Donna me prega* was living just a few miles from me, in the same comune, and that you are even the mayor! If I had known you were there, I would certainly have contacted you. But surely you must all come back very soon, say next week Tuesday, so that we can continue this conversation. Would that be possible?"

"We would like that very much," Stefano said. "Thank you for inviting us back."

"And next time," Bernardetto said, "we will not only talk about Guido Cavalcanti but also Giovanni Signoretti. People say that he is an obscure artist, but I must say that my wife and I collected more of his works than anyone else. They are housed in what used to be the monks' cells. Next week Tuesday I will show you every one."

SINCE THE ROADS were sheer ice and there was no oncoming traffic, their car simply slid perilously down to Sant'Antonio. When Donna greeted Ezio, and Mario greeted Anita, and Gino greeted Stefano, the tired travelers could only say, "I'm exhausted/worn out/ ready to drop so let's talk about it tomorrow."

Somehow, the word got out the next day about the three villagers visiting "that rich man in the hills." Amplified each time, the story quickly spread with a new version each time, and by the end of the day Signor Bernadetto Magnimassimo was not only presenting the village with millions of *lire* immediately but he also would bequeath his huge mansion with its priceless books and paintings. And there might be a ship or two involved.

Stefano, Ezio and Anita could only smile when questioned about their visit. They decided that their mutual response would be: "We need to meet again." They were well aware that March was looming and that the villagers were confident that work on the piazza would soon resume.

They were grateful for one thing. Bernadetto Magnimassimo apparently hadn't read, and perhaps didn't even know about, *Scandalo italiano.*

"He only reads Guido Cavalcanti," Ezio said.

"He's lost in his own world," Stefano said.

"With his wife," Anita said.

Laying out strategy before next Tuesday, they decided that they would have a written proposal to present, that Ezio would bring along the books about the piazza in the past and that Gino, a fine artist, would sketch a plan for the new piazza. Ezio also was assigned to bone up on the paintings of Giovanni Signoretti.

"We're set," Stefano said. "He's a great guy, and it was nice to get that praise, but I won't let him sidetrack us again."

On the morning of the visit, however, Anita had a crisis. Little Marianna's school was flooded in last week's storm and was closed. Mario had to go to Lucca for supplies. Anita couldn't leave the child at home alone, so the only alternative was to take her along.

"Now listen," Anita said, buttoning the child's blue-and-white dress. "We're going to a big beautiful house and you must be very good. And quiet. And don't touch anything. If somebody offers you a cookie, you can have one. Only one. Otherwise, I'll show you where to sit, and you just sit there until Mama is finished, OK?"

"OK, Mama."

"OK, let's go."

With the sun now warm and bright, the roads were mostly bare, and Emilio greeted them at the gate, this time without dogs. A smiling Amabilia ushered the visitors into the parlor again, delighted that Marianna had come along.

"Such a lovely little girl," she said. "Yes, you are beautiful. I like your dress. And your hair! Such long curls. What's your name?"

"Marianna, Signora."

"Marianna. What a lovely name. Stay here while I bring you some cookies and I'll tell Signor Magnimassimo that you're here."

She immediately returned with the silver plate of coffee and cookies, insisting, to Anita's displeasure, that Marianna have two.

When Bernadetto arrived he was surprised and pleased to find the little girl sitting in a corner munching a cookie. "What have we here?" was followed by more fussing over the child. Bernadetto was clearly smitten.

Stefano tried to get his attention. "Signor Magnimassimo . . . er, Bernadetto," Stefano said, "thank you for allowing us to intrude on your busy schedule again. We hope we won't take long."

"No, no," Bernadetto replied, leaving Marianna in the corner. "I have looked forward to this day ever since you left last week. I brought along a few more books of Guido's poetry so that we could discuss them some more . . ."

"We thought," Stefano said, taking the initiative, "that perhaps we could first take a brief look at your paintings by Giovanni Signoretti. Ezio here has admired his work for many years."

"Really! How exciting! Well, then, we must take a Giovanni Signoretti tour. Come, follow me."

"I think I should stay with Marianna," Anita said.

Bernadetto put his arm around Ezio's shoulder and led Stefano from the parlor to another room to a gilded lobby to a hallway and into what was once the monks' dormitory. In the reconstruction, walls in the tiny cells were knocked down, doubling the size of each, so that the paintings could be better displayed. Each room contained two or three paintings, depending on their size.

"This," Bernadetto said, "is the reason why I purchased this old monastery. I needed room to display all my works by Giovanni Signoretti. But, you know, even this isn't big enough for my collection. I have many more paintings from the Sienese School of painting in storage. I have been looking for a way to display them but so far haven't found any place. Do you know the works in the Sienese School?"

Ezio hesitated and tried not to get too specific.

"I know that Duccio di Buoninsegna is considered the father of Sienese painting. When my wife and I visited Siena last year we spent time in front of the Maestà in the Duomo. What an amazing work."

"Yes, on the front we see the Madonna and Child with saints and angels and on the reverse more than fifty scenes of the life of Christ. Fifty! Giotto's frescoes forecast painting in Florence, but certainly Duccio's Maestà became the reference point for all Sienese artists. And there were so many, from 1450 to 1500 alone, we have Bartolo di Fredi and Andrea Vanni and Niccolò di Bonaccorso . . ."

"And Niccolò di Ser Sozzo . . ."

"And Luca di Tommè and Taddeo di Bartolo and Paolo di Giovanni Fei . . . oh, so many."

For the next two hours, they moved from room to room, with Bernadetto pointing out minute details of each painting by Giovanni Signoretti.

"You see, in *The Adoration of the Shepherds,*" Bernadetto said, "how Signoretti softens the colors of the shepherds on the far right so that we can focus on the Baby Jesus."

Ezio, who had done his homework, said, "You know, this reminds me of Bartolo di Fredi's *Presentation of Mary in the Temple.* Of course, they were both members of the Sienese School."

Moving on to another room, they admired *Crucifixion with Two Slaves,* which both agreed was influenced by Francesco di Vannuccio's *Crucifixion.*

"Vannuccio inspired many painters in the Sienese School," Bernadetto said, "so that is not unusual."

There were more comparisons: Signoretti's *Madonna and Child* to a similar work by Luca di Tommè, and Signoretti's *Assumption of Mary* to Niccolò di Ser Sozzo's Ass*umption of the Virgin.*

"I've read that Niccolò's style is closest to that of Lippo Vanni and the Lorenzetti brothers, because he probably apprenticed with them," Ezio said, looking back at Stefano who was giving him the thumbs-up.

Stefano's own eyes were beginning to glaze over.

More paintings: *Agony in the Garden, Saint Bernardino of Siena, Saint Sebastian, Madonna and Child, Holy Family in Egypt.*

When, finally, they returned to the parlor, Bernadetto and Ezio were still discussing Signoretti's influence on other painters of the Sienese School. With Marianna still in the corner, Stefano and Anita pretended to be interested, and Bernadetto realized he should have been a better host.

"Signora Manconi, or may I call you Anita?" he said. "I have talked with Stefano about Guido Cavalcanti and with Ezio about Giovanni Signoretti, but tell me, what are your interests?"

"I . . . I'm afraid I don't know much about literature and art," Anita said. "I'm so busy with Marianna and taking care of the shop that I don't have much time for anything else."

"Ah yes. Amabilia told me you have a fine meat market in the village. Amabilia prefers to shop in Lucca, but she says she always finds what she needs when she stops in your shop."

"It's always a pleasure to see her," Anita said.

"And you have this lovely little daughter. You are very fortunate. My wife and I always wanted a child, and we tried for years. But I'm sorry to say that it was not possible. Sometimes I think my beloved Stella died of a broken heart."

Bernadetto got up and went to the corner where Marianna was sitting quietly, playing with her curls. He crouched down beside her.

"Hello, Marianna, can you tell me how old you are?"

"I'm six, Signor."

"Six. Tell me, Marianna, do you like to paint?"

"I like to draw."

"And what do you like to draw?"

"I draw my kitty. And houses. And balloons! I love to draw balloons. They're easy."

"What do you do with your drawings? Does your Mama put them on the refrigerator?"

"No, she puts them up in the meat market."

"Really? In the meat market. How lovely. And do people look at them?"

"Oh, yes. The signoras say I draw really well. Sometimes Mama gives them one."

"So everyone in Sant'Antonio can see your paintings."

"I guess so."

Bernadetto got up and went up to his wife's portrait, staring at it for a long time. Stefano tried to break the silence. "Bernadetto, I don't think I've ever seen you in the village."

"Sant'Antonio? No, no. I've never gone there. I'm afraid it would make me very sad, seeing people who are happy and live normal lives. No, I just stay here with my poetry and my paintings. Some people might say that I'm living in the past. Yes, the far distant past. But that's better for me than living in the present. Someday I hope I will join my Stella. Soon, I hope."

"But don't you get lonely?" Anita asked.

He returned to his seat on the sofa. "Amabilia and Emilio are always here, so if I need something, they come. I can't really talk to them, though."

"You seemed to enjoy talking to us," Ezio said.

"Enjoy! Ezio, your visits have been the most exciting things that have happened to me since I moved here. To talk to people who share my interests . . . well, I never imagined it could happen again after Stella left me. So I thank you very much for visiting me. And thank you for bringing little Marianna along today. It has been such a pleasure."

Stefano saw an opportunity.

"Bernadetto, as you know, we had something in mind when I wrote to you."

"Yes, yes, of course. And I am so sorry we haven't discussed it. What would you like to talk about?"

"Well, it's a big project, but let me begin."

Then, for the next forty-five minutes, Stefano, Ezio and Anita described what they hoped would be a piazza for Sant'Antonio, the new buildings, the landscaping, the desire to bring the community together. Stefano showed Gino's sketch of what a new piazza could look like. Ezio opened his old books, one showing the piazza centuries ago, the other of the ancient competitions. Although they did not specifically ask Bernadetto for money, they made it clear that the village was broke and could not proceed. They did not mention the article in *Scandalo italiano*.

Bernadetto listened to all this without comment. Then he got up and went to the portrait, standing in front of it for a long time. When he returned, he put the sketch of the old piazza next to the proposed one. He traced his finger over one, then the other.

"I see," he said slowly, "that in the past the piazza had the two markets, which thanks to Anita and Mario still exist. Then there is a place to eat and a rather official building."

"We think that was a town hall," Ezio said.

"It could be that, I suppose. Or perhaps something else? Thank you so much for coming to see me today."

"MY, THAT WAS STRANGE," Anita said as they drove back to Sant'Antonio. "He ended our meeting so abruptly. Did we say something wrong?"

"I don't think so," Stefano said. "We were just talking about the old piazza and the new one and suddenly he started staring into space as if he just thought of something. And then he looked at the painting of his wife. We didn't even have a chance to talk about money. Look, I've still got our proposal in my briefcase."

"Maybe that's the last we'll see of Bernadetto Magnimassimo," Ezio said. "You'll notice that he didn't invite us back."

"If he doesn't contact us in three or four days, I'll try to call," Stefano said. "Amabilia gave me the number."

Cradling the sleeping Marianna in her arms, Anita said, "You know, I feel so bad for him. He seems so terribly lonely. He has this sad look in his eyes all the time."

"The loss of his wife must have been devastating," Ezio said. "He must have loved her very much. But he seemed to enjoy being with us. I don't know why he doesn't come down to the village sometime. He might enjoy it. Donna could make him a great meal. Paolo could tell him funny stories . . . well, maybe not."

"As beautiful as that place is," Stefano said, "it seems like a prison."

At the Cielo that night, Ezio talked with Donna and Lucia and Paolo about the frustrating meeting. They agreed that it now seemed unlikely that Signor Magnimassimo would be the village's benefactor.

"Too bad," Paolo said. "It would have been great."

"I would have loved to meet the man," Lucia said. "All these rumors all these years. To think that one of the richest men in Europe lives in Sant'Antonio."

Ezio poured coffee for everyone as they sat around the living room. "Well, if there's going to be a piazza here, we'll have to figure out a way to do it ourselves."

"Agreed," Donna said. "I think we should think about what a piazza needs. It already has two shops, but it would need other things, too. From the piazzas Ezio and I have seen in Italy, it seems that many have something to anchor them, like a town hall or a palazzo or a church. Unfortunately, we don't need a town hall and there aren't any princes for a palazzo and we're not going to move the church, for God's sake."

"People go to a piazza to eat," Paolo said. "I think it needs a *restorante* or a *trattoria*. Nothing fancy, just good food. But it should be run locally. We don't want one of those chains."

"Or one run by the mob," Ezio said.

"Let's see," Paolo said, "I wonder if there is anyone here who could do that."

"You mean," Ezio said, "someone for example who might be a well-known cook who could open a restaurant?"

"Yes," Lucia said, "and maybe someone who actually has written a cookbook?"

"And someone who's used to cooking for large groups," Paolo said.

"Who could that be?" Ezio wondered. "I can't imagine."

Donna felt three pairs of eyes staring at her. "No! No! Don't even think of it."

"Why not?" her husband asked.

"Because, Ezio, I have enough work to do around here, because I still go on book tours, because I'm thinking of writing another cookbook and because . . ."

"Because, because, because," Lucia said. "Excuses, excuses, excuses."

"All good reasons, I guess," Ezio said. "Well, it's too bad all those people who will be coming from all over to see our new piazza won't be able to have an excellent meal from a world-famous cook who has written a best-selling cookbook. But that's OK, I'm sure there would be other cooks in the village. Signora Cardineli, for example. Of course, she sometimes forgets to put the chicken in the *chicken cacciatore*. Or Signora Notari. Her food is awfully spicy, but some people like it like that."

"Or," Paolo said, "even Lucia here. She's known far and wide for her ravioli."

Lucia kicked her husband.

"But . . . ," Donna said.

"And of course whoever did this, and I can't imagine who that would be, wouldn't have to be there all day."

"But . . . ," Donna said.

"The place could be open just at night, say, from 8 until 10 and not on Sunday or Monday. And meals could be served family style. There are places like that in Florence now. They just have a small group of diners and the cook makes just one entrée a night."

"But . . . ," Donna said.

"I bet," Ezio continued, "there would be several girls who would love to earn a little money by helping in the kitchen or being waitresses. And of course if there are any profits they could be put back into the piazza fund, so it would be good for the village, too. But, of course, if the person who has this place is selfish and doesn't want to give our poor village any money, that would be understood."

"But . . . ," Donna said.

"I wonder what a good name would be," Ezio said. "'Donna's *Cucina*'? Wouldn't that be an excellent name for a restaurant?"

Ezio nudged his wife.

"Oh, all right," she said. "I'll think about it. But that's all. I'll just think about it."

Ezio kissed her. He and Paolo and Lucia seemed very pleased with themselves.

"Of course," Ezio said, "that would mean the piazza would have a gathering place only at night. It would be great to have a place open in the mornings, say, from 8 until 11. Maybe a *bar* or a café, a place where people could get a cup of coffee and a croissant or something to eat. Maybe have tables outside where they could sit and read the newspaper."

"Yes," Paolo said. "I'd like to read *Gazzetto della sport.*"

"Sure. Or *La Repubblica* or *La Stampa.* There are a lot of newspapers."

"That sure would be nice," Paolo said. "Remember how we used to meet at the *bar* in Reboli every morning? I imagine, though, it would need someone with experience in managing a place like that. Someone, say, who ran a *pasticceria* in Reboli but retired far too soon and is tired of riding his motorcycle all over the hills and is looking for something to do."

"And," Lucia said, "someone who needs to get out of the house and from under his wife's feet all the time."

"Sounds like an interesting idea," Paolo said. "Maybe I'll think about it."

Although there were no final decisions, everyone ended the night pleased that perhaps the piazza could proceed—if someone would only provide the initial financing. After all, first there had to be buildings to house a restaurant and a *bar.*

The next day, villagers besieged Stefano, Ezio and Anita with more questions about when the money was going to arrive because they were very anxious to watch the construction in March, which was only weeks away. All they could say was, "We'll see."

They did not have to wait long to see. Two days later, Amabilia called Stefano. "Signor Magnimassimo would like to meet you all again. Could you come up this afternoon?"

They could and did.

When they arrived at Bernardetto's place they found their host flanked by two men. One was almost as tall as Bernardetto, the other considerably shorter. Both wore pin-striped suits.

"*Buongiorno!* I would like you to meet two longtime friends. Armando here is my legal counsel," he said, introducing the taller man, "and Renaldo is the architect who was in charge of all the renovations here. I have him to thank for the beauty of this place."

Interrupted by Amabilia with her usual refreshments, Bernadetto invited everyone to sit and continued. "I have been thinking about what we talked about a few days ago, and that's why I invited my legal counsel and architect to meet with you today. I'll need them if we are to continue with this project."

Stefano almost spilled his coffee because his knees suddenly began to shake.

Bernadetto spread Gino's sketch of the proposed piazza out on the table. "Renaldo has looked at this and says it is a fine start. He suggests having the meat market here, where it is now, a restaurant over here, across from the Leoni *bottega*, and then a *bar* over here, next to this building, so there could be a continual flow. People would go from the *bar* to your place, Anita, then to your husband's place and then to the restaurant and then to this building."

Anita's shoulders were shaking now.

"We're not sure what to do about the well, which we understand is dry," Renaldo said, "but we'll see if it can be restored."

Bernadetto pointed at the sketch again. "Over here we would like to have an open space so that every month vendors could set up their stalls for a market. They could sell crafts, food, clothing. People would come from miles around. And notice the central area is kept open so that there would be room for the annual festivals and competitions. Maybe the village could revive some of those medieval contests that were shown in Ezio's book. And of course every night the entire village would be out for the *passeggiata*."

"This is so exciting," Ezio said. "I can't believe you're even talking about it. But we wonder, well, all this is going to cost a lot of money, isn't it?"

Bernadetto put his hand on Ezio's shoulder. "Don't worry about that, my friend. That's why I invited Armando here. He'll take care of the legal work in transferring the funds to the comune's account."

Stefano, Ezio and Anita stared in amazement. A piazza for Sant'Antonio was going to be that simple? They hadn't even asked for any money.

"Oh, my God, Bernadetto," Stefano said. "We are so very grateful. The people of Sant'Antonio will be so excited to hear this. How can we ever thank you? You're so kind, so generous."

"Actually," Bernadetto said, "I do have an ulterior motive. Sit down. Let me tell you."

AMABILIA CAME IN WITH MORE COFFEE. She was smiling even more than usual, as if she knew that something significant was happening but, more important, that the man to whom she had devoted her life seemed so much happier.

"Let me explain," Bernadetto said. "You'll notice that there was a building we haven't talked about in the drawing. Here's my plan. I've told you that I have so many paintings from the Sienese School in storage. These are besides the ones by Giovanni Signoretti that you've seen. They're just sitting there. It's a crime, really, because people should be able to see them. I have not been able to figure out a way where they could be displayed.

"Well, when we were talking the other day, an idea suddenly came to me. Why not have a little museum in this new piazza where some of the paintings could be hung and everyone would be able to admire them? So I talked to Renaldo about this, and he came up with this brilliant proposal."

Renaldo pulled a large sheet of paper out of a cardboard tube and spread it next to the other drawings on the table.

"We want the museum to be compatible with everything else in the piazza," he said, "so I've designed one that would resemble a palazzo more than a stuffy old museum. You see, the façade would have arches and stained glass, not just stone. The entrance would be at street level, no steps. Inside, visitors would go from room to room as in a home, with couches, chairs, tables here and there. It would give the impression of someone who has opened his home and his artwork to the public."

Stefano, Ezio and Anita couldn't imagine a palazzo in Sant'Antonio.

Bernadetto interrupted. "Of course, this will be a small museum, so I plan to rotate my paintings there. Perhaps twenty or twenty-five at a time, and then a new batch will come in. Over time, people will be able to see all of them and appreciate the wonders of the Sienese School."

"As I said," Renaldo continued, "we want the palazzo to complement the other buildings around the piazza. So please look at this."

He pulled out another large sketch and placed it on top of the previous one. "This is a rendering of the piazza from several sides. If the comune allows us, we will also construct this building here for a restaurant and this one for a *bar* or café. Both would have the same arches and stained glass. And over here, we would construct new facades for the two business establishments now in place. I believe they are called Leoni's and Manconi's."

"My God," Ezio said, "this looks a little like the piazza in Pienza. Donna and I have always said it is our very favorite in all of Italy."

"I have to say," Renaldo said, "that we didn't intend to copy that little jewel, but we were inspired by it."

"I must ask," Bernadetto said, "do you like the plans?"

"Like them! They're gorgeous," Stefano said.

"Incredible!" Ezio said.

"I've never seen anything so beautiful," Anita said.

They noted that for the first time since they had met him, Bernadetto was smiling. He asked Amabilia to bring in dessert cakes and glasses of *limoncello*.

They talked more about what the piazza would be like and how the people of Sant'Antonio would enjoy it so much and be so very grateful. And then Stefano asked the question Ezio and Anita were waiting for him to ask.

"Bernadetto," he said, "we wonder why you are doing this. I mean, you could have simply ignored our plans, but you didn't even let us talk about them the other day. You suddenly wanted to do it. Why?"

Bernadetto rarely smoked cigars but now lit one up. "Stefano, my friend, and Ezio and Anita, my other friends, I know you were surprised, so I should tell you what happened. You asked me the other day, Anita, if I was lonely, and I know I evaded the question. It's something I haven't thought about and, you know, if you don't think about something, it isn't there.

"After my wife left me I didn't want to see anyone. I secluded myself in my villa in Capri. And then I looked for a place where I could be entirely alone with my paintings. I looked all over Italy for a place big enough and found this old monastery.

"Well, when we were looking at the plans for the piazza I kept thinking about your question. I kept thinking how selfish I have been all these years, hiding my paintings here for no one but me to see, but even more than that, keeping myself hidden for so long.

"And then . . . and then . . . when you brought little Marianna here I realized how much I have missed. I hadn't seen a little child in I don't know how long. And here she was, with her lovely smile and beautiful blond curls. What a treasure she is.

"Then she told me how you put her little drawings up in your market so that everyone in Sant'Antonio could see her work. You could have taken them home and put them on your refrigerator, but you wanted everyone to see them. Now I want everyone to see my paintings by Giovanni Signoretti and all the other Sienese artists."

Stefano voiced what the others were feeling. "Bernadetto, you are giving a priceless gift, not only to Sant'Antonio but to Italy, indeed to the world. People will come from all over to see these works."

"Not to mention," Ezio said, "that the village will benefit, too. I'm sure there will be artists and professors and others who will want to stay and spend time with these paintings."

Bernadetto signaled to his architect. "Renaldo, that's something we haven't considered. We will need a hotel somewhere to house these visitors. Maybe more than one. Armando, see to it that this is done."

"Of course," Renaldo and Armando said together.

"I can promise one thing," Stefano said, "when all this is completed we will have a big celebration and you will be the guest of honor. I don't know how we will honor you, but we'll think of something."

"That is very thoughtful," Bernadetto said, "but I want to remain as anonymous as possible. Certainly, have the celebration. But I won't be there."

"Of course you'll be there," Anita said.

"My paintings will be there, that's enough."

Stefano, Ezio and Anita thought that they would try to change his mind later, but they still had one question.

"I suppose I should ask," Stefano said, "when the work will begin."

Bernadetto smiled. "I think, oh, next week?"

SINCE BERNADETTO MAGNIMASSIMO could afford the most efficient and fastest workers, signs of what would happen began the following Tuesday with the arrival of a team of foremen and inspectors. The surveying work by the university students was duly approved and the red bricks that covered the area checked. That took the rest of the week, but by the next Monday the place was ready for construction.

Giovanni Bertollino, Nico Magnotti and Primo Scafidi were pleased that work was starting opposite Leoni's. They would have plenty of time to supervise before having to move from their white plastic chairs.

The first project was the *bar*, a small building that was completed in only five days. After the shell was erected, it simply needed a tile roof and a stone façade. Paolo was there every minute, making suggestions and otherwise getting in the way. The final touches were a door with the word *BAR* on the glass and a green-and-white striped awning.

After consulting with Stefano, who assured him that there suddenly were funds in the comune's bank account, Paolo ordered a glass case with shelves, a cash register, storage cabinets, and espresso and cappuccino makers. He would wait to order other items needed.

Then came the restaurant. After the foundation was dug, walls went up and then the tile roof. Since this place needed strong flooring, that was installed before everything else. Then the kitchen, which was even bigger than the dining area. With Donna's suggestions, the newest stove, sink, refrigerator and freezer surrounded long work tables. Stefano provided the funds, and she ordered five tables with six chairs each.

"This is going to be a family restaurant," Donna told Ezio. "We want to keep it small."

When the interior was completed and another green-and-white awning put up, a sign was etched on the glass window: "Donna's *Cucina*."

It was now mid-June and the biggest project would begin in the heat of summer. The same construction company that was used to convert the monastery now was in charge of erecting the palazzo that would house the Sienese paintings. Trucks carrying tons of stone parked near the village, entering one by one to unload their cargo in the piazza. Workers quickly retrieved the stones and began building the walls.

Bernadetto was not to be seen during any of this, but Renaldo was there, helmet on his head and architectural drawings in his hands. Through the summer, when more fortunate Italians fled to the seashore, the sweaty workers built walls. Through the fall, when the temperatures were plummeting, they installed the roof. Through the cold of winter, when they wore heavy jackets and two pairs of gloves, they finished the floors. And in spring, they painted the walls, installed the rugs and brought in the furniture.

Giovanni, Nico and Primo cheered them on every step of the way.

"You do good work," Giovanni said one day. "Want to come over and fix my garage door?"

With the weather better, Renaldo turned his attention to the well. Three men took turns going to the bottom to examine the pipes, which were not broken after all but merely needed cleaning.

"We have good news," Renaldo announced. "We could fix this so that it could be a well again, or there's an alternative. We could turn it into a fountain."

There was just one answer to that, and soon a three-pronged fountain gushed forth. Coins immediately littered the base.

When the palazzo was completed, the only remaining projects were installing new fronts on Leoni's and Manconi's. The workers tried to finish the job as quickly and with as little disruption as possible. Meanwhile, they completed a sleek six-story hotel, complete with a swimming pool, just beyond the village. It was named Hotel Stella.

On June 1, 1986, Stefano, members of the *Consiglio Comunale* and the *Giunta Comunale*, members of the feasibility committee and almost the entire village, along with Renaldo and Armando, gathered in the middle of the piazza. Stefano gave a little speech, thanking Bernadetto, of course, and announcing that a celebration would take place the following September.

Bernadetto himself was noticeably absent.

Delaying the celebration for three months allowed the villagers to get used to their new and wonderful piazza. Sometimes, people would simply bring lawn chairs and sit and admire the amazing views. After they closed their shops for the day, Mario and Anita brought little Marianna out to play with her friends on the red bricks. Unless they were sick in bed, everyone came out for the evening *passeggiata.*

Even Giovanni, Nico and Primo grudgingly acknowledged that the piazza was a vast improvement and they now had a lot more to talk about.

The first exhibit at the new Sienese School Museum opened on July 1 with a sampling of paintings by Francesco di Vannuccio, Luca di Tommè and Niccolò di Ser Sozzo. Stefano's partner, Gino Rubino, the travel agent in Lucca, alerted art critics throughout Italy and "The Sienese School: Vannuccio, Tommè and Ser Sozzo" was lavishly praised in newspapers and magazines.

Gino then began promoting Sant'Antonio with other tourist agencies, and the trickle of visitors grew so rapidly that the Hotel Stella was filled to capacity.

After restaurant reviews were published throughout Italy, reservations were needed at least two weeks in advance for Donna's *Cucina*. Donna hired two excellent cooks from Lucca to work two days a week so that she had to cook and manage the place only on Wednesday, Friday and Saturday.

Paolo's *bar* quickly became popular and he learned how to use the espresso maker and the cash register at the same time. He and a small group of friends were already planning for a medieval festival on the feast of Saint Anthony, next June 13. They regretted not having horses, shields and lances for the contests for the *contrada*, but, he said, "we'll just get into our costumes and go into the piazza and punch each other."

On the second Saturday of the month, vendors occupied the space next to the *bar*. Many were farmers from the nearby hills, eager to sell their fruits, vegetables, wines and olive oils, but there were also the ubiquitous leather-goods dealers who went from market to market.

On September 15, the official opening of the piazza began with a Mass during which Father Marcello thanked God and Bernadetto Magnimassimo equally for "this wonderful addition to our community." Then a parade of floats proceeded down the main street to the piazza: marching bands and drummers, the soccer team, children in their First Communion outfits, the Ladies Altar Society, nuns from the nearby Dominican convent, a contingent of men in medieval costumes—notably including Paolo in red-and-black tights—and even flag throwers from a town in Umbria. A fleet of flatbed trucks followed.

At 4 o'clock, it was clear that the piazza was full. There was no room for Paolo in his tights or the nuns or the flag throwers. Someone whispered to the drummers who whispered to the First Communicants who told the Ladies, and the word spread back to the end of the line. Suddenly, those who were walking climbed aboard the flatbed trucks. Led by the flag throwers, the makeshift parade began the ascent up the hill, around the bends and higher and higher to the very top.

It was 6 o'clock by the time the flag throwers arrived in front of Bernadetto Magnimassimo's estate. Frantically following the growling dogs, Emilio rushed to the gate.

"It's us, Emilio," Stefano yelled. "We want to see Bernadetto!"

Emilio opened the gate and a flood of humanity, young and old, men and women and children, some in costumes, flooded the lawn in front of the main house. And the chant began.

"Bernadetto! Bernadetto! Bernadetto!"

Amabilia appeared, flustered but smiling, looked over the crowd and dashed back into the house. Moments later, a tall man in a pin-striped suit stood on the steps. He lifted his arms in a grand salute, then took out his handkerchief.

And sobbed.

Everyone cheered and spread out on the lawn until darkness fell. The flag throwers threw their flags, the drummers drummed and the children got their white First Communion outfits very dirty.

When it was clear that it was too late and too dark to descend into the village, Bernadetto invited everyone into the rambling old monastery to spend the night. Although there were hundreds, everyone found a space on the floor to curl up. Amabilia apologized the next morning for not having enough coffee and croissants to go around.

"This," Bernardetto said as everyone prepared to leave, "has been the greatest night I can ever remember. You must all come again!"

"Only if you come to see us in the village!" Stefano said.

Bernardetto thought for only a few seconds. "I will!"

The following night, as they did every night since the piazza was completed, villagers began to gather there at 8 p.m. for their *passeggiata*. Then, arm in arm and in twos and threes, they slowly walked the perimeter of the piazza, talking softly and greeting their neighbors.

"*Buonasera,*" "*Buonasera,*" "*Buonasera.*"

Donna was with Ezio, Lucia with Paolo, Mario and Anita with Marianna in between, Stefano with Gino, Serafina and Salvo Marincola with Francesco, Clara and little Pasquale trailing behind, and dozens and dozens of others. Even Giovanni Bertollino, Nico Magnotti and Primo Scafidi hobbled along with their wives past Manconi's and Leoni's and the restaurant and the *bar* with a stop at the fountain to throw in a coin or two.

Outside the Sienese School Museum, they saw three figures emerge. With Amabilia on his arm on one side and Emilio on the other, Bernadetto waved to the crowd and joined the procession.

"*Buonasera,*" "*Buonasera,*" "*Buonasera.*"

It was only three months later when Mario untied a package of magazines and found the new copy of the popular *l'Espresso*. He always liked to read it, finding it more credible than other newsmagazines, and his opinion was shared by hundreds of thousands throughout Italy.

Keeping one copy out before he put the others on the stand of his *bottega*, he noticed a headline at the top of the cover. "Five Best Small Piazzas in Italy."

"I know Pienza will be on the list, maybe San Gimignano," he thought. "I don't know a lot of them. Well, let's see who made it."

He turned to page eleven and, sure enough, Pienza was the first. "No surprise there," he thought. Then he looked at Number Two.

"Oh, my God!"

Waving the magazine in the air, he ran across the street to the newly refurbished Manconi's.

"Anita! Look at this! You're not going to believe it!"

Dino Finds His Roots

ALTHOUGH THEY HAD BEEN MARRIED for nine years, Dino had never taken Sofia up the steep hill to visit his father's grave until now. He wasn't sure why he waited. Perhaps he had just wanted to keep his connection with his father, such as it was, so private that he didn't want to share it even with his wife.

Or, perhaps, he didn't want anything to interfere with the strong relationship he had with his stepfather, Paolo.

This week, he and Sofia had fled their jobs in Florence during the heat of mid-August and were spending time with his parents in Sant'Antonio. With little else to do, Dino suddenly asked his wife, "Want to see where my father is buried?"

"Of course."

"It's up near the Cielo, at the spot where he was killed during the war. I used to go up there a lot when I was a teenager, and then when I came home from studying at the Accademia in Florence. I'd go up there and tell my father all my troubles, how I had difficulty studying, how I didn't have any friends. All that stuff. Not that he ever answered. But then I met you."

"I'm glad."

"OK, let's go."

They put on straw hats and sunglasses and began the long and steep climb. A half-hour later, they arrived at the small cleared-out area about a quarter mile from the farmhouse. It was in the middle of an olive grove, but Ezio had keep this spot mowed and free of weeds. Seated close to each other, Dino and Sofia could see far into the distance, the rolling green hills dotted with other farmhouses, patches of vineyards and rows of cypress trees. A breeze kept the place cooler even on this hot August day.

"If I were to choose a spot to spend my eternity, this would be it," Dino said.

"I think your father would have felt the same way."

Dino leaned back on his elbows and gazed at the cloudless azure sky. "I wish I knew something about him. He died before I was born, but I feel he's still a part of me. I was named after him, after all. I don't even have a picture, so I have no idea what he looked like. Maybe I look like him. I just don't know."

They studied the small marble marker, one that Dino had ordered made six years ago to replace the rugged stone placed there shortly after the burial.

Dino Pezzino

1926-1944

"Only eighteen years old," Sofia said. "He had his whole life ahead of him. But it seems very strange to see 'Dino' on a gravestone, Dino. I don't like it."

"When I was little, everyone called me Little Dino. That was OK until I was a teenager. Boy, did I get mad when people called me that. My mother still does sometimes! I think Papa has stopped, but it took a long time."

"It's interesting that you call Paolo your Papa."

"He's the only father I've ever known, and he's been great. I guess I was a spoiled little kid, but he always kept me in line. Of course, he was my real father's best friend and saw him die. It seems strange to call the man who's buried here my 'real' father when Papa has always been my father."

Paolo had told him the whole story when Dino was ten years old. He wanted Dino to know the truth about his father.

It was the summer of 1944, and the height of the war in the area. With the Allies coming steadfastly northward through Italy, the Germans were fleeing in haste, but not before killing, raping and destroying everyone and everything in sight.

Since early in the summer, they had occupied the little village of Sant'Antonio and residents had literally escaped into the hills, taking shelter in abandoned farmhouses, stables and even the forests. One mother, Gina Sporenza, had brought her five children, ranging from a three-month-old baby to a sixteen-year-old daughter, Lucia, to stay with other villagers in the old farmhouse named the Cielo.

In the second week of September, the remnants of a Nazi battalion encountered a small band of partisans just outside the Cielo, and a fierce firefight ensued in this very olive grove. Paolo Ricci and Dino Pezzino were naïve young members of the partisan band. As Paolo watched horrified but helpless, he saw a bullet hit Dino in the neck and then more and more riddled his body.

When the firefight ended and the Nazis had fled, the villagers counted two men from their refuge also killed.

Although Paolo had been Dino's best friend, he knew nothing about his family, and so the battered body was buried on the spot.

"Papa has told me that he and my father were both from Montepulciano, but that's about all he knew about him. They didn't know each other until they joined the Italian army. They both hated it, so they deserted and joined the partisans."

"I know a lot of men did that," Sofia said. "Tell me again how your father and mother met."

"It should be a sweet story, but it's not. After Paolo and my father had deserted the Italian army, but before they joined the partisans, they were running through these very hills. Paolo hurt his ankle and they came upon the Cielo. My mother, Lucia, who was staying there with the rest of her family, saw them and offered to help Paolo. But she was really attracted to my father.

"He and Paolo managed to stay for a few weeks with an old guy in a hut nearby while Paolo's ankle healed. During that time, Lucia left the Cielo, which she wasn't supposed to do, and met my father in the fields. It must have been somewhere near here. Anyway, you can imagine what happened. She was an impulsive sixteen-year-old girl and he was a lusty eighteen-year-old boy."

"Somehow, I can't imagine your mother as an impulsive young girl," Sofia said.

"I guess people change as they get older. Anyway, it was after that when Paolo and my father left to join the partisans. Which, by the way, were led by Ezio . . . ."

". . . who married Donna after the war and they bought the Cielo and live there now."

"Yes. A full circle."

Dino got up to brush nasty flies from the tombstone. His hand lingered at the top and he traced the letters with his fingers. D-I-N-O

"This is like tracing a part of me, Sofia."

They lay on their backs, holding hands and looking up at the sky. "Dino," Sofia said, "did you ever think about trying to find out more about your father? I always liked it when my father told me stories about growing up in Calabria, how he went fishing with his friends, how he went swimming in the ocean. And about all his crazy relatives. When I think about those stories, I miss him even more."

Sofia's father, who owned a tobacco shop, was killed by the Mafia when Sofia was seventeen. She was alone then, her mother having died in childbirth, so she fled her village and moved to northern Italy.

"My mother tells me stories about growing up here," Dino said, "but she never mentions my father. All I know is what Papa told me."

"Wouldn't you like to know more?"

"I don't know how I could find out."

"Talk to your mother?"

"I'm not sure if she would want to talk about him. She never mentions him."

"You won't find out unless you ask her. Unless you think this will be hard for her and your Papa."

"I don't think it would be hard for Papa. He's told me how he started going to see my mother after my father was killed. They talked about how they missed him and over the months got very close and fell in love. He married her before I was born. And he's always loved me like his own son. I still remember what he told me the morning I went off to Florence to study. I remember the exact words. 'Dino, I didn't marry your mother because she was pregnant with you and I wanted the baby to have a father. I married her because I loved her.'"

"That's so sweet."

"Then he told me how much he loved me and how much he was going to miss me. We both cried. Paolo doesn't express his feelings very well but I know he loves my mother very much. Sure they tease each other a lot and joke around, but they're still very much in love. Did you see them last night at the *passeggiata* in the new piazza? They were holding hands like young lovers."

"Just as we were."

Dino helped her up and kissed her cheek. "Well, I'll try to talk to my mother. And Paolo. And also Ezio. He was the leader of the *banda* that my father was in. He must know something."

"Scared?"

"Yes. Who knows what I'm going to find."

BECAUSE THEY WERE SO CLOSE TO THE CIELO, Dino thought they might as well start by talking to Ezio. They arrived as Ezio and Donna were having coffee and reading sections of *Corriere della Sera.*

"Dino, Sofia!" Ezio said. "Good to see you! Having a good time with us country folks after cosmopolitan Florence?"

"We're always glad to get away from Florence," Sofia said. "More tourists every year, more pollution, more garbage in the streets."

"And now the Arno is starting to smell even worse," Dino added.

"And that," Donna said, "is why we like living up here. A visit to Florence twice a year is quite enough."

Ezio poured coffee and they sat around discussing the weather, the new prime minister and Sant'Antonio's new piazza.

"The best thing that's ever happened to the village," Ezio said.

Dino hesitated, then plunged in. "Ezio, I've become curious about my father. I'd like to find out more about him. How well did you know him?"

Ezio paused and thought a bit. "Your father. Well, it's been a long time, more than forty years. Sometimes I think my memory is going. I know he was Paolo's best friend, but you already know that. They joined my *banda* in the summer of 1944, but you know that, too. They were both from Montepulciano. I guess I'm not telling you anything new, right?"

"Not so far. Did you ever talk to him about anything?"

"In war, Dino, you don't talk a lot. At least we didn't. We had a job to do and we did it. I remember before that last battle, right in the olive grove near here, your father and Paolo had spent four days cutting telephone lines so that the Nazis in Sant'Antonio couldn't communicate with their unit in Reboli. Oh, and they also helped disconnect land mines that the Nazis had placed in these hills."

"Did he do any actual fighting?"

"Your father and Paolo were very important in playing cat-and-mouse with the Germans. They'd flush them out of their hiding places and then other guys would move in for the kill. I don't know if he actually shot anyone, though he was about to when that bloody

Nazi shot him. Your father was a hero, Dino. You can be very proud of him."

Dino was pleased to hear this and suddenly he was very proud of his father. But he still hadn't heard anything personal.

"How did he respond to orders?"

"Dino, you have to understand that your father and Paolo were only eighteen years old. They were the youngest in the group. Sometimes it took a while for them to grasp what we were going to do. Often we had to do things on the spur of the moment, and our men had to act quickly. Your father and Paolo might have been a little slow at first, but they caught on fast. When I asked them to do something, they did it. And they did it very well.

"I do remember, though, that he was kind of impetuous when we had to wait. Wanted to get started right away. Paolo was more laid-back."

Sofia laughed. "Well, Dino, you certainly haven't taken after your father in that regard. 'Impetuous' is about the last word I'd choose for you. 'Deliberate' is more like it."

"Hey," Dino said, "just because it took me thirteen years for me to ask you to marry me? I just wanted to make sure I made the right decision. And I did."

Dino was still looking for more personal information about his father. "Ezio, did you ever talk to him about growing up in Montepulciano? About his family? What did his father do? Did he have brothers or sisters? Did he have any friends?"

"Let me think. No, I can't say that I ever had a good talk with him. But then I didn't with the other partisans either. This was a very intense time. We were just focused on doing our jobs."

Pleased that he had learned this much, Dino was about to leave when Sofia turned back.

"Ezio," she said, "does Dino look anything like his father?"

"Oh, my, yes. At least you did when you were younger, Dino. Every time I looked at you when you were a teenager I saw your father. Tall, the slender build, the dark eyes, the curly hair, the smile, the freckles, though they seem to have faded now. Oh, and I hate to say this, but also the ears. His stuck out just like yours did."

"I wear my hair longer now so you can't see them so much," Dino said.

"Anyone who knew your father would know right away that you were his son, Dino. You can be very proud."

Donna had been listening to all of this quietly. Now she put her hand on Dino's arm. "Dino, let me say something. I think it's fine that you want to find out more about your father, but I think you should be prepared in case there are any surprises. They might not all be good surprises. Just a caution."

"I'll be careful, Donna. Thanks."

The heat was more intense as Dino and Sofia walked slowly down the hill to the village. "You know," Dino said, "I feel like my friend Giacomo, the newspaper reporter, asking questions like that."

"But this isn't a newspaper story," Sofia said. "It's your story."

"I'd like to think it's our story. Anyway, I hope it has a happy ending."

They found Lucia and Paolo suffering miserably from the heat in a stifling house. Lucia was in an armchair, her cotton dress unbuttoned at the neck, fanning herself with a newspaper. Paolo lay sprawled on the couch, his eyes closed. A rotating electric fan whirred in a corner, requiring everyone to talk louder.

"I had the windows opened but that just let more hot air in," Lucia said.

"This can't last long," Paolo muttered. "In a few weeks we'll be complaining about the cold."

"Not soon enough," his wife said. "Where did you two go?"

"We were up at the Cielo," Dino said.

"Oh. How are Donna and Ezio?"

"They're fine," her son said. "We stopped at my father's grave."

Lucia put the newspaper down. "That's nice." There was no expression in her voice.

"It's really nice up there. It even seemed a little cooler. Mama, can I ask you a few questions about him?"

Paolo sat up and Lucia stiffened. She stared straight ahead.

"Mama?"

"It's so hot today, Dino. Maybe some other time?"

"That's OK. If you don't want to talk about him, we don't have to."

She picked up the newspaper again and resumed fanning herself. "No, it's OK. I've often wondered when you'd ask. What do you want to know?"

"Mama, I hardly know anything about him. Ezio told me a few things just now about when he was in the *banda*. And Papa has told me how he was killed. But I just don't know anything about him personally. What was he like? Did he have any family, brothers and sisters?"

Paolo responded. "Dino, let me say something first. I knew your father for a year, from the time we met in the army and then when we deserted and joined the partisans. I can tell you for a fact that he never, ever, said anything about his family. I would talk about mine, how my father took me to soccer games in Montepulciano and how he taught me to play cards and stuff like that. How my mother was such a great cook but how she liked to sneak a little more wine than she should. How my little brother always followed me around. I don't think Dino liked it when I talked about my brother. His face got very strange and he changed the subject. He never said anything about his family, nothing. Not a word."

"You didn't know him in Montepulciano?"

"No. Had no idea he was from there until one night when some of us were playing cards and he happened to mention it. But that's all he ever said. I don't know what district he lived in. I don't remember any other Pezzinos in Montepulciano. He couldn't have belonged to our church or gone to my school or I would have known."

"Did he ever talk about what he wanted to do after the war?"

"Oh, yes. Travel the world, travel the world. That's all he talked about. 'I want to see the world,' he would say. I'd say, 'Don't you want to marry and have kids and settle down?' and he'd say, 'I want to see the world!' One time we went to Siena and he got so excited when he saw the Campo. Thought it was the most beautiful piazza in the world. Then he decided he wanted to see Florence and Rome. It was almost like he was running, running, running."

Lucia listened to all this without comment and without emotion and then went upstairs.

WHEN SHE RETURNED, Lucia carried a small plastic bag. She eased back into her chair and fanned herself some more.

"Paolo, I've never shown you this."

"What is it?"

"I kept it under my underwear in the bottom drawer of my dresser. Thank goodness you've never looked there."

"Good grief. Why would I look there?"

"You're always looking for candy."

"Sometimes I find some."

"Anyway, this is a diary I kept when we were trapped in the Cielo during the war. I wrote some things about your father here," she told Dino.

Dino leaned forward. He couldn't imagine his mother being a young girl in the first place and now he couldn't fathom her keeping a diary. This was not the woman he knew as his mother.

Lucia took out the little black leather-bound book tied with a pink ribbon. The cover was torn and scratched and some pages were falling out.

"See this? These pages were ripped out by that nasty Nazi soldier when they invaded the Cielo. He was laughing as he did it and I was crying. His name was Konrad, I remember the other soldier calling him that. I think he would have done even more to me if they hadn't been in a hurry. After they left my mother wanted to see what I had written but I wouldn't show her."

She paused and opened the book. "I started the diary when we first got to the Cielo. Mama, my two little brothers, Anna my sister, and the baby, Carlotta. I was so very lonely."

In a faltering voice, she began to read.

"*We are stuck up here on the hilltop. Now nobody knows when we will go back. I think we will be up here forever. There's no one but old people and us and Carlotta wakes me up every morning with her crying. God I hate some of those women. They think I'm still a child. How can I ever meet someone if we stay up here forever? I'm going to be an old spinster like Fausta Sanfilippo. Or worse, Anna and me are going to be like the Spinelli sisters. Maybe we'll wear our hair funny like them and keep our jewels on all the time. That wouldn't be so bad.*

"*Yesterday everyone decided that we can't go out alone up here. I tried to complain but they didn't even listen to me. They think I'm a child. Why can't I just go for a walk around the house? I can take care of myself.*

"*Mama's so busy with Carlotta and the others I don't have a chance to talk to her. She probably wouldn't listen anyway. We haven't talked for so long I wouldn't know what to say. I wish we would hear from Papa.*

Maybe he's been taken prisoner. Maybe it's something worse. I wish I was back home. I wish I could talk to Daniela and Carmella again. I don't even know where they were sent. God I wish I was home.'"

Paolo looked away and Sofia grabbed Lucia's hand. "Oh, Lucia, that's so awful. I feel so bad that you went through that."

"Well," Lucia said. "I know now it was wartime. I just didn't understand then. I guess I was so selfish, just thinking about myself and being alone. Here people were dying all around us."

"You were sixteen years old," Sofia said. "It was natural to feel that way."

"Well," Lucia said, "then Paolo and his friend arrived. Paolo had hurt his ankle and I got one of my nightgowns and tore it up to make a bandage."

"You made a bandage for Papa out of your nightgown?" Dino said. "I can't believe it."

"But," Paolo said, "you weren't really paying any attention to me. You just kept staring at my friend Dino."

"Oh, Paolo, that's not true," Lucia said. "I looked at you, too. But Dino said I was a pretty girl, and he asked me what my name was. I said Lucia, and he said, 'Like the light in the tower.'"

Her son groaned. "My father said that? How corny! God, what a line he had."

"Don't laugh," Lucia said. "Sure, I knew he was cocky. I even wrote it down here. *'The boy named Dino is more cocky than he should be. Still, he is kind of cute. And I like his smile. And his freckles.'*"

"His freckles! Mama, you wrote that?"

"Don't laugh, Dino," Sofia said. "She was sixteen years old. And anyway, I was attracted to your freckles when I first met you."

"My freckles? Good God."

"Well," Lucia said, "Paolo here still couldn't walk so he and Dino stayed in the old guy's hut nearby. His name was Gavino. And Dino came to visit me. Often. I guess you can imagine what happened."

"Yes," Dino said. "I happened."

"You have to understand," Lucia said. "Dino was my first real boyfriend. At least I thought he was. And I was so lonely and scared. Our father was off fighting somewhere and we didn't know where he was. We could hear bombs and we didn't know what was happening to our house in the village. And little Carlotta was getting sicker and sicker. It was such a terrible time."

Paolo got up and stood in back of Lucia's chair, his arms around his wife's shoulders. She turned a few more pages in her diary.

"Oh my. I don't think I should read this."

"You don't have to, Mama," Dino said.

"Well, you want to know about your father, so I will. Here's what it says. I wrote this after spending an afternoon with him. *'I think I'm in love!!!!! He is so cute. And sweet. I think he loves me too!!!! He hasn't said so yet, but I think he wants to marry me. I would do anything for him, anything.'"*

Paolo looked down at the book. "She drew a heart at the bottom of the page and wrote 'Lucia + Dino' inside," he told the others.

"Oh, Lucia," Sofia said. "That's so sweet."

Dino groaned again.

Lucia turned another page and looked at what was written before she read it aloud. "I guess I can read this. Remember this was how I was feeling then.

"'I just want to be with him forever. Sometimes he scares me when he talks about all the places he wants to go and what he wants to see. When he talks like that he doesn't seem to include me. Other times he tells me how much he loves me and how much he wants us to be together. That's the Dino I like.

"'I don't know how long they're going to stay at Gavino's. Paolo's foot is getting better. Dino says they shouldn't stay in one place too long. I asked him if I could go with them and he just laughed. I hate it when he treats me like a child. I'm going to be seventeen in November. A lot of girls get married when they're seventeen. Wouldn't that be something? I would have a simple little wedding. I know the dress I would wear. I saw it in Reboli. Daniela and Carmella will be my bridesmaids. Anna can be my flower girl. Even Roberto and Adolfo can be in it, maybe even Carlotta. Maybe Papa will be back by then and he can give me away. Maybe the war will be over by then and Dino wouldn't have to be running all the time. I don't know when I'll see him again now. He can't come here and I can't go there because someone will see us. I don't know how I can even get a message to him. I am so afraid.'"

"Mama, you don't have to read any more," Dino said. "Really, that's enough."

"No, I want to finish the story. I remember your father came the day after little Carlotta died. He said he and Paolo were going to join the partisans. I told him he wasn't a fighter and he said he would learn to be one. Can you imagine? Nobody thought straight in those days. We had a big fight. I begged him not to go, but he said he had to. I'll never forget the last words he said to me. He held me and he said, 'I'll always remember little Lucia, the light in the tower.'"

Another groan from Dino.

"Well, we know what happened," Lucia continued. "Mama and I even saw him being shot. I wanted to go down to him but Mama wouldn't let me."

"Lucia and some others helped me bury him," Paolo said.

"I never thought I'd find someone who would get me through this," Lucia said, holding Paolo's hand, "but I found the most wonderful man in the world. I know I don't say that often, but that's how I feel. He got me through all the pain and he never asked questions. And Paolo has been a good father, right?"

"The best anyone could wish for," Dino said.

Lucia turned a few more pages. "Here's the very last entry. I wrote it two days after you were born."

"*Dear Dino, I wish you could see our baby. He looks just like you. He has black curly hair and big ears and I think he's going to have freckles.*

"*I'm sorry we parted so angry. I have thought of you every day since then and I'm so sorry I said such awful things to you. I know now that you wanted to see so much more of the world than just our little village and I should have understood that. I wish we could have talked again.*

"*It's too late now. Wherever you are, I hope you can see Little Dino and know that he is the joy of my life now, just as you were for me for such a few short weeks. Know that I will love you always.*'

"I tied the diary with this pink ribbon, put it at the bottom of my dresser and I never looked at it again until now."

Paolo knelt on the floor next to his wife. "Lucia, I've never told you this, but I might as well tell you now. The night before the firefight, Dino told me he was thinking about you. I asked him why, since he never talked about other girls he'd been with. And he said you were different. He said you had a mind of your own and he'd never met another girl like you. And then he said, 'After the war is over, Paolo, I'm going to go to Sant'Antonio and find Lucia.' He really did love you, Lucia."

"And I loved him. But that was an eternity ago. I love you now. And I have Little Dino."

"Don't call me that!" Dino said, but he was smiling.

LUCIA RETIED THE DIARY WITH THE PINK RIBBON and returned it to the plastic bag. In the silence that followed, Dino and Sofia stared straight ahead, Paolo sat back on the couch and closed his eyes and Lucia resumed fanning herself.

"Mama," Dino finally said, "I've often wondered why you didn't give me my father's name, Pezzino? Or Papa's?"

"I don't know. Paolo and I were married by the time you were born so I could have called you a Ricci, even though you weren't Paolo's son. I guess I was still kind of mad at your father so I didn't give you his name. So you're a Sporenza, like me."

"It doesn't matter. Really," Dino said. "Still, Dino Pezzino has a nice rhythm to it, I think."

"Don't even think of changing it now, Dino," Sofia said.

"Not a chance. But now I'm curious about the Pezzinos. Are you sure there aren't any in Montepulciano, Paolo?"

"No, I'm not at all sure. I just said I didn't know any."

Dino looked at his wife. "Well, Sofia, guess we'd better look for ourselves. It's only Tuesday and we've got the week off. We can go tomorrow and spend a few days there."

"Tomorrow?" Lucia cried. "But you just got here! I was going to make ravioli tomorrow."

"Better go, Dino," Paolo said. "You don't know what fate you're missing."

So it was decided. Dino and Sofia would drive to the medieval hill town southeast of Siena in the morning. With luck they would be able to find a Pezzino family in Montepulciano that very day.

"And where are we going to begin, if I may ask, Dino?" Sofia said.

"Hmmm. Well, there must be telephone books. We can start there."

"Dino," Paolo said, "if you're going to go into your history, try the churches. They keep records of births, deaths, marriages. Just go to the church offices and ask someone to look up the name. My brother did this for our family years ago and he was able to trace generations back to the 1700s."

"Good idea. What churches?"

"The good news is that the churches keep records. The bad news is that there are a ton of churches in Montepulciano. There's the Church of Santa Maria dei Servi, and the Church of Saint Augustine, and the Church of the Gesù, and the Church of Saint Bernard, and, let's see, the Church of Santa Lucia, the Church of Saint Agnese, the Chapel of Saint Anthony, and of course the Duomo, the Cathedral of Santa Maria Assunta. And down in the valley is the Sanctuary of San Biago. That's mostly a tourist attraction these days, but they may have old records. I am probably forgetting some."

"Good God," Dino said. "Maybe we'd better start now."

"No!" Lucia cried. "You can go tomorrow."

And they did. Predictably, Lucia began crying as they were leaving, and Paolo took Dino aside before he stepped into the car.

"Dino, maybe I told you too much about your father. I was thinking last night after you went to bed. I know he said he wanted to see the world, but I wonder if that was just talk. I do know that he didn't want to go back to Montepulciano. So I don't know what you'll find there. It may not be pleasant, Dino. Just be prepared."

"You know, that's exactly what Donna said yesterday. I will, Papa, I will."

Paolo hugged Dino as tightly as on the day long ago when the boy went off to study in Florence.

The drive on the Autostrada from Sant'Antonio around Lucca and on to Florence went quickly, with little traffic on another hot August day. There was more traffic on the Florence interchanges, but then they switched to Via Chiantigiana on the way to Siena.

"My favorite drive," Dino said.

Sofia, who was driving, agreed.

Motoring between the Val d'Esla and the Valdarno, they went through miles of vineyards and pastures, with castles and towers in the green undulating hills in the distance. Then came the towns, Greve, Panzano, Castellina, each inviting a stop, but Dino and Sofia were too anxious to reach their destination.

They drove around Siena, remembering how Dino's father had liked it so much, and then on the winding road through the hills and the towns of Castelnuovo Berardenga, Rapolano Terme, Sinalunga, Torrita di Siena and Abbadia.

"Whoever made up these names must have been a poet," Sofia said.

"Or had a sense of humor," Dino said.

They parked their Fiat at the base of the hill and climbed the winding path to the Porta al Prato and then to the center of Montepulciano.

"The streets are almost as steep as Siena's," Dino said, breathing hard.

"Good for your legs," Sofia said.

They had a *panini* and coffee at an outdoor café that provided a little shade from the beastly sun, then asked the café manager if they could look at a telephone book. Not to feel too cheap, Dino bought a guidebook.

Montepulciano's phone book wasn't large, and the "Ps" took only a few pages. Dino recited the names.

"Perri, Perrone, Pesciano, Petrolo, Peverelli, Pezzati, Pezzino . . . Pezzino! There are two, Sofia! Take down these numbers."

They found a telephone booth near the Piazza Grande. Dino gripped the phone hard as he dropped the coins in the box and dialed.

"Doesn't look like there's anyone home," he told Sofia as she waited just outside. "Six rings now. Wait!"

He could hear a faint woman's voice on the other end. "*Pronto!*"

"*Buongiorno,*" Dino said, raising his voice. "Hello?"

"I don't think she can hear me," he told Sofia.

"Talk loud!"

"*Buongiorno!* Hello! Can you hear me?"

Nearby tourists started to stare at this crazy man in the telephone booth.

"Can you hear me?" Even louder.

"Good! Were you related to Dino Pezzino?"

He couldn't hear the response.

"Dino Pezzino! D-I-N-O P-E-Z-Z-I-N-O. Dino Pezzino! Were you related to him?"

Dino held the phone away from his ear.

"She hung up."

"Well," Sofia said, "if she had been related, she probably wouldn't have been able to tell us anything anyway. Try the other number."

This one responded after three rings.

"*Buongiorno!*" Dino shouted, not taking any chances. "Do you know if you were related to a man named Dino Pezzino? This would have been about forty years ago."

Pause while he listened.

"OK, I'll stop shouting. Do you know if you or your family were related to a man named Dino Pezzino? He lived in Montepulciano and he was killed in World War II."

Pause.

"Why do I want to know? I'm his son. I live in Florence."

Pause. Dino put his hand over the receiver and whispered to Sofia. "I think he's talking to his wife."

"Hello! Yes, I'm here."

Pause.

"You think you might be related somehow but you didn't know him? Do you have any relatives who might have known him?"

Dino's heart started beating faster.

"Cortona? You think there is somebody in Cortona?"

Pause.

"Yes, I heard. Cortona. I know where that is. Near Umbria. Who do you think is there?"

Pause.

"Maybe a distant cousin? Great. Do you know a name?"

Pause.

"That's OK. We can go there and I'll try to find him. Is it a him or a her?"

Pause.

"A him. OK. Do you know where he lives?"

Pause.

"That's OK. Why do I want to know? I'm trying to find out more about my father. I was born after he was killed in the war."

Pause.

"Yes, it was a terrible war."

Long pause.

"I know. The Fascists were terrible."

Another long pause.

"Yes, OK. Well, thank you very much. You've been very helpful. Oh, what's your name?"

Pause.

"Well, thank you, Salvatore Pezzino. *Molte grazie! Arriverderla!*" Dino hung up the phone. "He was starting a harangue about the Fascists and the partisans and I've heard too many of those."

"Well, at least he sounds like he was on the right side."

"Sofia! We've got a lead. We're going to Cortona!"

Sofia grabbed his arm. "Not so fast. We should check church records as long as we're here. Paolo said they have records of births, deaths, marriages."

"Oh, right," Dino said. "I almost forgot. And he also said there are tons of churches in Montepulciano. I have no idea where to start."

"The Duomo is over there. Might as well start there."

"That's the Duomo?"

IT WASN'T UNTIL THEY GOT TO THE MAIN DOOR that they saw the sign: *Chiuso!*

"Well, of course it's closed," Sofia said. "It's 1:30. Everybody's taking a nap."

As long as they had to wait, they found another small table in the shade opposite the cathedral and ordered another coffee.

Accustomed to the magnificent Duomo in Florence and the gleaming white marble edifices in Siena and Pisa, they couldn't believe that the imposing mass of gray stones before them was Montepulciano's cathedral.

"It's officially the Cathedral of Santa Maria Assunta," Dino said, reading from the guidebook. "'It was built between 1594 and 1680 and stands on the site of the old Church of Santa Maria. Its Florentine architectural style is characterized by austere and elegant lines. The façade is unfinished.'"

"Oh, so they're still working on it," Sofia said, "only four centuries later."

"This book says there are several masterpieces inside, the Assumption of the Virgin triptych painted by Taddeo di Bartolo, Michelozzo's Aragazzi funeral monument, the Madonna del Pilastro by Sano di Pietro . . ."

"Enough!" Sofia said. "My eyes glaze over if I have to see three masterpieces at one time. Anyway, we don't have time for a tour. I'd rather look at people. Look at that girl over there. She hardly has any clothes on."

"Yes, I noticed her before."

"I'm sure you did."

Trailing tour guides holding umbrellas aloft, lines of tourists traipsed past the cathedral to visit other sites, the Palazzo Comunale, the Palazzo Tarugi, the Palazzo Bucelli, on their way to the valley just outside to visit Montepulciano's masterpiece, the Renaissance church of San Biagio.

"When I was a student at the Accademia," Dino said, "our class took a tour of this whole area. I remember drinking wine but the only building I remember is San Biagio."

"My girlfriend and I drove down one Saturday years ago just to see it," Sofia said. "I'll never forget it either."

"It's magnificent."

More lines of tourists filed by, Germans, Americans, Germans, Japanese, English, Germans. Sofia and Dino began to nod off, but at last it was time to see if the church was open. It was.

They stumbled through the dark interior trying to find someone in charge. In the sacristy they found an elderly nun sorting candles in a box. Dino explained what they were looking for.

The nun shook her head. "I'm not the person in charge. You'll have to come back."

"When?"

"Next week sometime." She turned back to sorting her candles.

"But, Sister," Dino said, "we're here only for today. I really would like to find out if my father was baptized here. I never knew my father. He was killed in the war and I don't know anything about him. But I'm named after him and people say I look like him and . . ."

Sofia thought he was laying it on rather thick, but the nun melted.

"All right," she said, "come with me."

The huge room off the sacristy was lined on all four walls with bookshelves that climbed to the ceiling. Hundreds of thin leather-bound books filled the shelves, top to bottom.

"If we have to go back before 1745, we will have to go to another room," the nun said.

She explained that the books were arranged by year, marriages for a decade in one book, deaths for decade in another, baptisms in a third. There was an index for each year.

"This is a very good system," the nun said. "If your father is here, we will find him. Now, what year was he born?"

"Either 1925 or 1926," Dino said.

"And his full name?"

"Dino . . . no, it's actually Aldobrandino, Aldobrandino Pezzino."

Sofia stifled a laugh. She had forgotten Dino's full name but then remembered that it was on her own marriage certificate.

The nun pulled a ladder along the shelves and nimbly climbed to the third highest. She took down a book and brought it to a massive table in the middle of the room. So much dust exploded when she put it down that Sofia sneezed.

Engraved on the cover were the words "Baptisms, 1920-1929."

"All right, let's see if there are any Pezzinos in here," she said.

She turned to the "P's" and ran her thin finger down the list for 1920. Nothing. 1921. Nothing. 1922. Nothing.

"OK, you said maybe 1925. Maybe there will be something here." Nothing.

1926. Nothing, and nothing for the rest of the decade.

"I'm sorry, son. I wish I could help."

"What does this mean, Sister?"

"It means that there was no Pezzino baptized in the Duomo of Santa Maria Assunta in the 1920s. That doesn't mean that your father wasn't born someplace else. We only keep records for our church. You'll have to try the other churches."

"And there are many," Sofia said.

"Yes, we are very fortunate," the nun said as she climbed the ladder to return the book. *"Buona fortuna!"*

"Thank you very much," Dino said. "We'll need all the luck we can get."

Shielding their eyes from the brilliant sun as they left the church, Dino and Sofia leaned against the rough façade as more and more tourists trouped by.

"Well, one down," Dino said.

"Only four thousand more to go," Sofia said.

"Not that many." He consulted his guidebook. "But a few."

They decided that there wasn't time to visit another church that day and even the next day would be filled, so they found a pensione near Palazzo Cervini. Since they had planned to stay the week at Lucia and Paolo's, they had clothes to spare.

"We really should bring some wine back," Dino said. "*Montepulciano d'Abruzzo* is known all over the world and we can probably get it cheap here."

The half case they bought at one of the zillion wine shops in the city actually wasn't any cheaper than what they would have paid in Florence, but at least they could say they got it in Montepulciano.

The next morning, after going through the guidebook another time, they decided to whittle the list of churches down to six, with each of them taking three.

At the massive Church of Santa Maria dei Servi, Sofia found a frail elderly priest in the records room and had to climb a ladder and retrieve the index book by herself. Breathing hard, the priest seemed to take an eternity to find the right page. Nothing.

She walked past the Church of the Gesù three times, not realizing that the flat stone façade held a religious purpose. She was surprised by the lovely Baroque interior, and almost bumped into a cleaning lady who volunteered to check the records. Nothing.

At the Church of Saint Augustine, she almost had to get on her knees to get a very reluctant cleric to look up the records. Nothing.

Meanwhile, Dino was making his own futile search, finding no record of a Dino Pezzino being baptized in the 1920s in the Church of Saint Bernard, the Church of Saint Agnese or the Church of San Francisco.

Exhausted, Dino and Sofia met back at the pensione that evening and exchanged notes on their unsuccessful encounters. Dino was pleased to tell Sofia that the body of Saint Agnese was perfectly preserved under glass in the church named for her.

"I swear to God," he said.

"Good lord," Sofia said. "That's the same as Saint Zita in the Basilica of San Frediano in Lucca. If I go to church, which I don't very often, I don't want to stare at a dead body."

"It does give one a perspective, though," Dino said. "Anyway, I thought of something today as I was making my rounds. Paolo said that my father was from Montepulciano. That doesn't mean he was born here. He could have been born anywhere in Italy and the family moved here later, right?"

"Right," Sofia said, "but I'm really not up to visiting every church in Italy."

"No, of course not. I guess we should just go on to Cortona tomorrow and see if we can find that guy who is supposed to be related."

Before turning off the light, Dino looked at the Montepulciano guidebook one more time.

"Sofia!" he said, waking his wife. "I don't know how I missed this one. There's a little Church of Saint Lucia on a side street. Baroque. Built in 1653. Has a painting of the Madonna by Signorelli."

"I really don't care about Signorelli," Sofia said, "but let's stop before going to Cortona. I don't have much hope, though."

AFTER COFFEE AND HARD ROLLS THE NEXT MORNING, Dino and Sofia had to ask three people for directions to the Church of Saint Lucia.

"I think we've seen more of Montepulciano than I want to," Sofia said as they retraced their steps and started over. "Certainly more churches."

They were rewarded when they finally found the pretty little church, with its gray marble exterior in a classic Baroque style.

"I don't know why, Sofia, but I feel good about this one," Dino said.

Inside, they found another accommodating nun, Sister Colombina, who was delighted to look up records. She said she hadn't been asked to do so in more than a year.

"I love to think about all these people in these books," she said. "I wonder who they were and how they lived. I pray for all of them every night."

She climbed to the top shelf in the records room and pulled down the "Births: 1920-1929" volume.

Like every other book that had been retrieved for Dino and Sofia in the last two days, it was covered with dust. As if she were bathing a baby, Sister Colombina carefully wiped it off with a clean handkerchief and started looking at the "P's" year by year.

"Nothing so far," she said as she reached 1926. "Maybe this year. Let's see. Pennachia. What an interesting name. I wonder what little Luca is doing now. Perconti. I remember that family. Maria must have been the third. There were nine children. Perritino. I think the father had a tobacco shop. His wife died just last year."

Dino and Sofia were getting nervous.

"Now, here are more names. Pesce. Pesciano. Pezzino. Pezzino! That's what you are looking for, isn't it?"

"Yes!"

"Aldobrandino Pezzino! He was born June 9, 1926."

"That's him!" Dino said. "That would make him eighteen when he was killed. Oh, Sister, this is so exciting."

Dino was so excited, in fact, that he touched the name on the page as if to bring his father to life.

Sister Colombina traced her figure down the page. "Wait! There's another Pezzino. Alessandro Pezzino. Born June 9, 1926!"

"Twins!" Sofia exclaimed.

"My father had a twin brother? I could never have imagined that. Sister, we're even more grateful now."

"Twin boys," Sister Colombina said. "What blessings God gave your family. Twice as many, in fact. I have to say, though, I never knew any Pezzinos in our church. It could be, of course, that they didn't come to church, God bless their souls. I will pray for all your family."

Dino and Sofia were about to leave when the nun stopped them. "Wait. We can look up the actual baptism record."

She went to another wall, climbed a ladder and pulled down a book labeled "Baptisms, 1920-1929."

"Let's see. If they were born on June 9, they were probably baptized a few days later. That's what they did in those days."

She found the page and then the entry. Aldobrandino Pezzino. Baptized June 12, 1926. Next to it was an identical entry for Alessandro Pezzino.

"But here's the interesting thing," Sister Colombina said. "This tells us the names of the parents. See? Son of Giovanni Pezzino and Regina Bagni. Same for Alessandro."

"I don't know why women in Italy keep their surnames," Dino said. "It gets very confusing."

"So you want me to take your name?" Sofia said. "Not a chance."

"OK, never mind," Dino said. "Sister, is it possible now to look up a marriage record for Giovanni and Regina?"

"Of course!"

She went to a third wall and pulled down the "Marriages, 1920-1929" book and quickly found the record for a marriage on February 5, 1926.

"This gives their birthdates, too. Giovanni was born on January 15, 1890, and Regina was born on April 4, 1910."

Sofia was furiously taking notes. "That means your grandfather was thirty-six and your grandmother sixteen when they were married. Interesting."

Then the good nun volunteered to search the "Deaths" book.

"Oh, I'm so sorry," she said after finding the right page. "It seems that your grandmother, Regina, died on June 9, 1926. She must have died in childbirth. The poor woman, after giving birth to two beautiful boys. And so young! Just a child herself! Did you see the lovely painting of the Madonna by Signorelli in the church? Before you leave, stop there and say a prayer for your grandmother."

Sister Colombina made the sign of the cross.

The nun also searched other books to see if she could find a death record for Dino's grandfather Giovanni, but could not find any.

"Here's what I would like to think," Sister Colombina said, making up a story on the spot. "Your grandfather was so heartbroken by the death of his wife that he let a family member raise his sons and he entered a monastery and prayed night and day for the rest of his life."

"That's a nice thought, Sister," Dino said. "I don't know how to thank you for all you've done."

"Would you like me to go back further? Our records go back to 1710, although some of the early ones aren't as complete."

"No, thank you, Sister. We're pretty overwhelmed with what you've already told us. Thanks again."

"Well, say a prayer for the poor starving children in China. They need our prayers so badly."

She allowed Dino and Sofia to kiss her on both cheeks.

After a brief prayer before the Signorelli painting, they settled in their car and Sofia went through her notes to see what they had just learned.

"Let's see. Your grandfather and grandmother were married on February 5, 1926. Your father and his twin brother were born on June 9 of that year. That's only four months later, but we won't think about that. Your grandmother died in childbirth. Your father died in the war. That leaves only your grandfather Giovanni and your uncle Alessandro and we don't know where they are. Your grandfather would be ninety-eight so he's probably not with us anymore."

"Probably not, but I doubt if he spent his life in a monastery praying day and night."

"Your uncle would be about sixty-two now so he may not be with us anymore either."

"Like my father. Sofia, now I'm both scared and excited. They say twins are like each other. So Uncle Alessandro might be a lot like my father."

"You know what everyone has been telling you. Be prepared for some bad news."

"I thought I was, but now . . . well, I really want to find my uncle or at least something about him. I hope we can."

"Maybe the guy in Cortona will know something."

THEY COULD HAVE STAYED in Montepulciano for an early lunch but Dino was too eager to get going and Sofia said she wasn't hungry anyway. They ran down the hill to their car and Sofia veered out of the parking lot and onto the highway. It was another hot and steamy day but somehow they didn't notice.

"You're awfully quiet," Sofia said as they drove through the hills. "Worried?"

"Hmmm? No. Not worried. Just curious. I wonder if he'd be, what do they call it, a fraternal or identical twin. I hope he's identical."

"So that you look like him?"

"Maybe. But not if he's a jerk. Only if he's a nice guy. I'm joking, of course."

"Well, you know what they say, 'You can chose your friends but not your relatives.'"

"Sofia, I'm just so excited knowing that maybe soon I'll find some relatives on my father's side."

"I know, hon."

In less than an hour they had reached the ancient Etruscan city of Cortona.

"Look," Dino said, "there's a church in the valley that looks sort of like San Biagio in the valley just outside of Montepulciano. It's beautiful."

"I like San Biagio better, but this is nice."

With steep streets that curve around medieval buildings, with red tile roofs, with a grand piazza, with quaint fountains, with busy markets and with a surplus of fine churches, Cortona could be the prototype for every Tuscan hill town. Dino and Sofia had never been there before.

"This is really beautiful," Sofia said. "Look how far you can see in the distance."

"Somebody should make a movie here," Dino said.

"Maybe someday they will."

At a café, Dino purchased a guidebook and asked to borrow a telephone book. Over coffee and *paninis*, they went through the phone book, finding only one Pezzino.

"The name is Bruno," Dino said. "I'll make the call."

It took five rings before someone answered, and there seemed to be a lot of laughing and yelling in the background.

"Hello? Hello?"

The response was muffled.

"Hello? Can you hear me?"

The man seemed to be saying yes.

"My name is Dino and I'm looking for relatives of my father, Dino Pezzino."

Another muffle.

"Yes, I said Dino Pezzino. Are you related?"

Dino couldn't understand the response but forged ahead.

"I would like to talk to you! Where do you live?"

Dino asked Sofia to take down an address.

"OK. Via Guelfa 4. Near Palazzo Baldelli in the center of town. Got it."

More muffles.

"Yes, my wife is with me. We'll be over in a little while."

Dino put the phone down and returned the telephone book to the café. "I'm not sure what was going on there. Sounded like there were twenty people on the line."

"Just a nice Italian family having dinner," Sofia said.

It was easy to find Palazzo Baldelli and the old apartment building nearby. Dino's heart started beating faster again when he saw "Pezzino" on a nameplate on the door. He touched it gently and then pushed the button. He thought he heard "third floor" when the speaker turned on.

"Here we go, Sofia!"

Dino took the stairs two at a time, with Sofia climbing right after. They had barely arrived at the third floor when a door down the hall opened.

"Dino! Dino! Dino!"

Dino found himself engulfed in the arms of a man whose breath smelled strongly of garlic. The man looked nothing like Dino had expected and Dino wondered if they could possibly be related. The man was short while Dino was tall, fat while Dino was slim, bald while Dino had a head of curly black hair. No sign of freckles or big ears.

"Dino! I am so happy to meet you! Come in, come in!"

The man pushed Dino into the room, where a large table was spread with an assortment of half-eaten meals. Around the table, at least fifteen people, young and old and of every size, looked up to see their new guests.

"We were just having a bite to eat," the man said. "You must join us."

A short woman, similar in size to the man, stood up. "Bruno, what are you thinking? Introduce yourself! How do you think Dino knows who you are?"

She came around the table and grabbed Dino and then Sofia, smothering them with hugs and kisses.

"My name is Veronica, and of course this is my husband, Bruno. We are so happy to meet you. Please, sit, sit, sit."

She shooed two of the smaller children away from the table, ran to the kitchen for more plates and virtually shoved Dino and Sofia onto chairs next to the table. "We have chicken and veal and linguini. There's a salad over there. Here, I'll help."

In seconds, the plates of the newcomers were filled. "Eat, eat!" Veronica commanded.

Dino and Sofia had little choice. They also realized that they hadn't said a word since they arrived.

Bruno now took over. "OK, you eat, and I'll introduce my family. Over here is Veronica's father, Luigi, and her mother, Maria Elena." He pointed to a wizened man who wore dark sunglasses and a tiny woman with dyed red hair. The woman smiled and nodded but the man apparently was blind.

"And these are our children," Bruno continued. "Here is our daughter, Analisa, and her husband, Pippino. We call him Pippi."

Pippi had his arm around Analisa as they leaned against a wall. Analisa looked as if she would have her baby any minute.

"And these are the children of Pippi and Analisa. There's Lorenzo and Luca and Franca. What do you say, children?"

"We are happy to meet you, Dino," Lorenzo and Luca and Franca chorused loudly together.

A young man about twenty-five, holding the hand of a pretty woman about twenty-three, stepped forward. "I'll introduce myself. I'm Rudolfo, the oldest son, and this is my girlfriend, Roberta."

Bruno now pointed to two teenage boys who looked remarkably alike. "These are Massimo and Michele, our twins."

"Twins!" Dino whispered to Sofia. "It runs in the family!"

"And over here," Bruno pointed to a little girl of about three and a boy about two who were teasing a cat in the corner, "are Luciana and Silvio, our youngest."

Dino lost count but guessed that there were fifteen people in the family. He finally had a chance to say something.

"Signor Luigi, Signora Maria Elena, Signor Bruno, Signora Veronica, and all you others, I am so happy to meet you and I want you to meet my wife, Sofia."

"Sofia!" everyone whispered.

"Ah," Bruno said, "we must drink a toast to Sofia!" Two bottles were passed around, one of white, the other of red wine, and everyone except the smallest children filled their glasses.

"To Sofia!"

"And to Dino!" Bruno shouted.

Then it seemed as if everyone was talking to one another. Veronica pushed more chicken and veal and linguini onto Dino's and Sofia's plates. "Eat! Eat! We have lots of food. We cannot let it go to waste."

Dino and Sofia were virtually ignored as the rest of the family began a million conversations.

"What do you think is going on?" Sofia whispered.

"I don't know," Dino said. "They don't even know who we are or why we're here. Maybe they take in strangers every day."

"This is only Friday. What do they do on Sunday?"

"Well, it seems to be a very happy family. And you know what? I'd like to be a part of it. If they'd let me."

In about a half-hour, Analisa asked to be excused to lie down and her husband went into the bedroom with her. Maria Elena said her husband also wanted to nap and guided him into another room. Rudolfo and Roberta said they wanted to do some shopping, and the twins, Massimo and Michele, said they were going to see some friends. Dino couldn't help but scrutinize them.

"They must be identical," he told Sofia. "They really look alike."

The children, Lorenzo and Luca and Franca and Luciana and Silvio, seemed to disappear into thin air, along with the cat. Bruno and Veronica invited Dino and Sofia, who would later regret eating so much, to sit with them in the living room.

"I'm so happy, Dino, to meet you," Bruno repeated again. "Let me tell you a bit about myself."

This was followed by a long story of Bruno growing up on the outskirts of Cortona, how he served in the army for two years, how he went to the university to study business but didn't like it so he dropped out, how he found work as a tour guide and now had his own tourist business. The man talked nonstop, only taking a breath now and then for a sip of grappa. His wife listened as if she had never heard the stories before.

"I get such interesting tourists," Bruno continued, and plunged into a story about a German couple who couldn't believe all the coats of arms on the Palazzo Casali.

Dino tried to interrupt. "Bruno, I wonder . . ."

"And then," Bruno said, "there was a couple from England the other day. I don't like taking the English, they want everything just right and sometimes . . ." And he continued with stories about not two or three but a half-dozen English couples who had toured with him in recent years.

"But Bruno . . ." Dino said.

"Once I had a group of Americans. Now I always thought that Americans like to spend money so I took them to this wonderful leather store . . ." That story was followed by three tales of leather store excursions.

"Bruno, I'd really like to know . . ."

The stories continued through the afternoon. Even Veronica dozed off as her husband recounted tale after tale. After the huge meal, Sofia had trouble staying awake, too, and Dino knew he had to interrupt.

"Bruno . . . Bruno . . . Bruno . . ."

"Oh, Dino, I'm so sorry to be talking so much. As you can see, I love my job and I love to talk about it. There was a time . . ."

"Bruno, I have to tell you who I am and why I am here. Please, can I tell you?"

"Of course, Dino."

DINO THEN TOLD THE STORY about his father being killed in the war before Dino was born and how his mother had married his father's best friend. He said his father was buried where he was killed, at the top of a hill near the village of Sant'Antonio west of Lucca. He said he and Sofia had just come from Montepulciano and had found church records that showed that Dino's father had a twin brother and that his grandfather might still be alive. Dino said that he knew very little about his father and that he hoped he could find relatives who knew him or at least knew about him.

Bruno listened carefully. "I'm sorry to hear that your father is deceased, Dino. We have been out of touch with your family for so long. The war was a terrible thing. So many people died. Terrible war. Those Fascists . . ."

"Bruno, a man in Montepulciano said we might be related. How?"

"I can tell you."

He went to a desk and pulled out a brown envelope. Inside was a large piece of paper. Dino and Sofia leaned forward to look at it. So did Veronica.

"My brother did—what do you call it? Genealogical research? He made up this little family tree. See? There are a lot of other people here, but, look, he found that my grandfather, his name was Isadoro, was the brother of your grandfather. His name was Giovanni, right?"

"Yes! That's right!"

Sofia pulled a pen and a piece of paper from her purse.

"See how my grandfather had a son named Carlo and that your grandfather had twin sons, Aldobrandino and Alessandro. So you see this line? My father, Carlo, was a first cousin to your father and his brother. That would make us, you and me, distant cousins, second, third, I don't know. I never understand this cousin business. I suppose the reason I don't look like you is because I take after my mother's side. Just my bad luck, I guess."

"This is fascinating," Dino said. "Did you know my grandfather?"

"No. He had moved to the Garfagnana with Alessandro. We had lost all contact with him."

"The Garfagnana?" Dino said. "Really?"

"Oh, my," Sofia whispered.

"Why did you lose contact?" Dino asked. "He was your grandfather's brother. Wouldn't you have kept in contact?"

Bruno put the paper aside. "Dino, your grandfather, well, we heard stories that we didn't like."

"Stories?"

"They probably weren't even true. Stories about how he was acting, the enemies he made in the Garfagnana. We really didn't want to be connected anymore. Anyway, I suppose he's dead now."

"Did you have a fight?"

"A fight? No, no. We just got tired of all the talk."

"Talk? What kind of talk? I just don't understand."

"Oh . . . oh, just talk. I've said too much already."

Dino hoped that Bruno would say more, but he did not.

"What about," Dino said, "his son here, my uncle Alessandro?"

"I don't know, but I suppose he's still in the Garfagnana."

"You haven't been in touch with him either?"

"No, no. Dino, we have lost touch entirely."

"OK. If my uncle is still in the Garfagnana, do you know where he would live?"

"From what we've heard, Alessandro's father used to live near a village called Vagli Sotto. I don't know if Alessandro is still there. I don't even know if he's alive."

"Vagli Sotto? Maybe we should look for him there?"

"That's up to you, Dino. As you know, the Garfagnana is very difficult."

For a long time the only sounds in the room were made by the cat scratching a couch. Bruno, Veronica, Sofia and especially Dino knew what he would face if he attempted to find his uncle in the Garfagnana, especially in Vagli Sotto.

Stretching northward from Lucca between the Apuane Alps to the west and the Apennines to the east, the region known as Garfagnana is one of the most spectacular areas in Italy. Ancient villages, churches and fortresses dot the landscape among rugged high mountains and deep valleys along the Serchio River, reflecting a time and place little changed in a thousand years.

It is also one of the most treacherous places in Italy, with dense, almost impenetrable, forests, precipitous mountain slides and sudden changes in the terrain.

There are those who believe strange creatures have inhabited the Garfagnana, and stories about encounters with them sometimes spread from village to village, from isolated hut to isolated hut.

One of the strangest stories is about the small thirteenth-century town of Fabbriche di Carreggine. When a hydroelectric dam was built after World War II, a huge man-made lake was formed. In order to create the lake, Fabbriche di Carreggine had to be flooded and its residents were moved to the nearby town of Vagli Sotto. In 1958, 1974 and most recently in 1983, the lake was emptied for maintenance purposes, and what was left of the village of Fabbriche di Carreggine rose like an underwater Pompeii from the water. Its stone buildings, including the church of Saint Theodore with its ruined bell tower, a cemetery and a bridge, were frozen in time, and tourists could once again walk its muddy streets.

It is known as *Paese Fantasma,* the ghost village, and some in the Garfagnana say ghosts have been seen and strange events have occurred since the old village was flooded. On cold winter nights, some people say, the bells in the bell tower can be heard, no matter that the bells were removed long ago.

"I guess we all know the story of *Paese Fantasma*," Dino said. "I don't think I'm looking forward to going there."

"I've always thought the whole story was rather creepy," Sofia said.

It was now evening and suddenly everyone in the family materialized, Analisa and Pippi and Maria Elena and Luigi from their bedrooms, Rudolfo and Roberta from shopping, Massimo and Michele from watching a soccer game and Lorenzo, Luca, Franca, Luciana and Silvio from playing in other rooms.

"We will just have the leftovers," Veronica announced, bringing more plates out on the table.

Dino and Sofia could not imagine eating another bite and begged to be excused.

"It's been a long day," Dino said. "We really must get back to Florence. I think we will try to go to the Garfagnana tomorrow."

"No!" Veronica said. "You must have something to eat before you go. It's a long drive and you'll get hungry."

Dino insisted and Veronica insisted until she finally yielded, but only if she could pack up sandwiches for a trip that would take no longer than an hour and a half.

Before their guests left, the family lined up and each of them, including the very youngest, hugged and kissed so hard that Dino and Sofia were breathless.

"Now you have to promise me," Bruno said, "that you will come back. We never knew we had relatives from my father's side in Florence, so you have to come again."

"Perhaps next Sunday?" Veronica said. "I can make my special meal of . . ."

"No, no, I'm afraid not next Sunday. But I have your telephone number so I'll call you when we can come again. Soon, I hope."

On the way out the door, Bruno took Dino aside. "Be careful, Dino. You don't know what you will find."

On the way back to Florence, the sack of sandwiches in the backseat, Sofia asked Dino if he really meant it about visiting the family again.

"Sure. You know, Sofia, I really feel connected to them. I don't know if I could stand all those people and all those stories . . ."

"And all that food . . ."

". . . too often, but I feel that I'm starting to find my family. Now if we can only find my uncle."

"Unfortunately, in the Garfagnana."

THE NEXT MORNING, Sofia repacked Veronica's sandwiches, saying that they were "almost fresh," and wondered what she should wear for the trip to the Garfagnana.

"It's likely to be cool in the mountains," Dino said. "Put a sweater in the car."

Having lost a coin toss, Dino was elected to drive. As they often found on Saturday mornings, their car was wedged between two others with barely an inch to spare in the narrow space outside their apartment building. Muttering under his breath, Dino took almost a half-hour to free the Fiat and get the car on the road. After stopping at a tobacco shop to buy a map of the Garfagnana, they were off, heading west, first to Lucca, under another blazing sun.

"Dino," Sofia asked as they veered into the Autostrada, "have you ever been to the Garfagnana? I haven't."

"Hmmm. Well, Sofia, you're not going to believe this story, but I'll tell you anyway."

"I always love a good story."

When he was ten years old, Dino said, he sometimes got into trouble because he was so headstrong.

"You mean you were impetuous like your father, as Ezio said?"

"I guess so. Then."

"I don't believe it."

"Well, one day about ten years after the war, I found out that Papa and Ezio were going away to look for a Fascist who had taken part in a massacre in the war. As I've told you, Papa was in Ezio's *banda* and they had become good friends after the war.

"I didn't want Papa to leave. I followed him everywhere. I was practically his shadow. I said I wanted to go along and I guess I made a big scene. Mama said I couldn't go, it was too dangerous. I didn't listen. I had to go. So when no one was looking, I hid under a blanket in the backseat."

"You hid under a blanket? In the backseat? Dino! You didn't!"

"I did. I wasn't discovered until we were in Lucca. I remember my Papa telling me, 'I'll tell you, Little Dino, when you want something, nothing stops you.' Well, it was too late for them to bring me back home so they were stuck with me. And guess where we were going? To the Garfagnana!"

"I can't believe this."

"I'm just beginning. Papa and Ezio kept a close eye on me, but they were busy looking for the Fascist. They stopped several times, and one time I wandered off and I saw this little kid, about my size. Only he was all white and disfigured. He looked like a ghost. I wasn't afraid. In fact, we played a little until Papa called me back and when I turned around, the kid was gone. Papa and Ezio kept looking for the Fascist and I was tagging along and they found him in a big cave near Borgo a Mozzano. The guy was with this same little boy."

"Borgo a Mozzano. That's where the Devil's Bridge is," Sofia said.

"Yes. Well, the Fascist grabbed his son and ran toward the bridge with Papa and Ezio right after them. The boy got loose, climbed onto the bridge and got scared. He jumped into the river. The father then jumped into the river after him. They were never seen again. Later, Papa and Ezio found out that the father was innocent of the massacre and that the boy was disfigured because he had been burned in it."

"Ezio! That's an incredible story. You've never told me this. Why not?"

"It was so horrible. I didn't want to think about it. Still don't. I can still see that little boy jumping into the river. I used to have nightmares about it."

"I can see why."

"That's why I've never learned to swim. I don't even like being near rivers and lakes. That's why I won't go to Venice. Now we're going to Vagli Sotto where there's this huge lake and . . ."

Sofia grabbed Dino's arm. "OK, now you've got me nervous, too."

"After that trip, I never went into the Garfagnana again."

At Lucca, they turned north and drove along the Serchio River. Soon they were at the Devil's Bridge.

"I don't suppose you want to stop," Sofia said.

"No. Definitely not. I'm not even going to look at it."

"It's a funny story, though," she said. "The builder can't complete the bridge on time so he sells his soul to the devil, but then the builder tricks the devil who jumps into the river and is never seen again."

"It would be more funny if this were the only devil's bridge. But you know, Sofia, there are devil's bridges all over Europe, nine in Italy alone."

"People like to believe stories like that. It makes them feel good."

With his eyes almost closed, Dino drove past the bridge and toward the heart of the Garfagnana. The forests grew thicker and greener, the mountains higher. Soon the medieval town of Barga loomed on the right, the tower of the Duomo dominating the landscape.

"I had a friend who went to a '*sagra*' there," Sofia said, trying to keep their thoughts off their destination.

"A '*sagra*'?"

"It's a huge meal for hundreds of people. They eat in an orchard or vineyard and raise money for a cause. Hers was for an artist group."

Past Chifenti and Fornoli and on to Bolognana and Gallicano and then, after driving up and down the verdant mountainous route, they arrived at Castelnuovo di Garfagnana.

"This town is bigger than I had thought," Sofia said, consulting the map. "And look, there's all these other little towns, Piano di Pieve, Filicala, Poggio.

"If they were somewhere else, it would be fun to stop and visit. But not here. Not in the Garfagnana."

They saw a sign pointing west: Careggine. "Lovely little church," Sofia said as they slowed through the town. The mountains that surrounded them now were bare of forests, huge craggy gray masses crowned with snow.

And then another sign: Vagli Sotto. Dino felt sweat forming on his forehead, down his back and on his hands, and it wasn't from the heat.

"This is interesting," Sofia said, looking at the map even more closely. "There's a Vagli Sotto and a Vagli Sopra."

"'*Vagli*' means valley, '*sotto*' means below and '*sopra*' means above, so I guess there's a village in the valley below and another one above. We'd better try the one below. Here we go."

The Fiat made the slow descent into the valley.

"Well," Sofia said, "if your uncle does live here, he's in one of the most beautiful places on earth. This is gorgeous!"

Dino focused on driving down the hill and into the village. He easily found a parking place.

"Not much of a business district," he said.

In the center of the gray stone houses they could see a coffee shop, a restaurant, a pizzeria, a *gelateria* and a grocery shop. They tried the restaurant first.

A woman wearing a white apron was slicing bread behind the counter.

"Excuse me," Dino said, "would you know a Signor Pezzino who lives around here?"

Two men in overalls looked up from a nearby table.

"Pezzino?" the woman said. "No, I don't know a Pezzino around here."

"Maybe a sort of different name? Prezzano? Pizzano?"

"No, nothing. I'm very busy."

"OK, thanks. Oh, would you happen to have a telephone book for Vagli Sotto?"

The woman put down her knife and laughed. "A telephone book? You think Vagli Sotto is big enough for a telephone book?"

"OK, thanks."

The two men stared at Dino and Sofia as they left and then whispered to each other.

At the *gelateria,* a teenage boy leaned over the counter in deep conversation with a teenage girl.

"Excuse me," Dino said. "Excuse me! Excuse me!"

The boy finally looked up.

"I wonder if you know of a man named Signor Pezzino who lives around here."

"No." The boy went back to talking to the girl.

At the grocery shop, Dino waited in line at the cash register until the clerk was free. No, she didn't know the name. Two women behind him suddenly started whispering to themselves so Dino took a chance.

"Excuse me, do either of you know a Signor Pezzino?"

Both women appeared flustered and flushed. "No, no, we were just talking," one of them said, placing two cartons of milk and two dozen eggs next to the cash register.

"Do I get the impression that my uncle is actually here but nobody wants to talk about him?" Dino asked Sofia as they left the shop.

"I don't like conspiracy theories, but, yes, I think something's strange."

They almost missed a small building labeled *ufficio postale.*

"The post office!" Dino said. "They must know."

No one seemed to be inside and Dino shouted through the barred window at the counter. "Hello! Hello! Anyone here?"

It took several more "Hellos!" before an elderly man with a green eyeshade and a long black apron appeared. Dino explained that he was looking for Alessandro Pezzino, who was supposed to live in the area.

"Alessandro Pezzino? Why do you want to know?"

"He's my uncle."

The man examined Dino's face. "Your uncle."

"Yes."

"Possible."

"Where do you deliver his mail?"

The man had a crooked smile. "Mail? We haven't delivered mail to Alessandro Pezzino in months, maybe years. He never gets any mail."

"Do you think he's still alive?"

"Who knows?"

"Have you seen him lately?"

"No. Never."

"Well, can you tell me where he lives?"

"A mile and a half down a long dirt road. A little house with a flag." The man seemed to smirk. "Turn left at the church."

"Really! Great! Thanks!"

"Good luck, son."

AS THEY MADE THE TURN at the church, Sofia raised the subject they'd been avoiding since yesterday.

"Dino, your new cousin Bruno said that his family lost touch with yours because of all 'the talk.' What do you think he was talking about?"

"I wish I knew. He didn't want to go into detail. I suppose it's just gossip. Something happens and it's blown all out of proportion. Some people love that stuff."

"But it's usually based on some sort of facts, right? Something must have happened with your grandfather and your uncle."

"And you think that's why they moved from Montepulciano to the Garfagnana?"

"Possibly. Why would anyone move here without a reason? I mean, this is spectacular, the mountains so green, the valleys so picturesque. The little towns look as if they came out of picture books. But my God, it's isolated. I don't think I could live here for more than a week."

"That's just because you're used to Florence."

"But I grew up in a little village in Calabria, remember. This is different."

Dino, who was driving down the bumpy dirt road very slowly, tried to see if there were any houses in the distance,

"Oh, my God," he whispered. "Look over there. The lake!"

The huge lake was now in view, blue as the sky and surrounded by hills. There was no sign of life nearby, but a silent sentry in the middle of the lake announced what was below.

"It's the top of the bell tower of the ghost village!" Sofia cried. "It must have been dry here this summer so the water is lower."

Dino's hands were shaking. "*Paese Fantasma*. Even when the lake isn't drained you can see a part of it."

"Do you want to get out and go closer?"

"No! Let's keep driving."

They rounded a curve and came upon another mountain looming over them. Then another curve, another mountain.

"No small houses," Sofia said.

"Wait. Look over there."

Almost hidden by a cluster of pine trees, a little house stood far back from the road. Dino turned onto the dirt driveway.

"It doesn't look so bad," he said. "Rather nice, in fact."

Although the stone house was small, it was not dilapidated as they had expected. The red tile roof looked newly painted, and green shutters graced the two windows at the front of the house, matching the green door at the left. The most striking feature, however, was the flagpole that extended from the side of the house just below the roof. It displayed a multicolored striped flag with bold letters, "*PACE.*"

"It's a peace flag," Dino said. "I've seen a few of them in Florence, but not a lot."

"Interesting man, your uncle," Sofia said.

Dino knocked.

No answer.

He knocked again. The door slowly opened and Dino stepped back. The man was tall and thin, with dark curly hair that barely covered his protruding ears. His ruddy face had a faint hint of freckles. Dino felt if he were looking at his older self in a mirror. This, he thought, is what his father would have looked like.

"Signor . . . Signor . . . Pezzino?" Dino hesitated.

"Yes, I am Signor Pezzino."

"I am Dino. I am your nephew."

"My nephew? You mean . . . you mean you are . . . you are Dino's son?"

"Yes."

"My God! Come in, come in."

If they had expected the home of a single sixty-two-year-old man to be untidy, they were mistaken. Bookshelves, with volumes neatly in order, lined three walls. A blue-and-white afghan covered a couch next to a comfortable rocking chair that faced the television set. The wooden floor was polished to a shine. They could see a small kitchen off to one side and a bedroom to the other.

"My nephew! I can't believe it. You are Dino's son? Where is Dino? Was he killed in the war like we thought? Where are you from? Who is this with you? Your wife? How did you find me? I have so many questions I don't know where to begin."

Motioning to the couch, Alessandro invited Dino and Sofia to sit down, "but not on the lump." The lump came to life and a tan-and-white cat jumped out. "That's Bella. She loves company." When he pulled the rocker in front of them, Bella jumped onto his lap.

"Now, please tell me everything."

After introducing Sofia, Dino described how his father, Alessandro's twin brother, had joined the Italian army during the war but then deserted it and joined the Resistance, but he was killed in a firefight with Nazis in September 1944.

Alessandro sighed. "Well, I guess that's no surprise. We suspected as much when we didn't hear anything. Sometimes we hoped he escaped or was taken prisoner and then released, but that was just fanciful thinking. In our hearts, we knew he was dead."

"We?"

"My father and I. I'll get to that. How did you happen?"

Dino then told about how his mother had fallen in love with his father, leaving out the descriptions in her diary, and how she married his father's best friend.

"I was born after my father was killed," Dino said, "so I don't know anything about him, and lately I've been thinking about him a lot. So Sofia and I have started a search. We knew he was from Montepulciano, so we looked up records there and found a distant cousin in Cortona. His name is Bruno Pezzino."

"I'm afraid we lost track of all our relatives many years ago," Alessandro said.

"Bruno said that you might be living in Vagli Sotto, so that's why we're here. Uncle, you don't know how happy I am to find you."

Alessandro's eyes began to water. "I never, ever, knew that Dino had a child. And I never thought that I'd meet that child. And here you are. Imagine. My nephew! And you know, even if you hadn't told me, I would have known that you were Dino's son. You look so much like him."

He reached over and gripped Dino's hand.

"Oh, what am I thinking? You must be starving. I am so embarrassed. I have some bread and cheese, but I was going to the grocery this afternoon."

"Don't worry about it," Dino said. "We're just glad we're here."

"Wait!" Sofia said. She went to the car.

And so, seated around the small table and over day-old sandwiches and glasses of water, Alessandro began his story.

"AS YOU KNOW IF YOU'VE LOOKED AT THE RECORDS, my mother, your grandmother, died in childbirth. Father must have been devastated. I know there was a difference in their ages, but they must have loved each other very much. Father said she picked out our names, by the way. She had some other long ones if we'd turned out to be girls.

"Father didn't talk very much about my mother, but sometimes your father and I saw him holding her picture in the bedroom. He never married again.

"Somehow, he managed to raise your father and me on his own. People in Montepulciano knew us as the Pezzino twins. We may have looked alike, but we certainly didn't act alike. I don't think I was a problem, but your father? He was something. He didn't exactly disobey our dad, but he sure stretched the limit. Father would tell us to be home at 8 o'clock. Dino would come rushing in at 8:05. Father would wake us up at 7 o'clock to go to school. Dino would stay in bed until the last minute and then he'd gulp down his breakfast.

"I'll tell you, I was impressed. I wouldn't try any of that stuff, but I admired Dino so much. Father said I was the good twin and Dino was, well, you know."

Alessandro helped himself to another sandwich. Bella waited patiently by his feet.

"I was quite content in Montepulciano. I liked to read a lot and there were things for a teenager to do. But Dino wanted to do more. He was always saying that when he finished school he was going to do this or he was going to do that. He was going to leave Montepulciano and see the world. That's what he kept saying. I just laughed at him. I mean, who would be there to wake him up in the morning? He had such dreams! I admired that, too.

"He had a lot of friends, more than I did. But he didn't do very well in school. Father was always after him to do his homework. Study like your brother, he used to tell Dino. Dino didn't care. He just liked to have fun.

"When Mussolini came to power everything changed. Father hated him. He said that he was a dictator and that he would ruin Italy. Father would listen to the radio at night and get so angry. He knew that Mussolini would take Italy into war, and Father hated that. He was totally opposed to war. All war."

Alessandro paused to slip a piece of mozzarella to Bella.

"But then Dino decided to join the Italian army. He said it was a way to see the world. If the Italian army could go to Ethiopia, then it could go anywhere, he said, and he wanted to be a part of it.

"Father was so angry when Dino came home and told him that he'd lied about his age and enlisted. He yelled and screamed, but he couldn't do anything about it. The morning Dino left, Father took him aside and had a long talk with him. I couldn't hear. When Dino walked out the door Father cried and cried. I think he cried for days.

"So after Dino left it was only Father and me. He didn't want me in the army and he didn't want to be in any place where there was war. He checked out all the places in Italy and decided on the Garfagnana. The mountains were so thick with forests, the towns were so isolated. So we moved here to Vagli Sotto. The war would never find us here, he said. Well, we found out soon enough that it did, but I'll get to that.

"And we never saw Dino again. I'm not surprised that he deserted the army and joined the partisans. He probably got bored in the army and thought there would be more adventure with the partisans."

Alessandro paused to refill their glasses from the sink. Dino and Sofia noticed that his hands were shaking.

"I think it was after Dino left that Father became a real pacifist. Maybe it was *because* Dino left. Father had always hated Mussolini, and he also hated Hitler and the Nazis and the Italian Fascists. But he also hated the Communists. And he hated the Catholic Church. Why couldn't it be more like Saint Francis, he always said.

"I don't mean to say that he was a man filled with hate. He was a man filled with peace. He wanted people to put aside their differences and the politics and get along. He wanted people to do good. He wanted to help people.

"Of course, that didn't make him any friends here. The town was deeply divided during the war, those supporting the Fascists, those supporting the partisans. Sometimes it was brother against brother. But Father was the only one who didn't support either side.

"Then we found out that even the Garfagnana wasn't safe. Have you heard of the Christmas battle of Garfagnana in 1944?"

Dino said he'd heard of it, but didn't remember the details.

"The Germans called it Operation Winter Storm," Alessandro said. "It was an offensive by the Axis forces in the southern part of the Garfagnana and it began on December 26, 1944. German mountain troops and the Italian army wanted to capture Barga and rout the so-called Buffalo Division."

"I know about that division," Dino said. "It was composed entirely of African Americans."

"Yes. Well, the Allies sent in an Indian division for support, and the German and Italian forces withdrew. But then a week later those forces captured Barga and this whole area was occupied by the Germans until the end of the war the following May.

"This was a terrible time. You can't imagine life under the German occupation. I can't even talk about it. Father was terrified that I would be called up. I was eighteen and I could have been. So we kept moving. To Sillano, Corfino, Renaio. All these little towns where there weren't many Germans. He hid me in attics when the Germans were around.

"When the war ended we came back to Vagli Sotto and found this house. It was a wreck then, just a hut, really. But father and I did a lot of work on it and you can see it's in good shape now."

"It's beautiful," Sofia said. "You keep it up so well."

"What happened to your father after the war?" Dino wanted to know.

"We stayed in this house. We both got jobs in a manufacturing plant. Not much money but we didn't need it. We had a great garden out in back and raised chickens and rabbits so we had plenty to eat. It's still out there.

"Then Father really became interested in nonviolence and the peace movement. I suppose these days he'd be called a peacenik. He was way ahead of his time. There really hadn't been much discussion about those issues in Italy although there were movements in other European countries. He became active in the Italian Christian Workers Association, which was founded by partisans during the war to promote peace and justice, the very topics he was so interested in. He would have been so proud to know that his son, your father, was a partisan.

"He began to write long articles that were published in various journals. He became an officer of the workers association. He spoke at meetings. He really became pretty famous here, Dino. He even worked with Aldo Capitini, who was known as the Italian Gandhi."

"I've heard of Capitini," Dino said. "He was one of the first Italians to develop Gandhi's theories of nonviolence."

"Yes. And there were others. Priests and monks. My father knew all of these people. He respected them and they respected him. They were all important in the peace movement, but I tell you, Dino, your grandfather, Giovanni Pezzino, was an important man in the Garfagnana. People elsewhere probably never heard of him."

"How long was your father able to do this?"

Alessandro's face became flushed and he needed to get more water. He walked to the window and looked out. Dino and Sofia noticed then that the backyard contained a large vegetable garden that was now yielding tomatoes, zucchini, lettuce and squash. A half-dozen chickens squawked in a pen, and a couple of rabbits snoozed in another pen nearby.

Alessandro sat down again at the table. "You have heard," he said, "of the town of Fabbriche di Careggine?"

"Sure," Dino said. "It's the town that was flooded when they built a hydroelectric dam and a lake. They moved the people here to Vagli Sotto."

"And every so often," Sofia said, "they drain the lake and you see what's left of the town. Personally, I don't want to see it."

Alessandro smiled. "Let me tell you the real story of Fabbriche di Careggine. It's not as romantic as the tourist brochures say it is.

"The village was founded in the thirteenth century by a group of blacksmiths from Brescia. It became famous for the production of iron, and in fact at the end of the eighteenth century, the Duke of Modena, Francesco III, granted the people certain privileges, including tax exemptions and exemption from military service. But later there was a decline in the iron industry and residents became farmers and shepherds.

"At the beginning of the twentieth century, a small hydroelectric power plant was built on the Edron River to serve the village's needs. Then in 1941, a Fascist company decided it wanted to build a big dam for the power plant. And that dam would create a huge lake, the largest in Tuscany, but it would also submerge Fabbriche di Careggine. Wipe it out. Destroy it. My father became very angry and upset."

"That's terrible," Dino said.

"Some people said what did it matter?" Alessandro continued. "Fabbriche di Careggine had only thirty-one houses and a hundred forty-six inhabitants. And the company said they would be moved to new homes in Vagli Sotto that would be just like their old ones.

"But some residents strongly objected and tried to fight this. Fabbriche di Careggine was their home. They would lose houses that had been in their families for generations, even centuries. Living in Vagli Sotto would not be the same.

"The plan dragged on and on during and after the war. By then, all of the residents of Fabbriche di Careggine were worn out. They said they would accept the measly amount of money the company said it would give them, and they would move to Vagli Sotto.

"But my father wouldn't give up. He was the only person left opposed to the lake. I know people thought he was a crazy old man. He had long white hair and a beard and he didn't care about the clothes he wore. He marched up and down in front of the factory with signs. *Fermare il lago!* Stop the lake! *Salvare le nostre case!* Save our homes! I know a few people supported him, but they didn't say anything. He was the lone voice.

"Well, the company went ahead and did it. The residents of Fabbriche di Careggine started to move to Vagli Sotto. Slowly the lake started to fill up. My father walked around the town wearing hip boots and tried to object. Finally, the last burst of water filled the lake. Father was on a rooftop waving a sign, *No Lago!* I was watching from the shore. The water filled the basin. And he disappeared."

Alessandro picked up Bella and held her close.

"Just disappeared?" Dino said.

"I never saw him again."

THEY MOVED BACK INTO THE LIVING ROOM. Dino and Sofia remained silent, trying to absorb and understand what they had just heard. Bella jumped back on Alessandro's lap and purred loudly.

"Uncle," Dino said at last, "I've heard that the lake has been drained several times since it was flooded the first time. Did you . . . ?"

"Yes, it was drained in 1958, 1974 and 1983. I know what you're thinking, Dino. Yes, I looked and looked each time. There was no trace of him. There are a lot of crevices in those old houses and there are other places that could hide somebody, but I couldn't find him. It's just a mystery, that's all."

Alessandro stared at the bookcase. "Oh, you know, people make up stories. Somebody claimed to have seen an old man with a beard walking around the lake at midnight. Another said he saw an old man picketing the factory. It's all just talk. Just talk. He's gone.

"There were some people around here who didn't approve of him. Not only the Fascists, other people as well. They'd snicker, say things. We pretended we didn't hear. One time somebody tore down the peace flag that you saw outside. Just kids, I think. We got another one. I know there are still people who snicker when they hear his name."

"You must be very proud of all that he did," Sofia said.

"He was way ahead of his time. I know he would have taken part in the first peace march in Italy. It was from Perugia to Assisi in 1961. I know he would have supported the law that Parliament passed in 1972 that allowed for conscientious objection. And I know he would now support those who oppose the NATO missiles in Sicily.

"When I watched the civil rights battles in America in 1968, I knew he would have supported them. And of course, he would have been opposed to the war in Vietnam. Way ahead of his time. He's my hero."

"And you?" Dino said. "How have you been since your father . . . since your father . . . disappeared?"

"I retired from the factory a few years ago. I take care of the garden, and I go into the village to get a few groceries, but mostly I spend my days reading." He waved to the bookshelves. "Gandhi, Martin Luther King, Thoreau, works about Hinduism, Buddhism. I like to compare Christianity and Islam. I would like to take part in organizations and marches, but my health is not good."

He hugged Bella, who purred loudly and then scratched his hand.

Anticipating another question, he said, "No, I don't get lonely. I'm used to being alone. And I have Bella. If truth be told, she runs the house." He hugged her again. "And before Bella there was Chiara and before that there was Francesca and before that Zucca. So many."

Expecting yet another question, Alessandro said that until he found it too strenuous, he liked to walk around the lake. "No, I'm not hesitant around it. In fact, it gives me comfort. I think of my father and that makes me happy."

Dino and Sofia thought Alessandro looked tired and said they'd better be going.

"You don't know how happy we are to meet you," Dino said. "We've learned so much. We came looking for information about my father, and I feel that I know him more now. But you also told us about my grandfather. I didn't know anything about him, either, and I'm so proud of him. And of you, too."

"It's given me great pleasure to have met the son of my twin brother. You are quite exceptional, too."

Dino promised to return—"soon!"—so that they could continue the conversation.

"Before you go," Alessandro said, "I want to show you something." He went into the bedroom and returned with a framed photograph.

"This," he said, showing it to Dino and Sofia, "was taken when your father and I were sixteen years old, a year before Dino left to join the army. The Pezzino twins. And that's our father between us."

The photograph, in dark sepia, was taken in a studio, with a potted palm in the background. The boys, seated on stools, wore identical suit jackets and ties that were too tight. The one on the left smiled broadly, the one on the right was serious.

"I think you can guess which one is your father."

"Yes."

Dino held the photo as if it were a gem discovered in a forest. It was the first time Dino had seen a photo of his father. He ran his finger over the hair, the face, the shoulders.

"He looks like me when I was sixteen, doesn't he, Sofia? Remember that picture of me in the photo album Mama has?"

Sofia agreed.

"Uncle, we all look alike!" Dino said. "The hair, the eyes, the ears! Even your father here. He looks so proud of you and my father."

"He was. We were his life."

Now it really was time to leave. With strong hugs and a final pat for Bella, Dino and Sofia opened the door.

"There's one more thing," Alessandro said. "I hesitate to ask this, but I must. I know it might be awkward for your mother and stepfather, but I would very much like to visit my brother's grave."

"Oh, of course. I'll talk to them. And I'll call you and we can arrange it."

Alessandro followed them out the door and reached up to the tip of the flag. "Peace," he said.

"Peace," Dino and Sofia said together.

Lost in their thoughts, Dino and Sofia didn't speak until they reached Lucca.

"Amazing. That's all I can say," Dino said.

"What an incredible story," Sofia said. "Your grandfather! Working for peace and nonviolence. Trying to save Fabbriche di Careggine. And then just disappearing. What do you think really happened? Do you think he swam to shore and is somewhere living under another name?"

"That's more unlikely than his ghost suddenly appearing."

When they arrived in Sant'Antonio, it didn't take long for Dino to convince Lucia and Paolo that Alessandro should be permitted to come and visit his brother's grave.

"Of course," Lucia said. "There may be some reminders, but your father is long in the past for me."

"It would be interesting," Paolo said, "to see how the twin brothers are alike. Or different."

Two weeks later, Dino and Sofia drove again from Florence to Vagli Sotto, picked up Alessandro and then drove to Sant'Antonio.

Just as Dino had thought when he first met his uncle, Lucia recognized in Alessandro the man she had loved and Paolo recognized the man who was his best friend. Lucia began to cry, hesitated, and then took him into her arms. Since he was tall and she was short, this involved putting her arms around his waist.

"Oh," she said, "I can't believe it."

Paolo disengaged his wife and shook Alessandro's hand. "I can just see Dino now, at your age."

"I'm sixty-two."

"Sixty-two!" Lucia cried. "Dino, your father would have been sixty-two!"

"I know, Mama."

Over wine, coffee and biscotti, they all talked and talked for more than two hours. There was so much catching up to do. Like Dino and Sofia, Lucia and Paolo found the story of Giovanni Pezzino amazing and kept asking questions about the war and the aftermath.

"Dino," Lucia told her son, "you can be very proud of your grandfather and your uncle. I hope you've inherited some of that."

"I hope so, too, Mama."

In the late afternoon, Dino said it was getting late and they really should drive up by the Cielo. At the gravesite, Dino, Sofia, Lucia and Paolo stood back while Alessandro walked slowly up to the headstone. Staring down at the marble marker, he showed no emotion at first. It seemed to be just a name from the distant past. Then he crumpled to his knees and sobbed.

EVERY COUPLE OF WEEKS for the next months, Dino and Sofia drove up to the gorgeous mountainous area of Garfagnana and spent the afternoon with Alessandro. There were always more stories to tell, a few about his twin brother but mostly about his father.

They noticed, though, that the man had less and less energy. He had trouble breathing when he picked up Bella, and he ate only a single sandwich instead of two or three.

"I might as well tell you," he told his guests in February, "the doctor says I have maybe three more months."

"Oh, Alessandro, I'm so sorry," Dino and Sofia said together.

"It's all right. I'm ready. I may not be religious, but I believe in God and I think somehow I'll see my father and brother again. And maybe I'll see the mother I never knew."

Dino and Sofia visited every week after that, but didn't stay long. They just wanted to make sure Alessandro was all right. They passed the Devil's Bridge so often that Dino no longer closed his eyes when he saw it approaching, and he even got used to walking around Lago Vagli. "But I'm not going in," he said.

They also made a couple of trips to Cortona to visit Bruno and his family. They ate too much, listened to more of Bruno's long stories and witnessed the christening of Analisa and Pippi's new daughter, Rosalia. That event, of course, included an elaborate dining extravaganza.

"I like those people," Dino said after every visit.

In April, Alessandro made a request.

"Dino, I have been thinking about this. I can't be buried with my father because I don't know where he is. My mother is buried in Montepulciano, though I visited her grave only once. Do you think it would be possible for me to be with my brother?"

"Uncle, of course!" Dino said. "But let's not think about this, OK?"

Perhaps because the word had gotten out among Italian peace activists that Alessandro was very ill, sudden attention was being paid to his father. A feature article recounting his works appeared in *Panorama,* and RAI televised a short documentary about Fabbriche di Careggine. Giovanni was named the posthumous recipient of the Aldo Capitini award by the Center for Peace and Justice. Dino and Sofia drove a very frail Alessandro to Rome to accept the honor.

Wrapped in a shawl, he made only a brief speech. "My father was ahead of his time. Thank you very much for this honor."

At the end of May, they received the call they had dreaded for so long.

"Alessandro's lawyer?" Sofia asked.

"Yes."

"I'm sorry."

A few days later, a hearse from a mortuary in Lucca drove up the hill to the Cielo. Dino, Paolo and Ezio had dug the grave and Alessandro's plain wooden coffin was gently lowered. After the dirt and sod had been replaced, everyone made a circle and prayed in their own ways. After more than forty-five years, the Pezzino twins were together again.

Two weeks later, Dino received another call from Alessandro's attorney. Alessandro didn't have any wealth, but he had left his home to Dino and Sofia, saying, in his will, "perhaps your family can use it as a vacation retreat."

"Isn't that a great idea?" Dino said when he hung up the phone.

"It is!" Sofia said. "As I said, I wouldn't want to spend a lot of time in the Garfagnana, but a week every couple of months would be wonderful."

"Oh, and the attorney said we will also get Bella. She's staying at his house now."

"Really? You know, I've always wanted a cat."

He wasn't sure whether she actually meant that.

"We may have to make some changes to that house," he said, "but I know one thing that's not going to change."

"And that is?"

"The peace flag."

That night, Dino and Sofia held the photo of the Pezzino twins with their father and tried to recall everything that had happened. The trip to Montepulciano, Sister Colombina, Bruno and his welcoming family, Alessandro, Giovanni, Vagli Sotto, the ghost village.

"You know," Sofia said, "we learned a lot about your family, but what do you think you've learned about yourself? Aside from your fabulous good looks (cough, cough), what do you think you've inherited?"

"Hmmm. I don't really know. Maybe you can judge that better than I can."

"Well, if you were impetuous as a child like your father—good God, you hid under a blanket in a car when you were ten?—I think you have probably outgrown that. As I said, deliberate is a better word for you now."

"Yes, probably."

"But I also can't help thinking about who you are. I mean, how you helped people during the flood, how you're assisting poor people find housing now in your job, how you're getting people from the North and South together in our little groups—I can see your grandfather and your uncle looking down and smiling with approval."

"What about my father?"

"I don't think your father had a chance to really become what he could have been. He was eighteen years old and the world was wide open to him. He didn't want to think about Montepulciano and I suspect he probably felt guilty about leaving his family. That may be why he never wanted to talk about those things. But I think the war might have changed him. He would have found great opportunities to do things besides seeing the world. I think he would be very proud of you, too."

"He was cut down too soon," Dino said.

"Yes."

"Ten months ago," he said, "I didn't know anything about my father. Now I know what kind of a man, well, actually, a boy he was. I didn't know anything about my uncle Alessandro. And I didn't know anything about my amazing grandfather. I didn't even know they existed. I'm really lucky to have found my family, Sofia."

"Not to mention Bruno and his big family in Cortona."

"And," Dino said, "Bruno said he had a brother. So we'll have to look him up, too, because he knows about all those people in the family tree."

"And we were in such a hurry to get to Cortona we didn't even meet that relative in Montepulciano," Sofia said.

"I think his name was Salvatore Pezzino. We'll have to find him, too. And maybe he has relatives."

"Who have relatives who have relatives."

"Who have relatives. Who knows, Sofia, how big my family is or who these people are? I think we're starting an adventure."